For Mary Lynn . . . of course; and for Kelly "Rue" Drake, Haley Shay-Marie, and Pam and Eli. And especially for Bridget Marie Dunn, who knows the price of a horse.

> "*. . . They who speak above the ring of coin, who measure life beyond their breath . . . know the price of horses.*"

Special thanks to the owners of the St. James Hotel in Cimarron, New Mexico, for preserving such a splendid monument to our Wild West heritage. May the St. James stand at the top of every dust-swept trail, and remain forever woven in the wayfarer's dreams.

PRICE OF A HORSE

A JESTON NASH ADVENTURE

RALPH COTTON

St. Martin's Paperbacks

PRICE OF A HORSE: A JESTON NASH ADVENTURE

ISBN: 0-312-95793-9

Printed in the United States of America

St. Martin's Paperbacks edition/May 1996

10 9 8 7 6 5 4 3 2 1

◆ PROLOGUE ◆

When I came away from the great civil conflict, I had seven dollars, a six-shot single-action Colt, and a fine riding mare. While it might seem I was a bit shy of draw and possibles, I was broad on ambition; and like many a young man who'd rode guerilla along the border, I had not the slightest compulsion against cocking a hammer, filling a bag with money, and riding off with all eyes and muzzles flashing toward me. For awhile I thought the only way to leave a town was in a hurry—such is the workings of a young mind with the sound of war still rattling in it.

I fell in love with a young woman of respectable birth and breeding, and for a short time I thought I'd put my low-slung long-rider ways behind me. But her father soon found out what I was, sicced the law on me, and once again I was on the run, lonesome, lovesick, and now it appeared, bound forever to live the life of a fugitive.

During my short brush with respectability, I did manage to breed my mare to a top Thoroughbred stud named Star Of Dawn. The colt born of that union was a big, scrappy, wild-natured stallion, blacker than a bucket of midnight and of a temperament more akin to a grizzly than that of an equine. But I overlooked his shortcomings, as I'm sure he did mine, and because of the circumstances surrounding his birth, I loved him like the son I thought I'd never have and spoiled him something terrible.

A feller out of Memphis once tried every way in the world to buy the young stallion from me. When he'd exhausted every possible trade or cash offering, he finally looked at me from beneath a narrowed brow and asked in a pressing manner, "Just how far would you go to *keep* that stallion?"

I caught his veiled threat; knowing he was a *horse-trader,* and knowing he was from *Memphis,* and knowing what a powerful effect those two factors could bring to bear on bending a man's better nature, I slipped my hand to the pistol in my shoulder harness, stared right back at him and said, "Six shots farther than you'd wanta go to *take* him."

I reckon when a man only has one thing of importance in his life, it's easy to get greatly affixed to it. And so I did, with my black stallion . . . Buck.

PRICE OF A HORSE

PART I — ◆

Value of Virtue

• 1 •

"To you, Mister Beatty," Thomas Mackay said. He cleared his throat, smiled slightly behind a curl of smoke from a black cigar, and laid the remainder of the deck on the green felt. His hands were pale and delicate, but they moved with a sharpness, steady and precise, denoting an underlying strength and quickness that, like most gamblers, he'd prefer not to reveal. I'd just met him but I already admired his style. He handled his game like a banker handles gold: smooth, cool, and instinctively, with no regard for error. A spur-triggered Uhlinger pistol rested in the pocket of his silk vest beneath a drooping watch chain. It was a dainty little pistol, pearl-handled and too pretty to have ever been fired, I thought. I caught a glimpse of it and smiled to myself. *An ornament* . . . but one that said, "Caution—man at work."

Would he cheat? Sure he would. It was part of his profession, and though I would never know when or how, I knew he had to in order to make his living. Knowing it, I played around him, enough to let him know that I didn't care how he made his living as long as he didn't make it all off me. We'd both fared well. I stayed out of his way when he made a run on a hand; and I played close, learned the habits of the other two players and took a bite of their money anytime I felt hungry. Mackay saw what I was doing and he folded at all the right times. We weren't working together intentionally. We were just showing each other respect.

"Raise a thousand," I said, sliding two stacks of chips and a stack of greenbacks into the pot. I glanced at the big feller on my left. He tapped a finger against his string tie and studied his cards. I knew that for the rest of the hand he'd be bluffing. Fingering his tie was a giveaway. I shot Mackay a quick glance and saw his cards relax slightly in his hand. He would fold when I made my move. For the last few hands he'd been losing small amounts. I figured he'd won enough for one night and was easing out gradually. That's the way a smart gambler does it.

The big feller shoved in his chips with an air of confidence that didn't match the look in his eyes or the sheen of sweat on his wide brow. "And I'll raise five thousand," he said, sliding his hand back and shoving his whole stack into the pot. Next to him, an old feller with a draping gray beard pitched in his cards and scooted his chair back without saying a word. He hadn't lost over thirty dollars all night, but I saw it was thirty more than he could spare. Good, I thought, now it's down to the big dogs. I knew I'd win the pot. I'd drawn to a full house—aces over kings. All the big feller had was sweat under his eyes and nervous fingers on his neck tie.

"My, my," said Mackay, from behind a slight smile. "Aren't you two just the quintessential—"

"If you're out, shut the hell up," the big feller said with no show of manners.

Mackay shrugged, brushed a speck of ashes from his green silk vest, dropped his slim fingers to the table, and tapped them softly. "My apologies, sir," he said. But although his voice was a humble whisper, I noticed his fingers slipped away from the table absently, and rested against his vest. He toyed with the watch chain, an inch from the Uhlinger pistol.

I'd seen this big feller earlier at the auction, bidding high and reckless on any horse that showed above average qualities. He'd struck me as a man who used his money like a battering ram, who elbowed his way to the best seat at the table and left no tip. Now he was drinking just enough to be mouthy and losing enough to be mean. Mackay must've already seen trouble coming; maybe that's why he'd eased back.

I glanced around Lambert's Saloon and decided this would be my last hand for the night. The place was still packed with drovers and whores, well-dressed business men here from the auction and hustlers here for the play. Smoke hung so thick and low, I felt I'd bump my head on it if I stood up. At the bar, my friend and partner "Quiet" Jack Smith played pinch and giggle with a young Rumanian woman who'd introduced herself as Helova . . . Miss Helova Knight. That's all Jack had to hear.

Henri Lambert, the saloon owner, had his thirteen-year-old son working behind the bar—supposedly, having the kid there kept down trouble—and four or five German barmaids worked the room with bubbling blue eyes, hair of gold and silk, and forearms like lumberjacks. They slung steaks, drinks, and bosoms, all at the same time. It'd been a friendly crowd, but high-strung and ready for the least thing to set it off. The ceiling had a hundred or more bullet holes in it from other such gatherings. Earlier, someone had knocked a banjo player cold as a wedge. It seems he'd misused the lyrics to "Bound for the Rio Grande." Overall, this was a tense bunch.

"Well?" The big feller leaned forward on his elbows and glared into my eyes. "You gonna call . . . or pick grit with the chickens?"

The old man with the beard drifted up and away from the game. I laid my cards face down slowly and tapped my fingers on them, considering whether I wanted to win this hand and risk a squabble, or let this big fool have it—make him feel good—and I would still come out ahead.

My eyes swept past Mackay and he seemed to be reading

my thoughts. I took a deep breath, let it out slowly, and pitched my cards forward, face down. I slid another glance past Mackay and saw the trace of a smile. "Looks like you win, mister," I said, as polite as possible after his show of rudeness. He hadn't even bothered telling us his name.

"Yeah," he said, more to himself than anyone else, and he slapped his cards face down in front of him and raked in the pot. "Now deal 'em, and let's quit fooling around."

Mackay scooted his chair back a foot. "Gentlemen," he said, "I'm afraid *this* tired child must bid you-all a good evening." He raised and drained his tall glass of bourbon, and quietly stifled a cough with the back of his hand.

"Me too," I said, leaning back in my chair. "It's been a long night."

"What?" The big feller slapped a hand down on the table; glasses rattled. "What about me? What about my money? You can't quit while you're winner!" His words aimed straight at me as if Mackay wasn't even there. I saw he was about to come up from his chair, so I braced my feet on the floor. Heads turned toward us from the bar. Quiet Jack picked up his drink and drifted over casually, with his left arm looped around Miss Knight's waist.

"I *came* here to win," I said. I kept my voice respectful but firm. "We all did. You just happened to lose . . . that's poker, mister." I saw Jack lean against the wall near my chair; he switched his drink to his left hand at Miss Knight's waist; she ran her painted nails between his shirt buttons and giggled something in his ear. He smiled, but with his eyes searching the room and taking note. His right hand rested near his holster. We were strangers here in Cimarron; for all we knew the big feller could have lots of friends.

The big feller glanced around nervously, then back to me. He must've seen the wisdom in my words or the seriousness in my eyes. He eased back. "But you can give a man a chance to get even. That's only sporting." He wiped a thick hand across his beaded brow and tried to smile. His jaw twitched. Light from the chandelier sparkled off two large diamond rings.

I eased back too and let out a breath. My tie was pulled loose and my collar lay open. It *had* been a long night. "Some other time," I said. "I'm through for now."

I saw a flash of white anger sweep his eyes, but he swallowed it, reached over, picked up the deck and the discards, and shuffled them together. He lay the deck between us. I glanced at it, then back to him. "I told you, mister, I'm through for the night."

"One cut," he said. He nodded at the large pile of cash and chips before him. "Just one"—he raised a thick finger for emphasis—"one cut . . . double or nothing. What do you say?"

I studied his eyes and chewed the inside of my lip. I wanted out without a scene but his eyes told me there would be one, win or lose. "Look, mister . . . we're both tired—"

"One time," he said, cutting me off and leaning forward. "Winner takes all. Your luck's been good handling the cards, surely you're not afraid to just flip one over?" His eyes, words, and tone offered the slightest suggestion that I'd been cheating.

"Don't take any guff off this buzzard!" I saw Jack pull away from Miss Knight and lean toward the table. I grabbed his arm. How he got the name "Quiet" Jack was something I'd never figured out. Most times he was louder than a marching band. We'd been partners for several years, and riding with Jack was often like holding a mad hornet under a tin can. You had to keep a good grip and not let the noise rattle you.

At the next table sat Federal Marshall Newton Briggs and two of his deputies. They watched us like hounds waiting for someone to throw red meat in the air. Briggs looked gray and old, but hard as seasoned hickory. An early model Dance Brothers pistol hung from his waist. A drooping white mustache mantled his lip, and his eyes were backed deep into the sockets from years under a blazing sun. I didn't know him except by reputation, but that reputation stretched from Milk River to the Tularosa Valley. He was known as a tough knot. I, being wanted for killing a crooked sheriff back in Missouri, tried to maintain a narrow profile at all times. Anonymity is the only solace for a wanted man.

"All right," I said, just wanting off the spot. It was his money anyway. I could afford to lose one cut and still come out ahead. I spread my hands in a cautious show of peace. "I'll cut one time, double or nothing . . . but that's all, win or lose." Out the corner of my eye, I saw Briggs nod his approval to his deputies and I felt better seeing it. "Boys, there's a gentleman," I heard him murmur. His deputies just stared.

Beside me, Thomas Mackay drew on the cigar and watched with curiosity, his head slightly cocked to the side and his fingers still toying with his watch chain.

The big feller glanced around the table and rubbed his hands together. The crowd drew its breath and held it as his hand trembled slightly above the shiny deck. He took a shallow piece of the deck and turned it over slowly. I saw cruel evil in his eyes as his lips formed a smug grin; and the Jack of Hearts smiled up from the green felt. The crowd stirred, then held its breath again as I took the top card off the remaining deck and flipped it over.

The big feller stared down at the dark queen in disbelief, shaking his head. "Damn you, boy!" He slammed a fist on the table and swept the deck away. Cards fluttered in the air and fell. The crowd pulled back. I just stared at him, knowing that nothing I could say would make a difference. The storm was coming; all I could do was batten my hatches.

"My goodness, sir," Thomas Mackay chuckled. "Doesn't that just make you want to spit?" His vest pocket was now empty and his right hand had disappeared beneath the table.

"Shut up, you damn tinhorn!" The big feller shot straight up from his chair with his fists clenched. His face was red-blue, but too white around his mouth. "New deck," he shouted, glancing toward the bar. "Get a new deck over here, pronto!"

I stood up slowly, facing him. "I said one time only, mister, and I meant it." Without taking my eyes from his, I reached my arms over around the pile of winnings and raked it to me. Funny, I'd been prepared to lose it, had expected to lose it. Now that I'd won it, I didn't know what to think.

"Just one more cut," the big feller said. He started to grab my arm, but the look in my eyes stopped him. "One more, and that's it."

"Hunh-uh." I shook my head and nodded toward the bare table in front of him. "You're done in."

He reached inside his coat and I almost went for my pistol; but he pulled out a thin leather wallet and slapped it on the table. "Here's my marker. I'll draft a check for any amount—"

"No way," I said, cutting him off. "House rules says cash or chips. Besides, I'm calling it a night."

He kicked back his chair and started around the table. Marshall Briggs stood up, pointed a long finger, and said, "Hold it right there," and the big feller froze as if looking down the barrel of a gun. "I've seen enough of this." Briggs stepped over closer, his left arm still out, finger still pointing, his right palm resting on the bone-handled Dance Brothers pistol. "This young man has gone out of his way to accommodate you," Briggs continued in a low voice. "But you, sir, are acting like an ill-mannered—"

"That's my money!" The big feller clenched his fists so hard, they seemed to draw his arms into his sides.

"Used to be, sir," Mackay taunted under his breath.

"Enough out of you!" Briggs's finger swung toward Mackay. "And wipe your nose, right now!"

Mackay smiled sheepishly. "Thank you, marshall." He brought his empty right hand up slowly from under the table, rubbed a finger across his nose and laid both hands on the tabletop.

Briggs stepped closer, staring back at the big feller, picked up a pearl derby hat from an empty chair, and held it out arm's length. "Now, you . . . git!" The deputies stood up behind him.

The big feller seemed ready to explode as he snatched the hat and spun toward me. "You haven't heard the last—"

"I mean git!" Briggs's voice sounded like cannon fire. The big feller swept up his leather wallet and stomped off through the crowd with his long coattails flapping behind him. I let out a tense breath. Jack squeezed Miss Knight closer; she giggled and ran her hand inside his shirt. Mackay poured a glass of bourbon and I noticed the Uhlinger was back in his vest pocket. Briggs, his deputies, and I watched as the big feller disappeared out the front door. The crowd murmured and spread out back to the bar.

"Much obliged, Marshall," I said to Briggs, picking up my Stetson from an empty chair. I adjusted the dents in the crown and signaled a barmaid to gather my winnings, then I turned back to Briggs. "Can I buy you fellers a drink?" I felt I should show some appreciation, socialize enough to confirm his opinion of me as a gentleman. If I ducked out too soon it could draw suspicion.

Briggs nodded, "We'd be honored, Mister . . . ?"

"I'm Beatty . . . James Beatty," I said quickly, hoping he couldn't tell I was lying. My real name had been Jeston Nash years back, back before fate dealt me an outlaw's hand. I'd changed my name to Miller Crowe after the war, but was now wanted for killing a crooked lawman under *that* name. *Beatty* was my third attempt at going straight. I'd worn out names faster than some people wore out boots.

"Pleased to meet you, Mister Beatty," Briggs smiled. "I'm Newton Briggs. These are my deputies, One-eye Marvin Ingram, and Little Dick Duggins."

I glanced at Ingram and saw that both his eyes were sharp and clear. "Why do they call you One-eye?" I asked.

"Why shouldn't they?" he grinned.

I nodded and looked at "Little" Dick Duggins. "Don't ask," he said. "Just call me Richard."

"I will," I said respectfully, and I flagged another German barmaid and ordered a bottle of rye. It struck me that all these German barmaids looked identical, fair-skinned, tall and broad-shouldered, with biceps that could snap a man's neck. But they were big, gentle women who loped about the saloon like palomino workhorses, Schleswig warm-bloods in sweet-smelling gingham.

"So, Mister Beatty," Briggs said as we sat down at his table, "what brings you to Cimarron?"

"Horses," I said. "I'm a horse dealer out of Missouri." I gestured toward Jack who'd turned his full attention back to Miss Knight. "My friend there works with me . . . making the auction circuit." Of course part of my job as a horse dealer was procuring good riding stock for my cousins, the James-Younger Gang of Missouri—something I certainly wouldn't mention here.

"Well, Mister Beatty"—Briggs smiled and laid his hands flat on the table as a bottle and four fresh glasses appeared in front of us—"you certainly handled that incident like a young gentleman."

"Yeah," said Little Dick, "you had every right to kill him."

"Perhaps," I said, warming to the conversation but weighing my every word. I took the bottle and began pouring us a drink. "But I find violence needless and distasteful. As a horse trader, I find there are few things a man can't *deal* his way out of if he keeps his head. I believe in live and let live."

"That's a good attitude," Ingram said.

"Here, here," Briggs said, raising his glass. We all threw

back a shot and Little Dick poured us another. "I wish more folks felt that way." Briggs glanced at both his deputies and they nodded in agreement. "Sure would make our jobs a lot easier. We're looking for Ned Quarrels and his bunch. Don't know 'em, do you, Mister Beatty?"

"No," I said, "but believe me, if I did—"

"Ever heard of 'em?"

"Not really," I said, "except bits and pieces. I hear of such people now and then, of course. But for the most part, I steer clear of such hardcases. In fact, this is the first I've been in a saloon or played any poker for the longest time." I stopped for just a second to see if they believed a word I'd said. They seemed to. "Most times, I spend my nights in my hotel room." I checked their eyes again. "I'm studying the scriptures, you see. Always looking for the deeper meaning of life."

"Studying what?" Ingram glanced at Briggs.

"The bible, goddamn it!" Briggs spoke his words out the corner of his mouth. "This young man studies the bible."

"Oh," Ingram said. He took off his hat and laid it on the table.

"Do you happen to follow Emerson's Transcendentalists?" Briggs folded his hands.

"No, marshall," I said. "I avoid railroads as much as possible. I prefer horseback, although it gets weary sometimes." I watched his eyes to see if I'd said the right thing. Briggs glanced down at his hands with a patient smile.

"If you're religious . . . why was you playing poker?" Little Dick looked more confused than suspicious.

"That's my one occasional weakness, I'm afraid." I glanced around toward Jack. I'd stayed long enough to be sociable and express my thanks; it was time to go. "Dealing in horses can be a lonesome business. Many nights I just ponder the—"

My words were cut short by a woman's scream and the sound of boots and slippers scuffling away from the door.

"Look out!" someone shouted, "He's got a gun!"

I caught a glimpse of the pearl derby hat near the door as the crowd parted in a flurry of spilled beer and falling chairs; I spun up from the table toward the commotion, drawing my forty-four as the first bullet whistled past my head. In reflex, I stepped sideways cocking my pistol, swinging it up toward the big feller. Taking a split second to aim as his second shot exploded in a belch of smoke and fire, I raised my thumb and let the hammer fall with the impact of a mad judge's gavel.

It was the strangest thing I ever saw; but for the first time in my life I actually watched a bullet come out of my gun barrel. It spun out and upward in an arch—awfully slow for a bullet, I thought—then dropped down and smacked the big feller right in the face. There'd been no recoil and the shot sounded weak and muffled. I glanced at my pistol. The big feller stumbled back, raised the big shiny Russian forty-four again, and tried to aim it as a trickle of blood ran down his nose.

Frantically I recocked my hammer and let it fall. This time it made a sound like someone spitting tobacco, and the bullet dropped to the floor ten feet in front of me and skidded and rolled away into the crowd. "Lord-a-mighty!" I heard Jack bellow, "Quit fooling around!"

"I ain't fooling arou—!" In a near panic I shook the gun and slapped it against the palm of my hand, as if that would somehow fix it. I cocked it again—*"Jesus!"*—but by now the big feller had staggered backward with his gun hanging from his hand. I let out a tense breath as he fell against the wall and slid down. *"Bible,* my ass," I heard Ingram say. I stepped forward cautiously and saw blood run down from the hole between the big feller's eyes and drip off the tip of his nose.

"He ain't no horse trader," said Little Dick Duggins.

"Nor much of a gunman either," Ingram said.

I stopped, reached out a trembling foot and kicked away

the big forty-four. Bending down, I saw the hole between his closed eyes, eyes that were already swelling and turning purple, like a man who'd been smacked in the face with a barn slat. His mouth opened and closed slowly like a fish out of water. My mouth dropped open the same way as I looked closely and saw, of all things, my bullet sticking out of the skin on the bridge of his nose. "Jack," I said quietly and in awe. I reached back a hand and motioned Jack over. "Come here and look at this. . . ."

"There's a peculiar sight," Jack said, stepping in beside me. He reached down and plucked the bullet out with his fingers. The big feller groaned and dropped his head over on his shoulder. Behind us, I felt the crowd drawing close as Jack studied the bullet, then pitched it in the man's lap. "He's one lucky sumbitch," Jack chuckled. "You better learn to shoot a little harder."

I cocked an eyebrow. " 'Shoot a little harder?' "

Jack chuckled, took my gun from my hand and clicked it open. Briggs and his deputies gathered around us, watching as Jack took out a bullet and bit the end off it. He poured a tiny mound of powder in his hand and they all examined it closely. I reached down and slapped the big feller's face back and forth to bring him around. "You all right, mister?" I glanced over my shoulder at the bar. "Somebody bring a towel and some cold water." I looked back down at him, "And a bottle of rye."

"Yep," Jack said, "short loads, just like I suspected."

"Whoever sold you these bullets oughta be shot," Briggs said. "Where'd you get 'em?"

A German barmaid came running and knelt beside me with a bowl of water and a dirty bar towel. "Taos," I said over my shoulder, dipping a corner of the towel into the bowl and dabbing at the blue hole between his swollen eyes.

"Figures," Briggs said. "You gotta watch them boys in Taos. They'll sell you a horse turd and swear it's an emerald."

"Somebody get a doctor," I said. "And some ice . . . and an ice pack." I wiped away the blood and saw where the bullet had broken the skin; the bridge of his nose was busted flat. He forced his swelling eyes open and tried to focus on me. One eye cocked in toward his nose and swam up and down, as if surveying the damage.

"You . . . hit . . . me?" His voice honked like a sick goose; it sounded terrible. I pressed the wet rag against his nose and he winced in pain. He tried to shove my hand away.

"Take it easy," I said, "I've already sent for a doctor. I'm trying to help you here."

"On the contrary," I heard Thomas Mackay say beside me. I saw the toe of his polished dress shoe reach out and tap the barrel of the Russian forty-four. "You really should empty his big *shiny new* pistol into him and send him on to a better world. He *did* try to kill you, sir."

The barmaid took the rag from my hand and I stood up, stepped back beside Mackay, and tugged at my vest. "Well . . . luckily he didn't," I said. "And I reckon with a nose like that he'll think twice before stirring up any more trouble."

"With a nose like *that,* sir," said Mackay, "what will he really have to lose?" Mackay snapped a fresh handkerchief from his pocket and flipped it to me; I dried my hands. "Thanks."

"To hell with his nose," Briggs said. "Say the word and I'll have him locked up. Let his nose mend on its own in a jail cell."

"Naw, I reckon not," I said. "I figure he's learned a lesson in all this." All I was really thinking of was letting everything die down. I sure didn't want to bring charges against him and have to go to court, maybe run the risk of having somebody poking around and finding out who I was, or what I'd been up to for the past few years.

"You haven't seen the last of this man, sir," Mackay said. "No indeed! This man will not rest until he kills you."

Briggs reached down and picked up the Russian forty-four. He shoved it into his belt. "Like I said, Mister Beatty, just say the word and I'll put him on bread and water a few days. Let him fix that nose to suit himself."

"Live and let live," I said, spreading my hands. "He's had enough. Hopefully he'll ponder the consequences of his actions and be the better for it."

Briggs cocked an eye toward me from beneath a bushy brow. "I can see how a *young gentleman* like yourself might think that way. But believe me, Mister Beatty, you've no knowledge of these kinda rascals."

"Oh, I don't know, Marshall." I shot Jack a knowing glance and almost smiled. "I like to think I've seen my share of scoundrels. And I believe there's always a chance that a man will learn from the errors of his ways."

"That's a damn fine way of looking at it," Briggs said, "but I'm afraid I don't agree. Maybe I've just seen too much of the darker side of life." Evidently the old marshall thought I'd just dropped by after church.

"Well, I can't help but think we all deserve a chance—"

I heard Mackay disguise a laugh by coughing against the back of his hand. I turned toward him. "Sorry, Mister Beatty," he said. "But you, sir, are an *innocent* . . . very naive." I just looked at him as he rolled the black cigar around in his mouth and smiled. "Yes indeed," he said in a near whisper, staring down at the big feller with a strange gleam in his sharp eyes. "*Very* naive."

2

Later that night, I explained to an old doctor about the cheap bullets I'd bought in Taos, the card game and the shooting, while he worked the big feller over with a swab of iodine, stuck a couple of leeches under his eyes, and helped him upstairs to his room. Jack and I took the last available room in the St. James Hotel without realizing it was right above Lambert's Saloon. The hotel also belonged to Henri Lambert and was still under construction, being built against, onto, and directly *over* the ceiling with all the bullet holes in it.

No sooner than we'd stepped into the room, I looked down at the floor and saw candlelight shining up through bullet holes from the saloon below. "No wonder this was the last vacancy," I said, throwing my saddlebags across a wooden chair and leaning over the holes in the floor. "A man could get killed in his sleep here."

"Not if everybody bought their bullets where you got yours," Jack said. He'd grown a little sullen when Miss Knight told him she had to turn in early. Apparently she had another job during the day and only stayed up late on weekends. Jack grunted and dropped his gear on the floor. "And you better watch out, stringing that old lawman along the way you're doing."

"Ah, Jack, I'm just providing a good cover for myself.

You oughta know that." I backed close to the wall and stared at the riddled floor. "No harm in making him think I'm an upstanding citizen. I kinda enjoy it . . . you know?"

Jack grinned. "Just don't go thinking you are one. I know how you get sometimes."

After making a couple of slow circles around the room, staying close to the walls in case one of the loud yells from below was followed by a blast of gunfire, Jack walked to one of the small beds, stripped up the feather mattress and slung it up on top of an oak dresser. I leaned a straight-backed chair against the wall beside the door, for a fast getaway if any shooting started downstairs, stripped the other bed of its mattress, pressed it into the chair, and sank into it. I didn't like sleeping in my dress clothes, but I wasn't about to stand out on the floor long enough to change.

I only slept in short stretches that night. What time I wasn't dozing and waking to the sound of pitiful wailing from the big feller's room down the hall, I was jerked awake with a start every now and then as my chair tipped forward.

Through the veil of a dark dream, I kept seeing people sneaking into the saloon one and two at a time. Miners, whores, cowboys, barmaids—even the knocked-out banjo player. They gathered silently beneath us, all armed with pistols, shotguns, rifles, and other weapons of terrible intent. All night they gathered and waited, and at Henri Lambert's signal, they raised and fired their weapons as one; the explosion would jolt me awake with my breath heaving in my chest. Then I'd hear the big feller squall and moan through his shattered nose, and the whole terrible cycle would start all over. It was a long and trying night, and I welcomed the gray-gold of dawn when it finally seeped across the windowsill.

The next morning, I stepped barefoot carefully around the splintery, shot-up floor, steadying my hand against the wall until the leftover fog from a restless night lifted off my brain. When I finished changing into my everyday clothes and stuffed my suit in my saddlebags, I took a pan and a pitcher of tepid water out in the hall and shaved and brushed my teeth, using my reflection in a wavy window-pane. After Jack shaved and attended himself in the same manner, we headed down to breakfast, hooking up our suspenders as we went.

A deep mournful groan resounded as we passed the big feller's room, and I saw a pile of wet, bloody towels and an ice pack laying on a tray outside his door. "Poor sumbitch," Jack said. I just shook my head. It felt strange staying in the same hotel with a man I'd just shot . . . or *tried* to shoot. I didn't know what to expect when I ran into him face to face, but it was something I figured was bound to happen most anytime.

In the saloon, Thomas Mackay sat reading a newspaper. All we saw at first was a rising cloud of smoke from behind the fanned-out headlines. But upon hearing us, Mackay let down the paper and beckoned us to his table. He looked rested, except for the dark circles under his eyes, and neatly barbered, with a smell of peach blossoms and alcohol forming an aura around him. He smiled and looked us up and down as we seated ourselves. I reckon we didn't look like two men who'd had much sleep. My back felt stiff from the chair and I doubt if Jack's felt any better from sleeping drawn up in a ball on the hard dresser. "Let me offer a guess," Mackay said in his soft southern voice. "Henri must've rented you what I refer to as the *undertaker's* suite."

I glanced up at the ceiling and back at Mackay; Jack leaned back in his chair and craned his neck toward the smell of biscuits from the kitchen behind the bar. "I plan on mentioning it to Mister Lambert as soon as I see him," I said. There were only two other customers in the saloon at that hour of morning: one was a thin young cowboy who looked to be no more than sixteen. He lay passed out with his head on a table, cursing in his sleep like a lunatic. The other was a dandy dressed feller with a travel bag on his lap, who glanced nervously at the downed cowboy and looked out the window for the early stage into Santa Fe.

"It will do you no good, sir," Mackay said. "I'm afraid Mister Lambert has a very stringent 'no-refund' policy."

"We'll see about that," I said.

One of the German women showed up with a steaming blue and white porcelain pot and poured us coffee that was strong enough to float a pistol. Mackay sat silently smiling until we'd taken a couple sips and ordered a plate of eggs, grits, and elk steak. Seeing the coffee had kicked in and leveled our attitudes, Mackay leaned forward on his elbows when the waitress had left, and said, "At least he didn't rent you one of the *soft* rooms from his brochure."

"What's that?" Jack said, raising the cup as steam billowed around his lips.

Mackay reached into the empty chair beside him, picked up a fancy binder, and spread it out on the table. We leaned over and looked at ink sketchings of ornate rooms complete with overhead chandeliers and ice-chests. "I see nothing wrong with these," I said, "except they probably cost an arm and leg."

"Oh no," Mackay nodded, "these rooms rent for the same as your *undertaker's* suite. The difference is, they haven't been built yet. They're only staked off on the ground out back and outlined with a string. Thus, Henri refers to them as *soft* rooms." Mackay smiled and raised an eyebrow.

"You're kidding," I said, and Mackay swept an arm toward the window on the back wall, inviting me to see for myself. I walked over, leaned my hands down on the sill and sure enough, there sat two men in wooden chairs, one whittling a stick and the other gazing off at the sunrise. Their saddlebags lay in the dirt beside them and a blanket lay spread near a dirty string that separated their space from the next. The other space was empty but for a wooden chair and a rolled-up blanket. Before I turned away, the man whittling looked up at me with a blank-faced expression. "Now I've seen it all," I said, shaking my head as I returned and sat down at the table. We heard a stage pull up out front, and the dandy dressed feller stood up, walked wide around the babbling cowboy, and disappeared out the door.

"How the hell does he get by with stuff like that?" Jack chuckled. I couldn't help but laugh myself, thinking of that blank face staring back through the window.

Mackay puffed his cigar and smiled. "It is truly remarkable, sir. I asked him the same question when I arrived, and he replied quite indignantly that the rooms were every bit as nice as any other except they weren't finished yet."

As we ate our breakfast—food so good it couldn't be compared to anything I'd ever eaten—Thomas Mackay told us that Henri Lambert had settled in Cimarron after serving as President Abraham Lincoln's personal chef. From the quality of food, I could believe it.

After filling our bellies, I leaned back and sipped more strong coffee. "Well, maybe I won't complain," I said, letting out a breath. "We only took the room for one night. I reckon it was no worse a deal than them bullets I bought over in Taos."

"Yes," said Mackay. "That was rather extraordinary. Have you seen that miserable blackguard this morning?"

"No, but I heard him carry on all night down the hall. Why, have you seen him?"

"Oh . . . my, yes!" Mackay waved a hand as if swatting a fly. "He came down earlier for more ice. He is one very *wretched* individual." Mackay cupped his hand in front of his face. "Nose this large, sir. One eye crossed . . . both eyes swollen shut and black as a raccoon's. I must say, you showed him little kindness by sparing his life."

"Yeah . . . well, I hope to be away from here by the time he's up and around. I've never faced a man after having a shoot-out with him." I shrugged. "If you can call that a shoot-out."

"I don't know *what* you can call that," Jack said, reaching for the last biscuit on a platter. "But if I was you, I'd go straight back to Taos and take a chunk of meat off the sumbitch that sold you them bullets." He chewed the biscuit. "The hell'd you have in mind buying cheap bullets anyway?"

"I don't know," I said, finishing my coffee. "Just trying to save money, I reckon. It's easy getting *took* when you travel a lot."

"Yes," said Mackay, "it is indeed. Like you two gentlemen, I often find myself far from the comfort of hearth and kin. I fear gambling is not the glamorous life many folks have romanticized it to be." Mackay glanced out at the stage and folded his newspaper.

"Rolling on!" yelled a voice from the boardwalk.

"So, where are you headed?" Jack spoke over a mouthful of biscuit.

"Oh . . . wherever the spirit moves me, I suppose. I'm riding over to Gris this morning, to see how my luck runs with the miners. They have a new hotel and saloon there. Quite something, I hear." He drained his coffee cup and let out a shallow breath. "But I must say, this whole Santa Fe Trail experience hasn't quite lived up to my expectations." Mackay stood up, tugged at his vest, and cocked his head slightly. "Although meeting you gentlemen has truly been a pleasure I won't soon forget." He extended his hand and Jack and I both stood up to shake it.

"Good luck," I said. "Maybe we'll run into each other down the road." His hand felt cool and moist.

"I look forward to it," said Mackay.

We watched as Thomas Mackay left the saloon and stepped aboard the stage, carrying nothing but the newspaper folded under his arm. I noticed he wasn't much over five feet tall, and wouldn't weigh a hundred and twenty pounds with rocks in his pockets. "Now there goes a strange one," I said, watching the stage roll away and wiping my hands on a table napkin. "Like shaking hands with a dead man."

Jack and I sat down in our chairs and saw a broad-shouldered man with a black beard walk toward us from the kitchen. He wore a white apron that hung nearly to his ankles and a high silk top hat.

"That will be nine dollars even," he said, laying a bill on our table and smoothing it out with his broad, clean hand.

"For what?" I leaned over and studied the scribbling on the paper. "All's we had is breakfast!"

"Correct," he said. "Breakfast for *three*—two pots of coffee, two cigars, and the bottle of bourbon *your friend,* Mister Mackay, drank before you came down." He smiled across large white teeth behind his drooping mustache. "And one newspaper, of course."

I looked at Jack, shook my head and looked back up at the broad-faced man. "Are you Henri Lambert . . . the owner here?"

He tugged at the cuff of his shirt. "At your service." I noticed the slightest hint of a French accent.

"I've been wanting to talk to you about that room up there." I nodded toward the ceiling.

"Yes," he said. "It has an excellent view, doesn't it? You would be surprised how many famous people—and I mean heads of state and such—have slept there."

"Really?" I leaned forward and picked up the bill. "How many of them have gotten their heads blown off in their sleep?" I was prepared to demand our money back for the room.

"Aw." He waved his thick hand and smiled. "You're worried about the bullet holes . . . yes? Well, don't be." He leaned close, lowered his voice and winked. "You see, that's only to impress travelers from back east. Sure, I allow some of the locals to fire a few rounds now and then, but only if the room is empty." He spread his arms and glanced at the ceiling. "It's only for color, to provide atmosphere. . . . Although, I once had a cowardly idiot who was so afraid, he spent the night sleeping in a chair. But, gentlemen, use your head. Would anybody in their right mind subject a customer to sleeping under such conditions? What would it do to my business?"

I reached slowly for my wallet, feeling a little foolish. "You're right," I said, offering a sheepish grin. "You have to pardon us. We're not from here. But you oughta think about putting up a thicker ceiling. It'd make everybody feel better."

"I'll make a note of it," said Lambert. "We aim to please."

Jack shot him a frown. "What about these *soft* rooms?" He picked up the picture and pitched it across the table.

Henri shrugged his broad shoulders. "What about them?"

"We're told you rent them for the same price as the others."

"Yes," Henri said, "that is correct. So?"

"So?" I laid my wallet on the table with my hand on it. "So, how the hell can you charge people for a room that ain't even finished? Hell, it's just a string in the dirt . . . it ain't even started!"

Lambert's feelings looked hurt. He stiffened up. "You should see what you get over in Gris. They may be cheaper, but *ugh.*" He swiped a hand. "Besides, those are not mere *rooms* I'm renting, sir. Those are *dreams.* Dreams that are shared by only a few of us who have the vision and courage to see this place not as it *is,* but as it will someday be, given the support . . . the hope and faith of such gentlemen as you see out there in the dirt." Lambert's eyes watered up slightly. "Perhaps to people like you . . . and you—" he nodded at each of us in turn "—this place is nothing more than a rough spot in the road. But to some of us here in Cimarron, this is a beacon of refuge in a savage land. This represents our struggle . . . our manifest destin—"

"Hold it!" Jack said, and he turned to me. *"Please* . . . pay him!" He pointed a finger at Lambert. "Pay him whatever he wants and let's get the hell out of here."

"Nine dollars," Lambert said, clearing his throat and running a finger beneath his eye.

I pulled nine dollars from my wallet without taking my eyes off Lambert's. "Thank you," he said, folding the money and slipping it under his apron. He leaned toward me. "You wouldn't happen to be the gentleman they call 'Bullets' would you? The one who shot—or I should say, *tried* to shoot—Joe Alahambre between the eyes last night?"

I glanced at Jack and felt my face redden. "I've never been called 'Bullets' in my life. But, yes, I did have cause to shoot a man here last night. Is that his name? Joe Alahambre?"

"Yes," said Lambert. "Folks who know him, call him Two Diamond Joe—"

"Jesus," I said under my breath, and I saw the look in Jack's eyes. Joe Alahambre was, at one time, the fastest, meanest, most vicious gunman to ever stain the earth.

"Of course most folks don't know him anymore, not since he's settled down and taken up ranching instead of bounty hunting for a living."

"I shot 'Two Diamond' Joe Alahambre between the eyes with a cheap bullet? *Jesus,"* I whispered again.

"You most certainly did," Lambert said. "And I'm afraid you owe me money for it."

"What?" I couldn't believe it. I stared at Lambert as he fished out another bill from his pocket and slapped it on the table.

"Yes," he smiled and smoothed out the bill. "It comes to seven dollars and fifty cents."

"That's crazy! What the hell for?"

Lambert leaned over and ran a finger down the bill. "There's three towels, a pan of water, a bottle of rye, some ice . . . an ice pack, and a *one-dollar* fee from our town doctor for making a house call."

I shot straight up from my chair; Jack chuckled and shook his head. "I don't believe this!" I shouted. "All's I did was shoot him, I didn't take him to raise!"

"We pay for what we get, and we get what we pay for." Lambert smiled. "You did order some towels and water, didn't you?" He checked the bill as if making certain.

"Well . . . I—"

"A bottle of rye whiskey?"

"He was in pain—"

"An ice pack? You did send for a doctor, didn't you?" Lambert glanced up and smiled each time he mentioned another item. "It's all right here," he shrugged. "Has our service been adequate? Has there been a mistake? Because if one of my hurdy girls hasn't done her job or if she's lied about this bill, believe me, she's fired. You just say the word and she's out of here. She can spend her life in some dirty stinking San Francisco bordel—"

"She didn't lie." I glared at Lambert. "I ordered those things, but I did so just trying to help the man. It was done out of kindness—"

"Oh, certainly, I see, after your failed attempt at blowing his brains out." Lambert shrugged. "I provide good, clean rooms, good food and good service . . . at reasonable prices. I try to stay out of our guests' personal affairs."

"There's nothing personal about it," I said. "He threw down on me. I shot him. Now that's that . . . but I ain't paying his medical bill—"

"Well, perhaps I should call him down here and settle this." Lambert stepped quickly to the bottom of the stairs and called up in a loud voice, "Mister Alahambre . . . oh Mister—"

"Don't do that," I said, cutting him off. I don't know why, but I couldn't stand the thought of facing the man I'd shot the night before. Lambert smiled as if he knew how I felt about it. "I'll pay the damned bill," I grumbled.

"Hod-iz-it?" called a strained voice from upstairs. It sounded like a man talking through a tin can. I winced; Jack chuckled.

"Oh . . . never mind, Mister Alahambre," Lambert called out. He walked back to me, wiping his hands on his apron.

"Now there," I said, throwing eight dollars on the table. "Keep the damn change." I pointed a finger at Lambert. "But you make damned sure he knows that I paid the bill. And I don't want you charging nothing else to me." I glanced at Jack as he stood up shaking his head. "I hate getting taken like this," I hissed. "I oughta go up there and finish him off."

Jack shook his head. "Then you'd owe for a bloody mattress and a burying. Hell, it ain't Alahambre's fault you bought cheap bullets."

"Will you gentlemen be staying again tonight?" Lambert asked with a beaming smile. "I need to know in order to freshen your room." He raised a clean finger. "Service, service, service."

I just stared at him, picked up my hat, and shoved it down on my head. Outside the door, I heard Lambert say to the passed-out cowboy, "Wake up, sir. I've totaled your bill."

"Poor sumbitch," Jack chuckled under his breath.

When we got to the auction, I noticed several townsmen looking toward me and whispering back and forth, so I tipped my hat low to cover my face. Before the bidding began, I left Jack in the auction corral, walked to Buck's stall, and looked him over good. "Are you graining him proper?" I rubbed Buck's muzzle while I spoke to the young Mexican stable hand. Buck nipped at my cheek playfully.

"Si, señor. But the owner said he will need this stall to separate out the auction stock this evening."

"That's no problem," I said. "I'll be leaving before then. Did you pick his hooves clean and check his shoes?"

"Aw—si, Señor Bullets. I take most care of him, like he

is my own *caballo.*" He grinned, then his grin faded as he saw the look in my eyes.

"My—name—is—Beatty," I said, mouthing each word slowly. I raised a finger. "Now . . . don't call me Bullets ever again, *comprende?*"

He shrugged. "Si, but I say it in respect, Señor Bull—I mean Beatty. There is much talk of how you shot down Diamond Joe in a blazing pistol duel. They say you killed him between the eyes and wounded two of his *vaqueros.* It is an honor to—"

"No . . . no," I said, shaking my head. "That's not what happened. What happened is, Joe Alahambre threw down on me, and I shot him. He's not dead. I only wounded him."

"But you shot him between the eyes, señor." He tapped a finger on the bridge of his nose. "How can he be alive?"

"It's a strange story. You see—" I took a deep breath and started to explain about the cheap bullets I bought in Taos, about the card game and Joe Alahambre, but a voice cut me off.

"Around here we don't brag about shooting a man down like a dog, mister," said the voice behind me. I turned and faced a tall man in a black suit wearing a brace of pearl-handled forty-fours and a sheriff's badge.

"I was just trying to clear things up a little," I said. "The story has gotten blown out—"

"Yeah, I heard about it. You're lucky I wasn't here. I'll be keeping an eye on you, mister."

I glanced past him and saw Briggs and his deputies walking toward us. "You've got me wrong, sheriff," I said, keeping my hands well away from my sidearm. "Ask Briggs here about it. He was there. He saw what happened."

"Sure was," said Briggs, hearing the conversation as he stepped up beside us. His thumb lay hooked above the big Dance Brothers pistol at his waist. "Howdy, Mace," he said to the sheriff. The deputies stayed a couple of feet back like trained hounds.

"Briggs," the sheriff nodded. "I just heard this man bragging to the kid here about last night."

"Beatty here?" Briggs smiled and pushed back his stained Stetson. "Naw, you've misunderstood him, Mace. Beatty here is a clean-cut young gentleman. He was probably explaining it. I'll vouch for him. I called it a fair shooting. Hell, this young man knows the bible, religion and the like." He winked and nudged me with his elbow. "And not a bad hand at poker either, when the spirit moves him."

"Well," the sheriff said grudgingly, not wanting to give in too easy. "If I'd been here—"

"You'd say the same I'm saying." Briggs looked him in the eyes. "The feller didn't give him no choice."

"I respect your call." The sheriff cleared his throat and tugged at his drooping mustache.

"Good." Briggs grinned. "I only met him last night, but I'd store my faith in Beatty here any day." Briggs beamed so sincerely, I almost felt guilty. "Mister Beatty," he added, "meet Sheriff Mason Bowman, best damn sheriff a county ever had. Fastest gun in the territory"—now he nudged Bowman and winked—"and a damn good dancer, drunk or sober, eh, Mace?"

The sheriff let out a breath and smiled. "Sorry, Beatty." He reached out a hand and I shook it. "If Briggs says you're all right, then you must be. It just seems like we draw a lot of thugs and grifters here for these auctions. You never know when some of these high plains maniacs might come tearing through here. Lambert puts a lot of effort into these community events—hell, everybody here does." He swept a hand to take in all of the town. "I hate to see something go bad."

Briggs sighed. "Poor ole Lambert. He offers the finest accommodations west of St. Louis, but for some reason he attracts more than his share of lowlifers." Briggs shot me an apologetic glance. "Present company excluded, of course!"

I nodded; Bowman grinned. "So, what brings you and your deputies here?"

"Hunting for Ned Quarrels and his gang," Briggs said with a determined expression. "They hit the stage west of here last week for *forty thousand* dollars." Briggs slid a glance past me and back to Bowman. "Shot old Brody, scared the shit out of some lecturer on tour out of New Hampshire."

Jesus! Forty thousand, I thought, and I hoped they didn't see dollar signs flash across my eyes.

"Yeah, I heard about it," Bowman said. "Been meaning to hunt down RC and his boys and go kill ole Ned. I'm just waiting till after the auction. RC's on one of his wild drunks. Wouldn't do for him to bring Ned's head in and stick it on a pole right now. It'd look bad for business."

"I reckon," said Briggs. "RC can get a little out of hand sometimes. Good thing you're around to keep a rein on him."

Bowman sighed. "It ain't an easy job. But he's a lodge brother, so what can you say?"

"This is Lambert's auction?" I glanced from Bowman to Briggs.

"It's a town function," Briggs said, "but Henri backs most of it. It's a way of drawing folks here. Thinks the Saint James will be here a hundred years, I reckon."

"Lambert's a hell of a citizen," Bowman said. "Does everything to help Cimarron. You gotta love a man like that."

"Yeah," I nodded. "He sure has my support. What's that about sticking a head on a pole?"

"Aw, it ain't nothing . . . just some foolishness that happened here awhile back. Say . . . where's that friend of yours today?" Briggs asked. "That gambler, Mackay?"

"He got on a stage this morning," I said, "last I saw him; why?"

"Rascal stiffed me for a steak dinner last night after you

and your partner went to your room. He ordered dinner for me, the deputies, and himself—said he felt bad about what happened and all. But then he disappeared when it came time to pay."

I shook my head. "No kidding?"

"It don't matter none. He probably just forgot. But when you see him, rib him about it a little. Just in fun."

"Okay," I said. "But I don't really know the man. Only met him yesterday at the table."

"Well." Briggs looked down and nodded his head. "Turns out, he's just a real nice guy. I had to brace him down a little last night over that card game, but that wasn't nothing."

"Didn't have to smack him around none?" Bowman looked curious.

"Naw. He ain't belligerent like most gamblers." He rubbed his boot around in the dirty straw. "Ain't sure he'd take a smacking, to tell you the truth." Briggs looked up at me. "Now what about that snake you bung-holed in the forehead? Seen him again?"

"Naw, I ain't. But he's a mess. I heard him carrying on all night. Could hardly get any sleep for him moaning and groaning."

Sheriff Bowman's eyes narrowed. "He oughta be ashamed, keeping you up like that, after you trying to blow his nose out the back of his head."

"I didn't mean it that way," I said. I cleared my throat.

"Aw," Bowman said. "Maybe I misunderstood you again." He looked me up and down, turned to Briggs, and shook his head.

Briggs just smiled; and I didn't understand the look that passed between them.

"Maybe I better go find my partner," I said, after an uncomfortable stretch of silence. I felt ill at ease standing there looking at two shiny badges, and apparently I hadn't hit it off with Sheriff Bowman the way I had with Marshall Briggs.

"He is at the block, señor," said the Mexican kid. "I seen him there."

"Thanks," I said, and I tipped my hat. "If you-all will excuse me." I turned and started out of the barn toward the auction yard.

"Now don't forget to tease Mackay just a little if you see him," Briggs said. I glanced over my shoulder and smiled. Briggs held up a thumb and forefinger to show me just how much to tease Mackay. "A teeny bit," he grinned. I waved and walked out into the sunlight.

I was laughing quietly when I walked up beside Jack and propped my foot on the fence rail. "What's funny?" Jack asked. Across the corral, the auctioneer's voice rattled like marbles in a bucket. He slung his arms like a Holy Roller at a tent meeting. Around the block stood a tight throng of string ties, silk vests, and long dusters. Derbies, bowlers, Stetsons, and sombreros milled and bobbed in wavering sunlight. Hand-tooled knee boots, low-cuts, and lace-ups, all pointed their toes toward the center of the block and shifted back and forth in a low swirl of corral dust.

"Nothing," I said. "Just thinking about Marshall Briggs. For some reason he thinks snow wouldn't melt in my hand. He just vouched for me being a gentleman to the local sheriff." I shook my head. "Imagine that."

"Better watch . . . getting close to a lawman ain't a good idea, no matter what he thinks of ya."

"Aw, Jack . . . Briggs is just an old man who's a little frayed around the edges. He even let that gambler Mackay stiff him for a dinner."

"So? He got you for breakfast and a bottle of hootch. I didn't even get to sniff the cork."

"That ain't the point, Jack. If Briggs thinks I'm a *'fine young gentleman,'* what's the harm?"

Jack grinned. "Yeah. After seeing that shooting last

night, I reckon he figures you ain't apt to go kill nobody."

We watched the bidding and the flow of stock without seeing anything of any interest, save for a big chestnut bay that sold for twice what I thought she was worth. The bidding had stayed high and loose all three days, and since I'd came here to buy and brought nothing to sell, the whole auction had been a waste of time. But that's just horse dealing. At least I'd done well at poker, even if I did have to shoot my way through it.

In the separating pens across the corral, I watched a stock handler lead horse after horse into a corral near the barn. Each horse had a tag tied to its mane; when one got loose and circled the bidding corral, it stopped in front of us long enough for me to see the name "Alahambre" scribbled on its tag.

"Damn," Jack said, "if all those horses are Alahambre's, he must be running a pretty big spread somewhere."

I eyed the stock closer as the handler led two more away. "Yeah, but he'd be a fool to risk these kinda animals on an open range. Especially for the price they're bringing. These ain't ordinary cow ponies, Jack. Some of these horses are fine enough for a show ring . . . or at least a cavalry regiment."

I watched the horses mill and prance in the pens until someone tapped me on the shoulder; and I turned around and looked into the eyes of one of the German barmaids. "Excuse me," she said. "Are you Herr Beatty?" Her English was flawless but I could tell she was studying each word carefully before she spoke it.

"Yes, I'm Beatty." I looked her up and down.

"Mister Lambert must see you right away. Please come with me."

"Wait a minute," I said as she turned to walk away; she stopped and gave me a curious look. "What does he want? I'm kinda busy here."

"It is about your bill. He said if you do not come pay your bill, he will send for the sheriff."

"He's crazy! I paid for the room in advance, last night."

"He said you owe him for today," she said. Her voice was cool, calm, and without inflection. "You did not turn in your key. So you are still renting the room."

"Son of a bitch!" I yanked off my hat and slapped it against the fence rail. Dust billowed. I kicked the post and felt a pain shoot up my leg to my kneecap.

"I will tell him you are not coming," she said, and she turned and walked away.

"Naw, naw, naw!" I jammed my hat down on my head. "I'm coming! You better believe I'm coming!" I turned to Jack, wild-eyed. "I bet I kill that money-grubbing bastard," I hissed.

Jack shook his head and fell in beside me. "Then you better use a club," he said. "You'll just run up more debt if you shoot him."

• 3 •

With everybody at the auction, Lambert's Saloon was empty and quiet except for the young cowboy who'd been passed out earlier. He sat on the floor polishing a brass spittoon, mumbling under his breath. When I stepped inside the door, he glanced up at me with a sneer and ran the back of his hand across his mouth. "Where is he?" I said in a clipped voice. The cowboy pointed at the bar, blew his breath on the spittoon, and started rubbing it again without saying a word. He was bucktoothed as a beaver.

Jack stopped just inside the door and propped his boot up on a chair. The German barmaid scurried off into the kitchen as I stomped over to the bar wide-eyed with my shoulders leveled. I slapped both hands down on the bar and called out, "Lambert! Here I am. Get out here. Let's get settled, once and for all." I'd gained some control on my way over and made up my mind not to hurt him bad, maybe just bang his face down on the bar a time or two—a practice that had kept Missouri barkeepers in line for many years.

"Please, sir," said the thirteen-year-old bartender, stepping out from the kitchen, wiping his hands on a bar towel. "Please be a little quieter. My father is asleep. If you wake him up it'll be bad for me."

I looked down at his pleading eyes, cleared my throat, and lowered my voice. "Well, I'm afraid you'll *have* to wake him up, young man. He sent a lady over to get me. He said he needed to see me."

The little boy shrugged and looked a little frightened. "I'm sorry, sir. But it was I who sent her. My father said if I didn't collect the money for the room, he'd take it out of my hide."

I looked at him, wondering for a second if he might be pulling my leg. Whatever else Henri Lambert was, he didn't strike me as the kind of person who would mistreat a kid, but when it comes to money, you never know. "I don't know about you and your father's problems," I said. "But I don't owe anything on that room. Now go wake him up. We'll get this thing settled."

"Did he ask you this morning if you were going to spend another night?" The boy watched for my answer as if he already knew it.

"Well," I cleared my throat, "he might've. I ain't sure."

"You did read the notice, didn't you, sir?" He pointed a slim young finger to a small—really small—sign on the wall behind him.

I leaned against the bar and squinted my eyes. I heard Jack chuckle from his perch inside the door. "Here," said the boy, "let me get it for you." He unhooked the sign and laid it on the bar. Even up close the print looked awfully small.

"It says," the skinny young cowboy called out from the floor, " 'All guests will be responsible for room rental until such time as the key is turned in at the bar. Any rental due is subject to collection procedures as deemed necessary—' "

"You know it by heart?" I glanced around at the cowboy.

"I oughta," he said. He shook his head and turned back to polishing.

"Damned if I'll be taken in like this!" I slapped my hand on the bar. "Go wake him up, right now."

"Okay, sir," said young Lambert, raising his hands. "I'll go wake him." I saw his eyes begin to water; his shoulders shook slightly. "I'm sorry if I caused you any trouble. I certainly didn't mean to—"

"Just a minute, kid," I said, my voice easing down some. I glanced around at Jack; Jack shrugged and spread his hands. I reached into my pocket, pulled out the key by its big brass tag, and dropped it clattering on the bar. "Just give him the key and tell him it was all a mistake, okay? Will that get you off the hook?"

"It might help . . . some." He lowered his eyes toward the floor behind the bar. "I'll spend a few nights in the woodshed . . . but I've done that before."

Again I glanced around at Jack: he pushed up his hat, gazed up at the ceiling, smiling, scratching his chin. I let out a breath, slumped on my elbows and pulled a clip of bills from my shirt pocket. "It ain't worth all this." I shook my head, peeled off four dollars onto the bar and stuck the clip back in my pocket. "There, I know when I'm whipped. Now . . . are we free and clear?"

"Yes, sir," he said. His demeanor changed instantly. "And here's your key back." He slid it toward me. I jumped back from it like it was a scorpion.

"Oh no!" I raised my hands. "You keep it. I just want out of here without losing my shirt." I backed away and turned toward the door. "There's such a thing as the Emancipation Proclamation," I said, gazing down at the skinny cowboy as I crossed the floor.

"Tell me about it," he hissed. He slapped the rag around the spittoon and shined it like you'd shine a boot. He *really* was bucktoothed as a beaver.

"Nuu sufa-bintch!" I heard a terrible grating voice from the stairs and turned quickly to see Diamond Joe standing on the third step holding the banister with much effort. A young cowboy stood beside him steadying him as he wobbled back and forth. Joe's face looked like a jack-o'-lantern, swollen, sickly orange, with purple slits of eyes separated by a bloody bundle of gauze. A black leech hung under each eyelid like a large dark teardrop. White strips of tape banded his forehead and jaws. It hurt to look at him.

"Sufa-bintch!" he said again. Jack chuckled behind me.

"Oh, Mister Alahambre. *Jesus,*" I said, looking at his face. I took a cautious step toward him, not knowing quite what to say or do.

The cowboy glared at me and spoke across a tight jaw. "You the one did this?"

"Yeah," I said, "but . . . whew!" My voice sounded hushed. "I've never seen such a face on a living human being. That must be awfully painful."

Diamond Joe's face seemed to swell even more each time I opened my mouth. He took a step down on shaky legs, stumbled, and the cowboy caught him. I threw up a hand, "Careful there, Mister Alahambre!" I said in earnest. "Watch your step."

He looked at me, shaking all over; his chest heaved in rage. His hand squeezed the railing.

"I mean, you don't want to go bumping that nose." I didn't know what else to say. Jack snorted to keep from laughing.

"Get out of here, mister," the cowboy hissed.

"I'll-kahill-nuu!" shouted Diamond Joe. He rocked forward. His shaky legs buckled. He turned loose of the cowboy and threw both arms out toward me. For a split second he seemed to hang in the air.

"Careful!" I shouted.

The cowboy grabbed him around the waist as he lunged forward and down. "Get out!" The young cowboy shouted at me as they struggled. And I backed up just as the two of them tumbled off the last step. Diamond Joe landed facedown with a loud thump, his arms spread out on the hard wooden floor. The cowboy landed on top of him. I winced, clenching my teeth at the sound of swollen flesh meeting hard pine.

"Good Lord!" I yelled, but my voice was drowned out by

anyway. Everybody's afraid of his bunch because the gang's gotten so big."

"How big?" I was just asking to make conversation.

"Oh . . . probably twenty or more men, by now. They've been left alone by most of the local lawmen, so now they've got big, wild, and out of control." A look of concern swept Briggs's face, then disappeared behind a worn smile. "That's how it happens sometimes. Things go unattended till they get out of control, then it's left up to somebody like me to go straighten it out. These young lawmen are too interested in making a quick name for themselves taming a town somewhere. They've got no stomach for trekking out across the desert. No glamour in it, I reckon. But there's more to settling a land than just cutting trees, throwing up buildings, and pistol-whipping a few drunks, you know."

"I reckon so," I said.

Briggs sighed. "But, enough about that. Here's something you might get a kick out of, being from Missouri and all. He pulled up a stack of professionally drawn posters that were dog-eared and dusty. "The boys," he said, and I felt my stomach tighten as he spread them on his desk. "Now there's a bunch of *real* desperados for ya. Jesse, Frank, Cole Younger, Miller Crowe. What a bunch, huh? Ned Quarrels couldn't hold these boys' horses, could he?" He shook off the dust. "These are posters a man can be proud of."

I slid a glance across my own poster, then Cousin Jesse's, then Frank's, then Cole's, then smiled and sipped my drink. "Yeah, I reckon they've had quite a stand at it." I looked Briggs in the eye, but saw no sign of recognition. Maybe he was getting too old. Maybe he just couldn't see the obvious. Of course, I had done a fair job of presenting myself as a young business man . . . and a *gentleman* to boot. "I suppose you've looked for them for a long time?"

"The Jameses Gang? Naw, not really. They don't get over this way much. I've always thought of them more as soldiers than common outlaws. If anybody hunts them it oughta be the army. They're the ones caused the James Gang . . . the war and all. I believe the Jameses would settle down if the law would let them."

I slid Jack a glance. "You might be right, marshall. They don't seem as bad as some scoundrels I've heard of."

"No sir," Briggs said, "nothing like Quarrels's bunch." Briggs sighed. "I know I shouldn't think of it, me being a lawman and all but I'd almost give that forty thousand just to see what Quarrels would do if he ever locked horns with a couple of 'the boys' here." Briggs tapped a finger on the posters. "Bet he'd fill his boots, huh?"

I grinned. "Never know."

Briggs shuffled the posters into a stack with mine on top. "Say now," he said, cocking an eye at my poster, then up at me. He held the poster over for Jack to see. "Look at Crowe's picture, then look at Beatty here."

"I'll be damned," Jack said. I glanced back and forth, felt my heart pound, but stayed calm on the surface. "You're under arrest!" Jack shouted, and slapped his hand to his holster. Briggs stiffened, then laughed as he saw Jack was only playing. My heart made one big thump and nearly fell out the seat of my britches.

"What's so funny?" I said with a weak smile.

Jack flipped the poster of me on the desk. "Look at that. He looks just like you." Jack craned his neck and looked again. "Well . . . not *just* like you, but some."

I studied the poster a second and threw up my hands. "You got me, marshall," I laughed. "I'm Miller Crowe—guilty as charged."

"Aw—" Briggs swiped a hand across the air. "You're too well-mannered to be that snake. Besides, if you *was* one of them, I'd want you to be Jesse himself." He grinned. "Always better to get the leader, you know."

"All right," I laughed, playing it to the hilt, "*I'm* Jesse James. Now do your worst."

"Aw," Briggs laughed and swiped his hand again, looked down and poured a drink. I shot Jack a glance and let out a sigh of relief. "That Crowe feller," Jack said. "I heard awhile back that he'd gotten skinned and gutted up at Powder River. Is that true?"

"I heard that myself." Briggs tossed back a sip, swallowed, and belched. "It's probably true. Nobody's heard nothing out of him lately." Briggs shrugged. "He wasn't much anyway . . . just held the horses for the rest of 'em." Briggs chuckled. "What does that tell you?"

Jack snorted a laugh; I felt my face redden. "Well, I reckon being the horse-man could get just as—"

Jack cut me off quickly. "Reckon we wouldn't know"—he shot me a glance—"since we never consort with *those* kind of people."

"Of course not." Briggs tapped a finger on his desk. "You're good honest boys, out here trying to make yourselves a decent living the hard way—the *honest* way."

"Thank you, marshall," Jack said. "It's good to be appreciated now and then." He looked a little embarrassed.

Briggs swept up the posters. "But still . . . " He sighed and dropped them in the drawer. "It'd be something to see. Like I told you, I got no riff with Jesse and his bunch. It's bastards like Quarrels . . . out there in the desert festering like a boil. Sitting on forty thousand dollars that he can't even spend except in some pig-sty like Gris . . . for fear of getting caught." Briggs shook his head. "All that money . . . probably hidden under a rock somewhere. Think about that."

I did think about it. I thought about it and almost licked my lips. "What business does a stage have carrying that much money, forty thousand?"

"None really. They carried a payroll for a mine near here. Tried to be clever, figuring nobody would suspect that much money on a four-wheeler. But Quarrels did . . . knew just where to look, too. Ripped out a seat, and there it was. . . . Easy pickings."

I saw the look in Jack's eyes. Somebody had to have tipped Quarrels off. Nobody rips a seat out of a stage for no reason. I wasn't even a stage man, but I knew better than that. Briggs had to know it too, unless he'd spent too many nights sleeping with his head on a cold rock. I poured another drink and sat on the edge of his desk. "I bet it's interesting work, looking for a pile of money? How do you even know where to start?"

Briggs looked back and forth between us. "Boys, it ain't easy. But it can sure be done."

"No kidding?" Jack sat down also, poured another drink, and we spent over two hours drinking and talking, talking about Ned Quarrels, his habits, his gang, and above all else, where a man like Quarrels might hide that much money along the high ridges of *Nuevo Mejico.*

It was midafternoon by the time we finished the bottle of rye. By then, I lay sprawled on a blanket-covered cot against the wall with my back propped up against an old saddle and my hat down almost to my nose. Jack was leaned back in a wooden chair with his boots on Briggs's desk. Briggs sat the same way on the other side. Now the shadows of the bars had crawled long across the floor and climbed the wall. I felt my belly rumble and I sat up on the side of the cot. "Anybody feel like eating?"

"I could use something hot wrapped around a scoop of beans," Jack said. "What about you, marshall?" He reached a boot over and tapped it against Briggs's ankle.

Briggs stirred enough to raise a hand. "Naw, I'm gonna stay right here where the dogs don't bite. But you boys feel free. There's Mama Lopez's a block from the livery barn. Tell her you know me."

"Why's that?" I stood up, pressing my hands to the small of my back.

"So she won't poison ya." Briggs ran a leathery hand across his white mustache. "She don't like gringos."

I smiled. Briggs was a good enough old feller. "It's been

nice visiting with you, marshall," I said. "I reckon we'll get a bite and be pushing on. Long ride across Kansas."

"Be careful, boys. This is a rough land full of dangerous people, just waiting to take advantage." Briggs waved a hand without looking up. Jack and I walked out into the evening sun.

"Boy have I ever greased his wheels," I said, as we started off up the dirt street.

"I don't know who's greasing who," Jack said. He glanced over his shoulder as we walked through an alley. "But I'd hate to see Quarrels hurt his back, carrying all that money around. Think we oughta take it?"

"Seems like we should," I said. We walked out onto the street and turned toward the barn. "But Briggs knows this country and *he* ain't found it. What makes you think we could?"

"Because we're outlaws." Jack spread his hands. "We think like outlaws. Make any sense?"

"Maybe," I said. Up the street, the Mexican kid from the stables spotted us and ran toward me. "But these are New Mexican outlaws. We're Missouri outlaws," I said to Jack.

"So?"

"Maybe we think different. The way Briggs talks, this Quarrels Gang ain't nothing like us." I grinned and winked at Jack. "We're *good* outlaws, remember?"

Jack grinned, but with reserve. "I'm telling ya, you're getting too close with that old boy. Don't forget he wears a badge. No matter how much a *gentleman* he thinks you are, he's still on the other side of the fence."

"Hell, I know it, Jack. But it don't hurt for *somebody* to think we're decent law-abiding citizens, especially in a *rough land full of dangerous people who're just waiting to take—"*

"That's enough," Jack said. "You ain't heard a word I said about him, have ya?"

"Sure I have. And I hear you about the money too. All's I'm saying is—"

"Señor!" I stopped and watched the kid slide to a halt. He looked frantic. "I have been looking everywhere for you! You must come quick! Your horse, señor! Your horse!"

I grabbed him by both shoulders. "What is it? What's wrong with Buck?"

"Do not beat me, señor! I could not help it."

"Easy, son, nobody's gonna beat ya. What's wrong with Buck?"

"He is gone, señor! He got mixed into Alahambre's horses. They took him! He is gone!"

I turned him loose and ran the last block to the livery barn. When I jumped the fence and slung open the doors, the owner, Migueal, sat on a bale of hay in front of Buck's empty stall. He raised his head from his hands and looked at me through sad and frightened eyes. "This is terrible, señor . . . terrible."

As if I couldn't believe what had happened, I jumped in front of the stall and looked all around. The stall was empty, save for my saddle, tack, and coat thrown in a corner, but I kept looking around, feeling the way a person must feel when a child is missing. I heard someone behind me, swung around and saw Jack. He too kept looking into the empty stall. "It is all a simple mistake, señor," Migueal said. "If you find the man and explain it, he will give you back your horse, no?"

"I don't know, Migueal," I said, chafing the back of my neck trying to think.

"What do you figure?" Jack asked in a low voice. "Accident, coincidence?"

"Maybe," I said. "How would he know it's my horse? And if he knew it, why would he take a chance getting caught stealing it? He's no horse thief."

"Revenge makes a man do crazy things." Jack went to the stall at the other end of the barn. "But mine's still here, so maybe it *was* a mistake."

"It might've started out that way, Jack. But what's he

going to do when he sees *me* riding onto his spread asking for my horse?"

Jack shook his head. "Should've killed him . . . I knew it."

"Mister Beatty," said Migueal, "I told the boy this morning to tell you I would need the stables for the auction horses."

"He told me, Migueal. I'm not blaming either of you."

"Oh, thank you, señor. I was worried."

"Where is Alahambre's spread? How far is it?"

"It is near Gris, señor. Out near the foothills. Do you know the country?"

"No, but I'll learn it." I walked back and forth looking in stall after empty stall for something to ride. "Where's all the horses?"

"There are none left, señor. They have all been sold. Only Señor Lambert has any horses left."

"Lambert? Damnit! I hate going to him." I spun around and stomped out of the barn with Jack right beside me.

"Does this kill any notion of looking for the money?"

I didn't answer. At the corral gate, I studied the land past Cimarron, the outline of ridges beyond the stretch of flatland rolling ever upward, dotted with dark shadows of mesquite, low-hanging juniper, knurled pinyon pine; beyond, the jagged lofty lines of the Sangre de Cristos stretching upward into a marbled gray and purple sky.

• 4 •

Lambert's Saloon was alive, kicking high, when I squeezed through the door and shouldered my way toward the bar. The banjo player was back at work strumming, bleating out the lyrics to "Bound for the Rio Grande," his words more clearly and cautiously pronounced than the night before. I caught a glimpse of a large blue knot on top of his bald head. Beside him, a heavy-set woman wearing thick rouge beat on a tambourine as if it owed her money. I jumped when a shot went off. I saw a splinter fall from the ceiling. Even above the noise, I heard someone cuss and stomp on the floor upstairs. I just shook my head and elbowed on through the crowd.

"Oh, it's you," said a laughing voice beside me. Miss Helova Knight took hold of my coat sleeve as I tugged slightly and tried to press onward to the bar. "Where's your friend, the admiral?" she said above the deafening roar. "I hoped I'd see him here tonight."

"The what?" I kept moving but she shouldered right along with me. Beer sloshed out of a mug. I felt it splatter on my boot. "You know," she said, "the admiral . . . from last night? He told me he owned a fleet of ships."

I caught a glimpse of Lambert's top hat and tried to maneuver toward it. One of the barmaids squeezed past me carrying three mugs of beer in each hand. She clipped me with her forearm, almost knocking me down. "Oh, the admiral . . . yeah, he does," I said, steadying myself on somebody's shoulder until I caught my balance. "He's getting packed, we're headed out." I managed to shake her loose without kicking her, reached between two big bellies in silk vests, grabbed the bar, and pulled myself to it. The bellies rolled apart for me grudgingly, like boulders guarding a great treasure. "Lambert," I shouted down the bar. His top hat rose for a second, looked around, then bent back to pouring whiskey. "Damn it!" I said out loud; and without a second thought I jumped the bar and started walking quickly toward him.

Faces stared wide-eyed through the heavy smoke—a woman even shrieked—and I raised my hands chest high to show that I meant no harm. Of everything I'd ever done, nothing felt more blasphemous, sacrilegious, *unforgivable,* than walking along that wooden catwalk above the vapor of stale whiskey and puddles of spilled beer. Out the corner of my eye, I saw beneath the bar a snub-barreled shotgun, four billy bats, two pistols, a short-handled ax, and a coiled-up rope with a noose tied in it. All these tools of the bartending trade were strategically placed at arm's length at any point along the bar.

Lambert looked up at me and his eyes grew large. "You can't be back here! The hell's the matter with you?" I thought I saw his hair actually stand out around his ears. His nostrils flared.

"It's an emergency! I've got to talk to you." I reached to tug at his sleeve; he jerked it away.

"An emergency?" He looked me up and down and slung a towel over his shoulder. His hand started instinctively toward the short-handled ax and stopped close to the handle. He rolled his eyes past the smoke, the crowd, and the wavering sea of upturned glasses. "What do you call this?" he shouted.

From the kitchen behind us came a long loud sizzle, like

someone had dropped a cow in a volcano. The smell of beef grease and mesquite lay heavy. From the crowd someone yelled, "Get it *right*, you son of a bitch!" There was a loud thud and the banjo stopped abruptly, but the tambourine rattled on in a high fervent solo.

"Please, Lambert, damn it!" I snatched my money clip from my shirt pocket and waved it up and down. His head followed it. "I'll pay! I've got to talk to you."

Lambert snatched one of the German barmaids as she sailed past to the kitchen. "Watch the bar a second," he yelled above the noise.

"But I can't count!" She looked terrified at the thought of it.

"It doesn't matter," he said, shoving a bar towel into her hand. "Whatever they give you, just look at them like it ain't enough." He nodded me toward the kitchen door, then turned toward her before we stepped through it. "For god-sakes, don't give them any change!"

Just inside the door, I looked up and saw there was no roof over the kitchen. A thousand stars winked and glittered through a rising rush of mesquite smoke. Lambert held out a hand, snapped his fingers, and nodded toward my money clip. "That'll be two dollars . . . for the talk."

I peeled off the bills and watched them disappear from between my fingers. "I've got to buy one of your horses, right now," I said quickly. "It's an emergency!"

"How's that? What kind of emergency?"

"My horse got taken—"

"Coming through," said a voice from behind a wide tray of sizzling steaks. I pressed back against the wall, and saw the bucktoothed cowboy with sweat streaming down his face. He pushed between us, glanced at me, "Emancipation Proclamation?" shook his head and walked past in wobbling boots, forcing his way into a writhing wave of hungry thirsty humanity.

"—My horse got taken along with a string of auction

horses. I've got to catch up to them and get it back. You've got to help me!"

Lambert ran a hand across his sweaty brow as I took a quick breath and explained what had happened, about Alahambre and my horse . . . Buck. He already knew about the shooting and the cheap bullets I'd bought in Taos.

When I'd finished, he just stared at me. I could picture a large bag of money with wings on it; and it sailed along, waved its way out of my window and into Lambert's. "So you need a horse that bad, huh?" He studied my eyes. "Bad enough that you'd come to me after the shameless way you acted here earlier?" He shook his head. "The stallion must be something special. Worth a lot?"

"Yes, to me he is," I said flatly, letting out a long breath, the longest breath I'd be able to afford once he got through with me.

"So, will you sell me a horse?" I shook the money clip. "I won't dicker with you. Just name a price."

Lambert closed his sweaty hand around my money clip and squeezed it into my hand. "You have misjudged me, young man. What man with a heart could *sell* you a horse in a time like this?" He pressed my hand against my shirt pocket. "Put your money away and go, go tell Migueal to take you into my private corral and put you on the horse of your choosing. I would not think of *selling* you a horse—"

"Well . . . thanks, Mister Lambert." I almost had to run a finger beneath my eye. I felt like a low-down dog for what I'd been thinking of this fine and decent man.

He patted my shoulder. "Call me Henri," he said. "Or better still, just call me Hank." He raised a finger. "I only ask that you bring my horse back safe and sound, *comprende?*" Before I could even answer, he yelled back to his son who stood bowed over a wide parrilla full of hissing, smoking steaks. "Junior . . . wrap up some of those belly stretchers for Mister Beatty here and throw in a couple of baked trout. He's got a long ride coming."

"I don't know what to say, Mister Lam—Hen—Hank," I said. "I'm sorry if I've been difficult—"

"There is nothing to say." He swept a hand to take in the breadth of heaven and earth. "Isn't this why we are all put here? To help one another?" Beyond the kitchen door, I heard another belch of gunfire, followed by more heavy pounding from the room above.

"Are you sure you didn't take a knife to his finger joints?" Jack held a baked trout by its head, ate the side of it, and spit the bones so straight up that one had fallen on his hat brim.

"Naw, Jack, I swear," I said, wrapping a turn in the latigo and sliding the strap tight. I grabbed the saddle with both hands and tested it before letting the stirrup down the side of the liver-chestnut. The big mare quivered her skin, stomped a hoof, blew out a breath and shook her mane. "I was wrong about Lambert, and I'm sorry for it. I reckon he's some kind of a visionary—musta got that way working for ole Honest Abe Lincoln. I don't know." I slung up my saddlebags and checked them down, slid my hog-leg ten-gauge beneath my bedroll, and shoved my rifle into its boot. "Anyway . . . I reckon Mace Bowman was right . . . 'you gotta love a man like that.' "

Jack threw the trout's skeleton in a garbage bucket, picked a tooth, wiped a hand down his shirt, and unwrapped a thick steak. "I don't know about that, but he sure is a wizard with a skillet. I'm surprised ole Abe didn't put on more weight." Jack washed down the trout with a long swig of bourbon from his canteen.

I stopped and looked at him: "Are you ready?"

"Been ready," he said. He belched and took a big bite of steak.

I wasn't about to tell "Admiral" Jack that Miss Knight had stopped me and asked about him *once again* as I left Lambert's Saloon. I'd once again told her that we were headed out, but before I could shake her loose without poking her in the eye, she'd jerked me to a halt, propped a high heel on a chair arm, and threw open a slit in her long red dress. "Now tell the truth," she'd said, bold as brass. "Have you ever seen a thigh as white as this in your *whole* life?" She ran her hand slowly up along her inner thigh, her painted nails leaving tiny goose bumps that spread all the way from her leg clear up the back of my neck.

"Lord-God-have-mercy-on-my-soul!" said the man in the chair. He reached out a rough dirty hand, but she smacked it away, thumped his forehead with her palm and turned back to me, smiling.

"No, ma'am," I said in a hushed voice beneath all the racket, "as God's my witness . . . I *never* have . . . nor am I *ever* likely to."

"Feel free to tell the admiral about it," she winked. "Tell him it's perfect—" She took my hand and ran it from her knee upward. It was like sliding along a warm ribbon of silk that led to a steam boiler. My whole arm seemed to go numb. "And tell him I'm free—all night long." She smiled, dropped my hand, ran one long polished nail down her thigh to her knee, and flipped her dress shut.

"Yes, ma'am." I'd swallowed hard, backed up, stepped over the knocked-out banjo player and on out the door, needing air. I wasn't going to tell Jack about it tonight, and if I ever told him later on, I hoped I wouldn't have to fight him over it.

But now, as I looked at Jack chewing on the steak, ready to ride off with me into the wilderness, I couldn't help but feel a little bad about questioning his priorities. We'd been friends too long for Jack to let me ride off alone, to face a man whose nose I'd deformed for life. I knew Jack better than that . . . creamy thigh or no. It wouldn't be right, not telling him. I felt like I had to.

"Uh . . . Jack? There's something I meant to say."

"Yeah?" He smacked his lips.

"That woman last night . . . the one with the funny name?"

"You mean Helova, the Rumanian? What about her?"

I pushed up my hat and bit my lip. "Well, Jack—"

"There you boys are," Briggs said in a booming voice, stepping into the livery barn, into the glow of a lantern. He peeled off his stained Stetson and slapped it against his leg. "I heard what happened from the Mexican kid." He ran his leathery fingers back through hair the color of snow and wood smoke. "I say it was low down and deliberately down. What say you, Beatty? You gonna kill him this time? Kill him like the ill-mannered dog that he is?"

Just out of nervousness, I checked my saddle again. "Marshall, right now I can't say what I'm apt to do. I can't tell you how much that stallion means to me." I unsnapped my gunbelt and laid it in front of my saddle, butt forward, guerilla style, for a riding draw.

"Worth a lot of money, huh?"

"It's not that," I said. "It's that I hand-raised him from a colt. He thinks he's a part of me, marshall. Ever been that close with an animal?"

"Not really, but I know how you feel. Everybody's got something that they hold above everything else, I reckon. Something you can't really set a price on . . . something that only comes along once in a lifetime." He glanced from me to Jack, then back to me. "You boys ever rode this end of the high cutoff?"

"No," I said, "but if that's the quickest way to Gris, I reckon we're *fixin'* to. He's got about a four-hour start on us. We'll need to move quick."

Briggs shook his head slowly and looked at the ground. "It's a shaky proposition at night . . . if you don't know the trail. It's straight up and straight down. Real easy to ride off the edge of a ridge."

"We'll just have to be careful," I said.

Briggs sucked his teeth and chafed the back of his neck

for a second, then shook his head and looked up at me. "Boys, I can't let yas go . . . not alone. . . . Yas being the kinda boys you are and all."

I shot Jack a glance; he lowered the steak. Juice dripped. "Nawsir, it's too dangerous," Briggs said, still shaking his head. "I'm gonna ride along with you . . . at least till I see that that snake, Alahambre, does what's right. He's just the kind of person I warned ya about."

"Thanks just the same," I said. "We'll be all right, so long as—"

"Boys, this ain't Missouri," Briggs said, looking back and forth. "Boys, this ain't even *Tejas.* Boys, this is *Nuevo Mejico,* is what this is. There's forms of life out there would backhand an alligator, and I'm betting Alahambre's one of 'em. I'm the federal law here . . . and it's my duty to protect gentlemen like ya'selves." He hooked his thumbs in his belt. "Boys, I'm going"—he jutted his sharp chin—"And that's all there are to it."

I glanced at Jack; he looked puzzled. I couldn't imagine what Briggs pictured us to be. He had to see enough hardware hanging on the liver-chestnut to hold back a small army. Maybe he was blind. Since the last year of the civil conflict, Jack and I had robbed, burnt, shot, stabbed, and bludgeoned our way through everything but the gates of hell—done things I'd spend the rest of my natural life regretting. But Briggs wasn't seeing us in that light. I didn't know *what* he saw, but whatever it was, he was sure out to protect us, to save us from *something.* Maybe he was more than just old . . . maybe he was a little crazy.

The only way I ever saw myself riding with a lawman was strapped belly-down on the horse behind him, but I had to realize, having Briggs along might keep Alahambre on a short leash long enough for me to get Buck away from him without a fight.

"You sure, marshall?" He watched blank-faced as I pulled the small-caliber hideaway pistol from the back of my waist, checked it, twirled it, put it back, and adjusted the forty-four in the shoulder harness under my left arm. "We don't want to impose. What about your deputies? What'll they do while you're gone?" I even reached down, slid my glades knife from my boot, ran my thumb along the glistening edge and dropped it back down. Briggs didn't seem to notice.

"They'll stay drunk, if I'm any judge," he said. "But it don't matter. I couldn't face myself, letting a couple of boys like you two ride out there on your own." He waved a hand as he turned toward the door. "I've got lots of coffee and a spin of dried shank on my horse. I'm ready when you boys are. So there." He walked out with his duster tails licking gently at his boot heels.

I looked at Jack, shrugged, and picked up the reins to the liver-chestnut. "So there," I said.

Jack looked at me from under the brim of his long oval, ran the steak bone through his teeth sucking it clean, belched, and pitched the bone in the garbage bucket. "I hope you know what you're doing." He wiped both hands down his shirt and picked up the reins to his silver-gray. "Now . . . what were you saying about the woman?"

"The woman?" For a second I'd gone blank, thinking about Buck, wondering if he was all right. Knowing he'd be confused as to why a stranger had led him away from me, wondering if I'd forsaken him. Wondering if he was at that second calling out to me from somewhere high atop a cold lonely ridge, scared, and missing me.

"Yeah," Jack said, "the Rumanian."

"Oh . . . that was all," I said, "just that." I'd been on the verge of telling him about the creamy white thigh, hoping it wouldn't change his mind about going with me tonight. Now that Briggs was riding with us, I wasn't about to take the chance.

"Just what, goddamn it?" Jack gave me a puzzled look.

"Uh . . . you know. Just wondering—is she *really* Rumanian?"

Jack stopped and just stared at me. "Yes," he said flatly, "she is, *really* Rumanian." He dealt me a dubious gaze. "Is that all?"

"Uh . . . yeah." I nodded. I looked at him standing there in his long duster, a fish bone on the brim of his hat, a grease spot on the front of his wool shirt with a gnat circling it, and reins hanging from his hand. Between him and me I envisioned that white thigh and those nails sliding up it; I pictured Jack somewhere along the high rocky stretch between Cimarron and Gris, sleeping on the hard ground, snuggled up to a steel rifle barrel. I looked away from him, bit my lip, and led the liver-chestnut out of the barn.

"You can think of the most damndest things at the most damndest times than anybody I ever seen," he said, leading his silver-gray beside me. I remembered the feel of that white thigh, felt the pale creamy warmth of it against my hand. My hand tingled. Someday I would have to tell him, but not now. I would tell him later on, someday when we were both old men . . . too old to kill each other over it.

"I reckon so," I said, and I stepped up in the stirrup, again thinking of Buck, knowing that no one understood the young stallion like I understood him, or handled him the way I handled him . . . and had handled him, since the first day he'd stood up on spindly legs and wobbled at his mama's flank. "Damn it, Buck," I whispered softly. I glanced at Marshall Newton Briggs and "Quiet" Jack Smith. They both tugged at their hat brims and glanced down; and I tapped the big liver-chestnut with my heels, felt her snap forward . . . and I rode ahead of them a ways, past the glow and the din of Lambert's Saloon, past scattered adobes curling thin smoke from their *chimeneas,* out across the dirt road . . . into the thin, chilled air.

• 5 •

According to Briggs, with a long string of horses Alahambre's wranglers would've had to have taken the long flat trail out of Cimarron, winding through miles of buttes and mesas. By taking the cutoff, we would swing up around a stretch of high ridges saving ourselves twenty or more miles of riding, and drop down and intercept them by midmorning. With a half moon lighting the sky, we turned at a fork in the main trail and reined our horses along a rock ledge curving upward into a dark, lofty world of towering spruce and ancient pines.

Long past midnight we rode in silence, Briggs leading, then me, then Jack, our horses hugging near a wall of high smooth stone on our left, and on our right less than three feet away, a sheer drop of over two hundred feet. I said a thankful prayer for having Briggs with us as I gazed out and down at the dark pointed tops of aspen and spruce swaying like ghosts in the pale moonlight.

Somewhere above us I heard the snarl of an animal and the scurry of many quiet and padded paws searching the rocks. I felt the mare tense up under me and heard Jack wrestle his reins to keep his silver-gray in hand. "Wolves," said Briggs calmly, glancing up the wall.

"Wolves." I relayed his words over my shoulder, and saw Jack slip his rifle from its boot.

"I heard," Jack said softly.

"No problem, though," Briggs said, "long as they don't spook the horses off the edge or jump us when we round a turn." The indifference in his voice caused me to breathe easy as I turned to pass along the information; but then his words sunk in and I tensed with a chill up my spine.

"I heard," said Jack again, staring at me in the darkness.

My hand trembled slightly as I snatched out my rifle and swung it over my lap.

"Knowed an ole boy once got et by wolves," Briggs said. His voice was no different than a man talking about the weather. I watched his silhouette in the darkness, tall in his saddle but relaxed and now gazing off across the drop on our right. "A wolf has to be starving before he'll eat a human, but once he does, you know he'll eat a man while he's still alive?"

"No—!" I gazed up the wall, then leaned enough to look back behind Jack, then enough to look ahead around Briggs, then back up the wall. "I didn't know that. Jack, did you know that?"

Jack chuckled under his breath. "I know it *now.*"

"They sure will," said Briggs. "Heard that ole boy carry on for nearly an hour while the wolves et him."

"Jesus," I said. "You couldn't do nothing?"

"Nope. I was tracking him anyway. He was gonna hang. I figured at least them starving wolves got something out of it."

I swallowed and watched Briggs's dark outline ride along slowly in front of me. I hadn't yet decided what I'd say when we caught up with Alahambre's wranglers. I wondered—hoped—that maybe Diamond Joe had rode on ahead of them. If he had, maybe I could explain what'd happened to the wranglers, pick up Buck, and take the main trail back into Cimarron to return Lambert's mare. This could've all been a simple mistake, I thought, and with any luck, especially with a federal marshall riding with me, I could be back in Cimarron by tomorrow night and headed home on Buck the following morning.

We'd ridden another mile upward when the rock wall on our left gradually shortened and the narrow trail widened. On our right, the sheer drop sloped upward and turned into a summit of brown flat rock. I breathed easier as the ground leveled, and relaxed in the saddle, watching the first thin slice of morning sparkle on the horizon. Fifty yards across the bald summit, I glimpsed a bushy tail disappearing over the edge of a rock into the gray of dawn.

"You were right," I said to Briggs. He'd stopped his horse and crossed his wrists on the saddlehorn. Jack and I drifted up beside him. "That could've turned into an ugly night for somebody not knowing the trail." I raised my hat and ran a hand back over my head. Even in the chill of night, I'd perspired some around the hat band.

"Over there's Indian Run," Briggs said, raising slightly in his stirrups, pointing a long finger, "a hundred yards, give or take. We'll pick it up and head down to the cutoff." He grinned. "Three hours at the most, we'll be down on the main trail."

We stepped down from our horses and stopped long enough to rest them while we ate the rest of the cold steak from Lambert's tavern. Jack took out a twist of tobacco, cut a plug, and passed it to Briggs. Briggs took a cut and worked it into his jaw. I gazed out across the wide summit and watched an eagle appear up past the far edge as if coming out of the ground. "So, marshall," I heard Jack say. "How do you go about hunting a gang like Quarrels's in this kinda land?" I knew Jack was just trying to find out what he could about the forty thousand.

"It's hard to do," Briggs said, "but every animal has a watering hole. He'll slip up, show his face around a town or something. Somebody will tip me off. I'll isolate him from his pack and kill 'im."

I shot a glance at Jack, then Briggs. "I thought you was hunting the whole gang?"

"I am, but Ned's the main one. I get him and the rest will—"

"Kill him?" I saw Jack staring at Briggs. "What about a trial? How do you know he's guilty?"

"Aw"—Briggs swiped a hand—"he's guilty, sure enough. No need in it taking twelve jurors a week to figure out what I already know."

I shook my head. "What about the letter of the law, marshall? Everybody gets their day in court, don't they?"

Briggs chuckled and spit. "I see you boys've got a lot to learn about justice. A man like Quarrels don't get a chance to prove nothing except that he'll do the same again, rob, kill. Naw sir, the law is to protect the innocent—people like yourselves. But for Quarrels, it don't matter if I catch him with the money dead on him or if I catch him dead on the money. Either way, once I catch him . . . he's dead."

Briggs saw me staring at Jack, and he grinned. "That's just how it is, boys. I know it ain't pretty, but it's the world I live in." He thumbed toward Cimarron. "Back there, you got your town marshall, sheriffs, constables, and the like. They've got time for court and trials and such. But once the problem comes out here, they don't even want to know how I handle it. They just want it handled. You might say I get the ones hell wouldn't have." Briggs gazed away for a second.

I looked at Jack; Jack studied Briggs up and down. "Sounds tough all right."

"Umm," Briggs said as if remembering something horrible; but instead of saying what it was, he just shook his head, picked up his reins, and led his horse toward the other end of the summit. I glanced at Jack, and we fell in behind him, leading our horses until we crossed the stretch of brown flat rock and came to the start of a narrow path down the other side.

"There you are, boys," Briggs said, stopping and readjusting his cinch. "This's Indian Run. It's steep, but all downhill." Jack and I adjusted our cinches and stepped up in our stirrups alongside Briggs. "Nothing to fear from here down 'cept cougars, bears, and rattlesnakes."

I looked at Jack; Jack rolled his eyes upwards and tapped his silver-gray forward behind Briggs. I fell the liver-chestnut in behind Jack and we leaned back in our saddles as the horses stepped over the edge onto the narrow downhill path.

Twenty or so minutes down the steep terrain, we looked out across the valley to our right and saw smoke curling from the chimney of a cabin a hundred feet below, nestled amid towering aspen and pine.

"Hold it, boys." Briggs held up a hand and stared down with a suspicious gleam in his eyes. A stream cut along the valley floor fifteen yards from the cabin and disappeared back under a rock ledge. Sunlight danced on the glittering water. "That cabin's been deserted for as long as I can remember." He slipped out his rifle and slid down from his saddle. Jack and I glanced at each other and did the same.

"What is it, marshall?"

Briggs crouched and stepped to the edge of the trail. "It could be Quarrels's bunch."

I glanced at Jack; his eyes lit up. "Forty thousand?" His voice was a trembling whisper.

I thought about Buck. "Damnit, marshall. I ain't got time for this."

I started to step over beside him when I heard a rifle cock from along the rock wall behind us. "Up with your hands, pronto!" said a voice; and we all three spun, ready to fire, then stood stunned looking into the face of one of the most beautiful women I'd ever seen. She stood across the narrow trail with a rifle cocked and aimed. "What do you want here?" I caught a trace of a Spanish accent. Her skin was the color of dark honey; her black hair glistened down her shoulders.

The three of us let out a tense breath. "Easy, ma'am," I said, taking a step toward her with my rifle out at my side and one hand in the air. "We're just heading—"

The rifle bucked in her hands; shattered rock spit against my boot and I jumped back as she jacked another round into the chamber. *"Jesus!"* I felt my heart thump in my chest. Jack chuckled beside me.

"Who are you? What are you doing here?" Her voice was strong but I heard a slight quiver in it.

I bent down slowly, laid my rifle on the ground, and raised my hands as I stood up. "We mean you no harm, ma'am." I motioned for Jack and Briggs to lay down their rifles.

"Watch them," said a voice from behind the rocks. "They still have pistols." I saw another woman stand up slowly. Her skin was pale, her hair the color of wheat.

I tried a friendly smile. "I hope we haven't frightened you gals," I said, "but we're just passing through on our way—"

"Gals? We are not your *gals,*" said the dark-skinned woman. "Now what are you doing here?"

I started to take another step forward. "If you'll let me explain—" I saw her hand tense up for another shot.

"Hold your fire there," Briggs said. "I'm a federal marshall." I turned slowly and saw sunlight glint off Briggs's badge as he held it up. "So there," he said.

"How do we know it's real?" the pale woman said to the dark woman.

"Yes, how do we know it's real?" the dark-skinned woman said to Briggs.

I slumped my shoulders and shook my head.

"You don't," Briggs said, "but you gotta trust something."

I heard Jack chuckle again; the dark-skinned woman narrowed a gaze toward him.

"We spotted smoke coming from that cabin down there and thought you might be the Quarrels Gang," Briggs continued. "I've been looking for them."

She swung the rifle barrel from me and toward Jack. "Why is this one laughing?"

I turned slightly and looked at Jack. "I'm just a happy man," he said, eyeing them up and down.

She relaxed her rifle and they both stepped forward. "We have also been looking out for Quarrels and his gang. They came through here a week ago, shooting their big pistols and acting like lunatics. We had to run and hide from them. Why doesn't the law do something?"

"I plan to," said Briggs, "just as soon as they get in killing range."

Again Jack chuckled. "Is he an imbecile?" The dark-skinned woman gestured the rifle barrel toward him.

"No, ma'am," I said. "He's from New Jersey."

She glanced between Jack and me. "And you two are deputies?"

"Yes, in a manner of speaking," Briggs said.

"Not in *any* manner of speaking," I said. I squinted at Briggs and spoke to the woman. "We're just riding together a ways. Are you women alone out here?"

"What of it?" I saw her jut her chin.

"If you don't mind me asking, what are you two gals—I mean *women*—doing way out here?"

She took a deep breath and let it out slowly. "What are you *men* doing *way out here?*"

"Fair enough," I said, feeling my face redden. "I'm going to get my horse back. A feller took him from the auction barn in Cimarron. I have to get him back."

"He stole your horse? That is why the marshall is with you?"

"Well . . . no. I don't really think he stole him." I took a long breath and told her about what had happened, about Alahambre and the card game, the bullets I'd bought in

Taos, the shooting, and about my horse . . . Buck. When I finished, she stared at me curiously for a second and shook her head. "So, this horse of yours . . . he is valuable?"

"Well . . . to me he is. I raised him from a colt. He means a lot to me."

"Enough that you would risk your lives riding the high pass at night? That was foolish."

"Maybe so, but I'll do whatever I have to. He's kind of all I've got . . . if you know what I mean."

"I see." Her eyes seemed to soften as she searched my face. She hesitated a second as if considering something, then let out a breath. "You could've taken the valley trail through there." I was relieved to see her rifle hand relax slightly as she pointed down near the cabin.

"Valley trail?" I glanced from her to Briggs. "There's a trail that cuts through down there, back to the main road?"

"Now, hold on," Briggs said. "There's no trail down there. If there was, we'd've taken it."

"You are mistaken," she said. "There is one. I take it all the time . . . but it is hidden."

Briggs scratched his jaw. "Well, if it's hidden, you can't blame me for not knowing about it."

"You mean we could've rode right through there last night, across flat land?" I shook my head.

Jack nodded toward the stream near the cabin. "Is there a path leading down there, so's we can water our horses and take the valley trail?"

"Don't tell them," the pale woman said in a cautious voice.

The dark woman hesitated. "I will show you. But first you must help me lay planks across a washout just around the bend"—she pointed up the trail—"so some idiots do not come riding through in the night and plunge to their death."

When we'd finished dragging heavy planks across a ten-foot washout, we followed the women down a steep path that led to the stream and then the cabin fifteen yards away on a rise. As we watered our horses, I looked about the place and noticed the broken barn door was riddled with bullet holes, and I now saw that it appeared to have been torn from its hinge by a great force. Then I took note of the boarded-up windows on the cabin, and I saw that the small garden near the cabin looked as if it had recently been trampled by many pounding hoofs.

"This is what they did to our lodge." The dark woman swept a hand taking in the whole place. "This is what they leave behind."

"Your lodge?"

"Yes, we are a private lodge, owned by the American Women's League. We came here last year. Greta and I live here year around to look after the place."

I looked at Briggs and Jack; they looked amazed. I stared around the empty yard and nodded. "Oh," I said. "So you two are alone out here . . . most of the time?"

"What of it?" The dark woman shot me a cold stare.

"Easy," I said, raising my hands slightly. "Just don't seem safe, the two of you without—" I hesitated.

"A man to look after us?" She scowled.

"Well, you have to admit . . ." I felt my face redden.

She flipped the rifle up on her shoulder, and the two of them started wading across the shallow stream. She stopped and turned. "When you finish watering your horses, you must leave. The lodge is for women only." She pointed toward a thin path leading across the valley and into what looked like a solid wall of ancient pine.

"Stay on the path. It will widen and lead you back to the main road. Do not tell others about it."

"Thanks for the water," I said, staring into her cold gaze for a second before she turned and followed the pale woman to the cabin.

"Now there's some strange ones if ever I've seen any," I

said, leaning down and washing my hands and face in the cold clear water.

Jack sucked a mouthful of water from his cupped hands, swished it around, and spit a stream. "*Strange* could be nice, especially if one is stranger than the other."

"I've heard of these kinda women," Briggs said. He craned his neck as he studied the cabin. "They're progressives . . . freethinkers . . . libertarians, is what."

I stood and dried my hands on my shirt. "Well, I don't know what a libertarian is, but I reckon freethinking never hurt nothing."

"You just don't understand, Beatty." Briggs shook his head. "This Woman's League is just another name for wanting to cut off a tree and split the stump. They're a sick, twisted, and unnatural bunch. They're hollering to get paid the same wage as men . . . if you can believe that."

"My goodness!" I shook my head, but grinned at Jack as I stepped up into the saddle. "What's the world coming to?"

"Aw . . . you're just funning me," Briggs said. "But the fact is, they're claiming they've even got the right to vote, same as a man does." He shook his head. "It ain't decent. They're out to take over the world."

"Well, before they do"—I swung the mare and tapped her gently—"I'd like to catch up to Alahambre and get my horse back."

Briggs gigged his horse forward, bolted around me, and took the lead. I rode up beside Jack as we stepped from the stream. "I know," Jack said, raising a hand to keep me from saying anything. "But let him babble all he wants, so long as he gets us close to that money."

I just stared at Jack; apparently he'd forgotten my reason for being there.

6

It was midafternoon by the time we followed the valley trail to the main road. By my calculation we'd have made better time overall if we'd taken the hidden valley trail all the way, or else stayed on the main road out of Cimarron to begin with. I estimated that Briggs's shortcut had cost us a good two hours. I tried to hurry him up, but he wouldn't hear of it.

"Don't want to get in a rush now," he said. "We'll just wear out our animals. Might as well ride easy till we see their dust. There's water 'bout seven miles on. If we're lucky, we might catch them there. If not, we'll keep pressing."

I fidgeted with my reins. "Maybe I could run on ahead and—"

"Now listen to me, Mister Beatty," Briggs said, swiping a hand in the air. "I know you're worried about your horse and I can't blame you. But it won't do him or us any good if you get out there and get waylaid or run that mare to death. You're gonna have to trust my judgment. You boys ain't accustomed to this kinda—"

"Marshall," I said, cutting him off. "Maybe you've gotten the wrong impression. But I can take pretty good care of myself. The fact is—"

"The marshall's right," Jack said, seeing I was getting a little too testy, and maybe thinking I would say something

I shouldn't. He gave me a look of warning. "You're getting too anxious. Buck's all right . . . we just need to keep our heads here."

"You're right," I said, letting go a breath. I reined up beside Jack and let Briggs drift into the lead. He walked his horse along slowly, leaning out, gazing down at the hoof-prints.

I let Briggs get a full ten yards ahead. "Damn it, Jack, all you're thinking about is getting your hands on that forty thousand."

"Imagine." Jack shook his head and gazed upward. "Me, an outlaw, thinking about *money!* What *is* this world coming—"

"*Damn it,* Jack, you know what I mean." I spoke in a low voice, wiping a hand across my forehead. "You know as well as I do this is taking too long. Ain't we being a little *too* cautious here?"

Jack spit and grinned. "I don't know." He nodded ahead toward Briggs. "As many men as he's seen die in some terrible way or another, I reckon he's learned something. He's still alive." Jack grinned and cocked an eye toward me. "Besides, I told ya you was getting in too close with him, so don't blame me. Now we just gotta play it out till we can get rid of him."

"But I've never seen a man so damn careful about so many things in my life. It ain't normal."

For the next seven miles, we rode behind Briggs, so slow that at one point, I felt like the mare had gone to sleep beneath me. When Briggs reined up in the road ten yards ahead, I wouldn't have known he'd stopped if he hadn't raised a hand and started looking bigger to me. I gigged the mare. She jerked forward, startled. "Wake up," I said to her; but beside me I noticed Jack bolt upright.

"Am awake," he said in a groggy voice.

"What is it?" I called to Briggs, sliding the mare in beside him.

"Peculiar, is what," he replied, pointing down to where part of the hoofprints cut away from the rest and headed out through a rolling stretch of creosote and mesquite. I gazed out across the ten mile stretch of land that reached up into the foothills.

"How far are we from Alahambre's spread? Maybe he sent part of 'em to a line camp."

"Naw," said Briggs, studying the disappearing hoof-prints. "Migueal said his spread's the other side of Gris. That's still more than fifteen miles ahead."

I studied both paths of footprints, feeling my heart drop. Now I had no idea which string Buck was in. "Damn it," I said, "what next?"

Jack rode up wiping his hand across his eyes. "What's going on?"

"They've split off, Jack." I stared off across the sweep of land rising in to the foothills.

Jack studied the ground for a second. "Then let's split off with them. You two head on toward Gris and I'll follow these tracks."

"I wouldn't advise it," said Briggs. He nodded toward the distant foothills. "That's bad country if you don't know your way. I once knew an ole boy—"

"Then you go with me," Jack said to Briggs. He nodded to me, "And you go on to Gris. Can you do that without shooting Alahambre again?"

"I'll try," I said. I glanced back and forth between them. "Whoever finds Buck brings him to Gris, right?"

They both nodded; I backed the liver-chestnut a step and turned her in the trail. I looked over my shoulder at Jack, saw him slumped in his saddle watching me leave. "I gotta get him back, Jack. You know that, don't you?"

"We gotta do what we *gotta* do, right?" I saw the gleam in his eye. He winked, spit a stream, and waved me away with his hand. "Now tell me about that ole boy you once knew," I heard him say to Briggs as I slapped my boots against the mare.

I rode at a brisk clip for the next hour, reining the mare down every ten or fifteen minutes and letting her blow and shake herself out for a mile or so. Then I'd tap her again and run her some more. By the time we made a turn around a low butte and followed a wooden sign pointing to Gris, she was winded but still holding her own.

I cantered the mare into Gris sideways and reined down to a walk along a dusty street the color of burnt copper. Gris looked like every town I'd seen west of Missouri, except most of it was still being built. Everywhere I looked, I saw ladders sticking up the side of unfinished buildings. As I weaved the mare back and forth between slow rolling buckboards and lumber wagons, I even saw an old carpenter in a pair of bib overalls bent over a sawhorse at the corner of an ally, building more ladders.

I turned the mare between a pile of weatherboard and a stack of roofing and guided her to a hitch rail. As I stepped down and spun her reins, I couldn't help but notice that the saloon before me was so crooked it looked ready to topple over. I looked down at the boardwalk; it was crooked too. As I stepped up, I realized that whoever built the place had built it smack on the ground instead of leveling a foundation, then just built it straight up instead of allowing for the lay of the land.

I walked in looking up and down and all about the lopsided place. A dusty picture of a naked woman tied to a horse hung out a full six inches or more from the wall at the bottom of the frame. It swayed in and out, tapping the wall as I walked across the floor. I had to stop and just stare at it a second.

"Lose something, mister?" said a gruff voice from behind the bar. I turned and looked at him, started to ask him about the place but decided not to. "I'm the owner," he said, "can I help you?" He saw me gawking at the place and

I could tell he didn't appreciate it. I cleared my throat and swept off my hat. Dust fell from my brim.

"I'm looking for the Alahambre spread," I said slapping dust off my trousers and shirt. As soon as I did it I saw the cloud of dust roll out around me like a storm cloud, and I fanned it away with my hat.

"Gonna need a room? Or'd you just come in to tidy up?" The owner spoke from between two sagging jaws. He looked all around at the billowing dust.

"Sorry," I said. He tossed a hand and growled something under his breath toward the ceiling. He was bald on top, but his hair was long on one side, parted at ear level, swept up over his head and plastered there with enough lard to draw flies.

"Where you coming from? Gonna need a room?"

I gazed around the place. "Coming from Cimarron," I said. "I won't need a room."

He looked away from me to a curly-headed young man in an apron, and drew his lip up in contempt. "Hear that, Goose-stuff?" He jerked his head toward me. "Came from *Cimarron. Won't need a room.*" The curly-headed young man looked down and wiped his hands on his apron. He seemed disappointed.

"Huh," the owner said with a shrug of one shoulder. "I suppose after being in *Lambert's,* at the fashionable *Saint James,* nothing else quite measures up."

I unconsciously slapped more dust from my shirt, caught myself, and stopped. "Naw sir, that's not it." I glanced around again. "This is a fine place you've got here." I saw a breeze blow through a crack in one wall and stand a calendar straight out from its hook. The building creaked. The floor under me was so tilted, I took a step toward the bar and had to keep my legs from running out from under me. "I'm just in a hurry right now. Probably stay here on my way back, though, if time allows." I caught myself against the bar and stopped. The bar was as crooked as everything else. When I jarred to a stop against it, two ashtrays slid off and broke at the barkeeper's feet. He looked down, then slowly back up at me with a sour expression.

"How about a drink, now that the bar's nice and cleared?"

"I'll take a quick beer," I said, feeling like I oughta order something just to show respect. "Can you tell me how to get to the Alahambre spread?"

He drew a beer, sat it on the bar, and kept it from sliding backwards with his thumb. I picked it up, took a long foamy drink and sat it down carefully. "Sure," he said. "I can tell you. But I doubt he'll be welcoming any company. I saw him riding through this morning." The owner shook his head. "You've never seen such a honker on a human being." He held his hand in front of his face to indicate Alahambre's nose.

I nodded. "I don't know the man . . . just need to meet him on a business matter. If you could point me toward his place."

"I don't know him much myself," said the barkeeper. "He keeps to himself a lot. He's got a pretty wife. From what I've heard, he's a jealous man." The barkeeper grinned, and looked toward the young man in the apron. "With a nose like *that,* he'll have reason to be from now on." He let out a laugh that turned into a cough, then a deep wheeze; he slapped the crooked bar to get himself breathing again. "Oh, God! I kill myself." His face turned a dangerous red.

I felt a twinge of guilt as they laughed about Diamond Joe's nose, but I reminded myself he *had* tried to kill me. Now that I knew I was this close to getting Buck back, I wished Briggs was with me. I took two long sips and sat the empty mug down on the bar.

He wiped a hand across his eyes, looked down, shook his head for a second to compose himself, then sighed and looked back up. "So, you came from Cimarron? I suppose after drinking at *Lambert's Saloon—*" he rolled his eyes past the young man, sneered, then turned back to me "—it's hard to drink a beer in a place like this?"

"A beer's a beer," I shrugged. I looked around the place and tried to think of something nice to say about it. I couldn't come up with nothing.

"I mean, I don't have a flock of them big German hurdy girls, shaking their butts." He raised his arms and rolled his belly back and forth mimicking them. "And I don't have a banjo or a tambourine—"

"Could you tell me how to get to Alahambre's place from here?" I saw he was heading to that strange place where a bartender sometimes goes, and I thought I'd try to stop him.

He slid my empty mug under the tap and filled it, slid it back to me and leaned forward. "But I'll tell you this: I've got his prices beat all to hell, and he knows it. And it won't be long before his place will be a bare spot in the road." He thumbed himself on the chest. "I'll still be here." He nodded firmly, twisting his neck toward the young man. "Right, Goose-stuff?"

The young man took it as his cue to ease up and slip in beside the barkeeper. He wiped his hands on the apron and pushed a pair of wire-rims up on his nose. "I hear Lambert has trouble cooling his beer? I also heard you have to really count your change, and keep a close eye on what you eat there." He stared at me in expectation, his eyes bulged, his head nodding.

"I only stayed there one night," I said. "I can't say much about the place, 'cept the food was good and the beer was cold . . . while I was there anyway."

"Oh . . ." They both looked disappointed. I tried to think of something to say. "He *did* rent me a room with bullet holes all over the floor. I wasn't real happy with that. I started to ask for my money back but I heard he has a strict 'no-refund' policy."

"Well . . . there you are. See!" The barkeeper slapped a hand on the bar. "Take a look up there, mister . . . ?"

"Beatty . . . James Beatty," I said. "I'm a horse dealer out of—"

"No bullet holes in *my* ceiling, is there?"

"None that I see." I glanced up; a chandelier hung from the crooked ceiling. "I'm Gustav," said the young man in the apron. He slipped a little pointed hand across the bar and I shook it. "I've never cooked for the *president,* like Lambert has. But you name any fancy dish and I can tell you how to prepare it."

"Is there?" The barkeeper still pointed up.

"That's great," I said, nodding to Gustav, then glancing at the ceiling. "Not a damn one, far as I can tell," I said to the barkeeper.

"Go on—name one," Gustav said. "Just try."

"I don't know any fancy dish," I said, " 'less maybe it would be macaroni pie?" I shrugged.

"That's easy." He waved a hand. "With what base? Beef? Elk? Buffalo?"

"Look," I said, "I really need to get out to Alahambre's spread. I'll be coming back later—"

" 'Cause I wouldn't *allow* that kind of crap," the barkeeper said, still talking about the ceiling and glancing up at it. "I'd bust a sumbitch in the head that shot a hole in my ceiling."

I saw the old carpenter in the bib overalls walk in slowly, steadying himself with his hands out as he walked over to the bar. Gustav hurried down to him and sat a bottle and a shot glass before him. I saw it as my chance to get away. "Well . . . I've enjoyed talking with you, mister . . . ?"

"Fortenay." He grinned, spreading his hands. " 'Fortenay's On The Frontier.' That's what I'll call it"—he shot the carpenter a dark glance and raised his voice—"soon as somebody finishes making my sign!" The carpenter just stared into his glass of whiskey and nodded his head. The barkeeper leaned on an elbow and lowered his voice between us. "I wanted to just call it Fortenay's Saloon, but I didn't want people thinking I copied Lambert, you know? Didn't want them goody-gooders in Cimarron thinking I copied anything of theirs. Them and their"—he made a face and waved his hands up and down in a limp gesture—" '*oh! How we love our town . . . and do everything to make it a decent, respectable . . .*' " His words ended in a deep growl; his face swelled red. "Them rotten, goddamn, mealy-mouthed, tight-assed sons a bitches! I could eat sawdust and shit a better town!" He slammed a hand on the bar. The floor trembled.

I stared at him a second and cleared my throat. "Yeah . . . well. Would you mind pointing me toward Alahambre's place? I need to get moving."

"Aw, sure." He shook his head as if to snap out of a trance. "I just get carried away sometimes, thinking about"—he twisted his face—"*Ci-mar-ron.* Them and their whole goddamned, sickening *we-always-try-to-do-what's-right attitude.* Like they've got some kind of goddamned future—"

"Hold it!" I raised my hands chest high.

"Sorry," he said. He took a deep breath and wiped a hand across his mouth.

When he'd finished giving me directions, I climbed across the floor, out to the hitch rail, and looked around as I spun my reins loose. I cocked my head to get a good look at Fortenay's On The Frontier. It was the only crooked building in a row of buildings that were either new or being finished. The air was heavy with the scent of paint and freshly cut pine. As I stepped up in the saddle, I saw a skinny hound lope out of an alley with a streak of paint on the side of its head. "Boom town," I said to myself; and I backed the mare out into the dirt street and began to weave my way through delivery wagons and stacks of lumber.

Halfway out of town, a tall feller stepped out from behind

a pile of roof sheeting and blocked my way. I had to rein the mare up quick, sideways, to keep her from bumping him. "You looking for work?" He spoke quickly, glancing about, as if afraid someone else would hear. I backed the mare, letting my hand fall from my holster.

"No sir," I said. "I'm in kind of a hurry—"

" 'Cause I can use a good hand."

"I got some important business to take—"

"You don't even have to have your own tools, long as you can hammer straight."

I settled the mare and stared down at him just as another man came walking out briskly from across the street. "Mister," I said, "I'm just passing through. Now get out of my way . . . *please.*"

"I'll pay more," I heard the other man say. He stopped beside the mare, looked up at me with his hands on his hips.

"Keep out of this, Bryce," the man in front of me warned.

I reined the mare to the side and started around him. The man beside me followed along. "Pay him no mind," he said. "You can work for whoever you want to."

"I already offered him a job, Bryce," the first man yelled, "so butt out."

"Go to hell, Erlander!" The man beside me pulled a shiny pistol from the nail pouch at his waist and let it hang down his side.

I gigged the mare forward, away from both of them, saw an open alley and reined toward it as the two of them squared off into a shouting contest. I saw another paint-streaked hound slip from beneath a half-finished porch. It ran along in front of me like a guide. I followed the dog until I got clear of the stacks of building material and the smell of roof tar, then reined back onto the main trail, gigged the mare, and rode away looking back over my shoulder.

7

I followed Fortenay's directions, riding quickly for the next few miles until I found the road back into Alahambre's spread. I still wasn't sure what to do or say when I met up with him, but I hoped he would listen to reason. If not, I was prepared to take Buck back by any means necessary.

I gazed back and forth on both sides as I followed the long road toward the weathered ranch house. The place looked ill kept, with fence rails loosened by wind and hanging down into the dirt. I saw no cattle save for a couple of scrawny milk cows grazing the short grass near the yard fence. They looked up at me and went back to grazing. Stopping ten yards from the front door, I glanced toward the corral but saw no horses. Here goes, I thought, wondering why someone hadn't already come to the door. I let out a breath and kept my hand hanging free near my holster. "Hello, the house," I called out. I sat waiting, but heard nothing, just the wind off the flatlands.

I'd raised in my saddle and started to call a little louder when a woman's voice called out softly, "What do you want?"

"I'm looking for Mister Alahambre," I called out. "Need to see him about a horse."

"He's not here."

"Where can I find him? It's real important—" I'd stood

up to swing out of my saddle, but I heard a rifle cock and I sat back down slowly. "I mean no harm here," I said; but I kept my hand ready to throw down in case he really was here and came stepping out with a rifle pointed at me.

"He's gone to the line camp. I don't know when he'll be back."

"Could you direct me—?"

"I don't know where he's at," the voice said flatly. "You'll have to go find him for yourself." I saw a slim attractive woman step slowly out of the doorway holding a rifle leveled at me. "He's not in a very good mood today. He's suffered an accident," she said.

"Oh, I see." I sat there for an awkward second. "You mean his nose, ma'am?"

She gazed at me curiously. "Yes . . . his nose. Do you know what happened?"

"Kind of." I coughed and cleared my throat.

"Oh?" She stepped forward on the porch.

"The fact is, ma'am—" I coughed and cleared my throat again. "I'm the one who shot him in his nose." I sat still, waiting. After a few seconds she lowered the rifle. I saw a splotch of red along one cheek, like she'd been sleeping on a wrinkled wool blanket. "You're the one? The one who shot my husband?" She slumped with the rifle hanging from her hand. A gust of wind blew a strand of hair across her face. She smoothed it back with her hand.

"Well . . . yes, ma'am. I can't deny it."

Her fingers touched her cheek carefully, then gathered her dress at the collar. She seemed to shiver for a second. "Are you here to kill him?"

"Uh . . . no, ma'am. I . . . that is he, or one of his wranglers, took my horse . . . *purely* by mistake, I'm sure. I'm just here to get it back, is all." I'm real sorry I shot him in the nose." I shook my head and raised my hat brim. "I just wish stuff like that never happened."

"I see." She lowered the rifle more; for a second she

looked almost disappointed. "You must have *some* nerve, coming here. Do you realize who my husband is? He made his living killing men."

"I heard he used to be a bounty hunter, ma'am. But I ain't here for no trouble. I just want my horse, is all. I'm hoping he'll listen to reason."

"After being shot? You think he'll care about *you* or your horse?" She bit her lip and gazed off for a second.

"Ma'am, what choice do I have? It's *my* horse. I have to get him back."

"I see," she said. "Well, at any rate, he isn't here. He was only here long enough to change shirts this morning, then he left." She nodded out toward the line of mountains in the distance. "He and his friends have taken the horses *somewhere.*" She swept a hand as if having long given up on knowing anything of her husband's comings and goings. I squinted and looked all around.

She watched me for a second. "The horse must mean a lot to you, coming here like this."

"Yes, ma'am," I said. "Look . . . would you have *any* idea where he's headed, any at all? I mean . . . I promise I'm only here for my horse. I'm not here to—"

"Oh, I believe you," she said. She sighed and leaned the rifle against the house. "But no, I haven't the slightest notion, except that he could be anywhere up there." Again she nodded toward the mountains. "My husband doesn't feel it's important to tell me where he's headed or where he's been—" She stopped and gazed off again. "Anyway, he'll probably kill you if he sees you. From the looks of his nose, I doubt if you'll be able to reason with him." Her hand drifted to her cheek, then back down to her collar.

"I know that, ma'am. But he'll have to listen to reason. I'm traveling with a federal marshall who's along to keep things from getting out of hand. Like I said, I don't want trouble . . . just my horse." I glanced around again. "If you don't mind me saying so, ma'am, this place looks a little sparse for someone needing a string of horses. Where's all your cattle?"

She nodded toward the sweep of foothills. "Up there somewhere, what's left of them." She looked back at me. "The herd was my father's . . . he died last spring. My husband now runs the place."

"I'm sorry," I said.

"So am I." There was bitter resolve in her voice. She stood silently for a second, then nodded toward the corral. "On the other side there. Maybe you can pick up their tracks . . . I don't know." She turned to walk back inside the house.

"I'll water this mare, ma'am, with your permission."

She glanced over her shoulder and gestured to the water trough. "Certainly. But please do it quickly, then leave. I don't think you realize what you're getting yourself into."

"Yes, ma'am." I stepped down, walked the mare over, loosened her cinch to let her blow, and let her drink while I walked around to the other side of the corral and found tracks leading off to the hills. Just as I'd started back to the mare, I saw a drift of dust on the horizon beneath the foothills. I visored my hand above my eyes and watched until I could make out the flapping coattails of one rider. "That's him," I heard the woman say from the porch. Her voice was flat, yet with the tone of someone predicting a storm.

"Thank you, ma'am," I said quietly, quickening my steps back to the mare.

"There's still time for you to get out of here." She looked me up and down as if appraising my chances against Diamond Joe. "It would be wise—"

"I'm sorry, ma'am, but I've got to have my horse." I drew the mare's cinch, then slipped my ten-gauge from beneath my bedroll and lay it across the pommel of my saddle. I glanced at the woman and saw her watching me closer. I wasn't sure what I read in her eyes. "It's only a precaution,"

I said. But she only looked away and stared at the lone rider as he drew closer, her hand at the collar of her dress and the wind whipping her hair out behind her.

When Diamond Joe neared the far side of the corral, he saw me through the rail fence and slowed his horse sideways almost to a stop, then righted his reins and stepped the horse around cautiously. I glanced at the woman, then back to him from across the back of the mare. My hand lay near the shotgun butt. "I'm not here to cause any trouble, Mister Alahambre," I called out. He may not have even recognized me yet; but on hearing my voice, he jerked upright and glared through purple swollen eyes, kicked his horse a sharp tap, and slid to a halt halfway around the corral.

"Whant are nuu doing here, nuu sufa-bintch?" His voice was still a terrible nasal twang. He ripped a pistol from his waist and stepped his horse closer, then saw the ten-gauge on my saddle and froze. Out the corner of my eye, I saw the woman take a step back, then stop. She watched with an air of detachment, I thought, for someone whose husband faced a stranger with a loaded shotgun.

"There's been a mistake made, Mister Alahambre," I called out quickly. Damnit, I thought, why hadn't I brought Briggs along with me? "One of your wranglers took my horse—purely by accident, I'm sure—and I've come to get it back." I stared at him, trying to read his eyes, but was unable to because of the swelling. The gauze on his nose was terribly stained from road dust, blood, and iodine. The leeches were gone from beneath his eyes. "It's nothing that can't be straightened out, Mister Alahambre—just a simple mistake—"

"Yeah, and you made it!" He tried stepping his horse around the mare. I jerked down the shotgun and stepped from behind her.

"He has a federal marshall with him!" The woman spoke fast, but not in a panic. Diamond Joe glanced around quickly, then at me.

"He's out there," I said, trying my best to keep from shooting him again and knowing that if I did, I'd have to kill him. I stared at him with the shotgun raised as he stared back at me. "Don't make me kill you, Diamond Joe," I said quickly. "You saw what I can do with a pistol. You don't want me rounding *this* thing out on ya." I watched his horse, saw the animal sense the tension between us. The big sorrel quivered, arched his neck, and struggled against the bit. Diamond Joe leaned back on the reins, pointing the pistol at me as the horse whinnied and stepped back and forth.

"You lent this banstard in here?" He spoke to her without taking his purple eyes off me. "Lent him wanter his hornse at *my* trough?"

She just hunched up and held her hand at her dress collar.

"She's no part of it," I said. I saw the sorrel ready to bolt. "All I want is my horse. My horse—and I'm out of here!"

"Whant's it loonk linke?" He spoke through clenched teeth. "If int's a mare I'll jill-flirt her. If int's a stud I'll canstrate him with a runsty knife."

He threw his pistol out arm's length, squinted to focus his eyes, and let off his reins to step the sorrel forward. Just as he let off the reins and braced for his shot, I jumped behind the mare, blasted one barrel of the shotgun straight up, then jumped back from behind her.

The big sorrel reared high, twisted in the air; Diamond Joe struggled with the reins, grabbing them with both hands, his pistol now up across his chest. I bolted forward, jumped into the sorrel, grabbing the bridle close to the bit and twisting the horse sideways as it came down. The pistol went off, but I knew it wasn't aimed at me. I heard Diamond Joe scream as he toppled backwards and landed on his head. Then he was silent as stone.

I turned loose the downed sorrel and the horse feinted away and rolled back up, shaking dust and blowing out a breath.

"He's dead, isn't he?" said Diamond Joe's wife, with no show of remorse. She leaned forward as she stepped from the porch and walked closer.

I stepped over with the shotgun pointed at him and kicked his gun away. It struck me odd that this was the second time I'd kicked a gun from this man's hand. I reached down and poked him in the ribs until I saw him take a breath. "No," I said, "he's alive, but he's knocked colder than last Christmas." I saw the streak of a powder burn up his jaw. His mustache was singed and smoking; I smelt the odor of burnt hair. "He's pock-marked himself with his pistol," I added.

I reached down and rolled him over to see if his neck was broken. It wasn't, but there was a knot the size of a goose egg on the back of his head. A flat rock stuck up from the ground where he had landed, and in the whole yard surrounding us, I couldn't see a single other rock. *"Jesus,"* I said under my breath. I turned to his wife. "Has your husband been on a run of bad luck lately?"

"We all make our own luck," she said in a flat tone. "I can't leave him out here." She gestured a hand down toward Diamond Joe. "Will you be so kind?"

"Oh, of course." I leaned down with her. Together we lugged Diamond Joe inside the house and laid him on a bed. I stared down at him while she fetched a pan of water and a rag and began dabbing at the knot on his head. The impact of skull against rock had left a deep gash. The fire from the pistol shot would leave a terrible black streak up the side of his face for a long time, if not for the rest of his life.

"I'll have to shave around the cut and sew his head up," she said, dabbing at the bloody knot and inspecting it closely.

"I'll help," I said.

"No." She raised a hand. "It would be best if you just left, before he wakes up . . . or one of his wranglers comes—"

"I'm not leaving without my horse," I said.

"Don't be a fool," she said. "You heard what he said. If he knew which horse was yours, what do you think he would do to it? My husband is a *dark*-minded man." She stopped dabbing long enough to look up at me, then dropped her eyes. "There's little doubt he'll kill *you,* let alone your horse."

I chafed the back of my neck. "I'm truly sorry it's going this way, ma'am. But he's giving me back my horse if I have to make him do it with a gun to his head. As soon as he comes to, he's taking me there."

"You don't know him, mister," she said. She plopped the wet rag on his head and stood facing me. "He'd die before he'd give in. Believe me. The best thing for you to do is wait. Hide somewhere until in the morning then track him back to the horses."

I gave her a suspicious look, but she raised a hand and shook her head. "Then do what you want. I'm telling you what I know about him. And believe me . . . I know a lot."

"You won't warn him?"

"No. I'll tell him you rode off looking for the new string of horses. He'll believe me. There's no reason he shouldn't."

"Why should I trust you?" I said, staring into her eyes, looking for the slightest flicker of deception.

"Because you have no other choice, do you?" she said, and she leaned back down and pressed the wet rag against the large knot. "Go somewhere and watch the house from a distance. I'll leave a lamp burning in the window. When he leaves, I'll turn it out. Then you'll know. Then you can track him."

I stepped back and studied her as she finished wiping the blood. She stood up, walked to a chest of drawers, took a sewing kit, and returned to the bed. I heard him groan. "Well?" She snapped her face toward me. "What are you waiting for? *Vamonos.* Get out of here before he wakes up."

* * *

I rode out nearly a mile from the house, camped myself on a low rise behind a scrub pinyon, and picketed the mare on the other side of the rise, just out of sight. Knowing I'd be up all night watching the house, I napped and awoke just as the western sky sank into darkness behind the mountain line. Below the ridge of the low rise, I risked a small fire of mesquite twigs long enough to make a pot of strong coffee; then I worked the fire down to a low glow of embers, warmed a strip of dried shank, poured my first cup, and began my vigil.

I might've dozed now and then through the night, but each time I caught myself and looked up, I saw the lamp burning and knew Alahambre was still in the house. By first light of dawn, the lamp was still burning, but I figured with a hurt nose, he might've slept a little extra. So I waited, watched, and even boiled up another pot of coffee with stale water from my canteen.

After two cups of coffee, the sun was full up past the horizon and I was pacing back and forth beneath the crest of the low rise. Now it was too light to see if the lamp was burning or not. I considered things for a second, then gathered my gear and rode down cautiously to the house. "Hello, the house," I called out. My rifle was across my lap, and I'd looped the shotgun sling over my shoulder, just to let him know I came prepared to kill him this time if I had to. I saw the door was half open, but there was no sign of anybody coming. I sat, listened, then called out again.

When my call still got no response, I stepped down cautiously and walked up on the porch. "Mister Alahambre?" I waited a second. "Missus Alahambre . . . ma'am?" Still no answer. I glanced all around and stepped inside the door. As soon as I looked around I could tell there'd been a fight—a bad one, judging from the overturned furniture and a streak of blood on the floor. I walked across broken china and into the next room. I heard a moan from the other side of a torn-up bed, and I swung my rifle toward the sound.

"Who's there?" I said; I stepped around and looked down at the woman.

Her face was bloody and swollen; her dress was ripped down the front and hanging open. One of her breasts had spilled partly from her dress, and it was terribly bruised. I winced at the sight of it.

"Oh Lord," I said, bending down and pulling her carefully up onto my lap. "He did this to you, ma'am?" I yanked off my dirty bandanna and pressed it to the blood on her forehead. I carefully folded the torn flap of fabric over her breast. "Can you speak? Why in God's name would he do such a thing?"

I leaned down close and watched her eyes swim about my face. She raised a hand and searched my face with her fingertips. "Mister Beatty?" Her voice was shallow and weak.

"Yes, it's me." I felt her shudder and I held her to me. "Don't worry, I'm here with you. He won't bother you again." I glanced out the open door across the grasslands, then back down at her. "Was this because you let me water my horse? Is that why he did this?" I bit my lip. "It is, isn't it?"

She didn't answer, but she didn't have to. I felt my jaw muscles tighten and I picked her up and laid her on the torn-up bed. "I'll be right back." I leaned the rifle against the bed, went and poured water from a bucket into a tin pan, and came back soaking my bandanna in it.

"Here," I said, laying the pan on the bed. "Let's get you up here." I raised her enough to get a pillow behind her back and she clenched my arm. Carefully I dabbed at her eyes and forehead with the wet bandanna until I got most of the dried blood off her face. He must've beaten her sometime during the night. Sometime while I'd sat dozing, listening to the sound of a coyote calling out, this poor woman was getting beat into the floor . . . because of me.

"Get me out of here," she gasped, holding one hand on her side. "Before he comes back."

"Don't worry, ma'am. I ain't leaving you here." I finished washing her face, looked around and found a large pin on a dresser, and fixed the front of her dress. "I wish the son of a bitch would come back right about now," I said under my breath, carefully touching her bruised cheek and picturing Diamond Joe staggering across the yard with the handle of my glades knife shining from his chest.

"No, please . . . let's go, let's go *now,*" she gasped.

"Yes, ma'am, take it easy." I glanced around for a shawl or something to throw over her, but saw none. I picked her up carefully and walked out through the house. On a coat-rack near the front door I saw a long cape, and I stepped over to grab it for her. When I reached for it, her foot tipped over the oil lamp still burning in the window. It shattered, and a streak of fire spread out across the floor. "Oh no!" I turned to sit her down, to grab the cape and slap out the fire.

"No!" She grasped my shoulder. "Leave it! Get . . . me away. . . ." Her voice trailed. Her face slumped against my chest.

"Aw, naw!" I stepped back and forth for a second, saw the flames lick up the curtains on the front window. "God-a-mighty!" I turned and walked quickly out the door to the liver-chestnut. The mare saw the flames and tossed her head up and down, stomping sideways against the reins. "Easy now." I loosened the reins with one hand, let the mare back away a couple steps, then turned her from seeing the flames and settled her. A billowing orange and black cloud rolled out of the door and mushroomed up in the porch ceiling. *"Jesus,"* I said, hurrying the woman into the saddle. I swung up behind her on the mare's rump, reached around her, and grabbed the reins. I could feel the heat on my back, hear the rush of the fire blowing through the house, and hear the crackling of wood as I gigged the mare away.

I glanced back at the rising smoke long after we'd topped

the low rise where I'd spent the night. It billowed upward and spread across the clear morning sky. *"My God,"* I said in a hushed voice; and I shook my head and tapped the mare forward, cradling the woman across my lap. So far, and with absolutely no malice whatsoever originally intended toward the man, I had shot his nose into his face, busted his head, pock-marked him for life, burnt down his house . . . and now, I rode away . . . with his wife in my arms.

PART II — ◆

Cost of Commitment

8

If there was any question whether or not Alahambre and I would kill one another the next time we met, I'd resolved it. The answer lay smoldering in the dirt back in the charred pile of cinders that used to be his home. It seemed almost eerie the way things had happened between the two of us, almost as if some dark force had determined we'd kill each other and was doing everything in its power to bring it about. Had it not been for leaving Buck behind, I would've rode off to home that morning and never looked back. I would've dropped the woman at Gris and not slowed down until I hit the Missouri border. But no matter what had happened between Alahambre and me, none of it was Buck's doings. I'd still get him back . . . or die trying.

Instead of riding into Gris and take a chance on running into Alahambre with his wife in my lap, I circled wide and headed back to the place where I'd split off from Briggs and Quiet Jack. The way things were stacking up, I figured it paid to have a federal marshall with me. There wasn't a jury between there and hell who wouldn't stretch my neck for everything I'd done to Alahambre, if they only heard his side of the story.

"Are you feeling any better, ma'am?" I turned the mare off the road and started following Briggs's and Jack's hoof-prints out across the stretch of ground leading to the foothills. The woman moaned but didn't answer. She glanced up for a second through swollen eyes, then drifted away.

Given the proper circumstances I could be made to feel guilty about most anything, including the weather. But I had to remind myself that Diamond Joe hadn't done this because his wife let me water my horse. This was the act of a madman, a coward, and a snake; he would have done this for any other reason, and probably had . . . many times. I just happened to be the reason last night. I looked down at her and held my hand near her face to shield her from the sun.

We must've rode for nearly an hour before I spotted Jack's horse tied to a scrub pine in the distance, and we rode another ten or fifteen minutes through scraping mesquite and rabbit sage until we reached it.

When I reined up closer, and saw Jack stand up from where he'd been watching me, I called out to him, "How about a hand here?" I looked all around but saw no sign of Briggs, just his horse tied beside Jack's and picking at a clump of buffalo grass. Jack leaned his rifle against the tree and walked out to us.

"Who's she?" Jack said, helping me lift the woman down from the saddle. She moaned and tried to press her hand against her side.

"Careful," I said. He cradled her in his arms and gazed at her battered face.

I shook my head. "You ain't gonna believe this, Jack. But she's Alahambre's wife."

I slipped from my saddle, took her back from Jack, and carried her carefully to the shade of a pine tree. Jack glanced at her battered face again. "So . . . you've started beating up his family?"

I shot Jack a frown. "You know better'n that. Alahambre did this to her . . . because she gave me water."

"Damn," Jack whistled low, studying her battered face. "Was they short?"

"No, Jack," I said slowly, trying to be patient. "They had plenty of water. This was just him taking it out on her because I caused him to bust his head and blaze himself in the face with his pistol. The man's a mess. You'd have to see him."

"How'd you do all that to him?"

"It's a long story," I said, glancing around the camp. "Where's Briggs?"

"Oh boy," Jack said, letting out a breath. "You ain't gonna like this, but he's over the ridge there. Thinks he's got a couple of Ned Quarrels's boys spotted down in a gulch, and he's just itching to shoot it out with them."

"Jesus," I said. "That's all I need right now." I propped the woman's head on Jack's saddle and picked up his canteen. "Watch about her while I go try talking some sense to him. Give her some of this when she wakes up." I glanced down at her. "I've got a feeling this poor lady's been through a lot in the past couple years."

Jack knelt beside her and brushed her hair from her eyes. I walked back to the mare and slipped out my rifle. "If you go to take a piss, watch out for rattlesnakes," Jack called softly as I started off toward the rocks leading up the ridge.

"What?" I glanced all around on the ground.

Jack chuckled. "Briggs once knew 'an ole boy who went to take a piss—' "

"Don't even tell me," I said, waving a hand.

I got close to the ridge line and saw Briggs laying behind a rock overlooking a deep gulch. He lay polishing his rifle with a bandanna, and as I crept forward quietly, I saw that he wore a pair of wire-framed spectacles. "Marshall," I said quietly. He looked up from his work, pulled the wire frames low on the bridge of his nose and waved me closer. "What's going on here, Marshall Briggs?" I glanced down and saw a brass and steel shooting scope on a wrapping cloth beside him.

"Got two of Quarrels's boys ready to shake hands with

the undertaker down there," he said nodding over his shoulder toward the gulch below. His voice was matter-of-fact as he pushed up his glasses and picked up the scope. "Been watching 'em awhile, hoping the rest of the gang would show up, but I reckon—"

"How many did you say are in the gang . . . *twenty or more?"* I peeped out and over the edge, saw two men sitting near a low flame cooking something on the end of a stick. They were a long ways from us, far enough that I saw no need to whisper.

"Yep, about twenty, give or take." Briggs shrugged and mounted the scope, tightening it with a small screwdriver.

"And you wanted to wait until they *all* showed up?" My apprehension must've shown in my voice.

Briggs smiled and swiped a hand. "Now, don't get troubled, Mister Beatty. It looks like the rest ain't gonna show. I'll just pick these two off slow and easy here and we'll go on 'bout our business. I'm sorry you and your friend have to witness something like this, but it can't be helped." He looked up, sighed, and went back to adjusting his scope. "I know law work ain't a pretty sight. Not something you and your friend oughta see." I just stared at him a second. He held the rifle to his shoulder, sighted it, and adjusted it more. "So there," he said, drawing the rifle back and patting it with his hand. "This baby would knock the berries off a running bobcat at two hundred yards."

"The thing is, marshall, I've got a woman back there beat all to hell. I don't think this is a good time to go sparking a gun battle. Maybe we could come back later or something?"

"Later?" He cocked a bushy eyebrow. "*Law* can't wait till later, now can it?"

"Maybe just this once?" I leaned down with my hands on my knees. "This woman is hurt pretty bad. There's only three of us against *twenty* riders—"

"Now listen to you, Mister Beatty. Your lack of experience is starting to get the better of you." He smiled, reached out a weathered hand and patted my forearm. "This is nothing to fret about." He turned and eased the rifle barrel out over the ridge, then glanced back over his shoulder at me. "I'm shooting high-grains, so you might wanta cover your ears."

"Damn it, marshall!" I felt like jerking his arm back, but if I did, and he missed, it would only make matters worse. "There's bound to be a better way—"

His shot exploded, sounded as loud as a field cannon. I saw his shoulder buck and his whole body bounced from the recoil. *"Damn,"* I said, staggering from the terrible jolt to my eardrums.

"There's one," I heard him say through the loud ringing in my ears. I glanced over the ridge, saw one of the men stretched out facedown in the dirt. The other ran in a crouch across the gully floor with his pistol drawn, scanning the ridge. Briggs jacked another round into his chamber, raised it, and hummed—actually hummed!—took aim again and squeezed off another round. This time I had my hands on my ears like the first time a kid watched his pa shoot a rabbit.

"Whew," I said, watching the other man slap the ground like a rag doll. He clawed the ground in front of him trying to crawl away. Briggs leaned back as if he'd just done no more than take a drink of whiskey. "There now." He let out a breath of satisfaction, and relaxed. "I shoulda let you had one of 'em . . . just for practice."

I stared at him.

"I left that one alive," he said, dismounting the scope and laying it back on the wrapping cloth. "I believe that's ole Ned's brother, Sonny. That'll stir things up some." He flipped the rag closed over the scope and pushed himself to his feet with his rifle stock. "We'll go down and get him . . . eat a bite and ride on." He grinned and dusted the seat of his pants. "Sound good to you?"

"Jesus," I whispered. Briggs acted as if he wasn't concerned that the wounded outlaw might crawl to his horse and ride away. I asked him about it as we walked back to Jack and the woman, him stepping along calmly with the rifle over his shoulder, and me walking in front trying to hurry him on. "Naw, he ain't going nowhere," Briggs said. "I punched him high in the right shoulder, just above the shoulder blade. He'll flounder awhile before he can make sense out of anything."

"Well," Jack said as we walked up, "I reckon if Quarrels's bunch is within ten miles, they *had* to hear that." He'd given the woman water and wiped her face again with a wet bandanna. She'd come around some and sat leaned against the tree holding the bandanna against her forehead. Jack slung his saddle up on his silver-gray. "Bet you didn't buy them rounds in Taos," he said to Briggs.

Briggs grinned and reached a hand down to the woman. "Federal Marshall Newton Briggs, at your service, ma'am." She took his hand and he raised her to her feet. "I'll be wanting a full report on what's happened to you as soon as we get settled up here. Whoever did this to you is gonna have to—"

"Christ-a-mighty, marshall!" I stepped in, took her hand and guided her toward my mare. "Can we get moving here? If Quarrels is around he'll be on us with both boots." I helped her up the side of the mare and climbed up behind her. She worked her head back and forth slowly.

Briggs pushed up his stained Stetson. "You'll have to pardon these young fellers, ma'am. They're not used to this kind of—"

"Marshall, *please!* Can we go get him and get the hell out of here?"

"Watch that language," Briggs said like a correcting father. "I know this all has you a little rattled, but there's never a cause to forget your manners."

I heard Jack chuckle as I turned the mare.

We were a full ten minutes riding to the end of the gully and another ten circling back to the dead and wounded outlaws. Three buzzards had already homed in overhead and begun their lazy circle by the time we got there.

I couldn't help but think that nobody who ever rode with my cousins and me would've hemmed themselves in like this. There was only one way in and out and the whole canyon lay exposed from either edge above it. "How dumb you suppose this Ned Quarrels bunch is?" I asked Jack in a quiet tone as we followed a few yards behind Briggs. Jack looked at me and I nodded, taking in the gully.

Jack spit a stream. "Maybe they're smart at robbing but not at hiding out. Nobody's perfect. Maybe they're dumb when it comes to hiding money, too." He winked and grinned.

We stopped when Briggs raised a hand, then watched him ride forward with his elbow bent and the big Dance Brothers pistol held up near the side of his head. Jack slipped down and walked forward with his rifle hanging from his hand; I drew my forty-four and lay it on my lap between me and the woman.

I sat behind my saddle with my arms around Diamond Joe's wife, her hair tickling my cheek ever so slightly in the breeze, and we watched Jack walk forward and roll the dead outlaw over with the toe of his boot. Most of the top of the man's head was missing. His hat lay six feet away with a large hole through the crown. Briggs had walked over and pulled the wounded outlaw to his feet. The man wobbled like a lopsided top. I was spun tighter than new rope, wanting to get away, get help for the woman, get rid of the outlaw, and somehow, some way, get Buck back from Alahambre and get out of here. I just clenched my teeth, knowing that nothing I'd say could hasten Briggs along. The man only had one speed.

"Boys," Briggs said, holding the outlaw up by the scruff of his collar, "meet Sonny Quarrels." He shook the man back and forth like a hand puppet. Blood ran down from Sonny's right shoulder where the bullet had come out. He was still dazed.

"What the fuck hit me?" The outlaw groaned.

Briggs thumped him on his forehead. "We'll have of none of *that* talk. There's a lady present—" He glanced at Jack, then me. "And a couple of young gentlemen here."

"I . . . know him," the woman said softly across swollen lips.

I reached up and brushed her hair back from her face. "I doubt it, ma'am. This is one of the Ned Quarrels Gang—"

"No." She shook her head slightly. "He's been to my place twice. He's picked up horses from my husband."

I felt a jolt of realization. Of course Diamond Joe hadn't bought that high-quality string of riding stock to run a herd of scrub cattle—any half-green mustang would've served that purpose—and of course he'd only bought the unbranded ones. Diamond Joe Alahambre was the horse-man for the Quarrels Gang, same as I was for the James-Youngers. I felt foolish for not having seen it all along.

"Are you sure?" I leaned around her and her face met me half way. She nodded, raised a hand to shade her bruised forehead, then dropped it to gather the front of her torn dress. "Marshall," I called out, still watching her eyes.

"I heard," Briggs said, stepping toward us and dragging the outlaw beside him. Jack walked up beside them and stuffed a hat down on the outlaw's head; dust billowed. He'd picked up a bandoleer of ammunition from beside the campfire and slung it over his shoulder.

Briggs slung back the outlaw's head and held him out toward the woman. "Now take a good look, ma'am—"

"I don't have to," she said. "I've seen him there. Him and another one—"

"You're dead, bitch," Sonny Quarrels growled in a dazed voice.

"I warned you," Briggs said; and he drew back his right

hand arm's length and swung the longest, slowest, and hardest slap I ever saw in my life. I winced at the sound and the sight of it. The outlaw's head snapped back, spun around on his shoulders, then dropped and bobbed on his chest.

"Damn! I mean—darn it, Briggs," said Jack. "The man's shot all to hel—I mean *heck.* You can't expect him to watch his language—"

"I don't tolerate sass from a prisoner," Briggs said. "It's a bad way to start him off on his road to rehabilitation."

I reached down, took up the canteen, uncapped it around the woman's waist, and held it up for her. I ran things through my mind as she sipped the water. Jack and I were becoming more and more drawn into a bad situation here, and I didn't know quite what to do next. Alahambre, Ned Quarrels, this poor woman, the marshall, the wounded outlaw . . . and my horse, Buck, all swirled in a tangled picture in my mind.

I looked at Jack. He shot a glance around the campsite, then back to me, and I knew what he was thinking about—the stage money. He'd searched around enough to know it wasn't here, but just getting this close to the forty thousand dollars had his blood pumping, same as it would've mine if not for my concern over Buck. I had to get Buck back whatever the cost, even it meant riding with a lawman and hunting down the Quarrels Gang.

The woman turned loose of the canteen and swooned against my chest. I studied Jack's eyes for a second, then looked down at Briggs. "Let's take her back to the women's lodge—they'll take care of her. Then we'll ride with you to get Quarrels and Alahambre." I stared at Briggs; he swiped his free hand.

"Naw . . . you boys ain't cut out for this. This is a crude, ugly business. It wouldn't be right dragging you into—"

"Look, marshall." I cut him off. "I'm going after Alahambre and getting my horse back, one way or another. Now, we ain't quite the dandies you think we are." I shot

Jack a glance and saw the look of caution in his eyes. "That is, we can handle ourselves as well as the next man," I said, changing my tone of voice. Sunlight sparkled off the butt of Jack's La Faucheux pistol. I couldn't believe Briggs not seeing what we were. "You need help with Quarrels and I need help getting my horse. There's no more to be said."

"Well—" Briggs drew out his pistol "—I feel so bad about yas having to be a part of it." He drew back the pistol, raised it high and busted Sonny across the head without raising his voice. "It just don't seem right dragging yas into all this."

Again I winced. The outlaw crumbled straight down. Briggs wiped his pistol barrel across his pants leg and dropped it back in his holster.

"Ease up, Briggs!" Jack leaned down to the outlaw. "Don't you think this poor sumbitch has had enough?"

"Nothing personal against him," Briggs said. "It's just been my experience that a prisoner's easier to handle if you strap him across a horse and crack his head now and then. Keeps 'em docile and easily managed. Teaches them some respect right off."

I watched Jack and Briggs drag Sonny Quarrels to a horse and pitch him across it. The woman moaned and turned her face against my chest. I wanted to touch her somehow in a way that would take away the pain, not just the pain of last night's beating, but all the pain, any pain . . . any she'd ever felt. I brushed her hair back carefully and held her. "You'll be all right, ma'am," I whispered, with my face pressed gently near her ear.

"I know," she said, as if speaking through a dream. "I know."

We turned our horses and rode back out of the gully watching the high ridge above us. The same thing that happened to Sonny Quarrels and the dead man could happen to us as well. I didn't breathe easy until we'd topped the trail back up to where we'd started. Briggs once again took the lead and stepped his horse along at a snail's pace, leading Sonny Quarrels knocked out over his horse. I rode beside Jack with the woman dozing against my chest. I looked back at the buzzards as we headed out to the main trail. They had circled lower; one had dropped out of sight.

The sun poured down fiercely on the parched land. Wavering heat swirled upward before us like a watery veil.

9

It was evening when I split off from Jack and Briggs and took the lower trail into the valley toward the women's lodge. We'd planned on Jack and Briggs taking the high cutoff and pulling the boards off the washout behind them, forcing Quarrels's gang to ride all the way back, and down to the main road. That would give Jack and Briggs a good three-hour lead. They would take the prisoner into Gris and I would meet them there after leaving Diamond Joe's wife with the two women.

According to Briggs, if Quarrels wanted his brother back he'd follow the three horses' hoofprints up the high cutoff. He might send a man or two to track me, but I convinced Briggs that I could handle them. Briggs appeared apprehensive as I left them at the fork in the dusty trail. "Anything happens to that young feller," I heard Briggs say to Jack as I turned the mare away, "and I'd just turn this old Dance around and blow my head off."

"I wouldn't worry, marshall," Jack replied. I heard him chuckle and talk loud enough for me to hear. "He don't look like much, but he'll manage . . . somehow." It was Jack's intention to get Sonny Quarrels alone and try to find out where the money was hidden. I figured he'd set up an opportunity where Sonny would offer him a bribe to let him loose, then Jack would grill him about the money until he found out something. Even if Sonny lied—and he would, most likely—it would be a place to start. Sometimes you could find out a lot just by finding out where *not* to look. At any rate, my main concern was finding Buck and getting him back. If the money came within grasp, so much the better, providing we could get it without running over Briggs. But Briggs was old, and I'd seen enough to know he wasn't pumping full steam. I saw no problem. He'd be easily fooled when and if the time came. Until then, I had to think about the woman.

I smiled and gigged the mare into a light trot. The woman reached out a hand and steadied herself on my leg. She had come around but was still dazed. I steadied her with my left arm around her waist, her hair blowing against my face, and I reined the mare with my right, off the trail, into the sprawling forest of aspen, pine, and cottonwoods, and deep into the valley until the sunlight faded above us.

She'd dozed again by the time darkness set in. I could've made it the rest of the way in another couple of hours, but I didn't want to risk it. The night would be moonless and blacker than a bucket of tar. If the mare lamed out in a pothole we'd be stranded, and as weak as the woman was, we'd be easy targets for Quarrels's men if any came searching for us.

In the last rays of grainy light, I followed a trickle of water toward a cliff overhang through a carpet of low juniper, stepping the mare back and forth carefully to cover our trail. Where the trickle turned into a thin stream, I walked the mare in, bearing back to the right, and midstream I turned around and walked the other direction a quarter of a mile until the overhang deepened farther back under the cliff. "Where are we?" The woman stirred and gazed around in the darkness.

I stopped, slipped down and lifted her down against me. She pushed back a step and tried standing on her own.

"We'll stay here tonight and ride on in come morning if you think you'll be all right."

"I can't seem to . . . stay awake." She twisted her head back and forth. "Can't seem to . . ." She swooned against me and I caught her by her shoulders.

"Here," I said, guiding her to a wide, flat rock. "Sit here a second." I stepped back to the mare, pulled down my bedroll from behind the saddle, and spread it on the soft sandy ground. I took off my duster, rolled it up, and laid it on my bedroll for a pillow. "Lie here," I said, "and I'll fix us something to eat. Can you eat something? Some dried shank? Some hot coffee?"

She leaned back against my rolled-up duster and touched her hand carefully to her jaw. "Coffee, maybe . . . "

"Good," I said.

I loosened the mare's cinch and walked her to the stream, let her drink her fill while I cleaned the coffee pot and filled it with water. When the mare finished drinking, raised her head, and let out a long blow, I picketed her in a narrow stretch of short grass while I gathered enough twigs and downed limbs to start a small fire.

After I'd started the coffee water and laid some dried shank on a clean rock close to the flames, I went back outside the overhang, brought in the mare, and tied her reins around a jut of rock in the wall. "Are we safe here?" I heard her voice unexpectedly and almost jumped, then let out a breath and turned toward her. "I'm sorry," she said. "I didn't mean to startle you."

I smiled and pushed up my hat brim. "It's all right, ma'am, I just thought you'd gone back to sleep." I glanced at her, then back to the fire. "Coffee's up," I said. I unbuttoned my shirt sleeve and lifted the pot with my cuff wrapped around the handle. I filled a metal cup, sat the pot back on the fire, and slung my hot hand back and forth.

"Careful," I said. She took the cup of coffee between her

hands and blew on it. Steam swirled and she raised her face above it, smelling it.

"It's strange . . . " Her words trailed away and she gazed up into the golden shadows of low flames on the ceiling of stone. Her bruised eyes glistened in the firelight and she squeezed them shut until something passed from her mind.

"Ma'am?" I asked quietly.

"Just strange." She shook her head slightly and her hair spilled forward hiding part of her face. "The warmth . . . the smell of this coffee." She sipped it like someone tasting it for the first time.

"You're feeling better, ma'am?" I noticed her voice sounded stronger.

"Yes . . . I think so." She ran her hand carefully across her side. "But I hurt in here, deep . . . deep in my side."

"We'll be there early in the morning," I said, "unless you don't think we should wait—"

"No . . . I think I'll be all right." She sipped the coffee. "This helps," and I saw her wince as the cup touched her swollen lips. I winced with her. She glanced toward the warm strips of dried shank. "Maybe I could . . . ?"

"Oh, yes, ma'am," I said, and as if afraid she might change her mind, I stepped quickly to the fire, flipped the warm meat onto the end of my glades knife, and held it out to her. "Sorry for the dinnerware," I said, smiling. She picked up a piece and ate it carefully. I watched, almost feeling the pain in her bruised cheek.

We ate in silence until she took the last strip from the knife. I wiped the blade across my boot, leaned in close to the fire, and cleaned the blade in the low flames. "I'll have to darken our camp," I said, and I nodded out toward the trail. "Hope you don't mind."

"I understand," she said.

I raked away the outer edge of the fire with the big knife, banked the pot on a bed of glowing embers, and mashed out the flames with the flat of the blade. In the glow of the embers, I walked over, took a sack of grain from my saddlebags, fed the mare three hands full, and rubbed her muzzle.

I slipped my rifle from its boot; when I walked back to the blanket, the woman was sleeping, facing the heat of the embers with her cup beside her and the blanket flipped over her. Her face glowed in the low embers, and I reached down and brushed back her hair. She stirred with a sharp intake of breath. "It's okay," I whispered, and she relaxed back into her sleep. . . .

I dozed with my rifle across my lap and my ear tuned to the darkness outside the overhang. In that nether world between sleep and consciousness where a hunted man must learn to live, I pictured this woman in the house alone with him, and I saw the terror in her eyes, and I heard the big calloused hand rise and fall again and again. I was somewhere inside that house, but try though I might, I could not reach her. I could see her, hear her, even reach out to her, but she was just past the tips of my fingers and I could get no closer. "No!" I jerked awake with a start just as I'd seen him raise a pistol toward her. I shivered and hunched up inside my shirt.

"What is it?" Her voice sounded hushed and frightened from the darkness.

"It's all right," I said, and I heard the tremble in my voice. "I must've been dreaming, is all."

I heard her stir from the blanket and I felt her hand find me in the darkness. She brushed her hand across my face. "You're freezing," she said.

"No, I'm fine, ma'am. Just had a dream—"

"Here," she tugged my arm. "Lie down and cover up in the blanket."

"No, I'm all right. You cover up. You need it more than I do. I'll be fine. I'm used to—"

"Come on," she said, and she tugged again, this time more persistent. "There's no harm in it. It's cold. We both need it."

I slept, and awoke in the gray of night just as early dawn crept down from atop the towering pines. I slipped quietly from the open edge of the blanket and lay it back over her softly. It had been a long time since I'd felt the warmth of a woman against me, even if it was only shelter from a cold night. I felt strange looking down at her, and I only did so for a second before walking to the coffee pot and placing my hand against it. It was barely warm.

While she slept, I fed small twigs into the faint glow of embers until I'd worked up a low flame. I sat hunkered near the fire, rocking on my boots with my arms around my knees, now and then stirring the flame and watching it lick up the side of the pot until I began to feel the slightest warmth of it against my face and the back of my hand.

I thought of Buck and wondered if I'd ever see him again. I thought of Jack and pictured the long white thighs of Helova Knight that he could've felt wrapped around him if only I'd have told him . . . if only he'd stayed in Cimarron.

I pictured Briggs and Jack and the outlaw, Sonny Quarrels. I wondered if they'd make it to the washout and pull up the boards behind them before Ned and his gang caught up to them. I wondered if I was being followed. And I thought of the poor battered woman behind me, sleeping peacefully in a world that had brought her such misery.

I remembered how warm she'd felt against me in the night, and how her warmth had moved into my spirit and awakened *something* like only the warmth of a woman can do. I'd slept in her warmth, but was careful not to hurt her. I'd felt her against me, longed to feel her against me again; and I shook that thought from my mind, feeling ashamed for thinking it. Then I reached out to the coffee pot, felt it hot against my hand, and I poured a cup and sipped it as I stared into the low flames.

"Mister Beatty?" I heard her voice behind me; she sounded frightened.

"I'm right here," I said, glancing over my shoulder. "Fixing some coffee for us if you don't mind warmed-over."

I heard her moan slightly and saw her stand up in the darkness and step over beside me. She leaned down, using my shoulder for support. "Feeling better?" I asked quietly.

She nodded and pushed back her hair. She reached for my cup and I gave it to her. She sipped it and I noticed she did so less carefully than she had last night. "Yes, thank you. I suppose sleep *is* good medicine." She rubbed her side carefully. "I still hurt all over . . . but I'm better."

I leaned back, reached and picked up her cup from beside the blanket. I poured the remainder of the leftover coffee into it and sipped it. "How long has that been going on with him . . . the beatings?" I stared into the low flame.

"Too long to talk about," she said. "Too *painful* to talk about." She sat silent for a second, then let out a breath. "I don't know what came over me. Somehow he forced his way into my life." She shook her head. "I never meant to let him in, but I did. I never intended marrying him, but I did." She sipped the coffee; I glanced at her, then back into the flames. "I don't know how it happened, but it did." She sighed heavily. "Now it's over. I'll die before I ever—" Her voice trembled and stopped short.

"It's okay," I said. "I shouldn't have brought it up."

She sniffed, ran her hand beneath her nose, and sipped her coffee. "Just promise me he won't kill you, Mister Beatty." I felt her hand on my arm. "You've been kind."

"He won't," I said flatly. "Or I don't think he will. He ain't done so good at it up to now." I smiled, then my smile faded. "But I'm getting my horse back either way."

"You told me the horse means a lot to you. Want to tell why?" She reached up a hand and brushed my hair from my forehead.

I felt her hand on my forehead, remembered the warmth of her in the night, and nodded my head away. She stopped her hand and drew it away slowly. "No, ma'am. If it's all the same with you, I'd rather not say why." I looked into her eyes. She was older than me, eight years, maybe ten, maybe more. "I reckon talking about that horse is like you talking about the beatings—just brings back the hurt, is all." I stared into the flames and sipped the coffee. "But that black stallion is like the son I never had."

"Oh," she said softly.

"Yeah . . . that's what it's like." And before I realized what I was doing or why I did it, I'd told her the story of why Buck meant so much to me, about losing my wife, about Buck's mama, the mare I'd taken from a dead man during the war, and about breeding her to the fine racehorse back near Kansas City. Of course I didn't mention any names, lest she realize that I was Miller Crowe the outlaw. I just told enough to let her know that to me, Buck was the most important thing in the world. When I'd finished, I threw back the last drink of coffee and shook out the grounds. "—And I'll get him back . . . or die in the process." I stood and dusted the seat of my trousers. I started to turn and gather the bedroll, but she reached up and took my forearm.

"I understand," she said.

"Yeah . . . well." I felt awkward and I looked all around and rubbed my jaw.

"And I want you to know . . . it's all right, Mister Beatty."

I stopped and looked down at her. "What?"

"Us . . . last night. It's all right. Us sleeping together. Two people who were just cold. We *slept* . . . nothing else. It was cold and we slept . . . all right?"

"Yeah," I said, and I let out a breath.

"Besides, I'm old enough to be your—" She stopped for a second and tried to smile. "Your older sister." She looked at me through hurt but healing eyes, and I saw in her eyes that even through her pain she'd felt the same things. She tugged at my arm for me to help her up. I did, and she moaned as she stood. "It was cold . . . people need to be warm." She smiled and I could tell it took much effort. "My name is Margaret," she said.

I smiled, "Yes, ma'am—Margaret. Thanks," I said.

When I'd finished drawing the mare's cinch and tying down the bedroll, I helped Margaret Alahambre into the saddle and led the mare out from beneath the cliff overhang. Rather than backtrack up the stream and take a chance on someone waiting along the trail, I slipped up behind the saddle and stepped the mare quietly along the stream in the other direction, then crossed a half mile below.

We worked our way through thick brush and heavy forest until I knew the trail lay a few yards ahead. But instead of riding out onto the trail, I stayed ten yards inside the cover of forest and headed toward the cabin. Margaret Alahambre struggled with the pain in her side as we crossed the rough terrain, and though she never made a sound, I could feel her tense up against my chest and gasp for breath.

"That's it . . . we're going up," I said in a whisper. I could not bear putting her through so much torture.

"No, please," she whispered in reply. "I'll be all right." She squeezed my leg against her pain.

"Huh-uh," I said, "we've got to get you there and get you looked after." And I eased the mare up near the edge of the road and looked in both directions.

I backed the mare a few feet and we sat silently for a minute, hearing no sound save for the scattered chatter of birds in the trees above us; then I eased the mare forward onto the road and gigged her gently. "See," I said, "there's no one here. They must've all taken the high—"

My words stopped short beneath the crack of rifle fire and the whistle of a bullet. I heard a loud yell behind us and swung the mare around, drawing my rifle as we spun. Another round whistled past. I saw two riders pounding toward us from seventy-five yards back up the trail.

There was no time to cut to cover and no time to help the woman down. "Hang on," I yelled. I ran my hand down the mare's reins quickly, wrapped a quick turn near the bit, and twisted her head back as hard as I could as I nailed my right spur to her. She let out a long neigh, rocked back on her haunches, and crumbled down on her left side. "Step off," I shouted, and with my rifle in hand, I threw my arm around the woman, still laying back on the reins, and we slipped off the saddle and onto the ground as the big mare stretched out on the trail with her hoofs thrashing the dust.

"Hold her head down!" I dropped behind the mare, cocking my rifle. Fifty yards—I aimed, locked the rifle down against the saddle as a bullet grazed off the pommel and spun away with a hiss. Thirty-five yards—I took a breath, exhaled it, and stopped; and I let my whole body settle into the shot, let my arm rise and fall with the mare's breathing, spaced it, timed it, squeezed it coming up, and saw my sights raise into his chest.

Twenty yards—I felt the rifle buck in my hand and the nearest rider flipped backwards as his horse tumbled in a spray of dust and loose rocks. Ten yards—I recocked as the other rider veered around the downed horse, slid his own horse down on its haunches, and turned sharp. Just when his horse had spun full turn and caught its balance, I felt the rifle kick again and saw his shoulder blades snap back like he'd been called to attention. Then he slumped forward as if dismissed and melted from his saddle as the horse bolted away.

I stood up slowly, recocking and scanning the road in both directions. "Are you okay?" I spoke down to her, still watching the road. She only nodded.

I reached down and drew her up carefully from over the mare's neck, picking up the reins at the same time. She moaned, but managed to stand. She held my arm and stood staring in disbelief at the bodies as dust settled around them in the silence of morning. Her hand tightened on my forearm. "I'm sorry you had to see this," I said quietly.

She didn't answer; I looked at her face and saw a trickle

of blood run down from her mouth. "Oh no!" I looked her up and down quickly but saw no wound.

"I hurt—bad," she moaned. She bent at the waist with her hand on her side and I caught her as she fell against me.

"Hold on to me," I said, pulling her against me as I yanked up on the reins. I kicked the mare in the rump and looped my leg over the saddle as the big animal rolled up from the ground, sweeping the woman and me up with her. "We've got to get there fast," I said. "I'm sorry! Hang on!" And I spun the mare and gigged her a solid punch.

I leaned over her and held her against me as the mare pounded down the trail. There was nothing I could do to lessen her pain, except to get the ride over with as quickly as possible. I sensed her hurt as hoofs met hard ground in the relentless thunder beneath us, and in a moment the woman slumped and lay limp in my arm. But I kept the mare bellied down until we rounded a turn into the clearing and slid to a halt outside the lodge.

I saw the cautious faces of the two women peeking through the front window as I jumped down and let Margaret Alahambre slip down to me. "Hello, the house," I called out, and I saw the door open.

"What has happened to her?" I forced my way past the dark-skinned woman and across the floor, carrying Diamond Joe's wife in my arms. "Answer me, I heard shots! Are you being followed? What happened to her?"

I laid Margaret Alahambre down carefully on a quilt-covered bed, then turned as the dark-skinned woman stepped past me and leaned over her. She touched Margaret's face gently. "She has been beaten like an animal." She shot me a cold stare.

"I didn't do it!" I said. "She's hurt! Help her."

"Then who did?" Her eyes swept over me, full of contempt.

"Please," Margaret Alahambre moaned in a weak voice. "He didn't do this. My husband—" Her voice failed her.

The dark-skinned woman glanced down at her. "Greta! Fetch some water and a towel, quickly," she called over her shoulder.

I stepped away and took off my hat. "I looked her over best I could," I said. "I don't know how bad it is under her garment."

She shot me another cold glance, then looked back down at the woman. "Even an animal does not do something like this to his mate."

"I know," I said. I held my hat against my chest and ran a hand back through my hair.

"Oh, do you?" She spoke without turning toward me. I felt her bitterness. Greta shot me a glance and slipped past me with a pan of water and a towel. Under her arm she carried a fresh dressing and a bottle of witch hazel. "Here," the dark-skinned woman said to Margaret Alahambre. She adjusted a pillow beneath her head, started unbuttoning her dress, then stopped and dealt me another hateful look. "Go! *Vamonos!*"

Margaret reached out a hand to mine as I turned to leave. "Don't go," she said just above a whisper. "Please . . . stay with me. . . . " Her voice trailed away.

The dark-skinned woman started to say something but I didn't give her a chance. "I won't leave you," I said. "I'll just be outside while they undress you and look you over. I'll stay close . . . I promise."

The dark-skinned woman cursed under her breath in Spanish. I let go of Margaret's hand and walked away shaking my head. At the door, I stopped and turned for a second. "Has anybody gone by on the high trail? Have you heard any—?"

"Yes," she said, without looking toward me. "We heard riders late in the night. They traveled fast—too fast for the trail."

"Was that all?"

"No. We heard more riders before dawn. That is all."

I turned, walked out on the porch, and breathed deep. Briggs had called it right. Quarrels had sent a couple men to follow me and the rest followed them. Now, with the wash-out stopping them on the high trail, all Quarrels could do was turn back. I took some comfort in knowing that Jack, Briggs, and for now at least, the woman and I were safe. But as I scanned the high ridge in the morning light, I thought of Buck. Was he somewhere in a hidden canyon with a dozen other horses, somewhere back near the Alahambre spread? Or had someone rode him along the high trail only hours ago? Had I been that close to him?

I slapped my hat against my leg and gazed upward along the high ridge, saw a hawk swing in a wide circle and soar out of sight behind the sheer wall of rock . . . and I stood there staring up the rock wall for the longest time.

10

While I waited, I walked the mare out across the yard, down into the stream, and gave her a good washing as she drank and blew and slung water with her muzzle. As she drank, I looked all around the base of the wall until I spotted the boards that Jack and Briggs had thrown off the washout once they'd crossed. Now there was no doubt they'd made it. But there was also no doubt that the Quarrels Gang would have to take the main road to Gris, or swing down through here.

I bathed quickly, pulled on a pair of wrinkled denim trousers from my saddlebags, and walked back up to the cabin carrying my saddle and leading the mare. I sat on the step of the porch cleaning my rifle when Greta stepped out carrying a plate of food. She looked down at me sitting there bare-chested and averted her eyes quickly. I saw her discomfort and I bent down to my saddle beside the steps, pulled a dirty shirt from my saddlebags, and slipped it on. It smelled of sweat, heat, and the road. I stood up and took the plate. "Thank you, Greta—ma'am," I said. She still looked away from my face.

"Carmilla says to tell you the woman is doing well. She has some broken ribs but they didn't puncture her lungs—"

"What about the blood? I saw blood."

Greta spoke as she focused past me toward the mare.

"She bit the inside of her cheek. She will be all right. . . . Carmilla says to tell you that."

"That's good." I sighed and nodded toward the door. "Can I see her for a second?"

"I told you she's all right." Greta's eyes snapped into mine for the first time, then slipped away.

"I know, but I'd like to just see for myself—"

"Very well." She hiked her long skirt and spun away, back through the door. I followed, carrying the plate of food.

"What do *you* want?" The dark-skinned woman, Carmilla, looked up at me through eyes of polished stone.

"I just want to see how she's doing."

Carmilla's face tightened. "Didn't Greta tell you?"

"It's okay, please," I heard Margaret Alahambre say from the bed. Her voice sounded tired and weak. She reached up a hand. I laid the plate on the table and stepped over to her. Carmilla moved aside and sat down in a chair near the bed.

"You're one tough woman, ma'am—Margaret," I said, squeezing her hand gently. "You must be from Pennsylvania."

She smiled and rolled her head back and forth slowly on the pillow. Her dress was unbuttoned nearly to her waist and I saw the tight wrapping around her ribs. "I can ride," she said, "any time you're ready."

"What?" Carmilla snapped up from her chair wagging a long finger. "That is out of the question!" She riveted her dark eyes on mine. "She cannot ride . . . not now. She needs rest."

"I've got to go with him!" Margaret tried to raise up but collapsed.

"Now look what you have done," said Carmilla, rushing between us and leaning down to her. I didn't know if she was talking to me or Margaret Alahambre. She stroked her forehead gently. "Lay still, *pobre caro.* Lay still and rest."

I backed up a step. Just having me around seemed to drive the dark-skinned woman to anger. *"Damn,"* I whispered; and I stepped over and picked up my plate.

"You cannot eat in here," Carmilla hissed, glancing around at me. "I told you, this lodge is for women—"

"Yes, ma'am," I hissed back. "I wouldn't eat in here if my *life* depended on it." I stomped out, down off the porch and across the yard to a large rock. I knew we had to leave. I had to take Margaret to Gris and I had to get busy finding Buck. "Damn headstrong bitch," I growled under my breath. I took a bite of food, started chewing, then stopped. I remembered what Briggs had said about Mama Lopez back in Cimarron. *"Jesus!"* I spit the food out on the ground, and ran my tongue around searching for any strange taste. Then I went to my saddlebags and yanked out some of the cold food that Briggs brought from Cimarron.

After I'd eaten a cut of stiff dried shank and a hard biscuit, I sat on the rock drinking water from my canteen. The cabin door opened and Carmilla stepped out, her shoulders squared and her chin at a cocky angle. I let out a breath and watched her walk over to me.

"I shouted at you," she said, and she looked up past me with her chin jutted. I had to admit, she was one of the most beautiful women I'd ever seen.

"Yeah? So?" I looked her up and down and reminded myself that beauty wasn't everything.

"I shouldn't have. That is all." She folded her arms, glanced down at me, then away. Somehow I got the impression she'd just apologized.

"Yeah . . . well, I was a little cross myself . . . I reckon." I wasn't about to offer any more of an apology than she did.

She stood silently for a second, then let out a breath. "She says her husband is crazy . . . and that he is a killer of men. She says he will kill you and her . . . and us for helping you."

"She knows him better than I do." I shrugged, capped my canteen, and dropped it at my feet. "You saw what he done to her just for letting me water my horse. I reckon you could call him a man of low character."

"Yes, I see." She glanced at flies buzzing the plate of food and the mouthful of food on the ground. "You did not eat?"

"No offense. I just had a real craving for something cold and stale." I stared at her, and felt she got my message.

"As you wish." She tossed back a ringlet of raven hair. "But now, because of what has happened, we must all leave here and go with you to Gris . . . for our own safety." Saying it made her face flush, as if someone had just jerked a knot in her intestines.

"Do you agree?" She still looked past me.

I didn't answer but I knew she was right. If it hadn't been for the two riders following me in, I could've left the women there. But now anyone with an eye for tracking could follow the hoofprints into the valley.

"This Diamond Joe . . . he rides with Ned Quarrels and his men? The ones who did this to our lodge?" She swept an arm, taking in the barn and garden.

"I think so," I said.

She shook her head in exasperation. "*Men.* You come up here with your trouble . . . your big long pistols . . . killing each other, then you think you can ride off as if it never happened? That is what you think you can do to us. Because we are *women.*" She bit her lip and gazed away.

"Look . . . I don't know what those men did to you and your friend, but I was no part of it. And I didn't start any of this. I'm looking for my horse and that's all. I didn't ask to come into your"—I waved my hand taking in all of the valley—"*lodge,* or whatever the hell this is. I brought her here because I thought that you and your friend, of all people, would want to help out another woman."

"You *men* start trouble by just being born. It is born in you, like venom in the rattlesnake. But I will not argue with you. For Greta's sake and the sake of that poor woman, we *are* going with you to Gris. If you forbid us . . . we will go anyway, and follow you. You cannot stop us."

"You blame this whole thing on me . . . like I planned it all just to come here and torment you. Now you've got the gall to want to ride out of here with me?"

"Only because there is strength in numbers." She stepped forward and snatched up the plate. "Do not think for a second that I would otherwise look to *you* for help . . . you or any other man."

She turned in a huff, hiked her skirt, and headed to the cabin.

"All right," I called out. "Go ahead . . . ride to Gris with me. You're welcome, more than welcome! But you're riding *behind* me!" I couldn't help spreading a devilish grin as she stomped toward the porch. "Hear that? *You* have to follow *me."* I thumbed my chest. "Ride *behind a man—"* I cupped my hand beside my mouth "—where you belong!"

"Get ready to ride." She raised a hand without turning and shot me an obscene gesture over her shoulder.

I let out a dark chuckle as she stepped into the cabin. "Stubborn hussy," I growled to myself. I spit and ran my hand across my mouth. "Prettier than any five women oughta be."

In a few minutes I'd gathered my gear, grained the mare, and gave her another long drink. When I'd filled my canteen and saddled up, I rode over to the cabin and looked down at Greta standing on the porch. "I better go get those two horses and roll the bodies out of the road." I saw her expression turn to terror; she bit her lip and stared away from me. "Sorry," I said, "but it needs to be done."

"Then just go and do it," Carmilla called from inside. "You do not have to tell her about it. She does not have to hear such—"

"All right," I shouted into the cabin, "I said I'm sorry." I tapped my hat brim toward Greta and reined the mare away.

I watched the low swing of buzzards as I rode the three-mile trek out to the bodies, and I turned my face from the sight of a large buzzard standing on one man's chest with its head bowed between its outstretched wings. I wasn't about to do anything now but let Nature have her way. Anybody within miles would see what was going on whether I rolled them off the road or not.

I stepped the mare wide, off the trail and around the grisly scene, and rode farther along until I spotted one of the horses standing near the trickle of water and grazing on a clump of grass. The big roan just stood staring as I stopped the mare, slid down and walked up slow and easy, talking in a soothing tone until I got within arm's reach, then eased out my hand and took up the loose reins. The horse slung its head a time or two against the reins, blew and stomped a hoof, then gave in and stepped along beside me as I walked back to the liver-chestnut.

I loosened the cinch on the roan a little and stepped into the saddle on the liver-chestnut. Leading the big roan, I searched around for the other horse a few minutes before turning and heading back to the cabin. There could be more of Quarrels's men roaming about, and following the circling buzzards would put them right on me.

Back at the cabin I spun both sets of reins around a post, and had stepped up on the porch when Greta came leading the burro from the barn. The small animal honked and whistled and kicked up its heels as if it hadn't been handled in a long time. I looked at them both and shook my head. "If you don't mind riding double, I'll put you and your friend on the roan there."

"The burro will do for me," she said, avoiding my eyes.

"You prefer *that* to a good riding horse?" I shook my head.

"She can ride what she chooses," called the voice from inside.

I threw up my hands. "Then you and that animal better

be able to keep up." Greta ignored me, picked up a wooden-frame pack saddle, and threw it on the burro's back.

Inside the cabin I walked to the bed where Margaret Alahambre sat leaning her weight on one arm, and holding a hand to her side. I squatted down and looked up at her. "We're gonna be leaving in a few minutes," I said. I pushed up my hat and laid a hand on her knee. "Are you gonna be up to it?"

She nodded without answering. "Good," I said, and I stood up.

Carmilla walked out from the next room wearing high-topped cavalry boots and tightening a leather belt around the waist of a pair of denim jeans. Her hair was pulled back and tied up under a long-oval Stetson. The handle of a long-barreled Smith & Wesson stuck up from her belt.

She wore a faded linsey-woolsey shirt with a bullet hole in the chest and a dark stain around it. But even in this rough getup, there was no denying her beauty; and I resented her beauty for some strange reason, looked for some flaw in it, the way the fox found fault in the grapes he knew he couldn't reach. "I'll tell you what I told Greta," I said. "You better be able to keep up." She ignored me and walked to the bed. I looked at the big boots as she crossed the floor and thought to myself that her feet were bound to stink when she took them off. I smiled to myself.

"Are you ready, Margaret?" she asked in a gentle voice. Margaret Alahambre nodded and started to stand. "Hold onto me," Carmilla said, and she swept Margaret up and cradled her in her long arms. "Get the door for me," she said without looking at me. It took a second for me to move. "Please!"

I snapped to the door and swung it open. She breezed past me, across the porch and sat the woman up in the saddle easily. I just stared until she turned and leaned a hand against the mare. "I will ride with her on the mare," she said. "You ride the roan. We will switch later."

I started to say something, but saw she was right. I didn't know the roan as well as I knew the mare. It would be better keeping Margaret Alahambre on the liver-chestnut for a while, then switch after I had ridden the roan and seen how he handled. Spreading the double load between the horses would also keep them both from wearing out. I just stood there staring.

"Well . . . do you agree with me?" Carmilla spread a crafty smile, as if she'd seen what I was thinking and knew I had to agree.

"That's what I was going to suggest," I said. "That, and walking the horses as much as possible to keep them both rested and even."

"Very good," she said. Her eyebrows arched. "It's a good thing you were here to notice something like that," she said in a smooth, even voice.

I wondered what she meant by that as I stepped up and brushed dust from my arm. I pulled on a pair of gloves and tightened them between my fingers. "If you gals—uh, *women* are ready, just follow me and I'll have us in Gris by supper time."

"As you wish, Señor Beatty," Carmilla said in a quiet, controlled voice. Greta gigged the little burro up beside the liver-chestnut. The mare looked down at it, blew, and stomped a hoof; the burro swished its tail back and forth, and raised its head high, like a silver charger. I shook my head and tapped the roan forward, cantered him sideways out across the yard, then reined him into a walk as he arched his head a few times and settled down.

We struck out across the clearing at a easy pace. I walked along in front of Carmilla and Margaret on the big mare with Greta beside them on the little burro. Near the far edge of the clearing the ground began a long, steady slope upwards into cedar, pine, and cottonwoods, and the flat, smooth bottomland turned gradually into rock and gullies along both sides of the path.

Inside the woods, we heard a pistol shot ring out from the high cutoff above the cabin and for a second we stopped and heard the strange-sounding voice of Diamond Joe Alahambre echo across the valley. "I know nuu're down nar, Marn-gret," he shouted from atop the rock wall. "Come ount and lent's talk. Hear me?" Another pistol shot popped from the high ridge. "Gondamn it, Marn-gret! We'll wornk nis ount . . . hear me?"

I looked at the woman and saw the fear, the dread, and the shame in her eyes. "Keep going," I said quietly, and we struck onward up the narrow trail. I led us back and forth in a maze of rock corridors that all stopped against the rock wall on our right. *"Damn,"* I said, after reaching another dead end. "I thought you called this the valley trail?"

"It is," Carmilla said quietly, "but only until we crossed the clearing." She stared at me without saying a word, until I finally let out a breath.

"All right," I said, feeling my face redden. "Would you mind taking the lead here?" She reined around and followed a thin path that seemed to roll back under the hillside, but then turned upwards onto a wider trail. When we rode onto it, she looked back at me and almost smiled; I shrugged and almost smiled in return.

After a couple of miles, I got off and walked the roan for a few minutes, then we stopped and moved Margaret Alahambre over to the roan, and I rode behind her while Carmilla walked the liver-chestnut. The constant uphill pull began taking a toll on both horses, and by the time the land leveled off, the burro had passed us both, walked well up the road, turned toward us and let out a honk. Greta righted the little animal. It kicked up its heels.

I caught myself smiling at Carmilla. "I hate a show-off."

She caught herself returning my smile and we both looked away at the same time. "There is water at the *junta* five miles farther." She pointed a finger.

"Good," I said. We rode on a few minutes, and I looked

down at her, watched the sway of her hips in the snug denim. "So . . . what is it your women's league does?" She shot me a glance without answering, then looked straight ahead. "I mean . . . do you get together and make quilts, swap recipes, nice things like that?" I grinned and prepared myself for her blow-up—watched her firm legs take long strides up the path—but it didn't come.

"Yes, of course." I saw her whole body stiffen, as if she'd been hit in the stomach; but she kept walking. "What else would you expect?" Her voice was tight with controlled anger, but beneath it, I sensed her humiliation, and I felt ashamed. I glanced at Margaret Alahambre's battered face against my chest, then back down at Carmilla.

I bit my lip, stopped the mare, and watched Carmilla lead the roan forward. "Damn it, ma'am, I'm sorry," I called out to her. "I truly am." But still she did not respond. She trudged forward up the path, as if carrying a heavy load.

By the time we traveled another three or four miles in silence, the trees along our left had thinned out and the heat of sunlight seemed to radiate off the rock wall like the stoked belly of a wood stove. I could see it waver out and up off the rocks, and up in long swirls from the trail in front of us.

Near the *junta*—the junction—Carmilla stopped; and when I caught up to her and Greta on the burro, I started to apologize again for what I'd said, but she placed a finger to her lips to keep me from speaking. "From here we must move very quietly." There was no more anger or hurt in her voice. "Sometimes hunters lay in wait around the water hole and ambush Mexicans or Indians for their scalps."

I just stared at her a second. "It is true," she said just above a whisper. "The government pays fifty dollars for a renegade Apache scalp—" she raised her hat slightly, then dropped it back on her head "—but who can tell the difference? A woman is an easy kill."

"I see," I said, avoiding her eyes. We switched Margaret Alahambre back to the liver-chestnut and when we'd remounted, I drew the rifle from my boot and laid it across my lap.

"What're we doing?" I heard Margaret Alahambre ask. She'd drifted in and out of consciousness the whole way.

"Be still," Carmilla said softly. She leaned her arms around her, took up the reins, and moved slowly around the bend and off the trail to the basin of runoff water. I waited until Greta followed her on the burro, then gigged the roan up over a steep rise of rocks and circled the water basin before slipping down the other side.

I watched from a broad, flat shelf above them, keeping my eyes shaded beneath my hat and studying each scrub pine and low bush around the basin as they watered their animals and themselves. When they finished watering, I backed the roan as they spread out back from the basin. Carmilla slipped a rifle from its boot and propped it up on her thigh; I slipped the roan down quietly to the basin, loosened his cinch, and let him drink and blow while I got down and filled my canteen with my rifle in my hand.

I'd just stepped up in the stirrups when we heard a rustling from a clump of mesquite bushes across the basin. Since I hadn't yet made it into my saddle, I squatted down quickly in one stirrup, snatched a handful of mane in one hand and propped my rifle across the saddle with the other. The roan stepped backward and forward.

"Easy, boy." I pivoted the rifle on the saddle and kept it trained on the bushes. Carmilla sat silent, one arm around Margaret Alahambre and one arm aiming the rifle. In a second, a large bird shot up from the bush with a loud squall and batted its wings off into the sun.

I let out a tense breath, saw Carmilla and Greta do the same, and I swung over into my saddle and gigged the roan over beside the liver-chestnut. "I still don't trust this place," I said. "Let's *vamonos.*" I scanned the trees and bushes around the basin and up the mountainside. I looked back and saw Carmilla watching me. She turned her face away and gigged the mare away to the trail. Greta fell in behind her with the little burro clicking its sharp hoofs across the flat stone path.

I backed the roan out around the stone path, then turned and gigged him quickly back to the trail. Of all the country I'd ever traveled I'd never seen any more perfect for an ambush than the high ridges of *Nuevo Mejico.*

We passed the junction, took a steep trail down a few hundred yards, then swung out onto a flat trail toward Gris. The evening sun now smoldered like a puddle of iron, glowing silver-red from behind the Sangre de Cristo mountain line. The colors of madness and magic streaked up into the sky as if God had swept a hand across the earth and smeared its blood and marrow into heaven.

We'd stopped once more and I now had Margaret Alahambre on the big roan. She'd sat up on her own for awhile, then drifted again. I brushed her hair back from her face, and held my hat out to shield her from the sun. As we rode on, Carmilla took off her Stetson, hung it on her saddlehorn, and shook out her long black hair. "So," she said to me, reaching out a hand and patting the mare's sweaty neck, "you have been a soldier, a cavalryman?"

"Some," I said, gazing ahead at Greta; she sat slumped on the burro as if asleep. The first breeze of evening swept past us.

"Some? What does that mean? *'Some.'* " She mimicked me in a lowered voice. I saw a trace of a smile.

"I rode for the stars and bars," I said. "Why?"

"I saw what you did back there at the water hole. That is something that a soldier does, sink down on a stirrup and use a poor horse as a shield?" I noticed the sharp edge in her voice.

"You don't let up, do you?" I shook my head. "I did it because I wasn't in the saddle and it was the best response

. . . right then." I gazed out across the land between us and the mountain line. An antelope darted across a rise and disappeared over the edge. "I'm not cruel to horses if that's where you're headed with this. Never was, never will be. I find horses are better company than humans." I glanced her up and down, couldn't help but notice the fine jut of her breasts and the way her body swayed gently with the movement of the horse. "Most humans, anyway," I added, glancing away from her.

We rode on in silence for a few seconds, listening to the sound of evening and our horses' hooves on the hard trail. "Yes," she said finally, her voice so quiet I wondered if she was speaking to herself. "I too find that to be true . . . in most cases."

We rode another few yards and I looked at her for a second, then back to the road. "I really am sorry about what I said back there." But she only shrugged and gazed ahead. "So," I said, after a second of silence, "we both agree that we like animals better than we do each other?" I smiled. Now that I'd tried to apologize, what more could I do? Her only response was another moment of silence. I chuckled. "We haven't exactly hit it off with each other, have we?"

She looked at me and leaned slightly toward me in her saddle, and I saw the outline of her breasts as the breeze pressed her shirt against them. "You must remember one thing—" Her voice softened for a second. She raised a finger. "It is a big world, Mister Beatty. . . . We don't *have* to be friends." She gigged her horse forward with a snap of her heels, and I sat there stunned, watching the breeze play through her hair as she rode away.

I felt my hands tremble and I folded them on the saddlehorn with my arms around Margaret Alahambre. She lay against my chest, still as stone. I gigged the roan forward. "There's a sound piece of wisdom if I ever heard any," I said under my breath.

• 11 •

"Stay close and let's not make any sudden moves," I said, when we stopped outside of town. "They might be a little jumpy." But Carmilla and Greta only looked at each other. I'd glanced down at the little burro; it cocked its head toward me and swished its tail. I shook my head and nudged the roan forward carefully.

I'm not sure what I expected riding into Gris. Knowing Briggs and Jack had rode in earlier with a member of the Quarrels gang strapped to his horse, and knowing that Ned Quarrels would be out to set his brother free, I must've thought the town would be up in arms, prepared for an attack. In the pale light of dusk, I spotted two wagons end to end in the street, and figured they'd been set up as a barricade. But as we rode closer, I saw a man standing in each wagon loading building materials from one to the other.

I glanced at Carmilla; she looked away. Gris was still busy at work, hammering and sawing, the same as before. We weaved around piles of lumber, nail kegs, and building blocks stacked in the street. A few heads turned up toward us for a second, then back to their work. "They are building a town here," Carmilla said. "What did you expect?"

I just stared at her as we guided our horses through the

building material and up to the hitch rail outside the crooked hotel.

"What is wrong with this place?" Carmilla turned her head sideways and stared with a bemused expression.

"Welcome to Fortenay's On The Frontier," I said wryly. "It's a little crooked . . . but it's home, for now."

"We cannot stay in such a place as this. What if it falls in the middle of the night?"

"Let's hope it doesn't. It's the only place in town, unless you want to sleep in a construction tent."

Carmilla stepped down and I eased Margaret Alahambre from the saddle and down to her. "I'm awake," Margaret said in a tired voice. She steadied herself and stood on her own. Carmilla looped her arm carefully around her and helped her to the boardwalk. Greta stepped off the burro and helped. "Are we really staying here?" I heard her ask Carmilla in a disbelieving whisper.

Carmilla shrugged without answering.

I stood back as they walked into Fortenay's On The Frontier, then walked in behind them. Jack turned from the bar, saw us, and raised a mug of beer. "About damned time," he grinned. The place was busier than before, but nothing like Lambert's. A couple of miners looked up from their whiskey glasses. They stared at the women and rubbed their eyes as if thinking they'd seen a mirage, then caught my cold stare and dropped their gaze back down to the bar.

At a table by the far wall, I saw Thomas Mackay dealing cards to a fat man in a tight vest and a young cowboy too drunk to know what he was doing. Mackay glanced up with a bored smile.

"Let me help you," Jack said, stepping over and reaching out for Margaret Alahambre. Carmilla shoved his hand away and the three women crossed the crooked floor to the far end of the bar. Jack looked at me.

I shrugged. "She don't take to male kindness," I said quietly.

"Gonna need rooms?" Fortenay asked, smiling, running a hand across his greasy hair and slapping at a fly. He hurried to a dusty guest register on the far end of the bar. Gustav stepped in from the kitchen and took Fortenay's place pouring beer.

I felt the floor tremble and rise slightly under my feet. I glanced down quickly. "That's nothing," Jack chuckled. "They've got a crew out in the alley trying to straighten this place up." I shot him a curious glance; he grinned. "I'm serious. They're raising it on railroad jacks . . . gonna build a foundation under it. This is *some* place."

I looked at the floor again and shook my head. Nails and timbers groaned. "Where's Briggs and the prisoner?"

"Sonny's in jail and Briggs is watching him. The jail ain't finished yet. There's no bars on it. We've been taking turns guarding him." Jack waved a hand taking in all of Gris. "This place is something you dream about after a bad meal. The town council is upset over Briggs bringing in Sonny." He shook his head. "I wish they had a bank here. I'd rob it and leave."

"I figured everybody would be pleased about Briggs bringing in Sonny Quarrels." I raised my hat and scratched my head. Dust swirled from my brim.

"They're not. Quarrels has spent a lot of money here. The mayor and councilmen all like him. The rest are too busy building this place to care one way or the other. Three builders offered me a job before I got off my horse. I thought they were gonna fight—"

"They did me the same way. Almost drug me off my horse. But the women are safe here, and Briggs has his prisoner. I'm heading out first thing tomorrow and getting Buck . . . some way, somehow."

"You might oughta hold up on that," Jack said. He glanced around as if someone might be listening, then lowered his voice. "I managed to talk to Sonny a little. He'd go along with anything to get away from Briggs." Jack let out a breath. "Poor sumbitch. Briggs keeps cracking his head. I'm sick of watching it."

"So, what're you saying, Jack? I ain't about to break Sonny Quarrels loose. Briggs might be a little heavy-handed, but he's done right by us—"

"I know," Jack said. "But if I can make Sonny think we're willing to take a bribe, maybe he'll tell me where to find the gang and the *money.*"

"You think?"

Jack shrugged. "It's worth a try. If you want Buck . . . where else can you start?" He leaned closer and spoke just above a whisper. "I've already made plans for my part of that forty thousand." He rubbed his hands together.

Fortenay had given the women keys to adjoining rooms, and Carmilla and Greta helped Margaret Alahambre up the crooked steps. Gustav slid a mug of beer in front of me and left. Margaret glanced over her shoulder at me as Carmilla guided her up the stairs. "We don't need their help," I heard Carmilla say. Good, I thought to myself. I had too much else on my mind.

I sipped the tepid beer. I understood what Jack was saying. All we had to do was *find* Ned Quarrels, we didn't have to *deal* with him. I'd stolen enough horses that I figured slipping into Quarrels's camp and stealing Buck was no big problem. Still, I knew how Sonny Quarrels felt being a prisoner and I felt bad making him think we'd help him, then not doing it. On the other hand, if we did work a deal to bust him loose, I'd be betraying old Briggs, and even though he was a lawman who would nail my hide to a board if he knew who I really was, he'd trusted us, been square with us—I couldn't see stabbing him in the back.

"So . . . what's the verdict?" Jack finished his beer and stared at me. I bit my lip and rubbed my hand up under my hat.

"I don't know, Jack," I said. "Let me figure it out."

"Sure," Jack said. "But figure this. I'll go along with

whatever you want to do. But I'm leaving here with forty thousand dollars hanging behind me, no ifs, ands, or buts—"

"Sure, Jack . . . so long as I get Buck back."

Jack left to relieve Briggs at the barless jail while I finished my beer and waved in another. "Have you thought of any gourmet dishes yet?" Gustav said when he slid the fresh beer before me. It took a second for me realize what he meant. "Remember?" He cocked an eye. "I asked you to name any fancy dish . . . any kind at all—"

"Aw . . . yeah," I nodded. "I remember, but no, I haven't really thought of any. I've been kind of busy since then—"

"Hasenpfeffer!" Gustav broadened his little chest and beamed.

"What?" I just stared at him. I had too much on my mind to deal with his culinary creations.

"Yes, hasenpfeffer," he said eagerly. "It's German, it's bold, robust, exciting!"

I shook my head and sipped. "I really ain't in the mood for this—"

"You take a fresh rabbit—although I'm certain you could substitute lamb in a pinch." He tapped a finger to his lips considering it.

I raised a hand. He was getting too carried away. "No offense. I'm sure you can outcook anybody who's ever slung a skillet, but I'm kinda busy right now—"

"Oh—" He thumped his palm on his forehead. "Listen to me rattle on, as if all you had to think of was recipes."

"Not that I don't appreciate it," I said, trying to be polite. "I'm just tired and got a lot on my mind—"

"Of course you are," he smiled. "Sometimes a good soak in a hot tub of water helps."

"Huh?" I stared at him, leaned my head, and sniffed my shirt.

He waved a hand. "Never mind. Why don't I just write down a few recipes for you?"

"Well . . . I reckon that'd be okay."

"Good, good. In fact I'll write down several. You never know. Sometimes when you're out there . . . tired of the same thing night after night, you may want to just whip up something different, something to perk you up—take the edge off?"

"Sure." I just stared at him, nodding, until he hurried away to find a pencil and paper. *"Jesus,"* I whispered under my breath. I heard someone cough and laugh beside me and I turned to face Thomas Mackay and a portly man in a striped vest and a strip of a goatee.

"Quite proud of his culinary expertise, isn't he?" Mackay nodded toward Gustav rummaging under the far end of the bar. "I can't tell you how happy I am to see you, sir." He extended a hand and I shook it; it was as cold and clammy as it had been in Cimarron.

"I'm afraid young Gustav has worn me out with his recipes ever since I arrived." I smiled at Mackay and looked the portly feller up and down until Mackay gestured toward him. "Mister Beatty, I'd like you to meet Mister Tripplet. I mentioned your altercation with Diamond Joe, and Mister Tripplet has been dying to make your acquaintance."

"Oh?" I looked at him closer. He stuck out a broad hand and I shook it. "Why's that?"

"You see," said Mackay, "Mister Tripplet here is a writer who—"

"—Searching for material for my upcoming book," Tripplet said, finishing Mackay's sentence. "Mister Mackay has informed me of your recent *extraordinary* events . . . and I must say you have quite a story there."

I shook my head. "Not interested, Mister Tripplet."

"Call me Frank." He grinned. I saw the shine of excitement in his dark eyes. "I think you'd really be impressed at what a good story in my book would do for you. You could wind up famous!"

"No offense, Mister Tripplet, but I've got enough to do

just straightening things out. No time to talk about it." I smiled, sipped the beer, and watched his eyes fade in disappointment. I didn't want to see nothing about me in his book, and I couldn't come out and tell him why. I nodded toward Mackay. "What about something on the life of a gambler?" I hoped to direct Tripplet's attention away from me.

Mackay chuckled. "Oh, I've known Frank here for quite some time. I'm afraid he sees nothing newsworthy in *my* life."

"Don't get me wrong, Doc," Tripplet said to Mackay. "You're an interesting fellow, and I'm sure it's exciting, traveling, seeing the West, and making your living at the game of chance—"

"Doc?" I looked at Mackay.

"A nickname," he shrugged.

"—but the readers want to hear about the rough-and-tumble aspect. . . . You know, man shoots another man over a card game, then man takes other man's horse." Tripplet rolled a thick hand around in front of him. "You know . . . something with the potential for danger, *gunfights, heroics* . . . that sort of thing."

I stared at Mackay. He reflected for a second, then raised a finger for emphasis. "There was an *ugly* incident in Texas awhile back, when I had to defend myself against—"

"And you did a fine job. I was there, remember?" Tripplet interrupted him, then turned back to me. "At least tell me this, Beatty." He snatched out his pencil and pad. "When you first started out after your horse, did you stop to think that—?"

"Sorry," I said in a firm tone, raising a hand. "I told you, I've got no story for you." I turned facing Mackay. "Doc? Are you a doctor?"

Mackay smiled and ducked his head slightly.

Out the corner of my eye I saw Gustav step up behind the bar folding a piece of paper. He slid it under my fingers and patted my hand before he drew his away. "Here," he said proudly. "Just something to start with. I'll work you up some more and give them to you tomorrow."

"Uh . . . thanks," I said; and I picked up the folded recipe and shoved it down in my shirt pocket as he turned and walked back along the bar. Tripplet and Mackay looked at me; I felt my face redden. "Why does he keep doing this?" I looked at Mackay and let out a tired breath.

"Perhaps he just likes you. Perhaps he feels he must measure up to Henri Lambert's reputation as a chef. Who knows, sir?" Mackay shook his head, rolled a black cigar in his mouth, and let go a stream of smoke. "Enough about him. I see you and your friends have taken a lot more on yourselves since last we met."

"Yeah." I took a deep breath, preparing to tell Mackay about Alahambre, his wife Margaret, Carmilla and Greta and their women's lodge, Sonny Quarrels, and my horse . . . Buck. But then I glanced at Tripplet's cocked pencil and stopped.

Mackay raised a hand. "No need, Mister Beatty. Your friend mentioned your situation. Let me say, sir, I empathize with you in your predicament. If there's a way I can help, don't hesitate—"

"Thanks." I sipped my beer and looked Mackay up and down. "But all I'm interested in is getting my horse back. Briggs will do all right with the Quarrels Gang. I suppose Diamond Joe's wife will be okay now that she's away from him." I cocked my head. "What kind of doctor are you, Mackay?"

"Merely a dentist—" He waved it away. "But what became of our rude and vulgar friend, Alahambre?" Mackay worked on the cigar, coughed and cleared his throat.

"Oh . . . he showed up as we left," I said. "Yelling like an idiot, shooting his pistol. I figure he'll come drifting this way." I shook my head. "It's not over between us, I'm certain of that." I gazed down the bar and saw Gustav scribbling again fervently. He looked up for a second as if remembering something, then tapped the pencil to his tongue and continued.

"I hesitate to remind you, sir," Mackay said. "But I *did* advise you to empty his *shiny* pistol into him the other night."

"I know. I almost wish I had. None of the rest of this would have happened." I glanced at Tripplet. "This is all just talk between us," I said, nodding toward his pencil.

"Oh, of course." I saw his grip on the pencil relax.

Mackay glanced at the pencil and beamed. "I find it always pays to simply kill a man, if there's the slightest chance he might cause you discomfort." He smiled. "You may quote me, sir."

"Yeah, right." Tripplet shoved the pencil into his vest pocket. "If you gentlemen will excuse me." He turned and walked away.

I studied Mackay. "So . . . you pull teeth?"

Mackay sighed. "Tripplet and his big mouth—" He leaned closer. "I hope I can trust your discretion, Mister Beatty?" He looked into my eyes intently. "You see, Thomas Mackay is an alias I acquired after that ugly incident in Texas. My real name is Holliday . . . Doctor John H. Holliday. But until my Texas attorney finds a way to grease the legal machinery, please continue to refer to me as Mackay."

"I understand," I said. "Your secret's safe with me."

"I felt I could trust you—" Mackay smiled and rolled the cigar around in his mouth "—and believe me, I meant what I said earlier about helping you any way I can."

I smiled. I couldn't see what possible help a dentist could be if it came down to a shoot-out. "Thanks, anyway," I said.

The wall behind the bar groaned and popped. I felt the floor raise a full inch. We looked down at it. There was a tremendous shudder beneath our feet and the whole place dropped with a heavy thud. Bottles rattled behind the bar. A miner nearly fell. "Goddamn it!" someone shouted from outside the wall.

I thought things over as I walked to the unfinished jail. I'd gone looking for Buck with Briggs's help and ended up with nothing, except another run-in with Diamond Joe. Briggs meant well, I was sure, but now that he had a hand on the Quarrels Gang, I figured I was on my own as far as getting Buck back. Jack's idea was probably best. I had no way of knowing where to look for my horse. If Sonny thought we were willing to help him bust loose, he'd have to point us to his brother Ned. Once we found Ned Quarrels we could play it by ear till I got my horse. What else could I do?

The noise of building had quieted down now that darkness had set in, and as I stepped on the boardwalk outside the jail, several workmen walked past smelling of sweat and sawdust. They looked me up and down and walked on toward the saloon. "Lazy sumbitch," one of them growled.

I heard heated words from inside the jail when I swung open the new, unpainted door and stepped inside over a small pile of sawdust and curly wood shavings. Briggs looked up from a chair behind a nail keg where he sat peeling an apple with his boots propped up. Jack stood leaning against the wall with his thumbs hooked in his belt, watching a big feller stomp back and forth waving his arms in the air. The big feller spun toward me, red faced and wide eyed. I saw the shine of a sheriff's badge inside his open suit coat.

"He's with us, Kersey," Briggs said calmly, raising a slice of apple on the edge of his pocketknife. "This here's Beatty. He's my deputy—"

"No I ain't." I shook my head.

Briggs gestured the slice of apple toward me, then bit it in half. "Beatty," he continued over the bite of apple, "this here's Town Sheriff Dan Kersey."

I tipped my finger to my hat. "Howdy, sheriff. Let me make it clear that I *ain't* no deputy."

But Sheriff Kersey had already turned back to Briggs. "I don't give a blue damn if you've got a dozen men backing you. This ain't the time or the place to go throwing down with Ned Quarrels." He swung an arm. "Now you've got the mayor giving me hell."

I glanced at Jack; he shrugged as the sheriff rattled on. I looked back into the shadows along the far wall and saw Sonny Quarrels seated on a nail keg with his elbows on his knees and his head in his hands. A string cut across the floor six feet in front of him. I figured it indicated where the bars would be.

"Tell me where the time and place is, then," Briggs said in a calm voice. He gestured the pocketknife over his shoulder toward Sonny Quarrels. "They broke the law. I'm holding him here and I ain't stopping till I get the others. It's your duty to assist me and my deputies here in carrying out our official—"

"We don't even have *bars,* for christsakes!" The big feller waved his arm again. "We're building a town! Nobody here cares about Quarrels. If you turned him loose right now . . . somebody would probably offer him a job!" He glared at Sonny Quarrels. "Quarrels, how fast can you nail?" Sonny didn't answer.

"You're the law here, Kersey," Briggs said, pointing the pocketknife toward the sheriff, "and I'm calling you to task. You've got two deputies and a jail." He waved the knife about the place. "You're obligated to assist a fellow officer in the pursuit of his duty. I shouldn't even have to ask."

The sheriff stopped in one spot long enough to wipe a hand across his face, then paced again, only slower. "Look . . . me and the deputies are covered up as it is. We spend day and night keeping these building contractors from killing each other." He stopped again, slumped his shoulders, and let out a breath. "Can't you just take him on to Cimarron? They've got a real jail—Sheriff Bowman's there."

"No time," Briggs said. "Besides . . . Bowman tells me ole RC is on a raging drunk. I ain't having him cut this boy's head off like we both *know* he's prone to do."

Sheriff Kersey snapped to attention. "RC ain't coming here, is he?"

"He's on a spree," Briggs said. "He's apt to show up anywhere."

I eased over beside Jack. "Who the hell is RC?" I whispered. Jack shrugged and looked back at the sheriff. I eased past Jack, back to the string across the floor, stepped over it and over to Sonny Quarrels. He looked up at me and I saw the shackles about his ankles and wrists. He dropped his head and I turned and walked back beside Jack.

"I heard what he done at Lambert's," Kersey said to Briggs. "I ain't having him in Gris. He's a crazy man!"

Briggs smiled, wiped the knife blade across his leg, snapped it shut and put it away. "He'll spend a lot of money. Ain't that all you folks care about? Ain't that what the mayor said—?"

"And he's right. Drinking and gambling is our life's blood. A town that chases off business ain't gonna last—"

"Then I reckon RC will be *your* problem if he shows up here. If you can't help me with the Quarrels bunch, I danged sure ain't helping you with RC."

Again I glanced at Jack. "RC?"

Jack glanced at me, then stepped forward. "I don't mean to interrupt here," he said to Briggs. "But if you don't get over to Fortenay's and get some grub pretty quick, there won't be none left."

"Who's RC?" I asked the sheriff.

Briggs stood up, grunted, adjusted his Stetson, and walked away.

"A damn lunatic, that's who," Kersey growled. He turned and followed Briggs out the door. We heard him griping until his voice faded away.

Jack and I glanced at each other, then back at Sonny Quarrels. Jack stepped over quickly, tipped back the nail keg Briggs had sat on, and pulled out a bottle of whiskey. "Here," he said to Quarrels, pulling the cork as he stepped over the string. Quarrels reached up his shackled hands and took the bottle.

I stepped in close and looked down at him, saw the bump on his head, and whistled low. "That's some knot," I said. I glanced at Jack, then back to Quarrels. He threw back a long drink and let out a whiskey hiss.

"All right," Jack said to Sonny, "you heard the marshall. RC could be here anytime, and you *know* what that crazy sumbitch will do." Jack ran his finger across his throat and looked at Sonny with a grim expression.

"Yeah," Sonny said in a low voice. He took another cut of whiskey, made another hiss. "RC don't like me anyway . . . never did." He glanced up at Jack, then at me with a look of uncertainty.

"He's all right," Jack said to Sonny. "We're partners."

Sonny looked back and forth again. "Yeah? How do I know I can trust either one of you?"

"You don't," I said. "But we're the best chance you've got right now. As many men as your brother's got riding with him, it ain't likely that the two of us are gonna ambush them."

Sonny rubbed his shackled hands against his cheeks and glanced down at the blood-stained bandage on his chest. "Shouldn't I be in a hospital or something? I hurt like hell. That ole marshall don't care if I live or die here." He looked up at me.

"Sorry," I said, "there's nothing we can do but try to cut a deal with your brother to get you out of here. As long as you're here, Briggs is in charge. He could skin you to the bone, and we couldn't stop him." I looked at Jack and back at Sonny Quarrels. "Now where can we find your brother? Where does he keep his horses?"

Sonny shook his head. "Nothing doing. Not 'til I've had time to think things out."

"What about the place where we found you? Is that a spot you boys use a lot?"

He shook his head. "No! We never go around there. That's the first time I ever saw the place." I caught the way his eyes darted off for a split second and I knew he was lying. I glanced at Jack; he saw it, too.

I leaned forward to say something more to Sonny, but I heard the door swing open. I straightened up quickly, turned, and saw the short deputy walk in chewing a toothpick. "You better think about it quick," I said to Sonny in a lowered voice. "I ain't offering the deal for long."

"Boy," the deputy said, belching from behind the toothpick and rubbing his belly. "Fortenay can call it steak if he wants to, but it looks, smells, and tastes like pure *mule* to me."

"Just checking the prisoner's chains here," I said to the deputy, reaching down and rattling the shackles. I saw the trace of an evil grin sweep across Sonny's face as Jack and I turned away.

"Now that you're here, I reckon we'll go get something to eat ourselves."

"Y'all be careful," the deputy said. "Them damned contractors are starting to feel their whiskey." He threw a glance over his shoulder. "And RC could ride in here any time."

"Thanks," I said, reaching for the door. I swung it open for us and followed Jack outside.

"Who the hell is this RC everybody keeps talking about?" I looked at Jack as we stepped into the street and headed for Fortenay's.

Jack chuckled and shook his head. "Damned if I know."

• 12 •

I saw something was wrong as soon as Jack and I stepped through the door of Fortenay's On The Frontier. We both stopped in our tracks. All the workmen stood back from the bar and gathered in the middle of the crooked floor. Two men stood faced off at the bar ten feet apart, ready to throw iron, the same two who'd stopped me on my way out of town. One stood braced with his hand near a leather nail apron laying on the bar. I saw the black handle of a Walker Colt sticking from the nail pouch. The other kept his hand down near a long-barreled Smith & Wesson hanging in the hammer loop on his overalls.

"You calling me a liar?" The one with the nail apron leaned forward an inch, braced and ready. Out the corner of my eye I saw Sheriff Kersey step cautiously through the crowd.

"I had forty squares of roof sheeting come in . . . ten of it's gone. I saw two of your men nailing it on the barber shop." His hand crept closer to the Smith & Wesson. "Yes, you're a liar, a lying, sneaking, snaking son of a—"

"Hold it, Erlander!" Sheriff Kersey's voice boomed, just as the man's hand started for the nail apron, then froze. Kersey pointed a long finger at the other man and kept his free hand on his forty-four Peacemaker. "And Bryce, you move another half inch for that Smitty and I'll clip your thumb off." The man's hand stopped and drew away slowly. Kersey stepped between them looking from one to the other. A deputy stepped from the crowd holding a shotgun.

"Now step away from that nail pouch"—Kersey spoke to Erlander and nodded toward the door—"and get out of here. Pick your gun and nail apron up in the morning after you've cooled off." Erlander hesitated a second, tossed back his drink, wiped his hand across his mouth, and walked away slowly, watching Bryce over his shoulder until he stepped out the door. Bryce stared back at him like a dog with its hackles up. "Okay, Bryce," Kersey said, once Erlander was out of sight, "unloop that Smitty and lay it on the bar."

"He started it," Bryce said. He was a big sandy-haired man with freckles burned deep into his face. "He's stealing building material with both hands."

"Then get a lawyer," Kersey said. He tapped a finger on the bar. The deputy leveled the shotgun. "Now shed it!"

Bryce bit the inside of his lip, then eased the Smith & Wesson out, up, and on the bar. Kersey moved over and picked it up. "You boys oughta be ashamed. I remember when Erlander and Bryce was the biggest building contractors west of—"

"He's a crook, damn it!" Bryce's big fist slammed down on the bar.

"What contractor ain't?" said a voice from the workers. The crowd laughed; Bryce's face turned red. A grin twisted at the edge of his lips, then disappeared. "You-all know what I mean," he said, and he tossed back his drink. He looked at the crowd and motioned them back to the bar. "Hell with it, let's get drunk. I'll kill him when the time comes."

Kersey and his deputy stepped away as the men gathered back at the bar. A thin little man in a slick bowler stepped in beside Bryce and I saw him flip a business card from his vest. "The sheriff's right," I heard him say quietly as I turned to Kersey. "You may need an attorney."

"I see what you mean, sheriff," I said. "Looks like these contractors are keeping you busy."

"You ain't seen nothing," he said, and he turned to the deputy. I expected him to say thanks, but instead he pointed a long finger at the man. "The mayor's on my ass about you coming to work early today."

The deputy shrugged. "I had to. Two bricklayers beat the hell out of a roofer. Said he stole their level."

"I don't give a damn," Kersey hissed at him. "From now on, you don't start work till six in the evening. That's final."

The deputy turned and walked away grumbling.

"See, Beatty?" The sheriff let out a breath and wiped his face. "See why I can't worry about Briggs and the Quarrels Gang? I spend all day keeping these builders from stealing each other blind, and all night keeping them from killing each other over it."

I just nodded and shot Jack a glance. I didn't know what to say.

The sheriff leaned close. "See . . . you boys don't know Briggs like I do. He gets something stuck in his craw and he won't listen to nothing. His day is over but he won't turn loose. He could bring in a federal posse if he would, but no! He's still riding down desperados—like a damn one-man army." Kersey waved an arm. "The rest of us have our hands full trying to build something out of this godforsaken wasteland!" His eyes glistened; I thought he was losing control.

"I understand, sheriff," I said, stepping away. Jack stepped along beside me.

"Well . . . that's good." Kersey raised a finger and pointed to Briggs, sitting at a table in the far corner with his head bent over a plate of steaming food. "Maybe you can talk sense to him. God knows I can't."

I eased over to Briggs's table and sat down. Jack leaned against the wall beside us. Briggs looked up, nodded, and spoke over a mouthful of hash. "Guess he was real surprised I didn't help him?" He grinned, swallowed, and poured a long drink of foamy beer down his throat. "That wasn't nothing." He sat down the mug and swiped a hand toward the bar. "What's a dead contractor more or less? He piddles around with stuff like that"—he waved a hand toward the door—"while men like Ned Quarrels are running loose." He poured back another drink and wiped foam from his mustache. "This country's gone to hell."

"Marshall," I said in a firm, even voice, nodding toward Jack, "we're heading out in the morning to get my horse. I know you've done everything you can, and I thank you for your help, but it looks like the only way I'll get Buck back is if I find Ned Quarrels and *take* him back."

"Can't let ya do it," he said, staring me straight in the eyes with a set jaw. "You boys are fine, decent young men—"

"Look, marshall." I cut him off, glanced up at Jack and cleared my throat. "I ain't been exactly honest about myself." Briggs's eyes searched mine curiously. I saw Jack look down and shake his head. "I ain't quite the dandy you think I am." Briggs just stared.

"The fact is, I rode for the stars and bars . . . did my share of killing along the border—" I hesitated a second, wondering how he would take it "—even rode guerilla"—his eyes narrowed and he leaned forward—"with Quantrill's forces—" I stopped, held my breath, then let it out slowly. "The *baddest* of the bad." I tilted my hat forward and stared at him from beneath the brim.

He swallowed slowly and let his hands down flat on the table without taking his eyes from mine. I'd said a lot; I hoped it wasn't too much. I tried to read his hard-set expression, but saw nothing past the dark gleam in his fixed stare. He glanced up at Jack, then back to me, scanning the shoulder holster hanging under my arm. I tensed, not sure what was coming, but certain he'd gotten my point.

He leaned forward slowly on his hands, silent as stone until his face was halfway across the table, then, "Naaaw," he said, and broke into a hard laugh that turned into a cough and ended in a wheeze. He slapped his hand on the table and wiped his eyes. *"Baddest* of the *bad?"* He slung his head back and forth.

I felt my face redden. "Damn it, marshall!" I rose half up from my chair. "Ned Quarrels couldn't fetch coffee for some of the bunch I've rode with—"

Jack stepped forward, saw I was going out of control, and placed a hand on my shoulder. "That's enough," he said.

"Please, Mister Beatty!" Briggs raised one hand, threw the other against his chest, and rocked back and forth. "You're killing me! Stop it now!" He laughed, coughed, and wheezed until he gasped for air. I just slumped in my chair, tapping my fingers on the tabletop and staring at him.

The next morning, an hour before daylight, I met Jack at the half-finished livery barn and we saddled our horses and walked them quietly out through the back door. A bushy-headed construction worker sprang through the flap of a tent carrying a pick handle. He stared back and forth between us and a row of toolboxes on the ground. I shook my head as we walked past. I knew Briggs was guarding Sonny Quarrels at the half-finished jail. After last night's talk with him, I decided the only way to get my horse back was to forget everybody else and do whatever I had to do. Briggs had no right telling me not to ride after Quarrels. Still, I couldn't help but feel we were sneaking out of town like two schoolboys going against their father's wishes.

We walked our horses out behind the row of construction workers' tents, mounted up, and rode away into the cool morning air, neither of us in a very good mood since we'd left without breakfast, coffee, or anybody's blessings. I heard the first rooster of the morning crow behind us a half mile out of town.

The night before, I'd given up on Briggs and gone up to my room early. Jack had stayed downstairs and worked into a poker game with Mackay and Tripplet. As I'd left, I called Jack to the side and told him my intentions of heading out early in the morning, even though I was bone tired from the ride and completely done in from Marshall Briggs and his stubbornness.

On the way up to my room, I'd stopped and gotten Margaret Alahambre's room number from Gustav, and after I'd winded the lopsided stairs I knocked quietly on her door. "Who is it?" Carmilla's voice demanded through the door. I stepped back and told her it was me, just checking on everybody.

She opened the door, shot me a knowing glance, and slipped past me into the hall. I leaned back and watched her walk to the next room in a huff, then I shook my head and closed the door behind me. Margaret Alahambre offered a weak smile from her bed and patted the mattress beside her. "She means well," she said softly. "Come sit beside me."

I took off my hat, walked across the crooked floor, and eased down on the mattress. "I've got some things to take care of come morning," I said. "I just wanted to see how you're doing before I turn in."

"Where's your room?" She looked up at me and brushed back her hair. I thought I saw a look of fear shadow her brow.

"Just two doors down," I said. "Don't worry, I'll be close enough if you need me for anything." But she held my forearm.

"No, please. Please stay here tonight."

I tugged my arm gently but she held firm. "It wouldn't look proper," I said.

"I don't care what looks proper." She ran her fingertips carefully across her bruised cheek. "Does this look proper? Does this look like something that happens to decent—?"

"Shhh," I said. Her eyes turned misty; I saw she could

easily lose control. "None of this was your fault. Try not to think about it until you're feeling better." I eased down alongside her. "I'll lie here awhile." She smiled and relaxed her face against my chest.

When I'd slipped away an hour later, eased out the door, and walked quietly to my room, Carmilla's door swung open a few inches and I saw the look of contempt on her face.

"This ain't what it looks like," I said.

"Oh, you slink in like a jackal and slip away like a snake?"

I stepped over to explain, but she'd quickly closed the door in my face. . . .

"Jesus," I said to myself, thinking about it as Jack and I rode around a turn in the trail and headed up toward the high pass.

"What?" Jack asked.

"Just thinking of everything," I said. "Everything that's happened since the night Alahambre raised that shiny pistol at me."

Jack chuckled. "All's well that ends well. . . . if it leads us to that forty thousand."

I looked at him and cocked an eye. "Once I get Buck back, of course."

"Yeah . . . of course."

We rode silently for a few seconds, then I said, "Jack, I don't know what to make of Margaret Alahambre. She's acted strange toward me ever since I met her . . . ever since I rode off with her." I told him about her wanting me to stay with her last night, and about sleeping with her on the way to the women's lodge.

"You mean . . . you just slept?" He almost drew his horse to a stop.

"That's right." I stared at him. "Jack, the woman's beat all to hell." I nudged the mare forward; we both nodded. "But I'm afraid she's got attached to me . . . like she thinks she ain't safe unless I'm around. I don't know how she's gonna act when she gets well."

He gazed away and then back. "Well . . . maybe you better think about it some. Behind all that black and blue, she is a beautiful woman. I reckon there's *worse* things than having a beautiful woman beholden to you."

"That ain't the point, Jack. I couldn't do nothing like that with her. Not after the way everything's happened."

"You mean you couldn't—" Jack drew a circle in the air and poked his finger in it "—just because she might be grateful to you for saving her life?"

I scratched my forehead beneath my hat. "I don't know, maybe. . . . I mean . . . it wouldn't seem right . . . somehow."

"Aw. Then you and Carmilla would make a good couple. She's fiery, beautiful, independent . . . and seems to genuinely hate the ground you walk on."

"I wouldn't say she *hates* me"—I grinned—"just that it's a big world, and her and I don't have to be friends." I gazed off toward the sliver of sunlight on the morning horizon. "But none of this has anything to do with me finding Buck." I gigged the mare forward into an easy trot and looked around for any sign of fresh tracks.

"Then let me ask you this," Jack said, trotting his silver-gray along beside me. "Just suppose we find Buck before we find the money. Does that mean you're heading out of here?"

"No, Jack. We'll get the money. Just to shut you up about it."

"What then? Are you gonna leave that woman to face Diamond Joe alone?"

"Briggs will take care of her."

"Yeah. Once he straightens out Sonny, Ned, and their gang, I reckon he'll have time."

I jolted the mare to a halt and glared at him; he jerked the silver-gray a full circle and stopped beside me. "What is this, Jack? I thought your main interest here is the money. I don't owe Briggs or the woman or anybody else. My main concern is Buck."

"I just know how you are," he said, reaching down and patting the silver-gray's neck. "I see how this whole situation could turn into one hell of a mess. We're partners. If it comes to it, I'm the one'll stand with ya till our faces hit the dirt." He grinned. "So don't go keeping nothing from me."

I let go a breath and pushed up my hat. "I never have . . . have I?" No sooner than I said it, I pictured Helova Knight's creamy white thigh, and I glanced away from Jack and down at my saddlehorn.

"No, you haven't," he said. He raised his reins and heeled the silver-gray forward. "So don't start." He grinned; again I caught a glimpse of the white thigh and the painted nails. "I just like to know what you're thinking sometimes, is all. Might start keeping a journal. Might get it published someday. Tripplet says there's a good deal of money to be made—"

"I get it," I said. "You've been talking to Tripplet? About us?"

"You know better than that. I got enough to do, keeping you from blurting something out to Briggs. But I've been thinking. What's to keep us from making something up and telling Tripplet? You know, just whatever comes to our minds. Hell . . . we'd get paid, and who'd ever know the difference?"

"I don't think it works like that, Jack. It could be a long time before we saw any money, and he'd have to check out everything and all. He'd never print something unless he knew it was true." I shook my head. "Naw, that's a bad idea. He'll get somebody like Briggs, I reckon, somebody that's done a lot of stuff with the *potential* for danger . . . *heroics, gunfights.*" I rolled my hand the way Tripplet had. *"That sort of thing."* I shot Jack a glance and smiled.

"We've done all that, and then some," Jack said.

"Yeah, but it ain't stuff we want to go telling."

Jack shrugged. "So? That's why I say, just make it up as we go along."

"It'd never work, Jack. Besides, Briggs is a lawman. Tripplet could take him and turn him into a living legend. And it would all be true."

"Bull." Jack rolled his head and grinned. "All Tripplet wants is a story. He couldn't give a damn if it's true or not. And you watch, he'll get one from somebody before it's over. That's how all them journalists are. They get paid just to *shoot* . . . it don't matter if they shoot *straight* or not."

I shook my head. "Boy, Jack. It must be terrible to not have any faith in anybody."

It was late morning when we stopped and looked down into the gully where Briggs had ambushed Sonny and the other outlaw. All that remained was a black smudge of their old campfire. We scanned the area closely before nudging our horses down the trail into the narrow passage between two high walls of rocks, both of us knowing that to be caught down there would be like going to hell and locking the door behind us.

Jack stayed back a full thirty yards with his rifle cocked and propped up from his saddle while I rode past the old campsite, followed a path of faded hoofprints past the picked-over remains of the dead outlaw, and on to the far end of the gully. Apparently the rest of Quarrels's bunch had been here but hadn't even bothered to bury their dead.

The hoofprints stopped, disappeared upwards into a steep rise of loose rocks that led into a sheer cliff no man or animal could've climbed; I slipped from my saddle and stood staring up, knowing there'd be no sense in going any farther. I looked down, truly puzzled. There were no prints leading back.

Just as I'd stepped back into the saddle, I felt the slightest whisper of a cool breeze lick at my shirt collar, and I gazed all around, then back toward Jack. Nothing stirred in the gully.

I raised my hat to better feel the breeze against my warm forehead and I backed the mare slowly, trying to pinpoint it. Searching the far side of the gully in the direction of the breeze, less than twenty yards away, I saw a dark shadow stretching upwards along the wall, and as I squinted toward it, I saw it was a narrow crevice almost completely hidden by a stack of boulders. That's it, I thought, the Quarrels Gang wasn't stupid enough to box themselves like this. There was a hidden passage—a hole in the wall.

I waved Jack toward me as I hooked the mare and rode over to the pile of boulders. Once there, I saw the hoofprints reappear from out of the loose rocks, and I smiled. "What's up?" Jack glanced all around. His silver-gray stepped around in a tight circle beside me.

I pointed at the loose rocks along the high wall, then down to the ground. "They ride up just enough to cover their tracks, circle around and come down here." I pointed at the prints on the ground beneath us and let my finger follow them into the narrow crevice.

"Aw . . . yeah," Jack said under his breath, grinning, stepping his horse forward around the boulders and into the shadow. "We could use something like this back in Missouri."

"Easy, now," I said, cautioning him, following him deeper into the crevice and looking back over my shoulder as sunlight faded behind us.

We rode quietly, in pitch darkness, letting our horses pick their way along a rough path of stones winding downward. They followed the cool breeze until it began to feel warmer, the path smoother, and the pitch darkness more gray, then faint silver before us. "There's the end," I said just above a whisper; and ahead we saw a wide shaft of sunlight wavering down and spilling across a tall, jagged pinyon pine.

We stepped our horses cautiously to the edge of a cliff

overlooking a wide valley of aspen, cottonwood, and juniper. On our left hoofprints led down a trail winding deeper into the valley. We followed them until we saw the wood-shingled roof of a cabin straight down beneath us built into the side of the cliff. As soon as we saw it, we both froze, backed our horses quietly and slipped down from our saddles.

On our bellies, we peeped down over the edge of the trail, saw the cabin roof fifty feet below, four horses tied to a post out front, and a corral full of horses twenty yards away. I studied the corral carefully until I was convinced that Buck was not among the horses, then turned to Jack. "That has to be Quarrels's bunch," I whispered. Jack nodded, and we lay watching the cabin. If I had any doubts, they vanished the second I saw Diamond Joe step from the cabin and swing up on one of the horses hitched out front. He turned the horse and heeled away across the valley. Beside me Jack drew out his La Faucheux and checked the action.

"How you want to do this? Want to go in shooting?"

I looked at him. "That's crazy, Jack." I nodded down toward the corral. "Buck ain't in there . . . so they must have other horses stashed somewhere. Diamond Joe's gonna *have* to come up this way. Get him, and I'll find Buck."

Jack shook his head. "I don't like it. It'd be a lot simpler to just ride in shooting—"

"Trust me, Jack, this has be handled right if I ever want to get Buck."

We tied our horses against the side of the rock wall. I crept forward a few yards and hid behind a loose boulder at the edge of the trail. For nearly a half hour, I sat watching the downward winding trail before I heard the first sounds of Diamond Joe's horse walking up toward me. I held my breath with my rifle ready as he walked on past me and around the bend where Jack waited. As soon as he disappeared around the trail, I eased out from behind the rock and trotted after him. With Jack in front and me behind there was no place for him to go. I'd told Jack not to shoot him unless he had to. Once I had him prisoner he'd either take me to Buck or I'd leave his body laying in the sun. Either way.

Diamond Joe jerked up on his horse and spotted Jack just as I stopped twenty feet behind him. Jack stood midtrail, smiling, with his La Faucheux cocked and pointed. He wagged a finger back and forth when Joe's hand started for his gun. Diamond Joe froze for a second, then started to spin his horse. "Don't try it," I said behind him, and he turned in his saddle and looked down at my raised rifle.

His face looked terrible. The bandage was gone from between his purple eyes and an ugly scab covered the bridge of his nose. One side of his mustache was gone and the black streak of powder ran up the side of his face. His nose looked like a ripe squash. "Sufa-bintch!" At the sight of me his hand trembled above his holster, but he fought the urge. "I'll kill nuu."

"You're taking me to my horse."

"I'd die firnst," he sneered. "One shont and nere'll be a donzen men rinding nis trail."

"But you won't be . . . ever again," I said. "Now slip it out slow and pitch it down easy."

I watched him bite his lip and think about it for a second, then he let out a breath. "All right." He reached his hand to his pistol slowly, but just as he went to pull it up, he snatched on the reins and spurred his horse. The horse spun sideways as Joe's pistol came up. A shot exploded from Jack's La Faucheux and Joe's pistol spun high in the air. I jumped forward to grab the reins, but just as I reached, his horse's rear hoof slipped from the edge of the trail and the animal's hindquarter sank down. Joe slipped backwards from the saddle as the horse struggled and gained its footing. I heard a long scream as I snatched the reins and jerked the horse away.

A loud crash echoed up from the valley, and Jack and I

looked down at the cloud of dust belching from the large hole in the cabin roof. *"Jesus,"* I said, staring down at the hole in the roof and watching Diamond Joe's hat sail away on a breeze.

"Let's ride!" Jack shoved me toward the horses. I hesitated, still staring down. "Damn it, let's go!" He shoved me again and this time I ran with him to the horses. "They'll be all over us as soon as they pick Diamond Joe outta their hair. I've never seen so many things go wrong in my life." Jack cussed and jumped into his saddle. Joe's horse had already bolted off up the trail. We hooked our horses and took off behind it, riding much too fast on such a narrow dangerous trail.

We followed Joe's fleeing horse and watched it disappear into the dark crevice. We'd have to slow down enough to let our horses pick their way through. "Push 'em some," I called out to Jack as we reached the crevice, "but not too hard!"

"I know how to ride a horse!" Jack yelled and gigged his silver-gray into the darkness. I followed, urging the big mare, but not enough to make her stumble. "Damn it," Jack yelled as the mare kept bumping his gelding.

"Keep moving, Jack!" I gigged the mare and felt her bump the gelding. The gelding snorted and kicked. I felt a rear hoof graze past my leg. "Don't let him kick!"

"Then quit pushing, damn it!" Jack yelled.

Ahead, I saw the sliver of light at the end of the crevice. I saw two riders turn into the crevice just as Joe's horse bolted between them. One rider flew from his saddle as his horse reared. "What the hell—?" The other spun and watched Joe's horse bolt past him with its loose reins whipping behind and saddlebags flapping up and down.

"Go, Jack!" I yelled, but Jack had seen the riders coming in and already bolted forward. I saw a blaze streak from the barrel of his pistol. The other rider's horse reared and spun in the air. By the time it settled, Jack thundered past him, bumping the horse against the side of the wall. The rider jerked up a pistol, but before he could aim, I slammed him back against the wall as my mare made the turn into the sunlight. I caught a glimpse of Jack slamming through four riders who'd just jumped away from Joe's horse as it shot around from the crevice. "Damn it!" somebody screamed. "There goes the money!"

I let out a rebel yell and tore through the horsemen, bumping them as they tried to right themselves. I saw a rifle sail in the air and heard a pistol explode. A horse fell before me as the rider spun it toward Jack. My mare sailed up and over it. I had my pistol out as the mare landed in a full run, and I cocked sideways low in the saddle, emptying all six shots into the pile of horses and men spinning and wallowing in a cloud of dust.

Jack pounded to the far end of the gully and spun his gelding. His La Faucheux exploded past me toward the riders. "Grab that horse!" I yelled as I drew closer. Joe's horse pounded on through the pass at the end of the gully.

"Damn that horse!" Jack yelled back, still firing, covering me. A shot ricocheted off a rock beside me.

"There's money on it!" I screamed. Jack's eyes widened. Another shot whistled past me; Jack returned fire and spun his gelding.

We pounded on through the pass; behind us shots pinged off rocks. By the time we'd cut upward toward the edge of the gully onto the flatland, I saw Jack reach down and catch Joe's horse by its loose reins. "Got it," he yelled over his shoulder.

I pounded forward toward him, and caught up just as he turned along the upper edge of the gully. Below us the sound of gunfire increased. I heard someone scream, and we spun to the edge just long enough to see a half dozen riders who'd followed us up from the cabin. They'd taken cover at the entrance to the crevice and were pounding out rounds at their own men. "Don't shoot," someone yelled. "It's us, goddamn it."

"Let's go!" I shot Jack a glance and we gigged our horses into a run across the flat stretch of mesquite and cactus. It would take a minute for them to get organized. We needed every second. We'd be sitting ducks across the flatland until we hit the stretch of ridges seven miles away.

I rode up on the other side of Joe's horse and unhitched the saddlebags as we ran. I slung them across my lap. "Turn him loose!" I yelled, above the thunder of our horses' hoofs.

Jack let go of the reins and Joe's horse veered away, out across the flatland in a swirl of sand. I opened a flap of the saddlebag, saw it crammed full of dollar bills, and let out a yell. A few bills spun up in the air and blew away. I slapped the flap shut.

"It's the mother lode, Jack!"

He stalled his silver-gray enough to fall back beside me. "The stage money?"

I raised the saddlebags and shook them. "The mother lode!"

13

When we reached the first line of low ridges, we stopped our horses and looked back at the cloud of dust five miles behind us. "One thing's for sure," I said, taking down my canteen and emptying it into my hat, "they can't ambush us. All we've got to do is keep our lead and not spend our horses out." I stuck my face down in the hat, into the water, took a mouthful and spit it back, then knelt before the mare and watered her. Jack did the same.

He ran a hand over his wet face and gazed back at the line of dust. "I feel a lot better, now that we got some money. I was starting to wonder what the hell I was doing here." He looked over at me, grinned, and nodded toward the bulging saddlebags. "Don't even mind dying, now that's there's something worth dying for." Dust turned to muddy streaks on his face and ran down his chin. He rubbed his face and ran his wet hand beneath his shirt collar.

"Now all I gotta do is get Buck," I said. The mare finished the water and rooted her muzzle in the hat for more.

"Yeah. But if you don't, at least we'll have something to show for it."

"I'm not even thinking about *'if I don't.'* I'm not stopping till I get him."

"For now, we better figure how we'll keep Briggs from knowing we got the money. If you think Quarrels wants his brother back, imagine how bad he'll miss his loot. Figure on that."

"I'm not only figuring on it, Jack, I'm *counting* on it." I stood and gazed back at the rising dust.

"Don't even think about giving him back the money," Jack said. "It ain't in my nature to return hard currency."

"I know, but I can make him think I'll give it back . . . for my horse. Now we're in a position to deal."

"He won't believe that." Jack shook his head and grinned. "Nobody would. Not for forty thousand. Not for a horse. The market ain't that good."

I slipped the hat back on my head and stepped into the saddle. "Well . . . that's what I'm willing to pay, as far as he's concerned. I want Buck as bad as he wants his money and his brother." I turned the mare as Jack stepped into his saddle and followed me. "That's how it's gonna go. Quarrels's bunch will deal with me"—I looked out across the endless land, saw a lone dust devil whip a stand of mesquite—"or else I'll kill 'em all."

With a safe ride straight to Gris we kept our horses at an even gait and checked over our shoulder every few seconds, keeping an eye on the rising dust. By the time we'd gotten close enough to town to see the unfinished roofs glisten in the evening sun, the dust behind us had faded into a thin streak on the horizon. Quarrels had slowed down. There wasn't a doubt in my mind he would follow all the way to Gris, then camp close by till he figured what to do. There also wasn't a doubt in my mind that with as many men as he had riding for him, he would strike Gris like a bolt of lightning. Briggs had predicted he'd do it to get his brother back—now there were forty thousand more reasons. I looked at Jack and almost told him to take the saddlebags and head for Missouri. He had the money. I had no right to ask him to stay.

As soon as we rode into Gris, we slowed our horses to a

walk. I slung the saddlebags over to Jack, and he rode on to the livery stable while I reined over to the unfinished jail. I stepped down and ran things through my mind as I walked up to the door. I had to warn Briggs, but I had to keep quiet about the money. Jack would stash it somewhere in the barn, and from then on it was our secret. If we captured Quarrels and his gang, it was their word against ours, and I knew whose word Briggs would have to take. I'd brought him the Quarrels Gang, and I'd fight them right beside him if need be. But when it came to the money . . . there were no refunds.

"Marshall Briggs," I said, as soon as I closed the door behind me. But instead of Briggs, I saw Thomas Mackay turn around from a nail keg sitting between him and Sonny Quarrels. I saw cards spread on the nail keg.

"Why, Mister Beatty," Mackay said. "I must tell you, you've caused us all a great deal of concern. We were beginning to think you'd gotten yourself shot."

"I came near," I said. I glanced around. "Where's Briggs? Where's Kersey?"

"Briggs went to eat supper, and Kersey and his deputies went to run a man out of town on a charge of indecent exposure . . . if you can imagine. There was no one available to watch young Quarrels, so I volunteered."

"Well, I hope you stay a little longer, 'cause I've got to let Briggs know that Ned Quarrels will be hitting this place most anytime."

"I think he's already aware of that, sir. Isn't that what he's been telling everybody?"

"Yeah . . . but things are even worse now," I said. "We come upon Quarrels's gang today. He chased us all the way here. I know he'll attack now that we've found his hideout."

"I see. Then perhaps you'd like to reconsider my offer of assistance? I'm quite capable of—" He broke into a deep cough before he finished talking.

"Thanks anyway." I shook my head and turned toward the door.

"Mister Beatty—" He wheezed and cleared his throat. "If you don't mind me asking . . . why is he more apt to attack today than yesterday? Have you gone and chastised the man somehow?"

"I don't have time for this," I said, glancing back. "I've got to tell Briggs."

Mackay shook his head and gazed back at the cards as I stepped through the door. "Busy, busy, busy," I heard him say to Sonny Quarrels. "Now where were we?"

I'd bounded out of the office and led the mare up the street at a brisk pace when I saw a crowd gathered outside the unfinished barber shop. I walked close enough to peep through and get a glimpse of a pistol butt rising and falling with a loud thump. Pushing my way through the crowd I saw one of the strangest sights I'd seen in my life.

There in the dirt street stood a man buck-naked, pistol-whipping the hell out of Sheriff Kersey, and at the same time screaming and crying like a school kid. Every time he swung the pistol, he'd come up off the ground. His bare feet would make a slapping sound on the dirt each time the long barrel met skin and bone. It was a horrible sight, and I stood stunned, wondering why nobody stopped it. Kersey's deputies stood six feet from me and neither of them offered to do a thing.

I glanced at the deputies and heard the shorter of the two say to the other, "Oughtn't we stop it, Charlie?"

The taller deputy shook his head slowly and spoke without taking his eyes off the beating. "I can't," he said in a low voice. "What time is it?"

"What time?" The short deputy shot the taller one a puzzled look. "Hell, I don't know. Shouldn't we do something here?"

"I don't go to work till six. That's *his* orders." He nodded toward Kersey's limp figure that was quickly looking more and more like a skinned buffalo. The whole crowd looked as if they were on the verge of doing something, yet not one of them made a move. I winced, and clenched my teeth each time the steel barrel fell.

"Damn it," I said. I shoved my reins into the short deputy's hand, "Hold these," and I'd just taken a step forward when the naked man turned loose of the sheriff and staggered back a step. I saw a red boil the size of a robin's egg on one side of his butt with a festered yellow head on it that looked ready to explode. The sheriff's blood ran down his chalk-white legs; his pistol was red, as were his forearms. His breath heaved in his chest.

He spun toward me just as I stopped; and in that second I noticed a terrible bullet scar on his left foot and saw him struggle to keep his balance. Two townsmen crept in, snatched up the battered sheriff, and took off with him while the naked man eyed me closely. I raised my left hand chest high in a cautious show of peace.

"The hell're you?" he said between gasps of breath.

"Just passing by," I said quietly. Now that it was over, all I wanted was out. I had to get to Briggs and tell him about Quarrels.

"Then pass by, damn you!" He waved me past with the bloody pistol; I led my horse slowly, my eyes fixed on his, and my right hand ready to drop the reins and snatch the forty-four from my shoulder rig. His eyes darted up and down me, fixed on the handle of the glades knife sticking above my boot, and widened in excitement. "You a knife fighter? Hunh? Are you, boy?"

I walked on without answering. "Know who I am? Hunh?" He seemed ready to go into another rage. If he did, I'd empty my forty-four, my thirty-six, my sleeve derringer, and anything I could grab from the crowd straight in his chest and keep walking. He'd have to kill me flat out before I'd let him do me like he'd done the sheriff. There was something sick, unwholesome, about a man standing naked with another man's blood running down his pale, spindly legs. Aw, yeah, if he made a move, I'd kill him . . . sure enough.

"I'm *RC* . . . RC Allison, boy! Crazy Clay Allison! Drunker than a crossed-eyed rooster!" he yelled, turning with a limp as I drifted away. "Mean anything to you?"

I felt the skin tighten on the back of my neck. Sure, I'd heard of Clay Allison, and now that I knew Clay and RC were the same person, I knew why everybody paled when they heard he was coming. I'd heard enough about him to make me want to jump on the mare and not slow down till I was well out of pistol range. Yes, I'd heard plenty, but I wouldn't let it show; instead I kept my eyes on him and held my slow pace as the crowd parted and stepped away a safe distance.

"Means nothing to me," I said, then I stopped, turned toward him, and dropped my reins. "Unless you raise that pistol."

It was done. I wasn't being brave; I was taking an edge. I'd never seen it pay to back down from a madman, and never seen it help to let one know that you're afraid. I had too much going on to have to fool with a lunatic. If I had to throw down on him, I wanted to do it now while his gun hand was slick with blood and his lungs pounded in his chest.

"Gun?" He looked astonished at his bloody pistol, then pitched it away. "Naw," he shook his head. "You're a knife fighter, ain't ya? I want you!" He pointed a bloody finger and limped toward me. I calmly drew, cocked, and aimed my forty-four. His being unarmed didn't bother me a bit, not after hearing who he was, not after seeing what he did to the sheriff. I'd splatter him like a gob of snot. He must've seen it, and at least had enough sense to stop in his bloody tracks.

"We'll dig a grave and get in it," he said. His eyes lit with a peculiar dark glow. I kept my finger snug on the trigger.

"I'm talking about a good old-fashioned carving match. Winner crawls out, loser goes to meet his ancestors." He let go a crazy laugh that started off toward me, then swung to the crowd. No one joined him.

"Damn! Ain't there nobody here enjoys a good knife fight?" He turned away from me, threw his hands in the air, and stalked toward the crowd, rocking back and forth on his crippled foot. "Bunch of goddamn lambs!"

I uncocked my pistol, eased it into my holster, picked up my reins, and stepped into the saddle while he chastised the crowd. I had bigger problems than Clay Allison. I turned the mare and tapped her into a trot, looking back over my shoulder until I pulled up outside of Fortenay's.

"Jesus," I said, walking inside and over to Briggs at a table by the far wall. "Do you know what's going on out there?" I thumbed over my shoulder. "Clay Allison just beat the breathing hell out of Kersey!" Fortenay's was empty except for Gustav behind the bar. As soon as he saw me, he reached down under the bar and pulled out a stack of paper.

"Yeah, I know," Briggs said over a mouthful of steak and gravy. "Everybody left to see it."

I spread my arms as Gustav came around from behind the bar. "Ain't you gonna do nothing?" I stared at Briggs.

He took a sip of coffee. "Is he still beating him?" Briggs patted a napkin to his lips as he spoke.

"No . . . he stopped." I saw Gustav standing beside me, proudly holding out the stack of paper.

"Then there ain't *much* I can do, is there?" Briggs smiled and turned back down to his plate. He belched and stabbed a forkload of steak. I couldn't believe it; I stared at him and walked to his table.

"I wrote down several dishes that I know you would enjoy, Mister Beatty," Gustav said, stepping along with me.

"Not now," I said, without looking at him.

"Oh . . . but these are simple to prepare, very palatable—"

I stopped and turned toward him. I saw my finger tremble as I held it up. "Not now!" I stopped and looked down at Briggs.

"You don't have to be rude," I heard Gustav say behind me.

"Sorry," I said glancing back at him, then back to Briggs.

"He is a rude person," I heard Carmilla say from the bottom of the crooked stairs. I shot her a glance and shook my head. "Here," she said to Gustav, "let me see your recipes."

"I know what you're thinking," Briggs said. He cocked an eye up at me. "You're thinking I shoulda done something to help ole Kersey." He raised a finger. "Well, the fact is, I warned him. You was right there when I told him if he wouldn't help me with Quarrels's bunch, I wouldn't help him if RC came riding in drunk. So there." Briggs lowered his finger and waved a hand toward the street. "All that's *town* business anyway. I'm federal." He grinned. "Now, where've you been . . . ? I've been worried about ya."

I took a deep breath and told him about us finding Quarrels's hideout, about Diamond Joe—about him falling through the roof, about us barely getting away, and about Quarrels's gang following us back to town. I didn't tell him about the money, didn't tell him that first chance I got I was going to find a way to make Quarrels think I'd hand over the money and his brother, just to get back my horse . . . Buck.

"Well . . . you're very lucky to be alive, is what," he said. He nodded in agreement with himself and sucked air through his teeth. "If something had happened to you boys out there, I don't how I could face—"

"Look, marshall," I cut him off. "They'll be coming. If I had any doubts before, I sure don't have any now."

Briggs eyed me curiously. "Why the sudden change?"

I cleared my throat and shrugged. "I don't know," I said. "But Quarrels means business. I figured Kersey would've had to help us once they rode in. But now . . . he's beat half to death by your ole buddy RC. So if you know of anybody who'll help us, you better get to calling on them . . . including that idiot out there screaming in the street."

"Aw," Briggs swiped a hand, "you're just nervous. Don't worry about RC, he'll be in there in a flash once trouble starts. Him and all his boys." Briggs slid a platter of biscuits toward me. "Here, sit down, I know you're hungry."

I ignored the biscuits and leaned my hands on the table. "How many are riding with RC? Are they any good?"

Briggs considered it over a sip of coffee. "All of RC's bunch are top hands; so's RC once he's sober. And if Mace Bowman is out looking for RC like he usually is, we can count on him. Can't always tell by looking at 'em, but RC and Mace are the two biggest guns in *Nuevo Mejico.*" A strange look swept across Briggs's eyes, and he smiled. "And there's that bucktoothed cowboy that was swamping for Lambert. He's young, brain-screwed, and crazy. But something tells me he'd drain a swamp and eat the alligators. He'll do."

I stared at Briggs and noticed he *had* given it some thought, all based on what he thought he knew about people. "Great," I said, letting go a breath, "a handful of drunks and a cock-eyed dishwasher."

Briggs chuckled, but his eyes were sharp. "Everybody's more than what they appear to be, Beatty. You, of all people, oughta know that." He shot a glance toward the street, then back to me. "Look at you and your partner. You appear to be fine young gentlemen, *businessmen*"—he grinned—"and in your case, a devoted bible student, savior of women in distress, and a sharp-eyed horse dealer."

I studied his eyes, wondering just what he was telling me.

He turned up a drink, swished it around, swallowed and hissed. "Yet . . . here you are, ready to toe straight up against the Quarrels Gang"—he raised a finger—"not out of duty, not for the money. Naw sir." He ran the finger across his mustache. "But for a horse." He drew his finger from his face, pointed it at me and winked. "See, lots of folks would call that crazy. But I like that about ya. Makes me think we'll do fine . . . just fine."

"Hold on, Briggs." I leaned forward and had to shake my head to clear it. He'd said more than I could understand all at one time, and he'd said it in a way that left a lot of doors open. "I mighta overpresented myself a little at first. But I showed you both sides of my picture. I told you I rode guerilla—let you know more about me than any lawman ought to know." I watched his eyes for a second. "But as far as *duty,* I don't *owe* any. As far as the money, if any falls in my path, I ain't gonna walk around it. But all I came in this for is my horse, marshall. That's the damn truth. If I get him back . . . the rest don't matter."

I saw him dismiss something from his mind. "That's understandable," he said, after a pause. He flipped a silver dollar from the edge of the table; it landed on his empty plate, rang like a bell, spun, wobbled down, and rattled, then stopped. He sighed. "You just won't believe how smooth things'll go once everybody gets situated."

I started to say something else when I heard a voice behind me. "Who'd you call a cocked-eyed dishwasher?" I turned and saw the bucktoothed cowboy. He'd appeared out of nowhere it seemed.

I felt my face redden. "I'm sorry, son," I said. "I meant no offense. We've got a bad problem here—"

"I ain't your *son.* My name's McCarty . . . *Mister* McCarty to you," he said. "I heard you talking. Don't worry, if Ned Quarrels rides in, I'll kick his ass and send him home to his mama."

I looked at Briggs, then at the young man, and grinned, knowing he meant well, but also knowing I wouldn't have the heart to send him out against a gang like Quarrels's. "Okay, *Mister* McCarty. Skin that iron and show us some gun-handling."

He grinned. "You got it, mister!" He threw open his coat and slapped his thigh, then his expression sagged as he looked down at his empty holster. "Hell, I've left my gun somewhere." He grinned sheepishly, ran his hands around on his coat, searching, then ducked his head. "I'll go find it and come right back."

I just shook my head as he slipped out the door, and I pulled out a chair across from Briggs and slumped down in it. "See," Briggs said, "this is how law work goes. Sometimes you sit around with nothing to do for a week or two, then all of a sudden, damned if you ain't three hands short and a foot over the edge. Never seen nothing like it, have you, Mister Beatty?" He picked up a biscuit and smeared butter on it. I sat and watched for a minute, not knowing what to say.

I turned, heard boots walk through the door, and saw Jack come in looking back over his shoulder. "There's people out there as naked as a stump." He thumbed back over his shoulder.

"That's the *RC,* we've been hearing about," I said. I glanced at Jack with a look that asked if he'd hidden the money in a safe place. His return look told me he had. "He's *Clay Allison.* Does that ring a bell?"

"No kidding?" Jack chuckled. "If he wants to keep his reputation as *big gun,* he better get his pants on." Jack looked embarrassed as we stared at him. "Not that I noticed, that is—I mean, I didn't look at—"

"Forget it, Jack," I said. I glanced at Briggs. "How'd you know Bowman would show up?"

"Only times he gets to go out drinking is when he rides out to bring RC home." Briggs grinned and rubbed his mustache. "That way, RC tells his woman the law was chasing him, and Mace tells everybody he's been hunting RC."

I stared at Briggs for a second, then at Jack.

"Mace Bowman? You mean the county sheriff from over around Cimarron?"

"Yeah," I said, "the one from the auction?"

"Sure," Jack said. "He's the other one out there. He's down to his underwear, accusing RC of hiding his clothes."

I started to go look, but Jack raised his hand. "It ain't a pretty sight."

Briggs laughed. "Now, now. These boys from Cimarron get a little wild sometimes. But they'll be all right. You boys are just letting this get to you, is all. You'll all do fine once I get you organized."

I looked at Briggs and wondered if I'd understood what he'd said moments before. Was he telling me he knew more about Jack and me than he'd let on? I wondered also if he'd understood what I said.

Jesus, I thought. I felt like telling him flat out who I was, where I'd been, who I'd killed, who I'd seen killed, and who I *would* kill if I ever got a chance, just to clear the air, just to let him know where I stood before the killing started.

Before I could say anything, Carmilla appeared beside me and dropped the stack of Gustav's recipes on the table. "He went to all this trouble for you. The least you can do is look at them . . . and thank him. Is that too much to ask from a big brave pistolero like yourself?" She stood tapping her foot with a hand on her hip.

"Jesus Christ!" I snatched up the recipes and started to throw them away, but I caught a glimpse of Gustav over by the bar. He looked like his feelings were hurt. I forced myself to smile. "Thanks, Gustav," I said. "I appreciate these. I really do." Then I stood and took Carmilla by the arm and jerked her away from the table. "Listen! I've had all of you I can—"

"Take your hands off me!" She shot out a small, hard fist that caught me square on the chin and nearly staggered me.

"Damn." I shoved her away with my hand to my jaw.

"Never jerk me around." She pointed a finger like a

dagger, spun on her cavalry boot heel, shot across the floor and up the stairs like a streak of dark smoke.

"What the hell got into her?" I stared at the empty stairs for a second.

Jack chuckled. "You said she don't take kindness from men. What made you think she'd accept abuse?"

• 14 •

My jaw throbbed as we left Fortenay's, and I leaned for a second against a crooked post and waved Jack and Briggs away. I watched them walk toward the barless jail; I breathed deep and tried to make sense of things. I wondered if Briggs had understood what I'd said. Then I thought about what he'd said and wondered if I'd understood him. Maybe things were getting to me. For some reason I felt like a puppet on the end of long strings. I could see the strings running off in many directions but couldn't see who was pulling them.

I rubbed my jaw. I had to calm down and take control. I must've been hoping until the last minute that something could stop what was about to happen. But it wouldn't. Maybe it took a rap on the jaw to jar me to the reality of it. We were on a runaway wagon here, and there was nothing to do but draw up and ride it out.

Just as I'd taken some deep breaths, turned and started off to join Briggs and Jack, I saw RC riding naked up the middle of the street wearing nothing but boots and a gunbelt. His naked behind made a slapping sound against the saddle leather. He fired an Army Colt in the air—a wild-eyed lunatic. He was splattered with mud. Streaks of Kersey's blood had dried to a dark crust down his pale legs. Jesus, I thought.

Near the jail, Mace Bowman leaned against an unfinished building, wrapped in a blanket with his gunbelt around his waist. I ducked my head and kept walking. "Damn it, RC!" Bowman bellowed. "I'm gonna be sick here. Believe I've been poisoned here. Give me back my clothes. Bring 'em back now, ya hear?"

Outside the unfinished jail, the bucktoothed cowboy came running up. "Found it," he said, out of breath. "Found this ole shooter." He slapped his holster; I saw the double-action Colt. "Still wanta see some iron work?" He grinned. I saw him puff a thick Mexican brown cigarette and inhale it deep.

"Not now, *Mister* McCarty," I said. I reached to open the door.

"Aw, heck . . . you don't really have to call me Mister McCarty. I just said that 'cause you was acting awful testy. My name's Henry, you can even call me Hank." He blew out a dark cloud of smoke and took a deep breath.

I looked him up and down and smiled. At least he was offering to help. "Okay, Kid—I mean, Henry. Thanks for your help. Sorry we got off on the wrong foot back there. You're right, I was a little testy."

"I know how it goes," he said. "I saw how Lambert screwed you around, and I heard about them bad bullets you got in Taos, and about your horse . . . Buck. I reckon you've had an awful lot on your mind"—he shook his head and winced—"not to mention getting punched by a woman. You oughta busted her head open for that, huh?"

"I've never hit a woman . . . yet." I felt the throb in my jaw. I wanted to raise my hand to it, but I didn't want to admit it hurt.

"Heck," said the kid, "I had to shoot a woman once." He shrugged. "She was just a whore."

"You don't say?" I eyed him skeptically. He knocked the fire off the tip of the Mexican brown, squeezed it between his fingertips, and dropped it in his shirt pocket.

"Yep." He grinned. "She was a hot one! You wouldn't believe how she could pick a gold coin off the table." He fanned away the smoke with his hand.

"I've heard of it, Kid—I mean Henry." I too fanned away the smoke, pushed open the door, and we walked inside. Briggs sat with one foot propped on a nail keg, Jack leaned against a wall. Kersey's deputies stood staring down at a white-haired old doctor who was busy wrapping a roll of gauze around Sheriff Kersey's head. All I could see was Kersey's right eye. The rest of his face looked like an Egyptian mummy. I winced.

"You told me not to start till six," said one deputy. "So don't go jumping on me for not doing nothing. I didn't want to get yelled at again."

Kersey groaned through the gauze, reached out a trembling hand toward the deputy, and tried to sit up on the blanket, but the doctor shoved him back down. His head thumped on the floor. "Be still, if you want this done right. Once heard of a man smothering to death because he got his beard wrapped up over his nose."

"Can't nobody blame you, Charlie," Briggs said to the deputy. "If he wanted you to start early, he shoulda said so. No time to worry about the town budget when somebody's wearing your head out with a pistol barrel." Briggs leaned forward slightly and spoke down to Kersey as if he was deaf. "Ain't that right, sheriff?" Briggs winked and wagged his finger at the battered sheriff. "Some days it don't pay to get out of bed . . . does it? Of course, if you'd been more cooperative, I'd have corrected RC right off."

Kersey just moaned and rolled his one eye to the ceiling.

Jack glanced my way, then back at Sonny Quarrels whose eyes shone from within the shadows along the back wall. I thought I heard Sonny laugh under his breath.

The old doctor stood up, wiped his hands on a bloody towel, and dropped the towel on Kersey's chest. "That's all I can do for now. Keep him drunk till it quits hurting. I've used enough thread on him to make a good quilt." He shook his head and clucked his cheek. "RC needs a good talking to." He turned and looked me up and down. "I heard what that woman did to you," he said, gazing above his spectacles. "Let me look at that jaw."

"Forget it," I said. I felt my face redden.

"She mighta broken a small bone." He leaned toward me.

"Naw she didn't, goddamn it," I said. I heard Jack snort to keep from laughing out loud.

"You might oughta let him take a look," Briggs said. "I once knew an ole boy—"

"I'm okay," I said, a little louder. "I think we need to make some plans or something, before Quarrels sweeps through here like a twister." I glanced from face to face about the room. On the floor, Kersey nodded his mummy head. The deputies looked at each other with a blank expression. Jack looked down and picked at his thumbnail.

Briggs folded his hands behind his head. "Doctor Eisenhower, this is Mister Beatty—he worries a lot."

The old doctor nodded toward me, reached down, and picked up his black bag. "No need in that, Mister Beatty. There's nothing you boys can do to each other that I can't fix . . . long as you're still alive."

I watched as the old doctor ambled out the door, then I turned to Briggs and started to speak. He held up a hand. "As soon as RC wears himself out, I'm gonna talk to him and Mace." He looked at the bucktoothed cowboy—"See you found your pistol"—then smiled at me. "See, everything is falling in place." He spread his hands. "All's I gotta do now is get you boys deputized and we'll be ready to romp."

"Deputized?" I looked from Briggs to Jack. Jack gave me a strange look, and I turned back to Briggs. "I ain't getting deputized, marshall."

"Yeah, you are." Briggs smiled. "You got to, for your own good. It'll make the difference later between you doing your duty or being tried for murder. That's all it's for. I'd hate to see a man hang for just getting his horse back. Now raise your right hand and say what I say."

"No," I said, but my hand made a halfhearted rise in the air. "This ain't necessary."

"You're right," Briggs said. "We don't need to say all the words. I ain't got but one extra badge for yas anyway." He took a badge from his shirt pocket, spit on it, rubbed it on his sleeve and pitched it to me. "So just consider yourselves deputized." He looked at the kid. "You too, cowboy."

The kid scratched his head. "I don't know, marshall. I never considered a career in law enforcement." His eyes were glassy and he seemed to be stifling a laugh.

I held the badge out to Briggs between my thumb and finger. "Maybe you should just hang onto this—"

Briggs pushed my hand back. "Wear it with pride, Mister Beatty. It ain't every day a man gets to uphold the law of the land."

"They don't get paid same as us, do they?" Charlie the deputy stepped forward. "I mean if federal deputy pays more—"

"You've got a full-time job," Briggs said. "These boys are temporary. Just till I get Quarrels and his gang. And they wouldn't think of taking pay for it."

"We wouldn't?" The kid looked at me and scratched his head.

Briggs grinned at me. "I hope you've changed bullets since the other night? I don't want you firing none of them floaters like you did at Alahambre."

I didn't even answer; I looked at Jack and nodded toward the door. I heard Kersey moaning as Jack and the kid followed me out.

"Where we going?" McCarty said, as the three of us stepped off the boardwalk and started up the street.

I stopped for a second, pinned the badge to my shirt and ran my sleeve across it. "The livery barn," I said over my shoulder. "I'm gonna find some wagons to set up a barricade. I ain't depending on nobody but us from now on. Briggs is either crazy or trying to get us all killed. From here on, Kid—I mean, Hank, you stick close. We'll look after ya."

"You don't have to look after me." He looked us over. "I'm better with a gun—"

We heard a shot from up the street near Fortenay's On The Frontier and the three of us ducked and drew our pistols. The sound of construction stopped. We turned in every direction, then back toward Fortenay's. "Thieving bastard!" a voice yelled, and we saw Erlander wave his pistol in the air. Bryce staggered to the middle of the street with one hand pressed to his stomach and the long-barreled Smith & Wesson hanging from his other. I glanced at Jack; he uncocked his pistol and we eased forward. Bryce turned around and tried to raise his pistol. "Don't try it!" Erlander shouted, his Walker Colt already aimed and cocked. Bryce staggered forward, tried again to raise it. Another shot exploded from Erlander; Bryce staggered back and dropped the gun.

"I'll . . . sue . . . you," Bryce said in a faltering voice. He sank straight down to his knees, swayed to both sides and pitched forward in the dirt.

I glanced at the kid, then back to the body in the street.

"Take a good look, Kid. That's what we've got to look forward to once Quarrels hits town."

"Aw—that ain't nothing." The kid spread a bucktoothed grin. "Seen more blood at family reunions." I just looked at him.

Several workers gathered around Bryce's body; several others drew close to Erlander.

"Now you've done it," I heard Clay Allison say to Erlander. He stepped out of Fortenay's wearing a bar towel stuffed down in his gunbelt like an Indian loincloth. "Now I'll cut your damn head off."

"You ain't the law, RC," said one of Erlander's crew.

"But he is." A worker raised a hand toward me and it took me a second to realize he was pointing at my badge. Faces turned and stared.

"Law?" RC waved the butcher knife toward us and laughed out loud. "You'll think *law*, when ole Ned eats 'em for breakfast."

"That son of a bitch," the kid hissed. He started across the street. I grabbed his arm and stopped him.

"Come on," I said, "they're all wind and no sail. Let 'em kill each other. We got work to do."

We walked on to the livery barn glancing back over our shoulders. I saw Mackay and Tripplet step out of Fortenay's; Mackay leaned against the front of the building watching the crowd and puffing on a cigar. Tripplet searched himself and jerked a pen and writing pad from his pocket. *"Jesus,"* I shook my head.

As we rounded the livery barn and started through the door, I ran into the owner and almost knocked him down. He'd been peeping around the half-opened door, watching the crowd up by Fortenay's. "I don't want no trouble," he said, scrambling backwards with his hands before his face.

"Good," I said, walking past him and looking around the barn. "You're the only son of a bitch who doesn't." Near the rear of the barn, I saw Mace Bowman leaning on one hand against a stall door with his head bowed and his other arm thrown across his belly. He'd found his trousers and one boot, and had a blanket thrown around his shoulders. He gagged violently. The barn smelled of sour whiskey.

"What're you looking for?" The owner stepped sideways along with me as I walked along the center bay toward the back door.

"Wagons," I said. "Any kind, any size."

"Something that'll stop bullets," I heard Jack say behind me.

"Bullets?" The owner's eyes opened even wider. "Now, hold on, mister."

I stopped and looked at him. "We're federal deputies of Marshall Briggs. You can check with him. We're fixin' to get hit by the Quarrels Gang. We're setting up a line of defense."

"I ain't got no wagons here," he said. "The contractors have everything rented except for two out back waiting for repairs."

"We'll take them," I said. "What else have you got that we can use?"

"You can't take my customers' wagons out there and get 'em shot up. I'm responsible for 'em!"

"The government will pay for any damage—" I stopped and looked at Jack. "I can do that, can't I?"

"They do it all the time," Jack said to the owner. He leaned close to me. "What the hell do you care?"

Mace Bowman wiped a hand across his mouth and straightened up when we approached him. "Deputies, huh?" he said. His eyes were bloodshot and still swimming in their sockets, but he'd sobered some. He looked us over and shook his head.

"That's right," I said. "Briggs just swore us in. Quarrels and his gang are gonna sweep through here like a swarm of hornets."

"You best get clear-eyed and sober," Jack said.

"Damn it," said Bowman. He jerked his gunbelt from off the stall door, threw it around his waist with shaking hands, and cinched it. "Why didn't somebody say something?"

"You and RC's been too drunk to know your own names since we left Cimarron," the kid said. "Rest of the boys has sobered up and rode on back." He shot me a grin, then turned back to Bowman. "But I reckon you'll know what to do now though, huh?"

Bowman swung open the stall door. "You're goddamn right!" He snatched the reins to a big pinto and pulled it from the stall. The three of us stepped back and watched as he shoved past us, leading the horse toward the door.

"Wait," I said. "You can't go after them by yourself."

"That's good advice," he said, running a shaking hand back through his tangled hair. "And I'm taking it." He stepped up into the saddle, threw a hand to his stomach for a second, and swallowed hard. His face turned gray for a second, then he let out a breath. "Only an idiot would stay here, knowing a gang like Quarrels's is on the way." He tapped a trembling finger to his hat brim. "See you boys later on . . . what's left of ya. I've got tons of paperwork back in Cimarron."

He turned the horse; I fell in beside him, stepping along with my hands spread. "But you're a lawman. It's your duty. You wear a badge."

"So do you, hero. Give 'em hell. Maybe somebody'll write a song about it. . . ."

"Damn it, Bowman! You can't leave. You owe these people something. You owe it to this town!"

"Ain't my town, ain't my people, ain't my duty. I couldn't even get me a free meal here." He sneered in contempt. "Had to pay for my own *whiskey!* If you want to die in this shit-hole . . . be my guest."

I trotted along beside him, hoping I could shame him into staying. "I thought you was the fastest gun in the territory?"

"Fastest, yes . . . dumbest, no." Bowman shook his head.

"What about your job, your reputation . . . *honor?"*

"Ha!" He tossed his head back. "You've been hanging around Briggs too long." He gigged the big pinto and pounded away up the dusty street. I stopped with my hands spread, turned toward Jack and the kid, then back toward Mace Bowman as he weaved around a pile of building material. We stared speechless until he was out of sight.

A skinny man wearing a brown derby stepped off the boardwalk and walked toward us, still looking back over his shoulder at the spot where Mace Bowman had disappeared into the stacks of sheeting and shingles. He had a long, rolled-up paper under his arm; and only when he stopped a few feet from us did I realize he was carrying a set of building plans. "Wasn't that Sheriff Bowman from over near Cimarron?" He swung the rolled-up plans from under his arm and used it as a pointer. We just stared at him. "What'd y'all say to him? Why's he leaving?" The skinny man cocked his head to the side and looked at us as if we owed him an explanation.

"Believe me, it ain't because we wanted him to, Mister . . . ?"

"Goodlet," he said, "Councilman Thornton Goodlet," and he stepped closer, drawn over at the shoulders and with his head still cocked to the side. "If you've said or done something to cause him to leave, I better not find out about it. We have a hard enough time drawing folks here from Cimarron, without some outsider poking his nose in—"

I glanced at Jack and shook my head. "We're federal deputies of Marshall Newton Briggs." I tapped my thumb against my badge. "And the fact is, I told Bowman the same as I'm telling you. Ned Quarrels is heading this way—"

"So what? He comes here all the time."

"Not like this. He's coming to get his brother."

"That damned Briggs." He shook his head. "I mighta figured. He can't go nowhere without stirring something up. He has no regard for anybody. Now he's got you three going around scaring everybody away."

"Look, Goodlet," I said. "We ain't trying to scare nobody away, but Quarrels is coming, there's no point in hiding it."

"Now, you don't know that, do you?" He threw a defiant hand on his hip and tapped the rolled-up plans against his leg.

I shot Jack a puzzled glance, then back to Goodlet. "Yeah," I said, a little put out. "I'm pretty damn sure. We ran into them out there today. Quarrels wants his brother back pretty bad."

"So give him back." He shrugged. "What the hell's the difference? We're building a town here. Take that bullshit out there in the desert somewhere. Don't bring it here. What's them boys done that's so bad anyway?"

"They robbed a stagecoach the other side of Cimarron, took off with the miner's payroll."

"Aw, hell." He swiped a hand through the air. "If you ask me, everybody around Cimarron is overpaid anyway. It might teach them a lesson to go without pay for a month or two. That whole damned town's nothing but a bunch of goody-gooders. Far as I'm concerned, Ned Quarrels's money will spend here same as the next fellow's."

I stared at him for a second, and couldn't believe the next words out of my mouth. "Mister," I said. "Maybe it don't mean anything to you, but the Quarrels Gang has broken the law." I tapped the badge on my chest again. "It's our job to stop them. If we overlook what they've done, pretty soon there'll be no law. Then what?"

I heard Jack and the kid chuckle beside me.

Goodlet looked back and forth among us. "The three of you would be out on your ass and have to find a respectable job, I suspect. You and that damned Briggs." He pointed the rolled-up plans at me. "What the hell could you do to stop Ned Quarrels anyway?" He looked me up and down and stepped forward. "If you ask me—"

"I ain't asking you . . . ain't asking you a damn thing." I stepped forward and slapped the plans aside; he backed up with a startled look in his eyes. "We're here to protect this town, and uphold the law, and I'll do it if I have to kick your ass all the way to the next Wednesday—"

"Smack that son of a bitch!" I heard the kid say beside me.

"—So you either get behind us and help us, or get your weasel ass out of our way. And don't you ever open your mealy mouth about Briggs again or I'll shut it with a pistol butt."

"Shoot him," the kid said, "smoke his oats!"

Goodlet backed away quickly, stumbling as he turned. "I'm getting the mayor, is what I'm doing. You can't talk to a councilman that way." He shook a finger as he backed farther away. "You'll see!" He stomped away, still looking back at us. I slapped my hand against my holster and he broke into a run.

"The hell's got into you?" Jack looked me up and down.

"I don't know, Jack. I guess I'm tired of everybody acting like there's something wrong with ole Briggs. I know he's a little crazy, but if this is the kind of people he's worked with all his life, I reckon I see why." I looked at the kid and nodded toward the barn. "See about them wagons, Kid."

"You shoulda shot him, cut him, kicked him, or something." He grinned, took out a Mexican brown, hung it from his lips, and walked away with his thumb hooked near his pistol.

"Don't go getting too carried away," Jack said to me, once the kid was gone. "Don't forget, that badge ain't got a thing to do with why we're here." He leaned close and rubbed his thumb and finger together in the universal sign of greed. "The *money,* remember? The old *long-green* stuff? The old' *'God! it's good to be alive'* stuff?"

I looked at him. "No. It's about my horse, Buck, remember?"

Jack rolled his eyes upward. "Okay . . . it's about the money *and* your horse. Just don't go getting—"

"No," I shook my head. "It's about *my horse,* then the money."

"Either way, don't let that piece of tin go to your head."

"I won't," I said. I ran my shirt cuff across the badge. "But damned if it don't feel good telling some asshole like Goodlet where to get off and knowing the whole United States government is standing behind me."

PART III — ◆

Measure of Merit

• 15 •

By dark, Jack, the kid, and I had managed to drag two long tandem freight wagons and a broken mail buggy out into the street and loaded them with thick chunks of firewood. For awhile it looked as though the construction crews would break into a shoot-out. We saw them curse and threaten each other out front of Fortenay's with Clay Allison right in the middle swinging a butcher knife, but they were all too drunk to do any real harm.

Finally, as the two opposing sides began shoving each other back and forth, drawing hammers and pistols and waving them in the air, Briggs sauntered down the boardwalk from the unfinished jail with a rifle hanging from his hands. For a moment he stood quietly, took off his hat and ran his hand back across his head. Then, smiling calmly, he walked up behind Crazy Clay Allison and busted him in the head with the rifle butt. Allison dropped like a bundle of rags.

"Now let that be the end of it," Briggs said to the hushed crowd. "Get Bryce's body off the street and y'all go on back to work." The crowd parted and watched as Briggs backed between Clay's legs, took an ankle in each hand and drug his naked behind up the dirt street to the barless jail.

Only then did I see Mackay take note of our wagons blocking the street. He nudged Tripplet who'd been watching Briggs and writing notes in a small pad. Mackay nodded toward us, and the two of them walked in our direction, Tripplet still writing as he walked. I turned around facing Jack and the kid. "Maybe Briggs will sober that lunatic up and get him to help us." I looked at Jack and nodded toward the firewood on one of the wagons. "Reckon we better get to work."

The bucktoothed kid grinned as Jack stepped over, took up some firewood, and pitched it into a small pile between the wagons. "If he sobers up, he'll probably cut and run," the kid said. "That's how RC is. He's a wildcat when he's drunk. Rest of the time he ain't got enough spit to wet his whiskers." He turned to set up the wood for a fire but Jack stopped him.

"How long you known him?" Jack asked. He looked around the small area to judge the size of the fire as he spoke.

"Just the past few weeks since I been in Cimarron. But I seen enough to know he's just *bottle* brave. If he ever messed with me, I'd put a hole through his head wide enough to run a freight train."

Jack smiled, "Sure, Kid," took some more of the wood from the pile, and pitched it to the side.

"It wouldn't be the first time," the kid said. He picked up a chunk of wood and started to throw it back on the pile. Jack stopped him. "I kilt me a sumbitch when I was fourteen, you know." The kid grinned. "Cleaved him with a knife from here to here." He drew a finger across his stomach. "Then when I was fifteen, I shot it out with a mess of renegades 'cause they attacked a wagon train of settlers. Then kilt me a Mexican over a whore, then kilt the whore 'cause she tried to kill me over the Mexican I kilt." He spread a grin at the irony of it.

"Jesus." I shook my head and watched Mackay and Tripplet walk closer.

Jack chuckled. "Just how old are you, McCarty?"

"Next year I'll be seventeen, 'less somebody stops me."

"So you're sixteen, huh?" Jack formed a tripod of firewood and laid other pieces against it. "Don't take this the wrong way. But how'd you crowd all that shooting, cutting, whoring, and everything else into *sixteen* years?"

"There ain't no age limit, is there?" The kid grinned, and for a second I thought I saw something in his eyes that said he really had done it all. But then I looked him up and down. He looked as spindly and awkward as a newborn calf. Ain't a way in the world, I said to myself.

"Let Jack handle the fire, Kid. It's his specialty," I said.

"I can build a fire as well as the next—"

"Not this kind, Kid," Jack said. "This is not a fire for warmth or light."

"The hell's it for, then?" He looked puzzled.

"Advertisement," I said, watching Jack bank dust around the pile of wood with his hands.

Jack smiled up at the kid. "You tell a pretty good story. Wanta make a couple bucks for it?"

"Sure—"

"Forget it, Jack," I said, watching Mackay and Tripplet step between the wagons.

"What's the harm?" Jack shrugged. "All's he has to do is tell Tripplet the same things he's telling us. It's worth some money—"

"How's that?" The kid leaned forward.

Jack stood up, dusted his hands, glanced at Mackay and Tripplet, then back at the kid. "Just tell this man what you told me, is all."

"My, my," Mackay said, as he and Tripplet stopped a few feet away. He gestured a hand at the loaded wagons. "Mister Beatty, I'm starting to suspect that you're one of those people who can't sit still for a moment." He shook his head and smiled. "Always busy, busy, busy. Always looking for what to do next." He gestured a hand, taking in our wagons, rifles, and ammunition. "I take it this is all done in honor of Ned Quarrels's arrival?"

"Yeah," I said, a little put out by his cavalier attitude. "It won't seem so peculiar when his bunch come blazing down the street." I thumbed the badge on my chest. "Briggs deputized us. So it's all on the up and up."

"No offense intended," Mackay said, looking around. "It's a fine barricade." He blew a stream of cigar smoke up in the air. "In fact, I wish you would reconsider my offer to help. I really am quite the cat's meow with a pistol." He reached a hand inside his coat. "I've never shown you this little dandy."

I held up a hand, stopping him. "We're kinda busy right now. I know you mean well and I appreciate it, but thanks anyway." I glanced Mackay up and down. I didn't want some sick dentist coughing his brains out in the middle of a shooting.

"I'd give my eyeteeth to cover something like this," Tripplet said. "If there really is a Quarrels Gang, and if they really are coming." He glanced both ways up and down the street. "Sometimes rumors get started."

I just glanced at Jack and shook my head.

"Oh, I can attest, there is a Quarrels Gang," said Mackay. "And if I'm any judge . . . I'm certain Mister Beatty has done something to assure his coming here." Mackay smiled at me. "Eh, Mister Beatty?"

I avoided his gaze and looked at Tripplet. "You can write what you want, far as I care. I just don't want to answer any questions, is all. I've got no time for it."

"You can write about me," the kid said through a bucktoothed smile. "I once shot it out with a band of Apaches. Saved a whole dern wagon train—" He glanced at Jack for approval. Jack grinned and nodded. "Kilt a Mexican over a whore, then kilt the whore because she—"

"Of course, son," Tripplet said, cutting him off. He tapped his pencil to his tongue and smiled at me. "Just a couple of questions, Mister Beatty? Perhaps a statement—how you feel right now, knowing that at any minute you could be—"

"You didn't let me finish, mister," the kid said to Tripplet.

"You really oughta listen to this young man," Jack said. "I think he's got the makings of a legend."

Tripplet turned to the kid with a patient smile. "I'm afraid young cowboys aren't in much demand right now. See me in a few years when you've sprouted some horns." He turned away from the kid, and Jack had to grab the boy's arm to keep him from cracking Tripplet in the back of his head. "Now then, Mister Beatty." Tripplet smiled and tapped the pencil to his tongue.

"Forget it," I said. I walked to the other end of the wagon and gazed off up the street.

"You said it was worth a few dollars," I heard the kid say to Jack.

"Not right now," Jack replied. "We'll talk to him later."

"Good luck, young man," Mackay said with a laugh that turned into a cough. "I've never been able to interest him in my story." He pressed his hand to his mouth and cleared his throat. "I'm afraid Mister Beatty has impressed him so profoundly, the rest of us don't have a chance."

"I'm sorry to say, gentlemen," said Tripplet. "But your stories just aren't newsworthy. I'm looking for real, as-it-happens adventure."

I looked away and up the dusty street. At Fortenay's the crowd had broken up and drifted off; but now a portly feller in a handsome dark suit stood talking to Gustav and nodding toward us. When Briggs came walking past them from the barless jail, the portly feller stepped along beside him, talking and waving his hands as they headed our way. Briggs stared straight ahead.

"And now, it appears we'll be visited by the esteemed mayor of this lovely hamlet," Mackay said with a slight chuckle. "Off hand, I'd say he isn't real pleased with your line of defense."

I smiled at Mackay. "Yeah, and I also threatened one of his councilmen."

"Did you really?" Tripplet sprang forward scratching rapidly with his pencil.

I raised a hand. "It's all off the record, Tripplet. Just a misunderstanding."

I heard the mayor cursing as he and Briggs rounded the corner of the wagon and stopped. "We don't care about any of this," the mayor said, grabbing Briggs's arm to get his attention. "I want the street cleared this instant!"

Briggs turned his face slowly down and stared at the mayor's hand. The mayor jerked his hand away from Briggs's arm as if it were a loaded bear trap. "Sorry, marshall," he said. "But this has gone too far. We have no problem with the Quarrels Gang. I won't allow you to turn this town into a shooting gallery!" He shot a finger up at me. "And I want that man out of this town immediately. He threatened the life of Councilman Goodlet! I won't stand for it."

"Is that true, Mister Beatty?" Briggs stared at me.

"Well . . . I might've gotten a little testy with him—"

"Testy?" the mayor fumed. "Marshall, he almost drew a gun on the man. He threatened to kill him. Goodlet is still shaken by it!"

"You didn't cuss him, did you, Mister Beatty?" Briggs cocked a bushy eyebrow. "You didn't blackguard or otherwise make any profane statements against his personage . . . his or his mama's or anybody near to him?"

"I don't think so," I said. I cleared my throat. "But I was pretty cross. He said some things he shouldn't have. Talked about you like a dog."

"There now, mayor, you see. Mister Beatty conducted himself like the young gentleman that he is."

The mayor looked around at us in exasperation and

waved his arms. "Look at all of you!" He turned to the kid, looked him up and down. "Young man, are you drunk? How long since you've had a haircut or a hot bath?"

The kid looked himself up and down, rubbed a hand across his shaggy hair, but didn't get a chance to answer.

"And you," the mayor said, swinging around, facing Mackay. "You've been gambling here for a week, and every miner in the area is borrowing against next month's pay to keep from starving to death."

Mackay shrugged; Tripplet chuckled and made notes.

"Mister Mackay is not one of my deputies," Briggs said. "If you have a problem with him, it's strictly a civilian matter."

"Civilia—? My God, Briggs. Listen to you. Do you think this is the army? Do you think you're in command of some military unit? This is the eighteen seventies, for christsakes! Wake up! We're building a prosperous community here. We don't need or want your protection." He swung a finger toward Jack and me. "What would these two be able to do anyway?" He shook his head. "Now clear this street and get the hell out of here!"

"I'll pretend I didn't hear that, Your Honor," said Briggs. "But you know as well as I do that no community will last if you ignore your problems. While you're building this place, trying to attract folks to come here, there's a lawless element that has grown wild and unattended right in your front yard. If you people had dealt with Ned Quarrels sooner, I wouldn't be here. But you didn't. So here I am . . . like it or not. And I'll take him and his whole bunch down if I have to level this town to do it."

"Pistol-whip him, Marshall Briggs," I heard the kid say; but Briggs ignored him.

"You're crazy, Briggs!" The mayor stepped back as if he'd just seen a streak of madness in the marshall's eyes. "That's it! I thought it before—everybody thought it—but now I see it plain as day. You're insane . . . and I'm going over your head." He shook his finger in the air. "Hear me? I'll go over your head on this!"

I heard the explosion without seeing the slightest flicker of movement. One second the old marshall stood staring at the mayor while the mayor ranted and raved; the next second, the mayor lay writhing in the dirt with blood shooting out of the hole in his boot, and Briggs's Dance Brothers forty-four hung smoking from his hand as he stepped forward.

"Over my head? Then you better go to God Almighty," Briggs said in a low tone, cocking the Dance and raising it until it leveled down a foot from the mayor's face. "There's nobody else over my head."

"Now you're cooking," the kid said. "Shoot him again!"

"Don't do it, marshall!" I heard myself yell above the ringing in my ears.

The mayor's face turned chalk white except for the blue vein that bulged in his forehead. His mouth dropped open staring up the barrel of Briggs's pistol, and a string of saliva stretched from one lip to the other. His hands clamped around his shattered foot; blood seeped between his fingers and dripped into the dirt.

"Oh God, oh God," he wailed, and I noticed the string of spit didn't break as he muttered what he thought would be his dying words.

I saw Briggs pull the trigger, even saw the hammer slam forward, but heard it stop with a click as Briggs caught it with his thumb just before it struck the bullet. The mayor slumped in the dirt as if his guts had melted. I swayed and let out a breath, glanced at Jack and saw him watching with a detached curiosity. "Whew," I said. Tripplet stood with his mouth hanging open and his pencil laying in the dirt at his feet.

"Had I been Ned Quarrels or one of his bunch," Briggs said in a quiet tone, "I wouldn't have let you gone over my head. But I let ya this once because I'm the law." He recocked the Dance. "Don't ever do it again . . . or I can't promise you a thing. When you belittle me, you belittle my office. I won't tolerate it."

From up the street, some of the construction workers had stopped long enough to look our way, then turned and went about their business. Mackay stepped close to the downed mayor to offer him a hand, but Briggs waved him back with the Dance forty-four. "Crawl out'n here, Your Honor," said Briggs. "You're no better than anybody else shot in the foot. Crawl on over to Doc Eisenhower's and get patched up. If there's a charge, tell 'em I'll pay it."

"Let *me* shoot him a time or two," said the kid. He started forward but Jack held out an arm, blocking him.

"Don't make him crawl in the dirt, marshall," I said, watching the mayor struggle along, whining like a pup.

Briggs let out a breath. "You're right." He holstered the Dance, stepped over, picked up the mayor's derby, brushed it off, and plopped it on his head. "Here, Your Honor." He looped the mayor's arm across his shoulder and helped him up. The mayor still whined as Briggs helped him away toward the unfinished doctor's office.

I watched and scratched my head. "Now there's you a story, Tripplet," I said over my shoulder. "There's a man who's already a legend. Write about what came over him to make him do such a thing."

"Yes, indeed," Tripplet said in a hushed voice.

"What about my story?" said the kid.

"Later," said Jack.

"My, my, Mister Tripplet." I heard Mackay chuckle. "Has our dear old marshall just stolen center stage? And all he had to do was blow the mayor's toes off?" Mackay chuckled and shook his head. "If I had only known . . ."

I turned and watched Tripplet pick up his pencil from the dirt. "Gentlemen, that defies simple explanation. I'm afraid no one would believe what just happened here."

"Looked simple to me," said the kid. "Briggs just popped

a cap on His Honor and put him on crutches for the next couple of weeks."

"Come now," Mackay said to Tripplet. "You aren't about to let that story slip past you, are you? If you do, sir, I'll have to question your credibility as a journalist."

Tripplet stared off and rubbed his strip of a goatee. "What do you suppose Briggs meant, *'Take it to God Almighty'*? Did he mean that by shooting him in the foot he was somehow answering the mayor's plea to a higher authority?" Triplet rolled his hand. "Sort of a, *'Take this over my head and this is what you'll get'*? Sort of an, *'I'm more responsive than God'* kind of thing?

I glanced among them and shook my head; Jack shrugged.

"Perhaps," Mackay said, taking out a fresh cigar. He rolled it around in his mouth. "But I saw great significance in Briggs pulling that trigger the second time but catching it with his thumb. As if to say that only the intervention of man can enact the will of God." He smiled at me and winked, as if I should understand. I just scratched my jaw and smiled back.

"In other words . . ." Tripplet drew out his writing pad slowly, and with a studious expression began jotting something down. Jack and the kid craned their necks to watch.

Mackay shrugged. "In other words, sir . . . Briggs becomes the personification of both goodness at bay and evil at large. A very fine line, I suspect. And like a circus performer, he now teeters on a tightwire above the dark abyss. He has assumed the role of both man's nature and God's will. He has become both the hammer that strikes the bullet and the thumb that keeps it from falling."

"Jesus," I said, chafing the back of my neck, "what a life," unsure if I was referring to Briggs, myself, or all of us gathered there in the dirt.

"I see," said Tripplet. He started to write something, then

stopped and stared at Mackay. "This may be a little too complex."

Jack rubbed his chin and spit. "I could use a drink."

"On the contrary, sir," Mackay said to Tripplet. "As a journalist, I should think you'd enjoy rising to the challenge."

I felt a deep, dull throb creep into my forehead, and wondered if it might be the aftereffect of Carmilla popping my jaw, either the pain of the physical act or the mental humiliation of it. Mackay's high thinking mighta had something to do with it.

"Y'all are nuts," said the kid. "Briggs is just a hard old feller sat in his ways. He just got tired of being fucked with."

Tripplet, studying the pad in his hand, looked up at the kid for a second. "You may have something there." He smiled and stepped over to Henry. "What did you say your name was? You know I've always felt it's best to stick to the rudiments and not get swept away by complex interpretation." Tripplet wagged the pencil in the air. "Simply, *'Mayor confronts federal marshall. Marshall shoots mayor in foot—'* "

"Hell yes," said the kid. He pulled the Mexican brown cigarette butt from his shirt and let it dangle from his lips. "Fancy thinking won't stop the bleeding, will it?" He spread a bucktoothed grin and searched himself for a match. "It's McCarty . . . Henry McCarty." He spelled out his name as Tripplet wrote it down. "But just call me Hank."

"Certainly," Tripplet said. He pulled a long match from his vest pocket and handed it to the kid. "So, Hank . . . you say you've had quite a few adventures? The wagon train . . . the Mexican, and so on?"

I turned to Jack and shook my head. "Life goes on, I reckon."

"Such as it is." Jack spit, ran a hand across his mouth, and leaned down to light the fire.

• 16 •

Near midnight the town had settled down and the only sound was the clinking of tools and the groaning of timbers as a night crew worked by lantern raising the side of Fortenay's On The Frontier. Jack had honed the fire into a bed of glowing embers beneath a layer of low, curling flames, providing a thin circle of light but revealing little. The three of us sat back at the edge of the firelight and kept an eye on each end of town. "This'll all look pretty foolish if the Quarrels Gang don't show up," Jack said. He spit a stream of tobacco.

"Not to mention the trouble Briggs is gonna be in for rounding down the mayor's shoe size." I gazed off and studied the flicker of a single dim lantern in the window of the barless jail. The glow of it looked small and lonesome against the backdrop of a wide dark night. "Wonder what Briggs is thinking right about now?" I pulled my coat collar up, tugged down my hat brim, and turned my eyes to the low flames.

"Probably thinking how good it is to be inside while we're out here in the dirt like fools." Jack spit a stream of tobacco and I heard it splat in the dust. He chuckled. "He sure ruined a good pair of boots for the mayor."

"Shoulda killed him flat out," said the kid. He sat cross-legged and played mumblety peg in the dirt with a short pocketknife. "Hell, he's the law. He coulda found some way to make it look legal."

I glanced over at Henry McCarty and back at the fire. "You've got a lot to learn, Kid."

"Yeah? Like what? I've been told that all my life, but nobody says what." He shrugged. "So I reckon nobody knows, or else they don't think I should."

Jack chuckled and spit a stream. "Where're you from, cowboy? You got any family?"

"I'm from west of here, but I was born back east. Naw, no family . . . worth mentioning. My ma died a couple years back, my pa died when I was a baby, but it don't matter. He wished I'd never been more than a wet spot on the sheet anyhow." He grinned and flipped the knife into the ground. "I was born standing up and been running ever since. Same as you two. I'm just an outlaw in the making, I reckon."

"What's that supposed to mean?" I shot him a glance.

"Means I see more than you think I do. I don't think you're smart enough to be a horse trader—no offense—and ain't neither one of you got the hands of a working man. I figure you're both a couple of outlaws, probably would steal a hot stove if you had thick enough gloves." He laughed under his breath and nodded at Jack. "You really take the cake, carrying that fancy La Faucheux pistol. Anybody carries one of them can kill a man so quick he'd think he died yesterday."

"You're talking crazy, Kid," Jack grunted, but I saw his eyes sweep over the kid in a new light. "This is a souvenir from the war. I took it off a dead soldier."

"Yeah? I bet you's the one made him that way. Bet you're faster with it than a rattlesnake."

"Yeah, Kid." Jack sipped a cup of coffee and studied the fire. "Faster than anybody I've ever come up against . . . so far. But there's more to life than being good with a gun."

"No there ain't." The kid beamed behind a dumb grin. "That's another one of them things people like you say all the time. But you don't mean it, or else why do you carry one? Why do you spend so much time practicing, to stay good at it?"

"I don't, Kid. It's just something I was born with, like some people are born to play the piano without ever having a lesson. If I didn't have it, I wouldn't miss it a bit. Nothing great about being good with a gun." Jack smiled slightly. "I'd take the piano any day."

"Yeah . . . I bet," the kid said.

I saw the dim firelight flicker in Jack's eyes. I knew there was a message for the kid in his words, but like most kids, Henry wouldn't hear it. At best, he would remember it someday, remember it and repeat it to some other crazy kid, but by the time he understood it, it'd be too late for him.

"He's telling you the truth, Kid." I glanced from Jack to the kid. "And you've got us wrong. We're just what we said we are. You can ask old Briggs, he'll tell you—"

He waved my words away. "Go on now. I don't know how y'all pulled that off, but Briggs is blind as a bat about the both of ya. Anybody with one eye and half sense can see what you are."

"I'm sorry you think that, Kid, but you're wrong."

"Hell, don't worry, I'm kinda a hardcase myself, 'cept I ain't been around as long as you. I won't say nothing. And I ain't looking for no money or nothing. I'm just along for the ride. But I want you to know, I ain't as dumb as I look."

"Well . . . *that* is good to hear." I smiled and nodded at Jack. "Ain't that good to hear?"

"I feel better knowing it." Jack smiled and sipped his coffee.

The kid looked embarrassed, grinned and shook his head. "See how y'all are? I swear, when this is all over, I might throw in with ya. After I get my yarn money from Tripplet."

"Don't forget, Kid." Jack tapped himself on the chest. "I get a finder's fee for coming up with the idea." He turned to me. "And I told you Tripplet don't care if it's true or not, didn't I?"

"But it is true," the kid said. "Every damn word."

Jack looked at me and rolled his eyes upward slightly. "Sure, Kid."

I saw someone walking our way from the barless jail and I swung my rifle up over the wagon tongue. "Who goes there?"

"Don't shoot! It's me, Clay Allison. Briggs says you boys need some help here. Can I come in?"

"Aw hell," I said in a hushed voice to Jack and the kid. "Now we'll get straddled with this idiot."

"It's one more gun in our favor," said Jack.

"I know," I said. I raised my head over the wagon tongue. "Are you sober?"

"Pretty much. As much as I oughta be."

"All right . . . come on in." I glanced at Jack and the kid. "If he goes nuts and I have to shoot him, I want you both to swear it's self-defense, or an accident, or something, all right?" I already knew Jack would; I was just checking on the kid.

"Sure." The kid shrugged. "We'll all shoot him if you want to."

I looked back across the wagon tongue at RC as he walked closer. "Jesus," I whispered, "he's still naked as hell."

But when he walked in between the wagons, I saw he was at least wearing the bar towel loincloth. "I don't know if I'm shaking from the cold or the whiskey," RC said, folding his arms across his chest. "I've been drunk for exactly two weeks." He shook his head and plopped down in the dirt near the fire. "I don't remember nothing about nothing."

"Uh . . . Mister Allison," I said. "I wouldn't sit too close to the fire if I was you. See, we've got—"

"Aw, don't worry about me. My skin's tougher than an allig—"

"—Ned Quarrels's coming any time, and you make a clear target there."

"Oh shit!" He scooted back quickly, leaving two wide cheek marks in the dirt, and ran a trembling hand back through his curly hair. "Don't know what I was thinking." He glanced around at us with a sheepish grin, then back to me. "Thanks, mister. I guess you know how it is to be on a bender."

"I'm Beatty," I said, and I motioned toward Jack. "This is my partner. You already know Henry here."

RC shot the kid a glance. "I do?"

"Hell, we rode here together, RC." The kid glared at him at first, but then chuckled and shook his head. Since RC didn't recognize the kid, I figured he remembered nothing about our confrontation in the street.

"Oh." RC considered it a second. "Wasn't Mace Bowman and some others with us?"

"They've gone back to Cimarron," said the kid.

"Did Mace know there was trouble coming?" RC scratched his head.

"Yeah, he knew," I said wryly. "Said he had tons of paperwork waiting on him."

"That's probably true," RC said. "He'll be back, though, if I know Mace." He motioned a finger toward the coffee pot on the edge of the fire.

"Help yourself." I picked up a tin cup from beside me and pitched it to him. But he missed it, and it bonked him on the bridge of his nose and fell in the dirt. "Jeez, sorry," I said. I held a breath for a second to see how he took it.

" 'S'okay," he said, rubbing his nose.

I heard Jack chuckle softly. "Here." He scooted forward, picked up the pot, and scooted close to RC. "I've had them blind staggers myself." Jack righted the cup on the ground and filled it halfway. Clay had to use both shaking hands to pick it up, then spilled most of it on the way to his mouth. Jack reached out, took him by the wrists and steadied his hands until he managed a long sip. "You ain't in no shape to spill something hot in your lap." Then he sat down the pot and scooted back out of the firelight.

"I know it," RC said in a humble tone.

We sat quietly watching RC struggle with his coffee. When he finished, he let out a coffee hiss that ended in a watery belch. "Boys . . . I'll just be honest with you. I hope I can do you some good. I'm a fair shot with a pistol. Better than average with a rifle. But I'd do better with a shotgun, if you've got one." He studied the low flame. "I dread getting shot. Shot my own self once . . . hurt like hell. Ain't nothing worse than a bullet cutting through ya. Blood flying. I've got a picture here of me after I shot myself." His hands searched around absently on his naked chest.

"Musta left it in your other suit," said Jack. He grinned.

"Huh?" Allison looked embarrassed. "Aw yeah." He offered a sheepish smile.

"Uh . . . RC," I said, to change the subject and hopefully boost his confidence. "You might not know it, but your reputation as a shootist has spread all the way across Missouri."

"No kidding?" He ducked his eyes and glanced up.

"Yep," Jack said, seeing what I was doing. "Probably on into Kentucky, Tennessee. . . . Hell, everybody's heard of you. You've got a *name* for yourself." Jack nodded his head for emphasis.

"Well . . . I don't wanta brag." RC ran a hand across his face. "I've come through some scrapes." He studied the fire again for a second. "But you never know when that next bullet is gonna poke through your belly and leave a hole the size—"

"You wouldn't happen to know where your clothes are, would you?" I tried to sound as polite as possible, but I didn't want to think of bullet holes right then. "I mean . . . you'd be a lot warmer—"

RC glanced down at himself, then back up. "Oh, right! I

think I left them behind Fortenay's. I can . . . uh, go get them?" He spread his hands, stood up and fumbled with the bar towel, smoothing it down. "I don't know why I do this. I just get a little drunk and there they go."

"Well," I said, "just get yourself dressed and comfortable, and come on back. We'll have plenty for you to do once Ned and his bunch gets here."

He hesitated a second. "You know, I'm actually a rancher by trade. Got a fair spread over near Cimarron. Nice place." He looked at each of us. "What about you fellows? Professionals?" He clicked his thumb back and forth like it was a gun hammer.

"No. Horse trader," I said, nodding. He looked at Jack.

Jack nodded toward me. "His partner."

"Oh, I see." RC looked a little let down and concerned as he eyed us.

"Dishwasher, cowboy, and general round-abouter," the kid said, spreading his toothy grin.

"Yeah?" RC looked worried, but nodded his head as if nothing bothered him. "Well, there we are. But we'll be fine. Sure will. Real good. Yep." He started to turn and walk away, but must've remembered his naked behind. "Nothing to worry about here. I'll just be back in a flash." He backed away to the edge of the wagon, then let out a breath. "Fellows, I might as well tell you, I've got a real bad feeling about this, you know?" He backed around the end of the wagon as we sat staring at him.

"He's scared to death, ain't he?" I smiled at Jack as we heard RC's bare feet slapping against the street in a dead run toward Fortenay's.

"Told ya," the kid said, "he's just *bottle* brave."

"Well, I reckon that's the last we'll see of him." I let out a breath and leaned against the wagon wheel. "Yep . . ." I crossed my boots and pulled my hat down over my face. Somehow, seeing a big gun like Clay Allison tremble in fear boosted my courage tremendously. I smiled to myself, ran a hand up, and patted the forty-four in my shoulder harness. "You're right about one thing, Kid. We're a couple of tough hombres." I grinned. "When *Tejas* gets too hot to handle and *Nuevo Mejico* gets too rough to ride, just call us ole boys from Missouri. We'll skin her down."

"Damn," Jack said. "Don't go getting cocky. *Please* don't!"

I just grunted under my breath.

I thought about Clay Allison, his trembling hands, and his bare ass with a boil on it. I thought of Briggs and pictured the mayor wallowing in the dirt holding his foot. I even thought about Carmilla, Greta, their women's lodge, and Margaret Alahambre. I thought of all these things to keep my mind off what I knew was coming. I pictured Diamond Joe's flat nose and heard him honk like a goose; saw him sailing off the cliff like a paper doll. And I recalled how warm it felt sleeping against his injured wife that night in the cave. For some reason I chuckled out loud.

"What's so funny?" I heard Jack say.

I just shook my head, and pictured the card game back at Lambert's, the posters of Ned Quarrels and his bunch with penciled-in lips and round eyes. I chuckled again and ran a finger under my nose.

"Damn it," said Jack. If you're gonna carry on like a hyena, let us in on it. If not, you'd better get a little shut-eye."

"It's nothing," I said, and I settled my mind beneath my hat. "I was just thinking." I let out a long breath.

"Thinking what?"

"Thinking . . . if I was Frank Tripplet . . . I'd be a full-blown millionaire."

After awhile, after trying to doze off and realizing I couldn't, I finally stood up, brushed off my seat and looked out toward the dim light in the window of the barless jail. I looked at Jack leaning against the wagon wheel, and I saw how his eyes studied me. "I gotta talk to him one more time," I said.

"Then go ahead, say what you've got to say. But hurry up. I'll keep the fire tended." He spit and ran a hand across his lips. The kid lay sleeping against the wagon tongue.

When I got to the jail, I stood to the side and knocked, lest Briggs think I was one of Quarrels's men and throw a few shots through the door. "It's me, Beatty," I said; and only when I heard a chair slide away and saw Briggs's face did I step over in front of the door.

Briggs saw what I'd done and he shook his head as I stepped inside. "Don't ever stand beside a door like that, Beatty. If anybody inside thinks you've come to kill 'em, they've already figured that's where you'll be. Knew an ole boy who got killed like that. Surprised the hell out of him, I reckon."

"I bet it did," I said. I looked past the circle of dim lamplight and saw Sonny asleep against the back wall, snoring like a yard hound.

"Don't seem right, does it?" Briggs nodded toward him. "He's the only one of us getting a full eight tonight."

"Yeah," I said. "Makes you wanta get him up and make him run around the room."

"Want me to?" Briggs looked serious.

"Not on my account." I walked over, propped a boot up on a nail keg, and stared down at it. For no reason, I reached down and brushed dust from my toe. "I wanta make sure we understood each other earlier, marshall. Things were a little confusing."

"We understood each other"—Briggs smiled, picked up two apples off another keg, and pitched me one—"I'm sure of it. I admire conversation that stretches farther than the weather. Don't get to use it a lot. Sometimes I almost forget how."

"Me too." I pushed up my hat and shoved the apple into my pocket for later. "Back in Cimarron, you said you'd almost give that forty thousand just to see Ned Quarrels lock horns with a couple of the boys." I looked into his eyes. "Is that what you think of me and my partner? Is that what you've thought of us all along"—I held a steady gaze—"that we're a couple of outlaws?"

Briggs flipped open his pocketknife with the snap of his thumb, held it against the apple and turned the apple with his fingertips, peeling it one-handed. "If you was, would you admit it?"

I watched the apple turn, saw the peel crawl down past his wrist. "If I did, would you arrest us?"

He grinned. "If I tried, would I have to kill yas?"

"Jesus," I said under my breath. "What do *you* think?" I looked down, hating to talk about such a thing.

"Yep, I'd have to. That's why I don't think it."

I looked back up. "Then we did understand each other."

"Sounds like it." He took a bite of the apple and let the long peeling dangle from his hand. It bobbed up and down like a weak spring. "All that talk about being an upstanding young man. Heck, you wasn't telling me what you are, you was telling me what you'd like to be." He chewed the apple slowly behind his drooping mustache. "Figured I'd give you a chance to be one. That's more than I've given a man for a long time."

"So you tricked me." I let out a breath, and thought of the morning he'd told us about justice, and people like Quarrels not getting a trial.

"You tricked yourself. You put on a nice suit, came into a nice town, got a washed-up old lawman believing in ya—" He shook his head and laughed. "—Went out of your way to keep from killing Alahambre. You musta been trying to prove something. I swear, Beatty. It's been a joy to watch you on your road to rehabilitation."

"You talk like I've been your prisoner—"

"Aw"—he swiped a hand—"how could you been my prisoner? You're my *star* deputy." He reached out and tapped the point of his pocketknife against the badge on my chest.

"Then what's to keep me from just riding out of here?" I wanted my temper to flare. I wanted to boil over, crack his head with a pistol butt, and be done with it. But all I felt was a strange resolve.

Briggs shrugged. "Your horse, the money . . . and a bunch of other stuff, I reckon. Sure, you could go strike a deal with Quarrels, get back your horse, and leave. You could even sell me out and cut Sonny loose." He glanced toward the sleeping outlaw, then back to me. "But you won't . . . not if you're the young *gentleman,* philosophizing, poker *playing—"* he chuckled "—sharp-eyed horse dealer I took ya for."

I shook my head slowly. "All lies—"

"Naw, Beatty. You ain't lied to me once. There's more to any man than just *one* thing. And I'm counting on you being everything you've said you are."

I just stared at him, and for reasons I didn't understand, I knew he was right. Somehow he'd read me like a nickel novel. Jack had warned me not to get too close, but I had. Now I was stuck with it. I breathed deep. "If anything happens to my friend because of this, I want you to know, the killing won't stop at the Quarrels Gang—"

"*That* one?" Briggs laughed, ignored my threat. "He'll outlive us all. He ain't gave nothing up, not even his name . . . if he's still got one. They'll have to knock him in the head come judgment day." Briggs flipped the apple core up and caught it on the point of his knife. He patted my shoulder. "He'll be all right. We all will, so long as you handle it right." He grinned again. "I've already got us community support."

I pictured the mayor wallowing in the dirt with his bloody foot. "Jesus. I feel like I'm making a deal with the devil."

"Naw sir. Just doing what you have to, to get your horse back."

I turned and walked to the door, started to pull it open and walk out, but his voice stopped me. "Remember one thing, Beatty. If I put my hand on the forty thousand, it all goes back to Cimarron. If I don't, I'll just figure the desert claimed it."

"Don't make me lie to you, marshall. I'd deal out the forty thousand if it'd get my horse back. If I *had* the forty thousand." I looked back at him over my shoulder, trying to see in his eyes if he had any suspicions about the money.

If he did, it didn't show. All I saw was the circle of dim light flicker on his face.

He smiled. With the snap of his fingers the pocketknife closed and disappeared. "Do what you've got to do, *deputy*. But give *me* Ned . . . and take the rest of 'em down."

• 17 •

"So what did you and Briggs talk about?" Jack lay sprawled against a wagon wheel with his rifle across his belly; but his eyes were open and scanning the dark street from beneath his hat brim. The kid lay asleep with his head on the wagon tongue and his pistol on the ground beside him. The night shift had stopped working on Fortenay's. I almost wished they hadn't.

"I ain't sure," I said. I heard a lone coyote cry out. I turned and leaned on my forearms against the wagons and gazed out across the darkness in that direction. I thought for a second of the conversation I'd just had with Briggs, and I let out a breath. "I just ain't sure."

I heard Jack chuckle and spit. "Musta really been something, if you can't repeat it."

"He knows what we are, Jack," I said quietly. "I think he's known it from the start." Again the coyote called out from the stretch of desert. "Probably lucky he didn't leave us laying off the side of a ridge."

There was a silence before Jack spoke. "Well, I ain't too surprised. Figured you'd let something go if you got too close."

I turned and looked down at him. "I didn't tell him nothing about us. You oughta know that."

"You didn't mean to, but you did. He's a lawman . . .

been one all his life. Think he'd live this long, not knowing how to see through a feller? That's why I've stayed back from him as much as I can."

"Then goddamn it, why didn't you stop me—?"

Jack chuckled and shook his head. "I tried . . . since the first day. You ain't listened. You been strung so tight over that horse, you ain't known bullshit from applebutter. You ain't even thrown your boots under that pretty woman's bed." He pinched the bridge of his nose. "Something's wrong there."

"What? Margaret? Come on, Jack, I ain't getting involved with her. She's had enough grief. Think how it would do her. She gets away from a son of a bitch who's nearly killed her, then takes up with me, horse-man for a band of road-agents." I shook my head. Another coyote cried out from another direction, then another. A hound bellowed from among the construction tents. We listened for a second.

"Road-agents." Jack chuckled. "I like that name. Has almost a businesslike ring to it." He spit. "But I wasn't talking about her. I was talking about Carmilla. And if you tell me she ain't as sweet and wild as a Gypsy wedding, I'll leave here tonight and tell everybody you got your head stuck and drowned in a water bucket." He spit, smiled, and shook his head. "*Road-agents.* I'll be goddamned."

"Carmilla hates me, Jack. Can't you see it? She hates nearly everybody . . . I think. But she hates me worse for some reason."

"She's a serious woman on a serious cause," Jack said. "Freedom. Freedom for *all* women. Think that ain't a hell of a job? But that don't make her no less a woman. Probably makes her more."

"Looks like you've put some thought into this."

"Just hate seeing you miss it—" he spit "—you being a friend."

"Yeah . . . well." I looked at him and pictured the creamy

thigh of Helova Knight. I felt bad, not telling him about her, and I took the apple from my pocket and pitched it to him. "Briggs sent it."

He caught it, rolled it around in his hand, and held it. "I've been watching you and her . . . and thinking." He shrugged. "Greta's a fine woman too." He gazed at the apple as he twisted it back and forth in his hand. "We shoulda forgot everything else and stayed with them at the lodge."

Now, what sounded like a whole pack of coyotes had gathered, and they wailed in the distance.

I squatted down and leaned against the wagon wheel. "You make it sound easy, Jack. But I don't think it would've happened." I picked my hat straight up from my head and laid it up on the wagon wheel behind me.

"Me neither. But it beats thinking about getting shot all night."

"I know it." I heard a hollowness in my voice. I slumped farther down, slipped out of my duster catching the shoulders in each hand, draped it back onto the spokes, and whispered to Jack, "How does that look?" Jack nodded. "I wanta blame Briggs for all this," I said, "but I can't really. I can't blame him for Alahambre taking Buck, and that's where it all started." I looked up at the stars. I'd blame the Lord, but he'd deny it. I slid the glades knife from my boot, and pulled the bandanna from around my neck, shook it out, and wadded it in my left hand.

"Briggs used it as a way of getting inside our circle. Now he's in with both feet." Jack spit and chuckled. He raised his hand and rubbed his thumb and finger together. His voice lowered. "Does he know we've got . . . *it?*"

I thought about it. "No." I thought again. "I mean yeah—I mean, hell, I don't know." I rubbed my forehead.

"Hell of a talk y'all had." Jack spit.

"The man's hard to pin down. He implies more than he says." The coyotes had quieted for a minute and now started again as they seemed to close the circle around the town. The hound started into a long howl that ended in a sharp yelp. "But . . . it's costing forty thousand for the band . . . I reckon somebody better dance." I took off the shiny badge and stuffed it in my pocket.

"Sounds like you musta struck *some* kind of understanding."

"Just that he wants Quarrels"—I shrugged—"same as it's always been."

"And you want Buck. Same as it's always been—"

"Yeah."

"And I want the money, same as always. So let's go on with it and keep it simple." He reached down in his lap and jacked a round into his rifle chamber. "Missouri sunrise?"

"Yeah," I said. "It'll let 'em know we're in the business." I looked at Jack's face in the thin glow of light. "You ever gonna learn to do this, some?"

"You ever gonna learn to shoot as good as me . . . so you can cover me?" His face leaned back out of the dim light, and I saw his hat raise up and lay on the wagon wheel, same as mine. I heard the rustle of his coat.

"If I do, will you do some of this?"

"No, I won't," he said.

"Then there you have it." I slid down from the wagon wheel, onto my belly, and beneath the wagon. A coyote let out a cry, and was answered from behind town, out past the tents. "Sounds just like one, don't it?" I said over to Jack, who hadn't moved an inch.

"They was born and raised here," he said. "They oughta know the language."

"Reckon they've seen enough in our firelight to get 'em interested?"

"I *know* how to tend a fire," Jack whispered.

"Hey—" The kid snapped his head up. "Where's he going?"

"Be quiet, Kid," Jack said, barely raising his voice to hearing level.

"Why?" He started to come over but Jack swung the rifle barrel toward him. He stopped. "What's going on here?"

"Just sit still, Kid . . . you're messing with our lives here," I heard Jack say as I turned and crawled along beneath the wagon, to the end of it, where I looked across and saw the deep shadow along the boardwalk. "It's a Missouri sunrise—guerilla style. You don't want to see it." I heard Jack's low voice fade as I rolled quickly across the open street between the wagons and the shadow, and edged along silently with the glades knife and bandanna in my hands, off toward the rows of construction tents and the scattered cries of coyotes moving closer.

I did not stop until I'd worked my way to the edge of the alley that ran back to the rows of tents. There, for a second, I looked back through the darkness at the flickering low light between the wagons, at the dark outline of mine and Jack's dusters draped on the wheels.

I continued on, like a snake, I thought, from shadow to shadow around the stacks of building material, toward the last sound I'd heard from the dog, and out past the tents. When I felt the warm puddle before me, I reached a hand slowly forward, felt the coarse hair of the dead hound, and stopped. It struck me that the first to die was always the innocent, the one that had no part or say in the dark game of bloodletting.

Past the dead hound, an inch at a time, I crawled until my fingertips felt the base of a mesquite bush; I curled myself around it, laying there, listening for the slightest sound of men in the dark.

When I heard a faint metallic click a few yards before me, my hearing targeted it, held its direction until finally I heard an ever-so-slight whisper. I followed it, silent as stone, leading with my fingertips, and listening.

"This is horseshit," I heard a voice whisper a few feet in

front of me, and I waited a second hoping they couldn't hear my heart pounding in my chest or the funeral drum beating in my head.

I inched forward. My fingers rested lightly on something hard and foreign to the sandy earth. And I froze there when I felt the slightest movement of it and realized it was a boot heel. "We could rush that shit-hole and get Sonny quicker than a cat can—"

"Shut up," a voice whispered a couple of feet away; and I drew a quick picture of their position. "This is how he wants it done. Says hit the tents tonight and the whole bunch will give up by morning."

I heard a low chuckle. "I could use a beer from Fortenay's."

"Just shut up," the other man growled.

I could smell them. I looked up and made out the outline of their hat brims against the dark sky. I took a deep silent breath and waited for a second; then I shot up, covering the man's back like a dark spirit, threw my left hand around and covered his mouth with my bandanna as I shoved the glades knife between his ribs, into his heart, and held him tight.

"The hell's wrong with you, Bob?" I heard the other man whisper as the man before me let out a muffled whimper and slumped against me. I looked past his shoulder and saw the other man's hat brim turn toward us. "Bob?" I saw him lean, trying to see from three feet away.

In one motion, I shoved the dead man away, shot forward with my left hand out, stuffing the bandanna against his mouth and clamping my fingers like talons into his jaws. He pitched backwards beneath me. I sank the big knife to the hilt where his ribs met, twisted the blade once quickly and felt him quiver, then melt, gone off to meet his friend somewhere in a place wider than the dark desert. Then I crawled away past them, my ears tuned to the night and my chest warm and gritty with blood and sand.

After my third stop in a wide swing around the tents, I crawled back toward town, back toward Jack's faint call of a night-bird. "God Almighty," a voice called out low and trembling in the darkness ten yards behind me. "Go get Ned, quick!" I heard the rustle of men moving back and forth, but I stopped for a second flat on the ground, to still my trembling, to silence the raging in my chest and let it flow out of me and into the earth. "Lord, look at this!" someone cried out, unable to keep quiet at the sight of what I'd left behind.

I crawled quickly back to the edge of the alley where I knew Jack would be waiting, covering me.

"Whew! How many?" He stared at the front of my wet glistening shirt. I held up four fingers without answering and leaned back against the pile of building material with my chest still heaving.

"Goddamn bastards!" someone raged out in the darkness. Shots spit orange and purple flames in the darkness and we heard bullets thump against the wagons twenty yards away. "Kill them sons a bitches!"

In seconds, I saw lanterns come on inside the tents. Past the tents, we heard the sound of men and horses scurrying away into the night.

I started to ask about the kid, but just then I saw his face in the darkness, four feet from me, staring slack-jawed. "I wanta learn that," he said in a tone that bordered on reverence. I avoided his stare, ignored his words, wiped the glades knife on the bandanna, and threw the bandanna away.

Jack spoke low. "Reckon the construction workers will thank us?"

"They don't even know what was about to happen . . . won't know till morning." I breathed deep.

"Ned'll have to go back now and think things over," Jack said.

"He'll see we ain't schoolboys." I shoved the glades knife

into my boot. "He'll have to come up with something better than coyotes."

"Coyotes, my ass. If I couldn't do better than that, I'd go back to school and take up ciphering for a living." He grinned and winked at the kid.

"Yeah," I said, still hearing the hollowness in my voice. "But they won't." I stripped out of my bloody shirt, wiped it around on my chest, and threw it under a pile of boards. "They'll be back, and it'll get worse before it gets better."

Jack bit off a fresh plug of tobacco and worked it into his jaw. "I'm starting to agree with Briggs. You do worry too much."

Come daylight, I stood up from a shallow, tortured sleep and saw Jack and the kid standing outside the wagons watching the construction workers throw the four bodies into a heap near the boardwalk outside the unfinished barber shop. Briggs stood close by, watching, holding a short rope that drooped down between his hand and Sonny Quarrels's neck. He shot me a curious glance and nodded me toward him as I stepped from between the wagons and stopped. I looked around and smoothed the front of the wrinkled shirt I'd taken from my saddlebags, but I wouldn't go any closer.

"That hound didn't do *this,*" said one of the workers.

"Well it damned sure was some kind of animal," said another. I glanced at the bodies just long enough to realize that the wilds of the desert had crept and fed upon the carnage I'd left behind, then crept back away. Quarrels's men hadn't even gathered their dead.

"I heard shots," said a worker.

"So did I," said another. "But I never saw nothing."

I saw Clay Allison standing on the boardwalk, fully dressed, with a hangover pallor to his face. Shaving cuts dotted his jaw. His eyes drifted down to the knife handle sticking out of my boot, then up to my face with stunned realization. I looked away. "Here," Briggs said, stepping up beside me. He avoided my eyes and stuck the rope into my hand. "Take Sonny to Fortenay's. I'll be along."

I turned, leading Sonny. Clay Allison drifted along the boardwalk, watching me closely, then stepped back as I stepped up and toward the crooked saloon. "I was coming back, you know." He looked me up and down, but I kept walking.

At the door, Sonny hesitated against the rope. "I'm ready to make a deal," he whispered.

I turned and looked at him. Past him, I saw Carmilla standing back up the boardwalk overlooking the bodies. She looked toward me. Her expression was that of someone watching a wild beast on the prowl. I jerked the rope, nearly dragging Sonny off his feet.

"Too late. The killin's commenced," I said in a bitter tone. Clay Allison stood staring as we stepped through the door of Fortenay's.

When I walked inside, I saw Mackay and Tripplet eating breakfast at a corner table, and I could tell by their expressions that they'd seen my gruesome handiwork laying in the street. But I said nothing as I walked to the bar, knocked Sonny from his feet and tied the rope around the bar rail. "Watch him," I called over to Mackay, and I wiped a dirty hand across my face and kept going.

At the foot of the stairs, I stopped and called out to Gustav in the kitchen behind the bar. He poked his head through the door and I ordered a cup of coffee. He nodded. His expression was the same as Carmilla's. Then I walked up the stairs noticing they were not nearly as lopsided as before. Upstairs, I knocked on Margaret Alahambre's door, and slipped inside when she opened it.

"Look at you," she said, standing back and gesturing a hand up and down my dusty clothes. "You look like you've slept in a buffalo wallow." Her face had cleared some. Her eyes looked rested. She wore a clean cotton dress she'd gotten from somewhere, and I noticed she stood much straighter.

"Almost," I said, and I tried to smile. "Looks like you're feeling better?" My voice still sounded tight.

"Yes, thank you." She tapped a hand to her hair. She'd washed her hair and I caught a scent of lilac. "I'm still sore, but I'll be fine." She stepped to the side and motioned me toward a chair. I walked over, took off my hat, and sat down.

"Margaret." I let out a breath. "I have to tell you what happened to Diamond Joe yesterday. I should've told you sooner but I've been kinda busy."

She nodded toward the window. "What's happened out there? I heard shots last night—"

"Somebody killed some of Quarrels's men." She seemed not to hear.

Her eyes drifted across the badge on my chest. "So you're a lawman now?"

"Yeah . . . it was Briggs's idea. It's just until we settle up with Ned Quarrels."

"Why, I think you'll make a fine marshall, Mister Beatty."

"Well, maybe." I suddenly felt ashamed. "But I don't think I'll do it for long."

"Perhaps you should. It's an honorable career. . . ."

I forced a smile. "Not around here, it ain't."

"Yes, I heard about Marshall Briggs shooting the mayor's toes off. That was dreadful."

"He didn't actually shoot his toes off," I said. "Just put a bullet through his foot, is all." I coughed and cleared my throat.

"Oh, I see," she said, as if that somehow lessened the severity of it. She watched my eyes, anticipating the news of her husband.

"And Diamond Joe? You said you have something to tell

me?" She eased down on the bed and folded her hands on her lap.

When I finished telling about her husband, she raised a hand to her dress collar and gazed away for a second. "I suppose I should feel *something* . . . but I don't." She moistened her lips and looked down at her hands. "I hope he didn't suffer, of course. But I would hope the same for anyone, regardless."

"I know," I said quietly. "I figure it was over the second he hit the roof face first. I reckon he was dead by the time he splattered all over the floor—" I saw her face tighten and tremble, and she blinked her eyes as they began to tear. "That is, no ma'am, I don't think he suffered much. I've . . . never . . . known anyone who has fallen off a cliff and through a roof. But as dying goes . . . there's worse ways . . . I reckon." I didn't really know what to say.

After a long second of silence, she took a deep breath, let it out with a sigh, raised her hands slightly, and let them fall back into her lap. "Well, that's that, I suppose. It's a part of my life that's over for good. Now that it's over, it all just seems like a terrible dream. I don't know how I ever allowed myself to become so . . . so trapped." She stopped and looked back down at her hands, as if ashamed.

I stood, stepped over, and knelt before her, laying my hands on hers. "The main thing is, it's over. Try to forget it ever happened and go on from here. You're not guilty of anything. You were an innocent bystander who got caught in the blast of a man's anger. The sooner you realize that, the sooner you can put it behind you and go on with your life."

She slipped a hand from beneath mine, pushed my hair back from my forehead, and rested her hand against my cheek. I felt the grit of dirt on my face; she wiped it away and smiled. "You've been so kind," she said softly. "And yet you still haven't got your horse back. . . ."

"Don't worry, Margaret. I'll get him back. I just want

you to be okay. That's the main thing right now." She looked deep into my eyes and I felt the strangest, strongest urge to kiss her, kiss her softly and gently, perhaps because I felt it had been so long since anyone had done so, and perhaps because I felt it would somehow calm the tremor deep inside my chest.

"Mister Beatty—Jim. When this is all over . . . where will you go?"

"Back to Missouri, for awhile, then back on the auction circuit, why?"

She glanced away. "I know I'm older than you." She touched nervous fingers against her cheek. "Please don't think of me as being forward—"

"Margaret," I said, seeing where she was headed and stopping her. "You're a fine woman." I stood up and stepped back. "You've been through a lot. Maybe you need to think awhile before—"

"I know." She touched her fingers to her lips. "You're right."

She stood up and smiled, reached out and brushed a hand across my shoulder. "Just be careful."

"I will." I touched a finger to my hat.

I left Margaret's room, and as soon as I closed the door, I saw Carmilla look at me from the door to her room. "Wait," I said, but she ducked her head and stepped inside.

I walked over and knocked on the door. When it opened slightly on its own, I peeped through. "I want to talk—"

Carmilla turned from the window with a pistol hanging from one hand, a wrinkled piece of paper from the other. I stopped when I saw a tear running down her cheek. She brushed it away. "What do you want?" Her voice was brittle with emotion. Glancing around the room, I noticed Greta was not there.

"Look," I said, stepping forward with a hand raised before me. I didn't like seeing a pistol in her hand, not after what she'd done to me yesterday, and not after what she'd seen in the street. "We've got to talk. I know what you're thinking. I know you don't like me"—I shrugged—"or anybody for that matter. But things could get a little ugly today—"

"Uglier than that?" She nodded toward the street.

"I'm sorry you saw that, ma'am, but it's going to get—"

"Greta is gone."

"What?" I glanced around the room. "Gone where?"

"She slipped away this morning before dawn . . . to Cimarron, to bring help." She pitched the wrinkled paper away and it fluttered to the bed. "I did not know until I found the note this morning."

"She rode out alone, knowing what could be waiting out there? Damn! Why didn't she say something to me first?"

"She does not need your permission to stay alive, or to keep others from dying—"

I stepped back and forth rubbing my neck.

Her dark eyes followed me. "—And I do not know *what* waits for her out there, but I know what is happening here. The violence has started. It started when the marshall, *your* boss"—she pointed at my badge—"shot the mayor's toes off. Now there are dead men in the street. Greta thought she could stop it."

"Briggs didn't actually shoot his toes off."

"It does not matter. Blood has been spilled, and it will cause more to spill, until someone stops it. You fought in the war, is this not what always happens?"

"Well, yes, but—"

"Then we must have help, si? Or is this all some crazy machismo game to you, some way of showing yourself, like the crazy man who rides naked in the street?"

I stared at her. I did not consider her words, for what was coming was past reasoning and consideration. "You're right," I said quietly. "Something terrible is happening here."

"And because Greta and I are women you expect us to

run and hide. To do as we are told, and watch as you kill each other?" Is that what you expect of women, Mister Beatty? That we be a part of this but have no say in it?"

"No." I slumped and pushed up my hat. "But she shoulda told me before riding out. I don't want her dying because of this."

"You mean because of you." She shook her head. "Briggs is here because of the law—his prisoner. Margaret is here because her pig of a husband beat her." She tossed a hand. "And of course, we all know about your horse . . . Buck. But because of these things, Greta and I had to flee from our home . . . our *home.* Do you *know* how that makes us feel?"

"Well . . . no," I said. "I mean, I hadn't looked at it that way."

"Of course you didn't." I watched her check the action of her pistol. "Did you expect us to cower like rabbits, until you *men* settle your bloody business?" She checked the Smith & Wesson and shoved it down in her waist. "So she went for help, without your permission." She wiped a hand beneath her eye. "And I will wait here and watch for her until she returns. Now go. They will all want to hear of your brave exploits in the night."

I felt low. "You've got me wrong there, ma'am." I looked down at the floor and shook my head. "Nobody hates this any worse than I do—"

"Just go away, Mister Beatty. I do not want to look at you. Go away with your bloody hands . . . and leave me alone."

◆ 18 ◆

Back down at the bar, Briggs stood a few feet away from where I'd tied Sonny to the bar rail. He stood spinning a silver dollar on the bar and looked up as I walked over from the stairs. I saw the drawn look on his face. "That was *some* piece of work," he said in a low tone. I didn't answer.

Gustav appeared with a cup of coffee, slid it before me with a cautious look, and backed into the kitchen without a word. I sipped and glanced around the tavern. Mackay sat dealing himself a game of solitaire, but Tripplet sat leaning from his chair with his ears tuned toward us. Down the bar Clay Allison stood, just staring at me as if in awe. Faces peeped in from the door, then jerked away. "I never expected something like that," Briggs said. "I figured on a straight-up shoot-out."

I looked at him and saw some apprehension in his face. "If you ride in my wagon, you go where I take ya." I took a breath. "See why I'd rather be looked at as a young *gentleman?"*

He looked away.

I saw Councilman Goodlet slip in and walk toward me, almost cowering like a kicked hound.

"I just wanted to let you know there's no hard feelings over yesterday, young man," he said. I saw the fear in his face. "I was a little abrasive—"

"Forget it," I said. I turned away and leaned on the bar beside Briggs.

"Everybody knows Ned Quarrels is a ruthless man, and we're all behind you one hundred per—"

"He said forget it!" Briggs swung around with one hand on the big Dance and looked down at Goodlet's foot. Goodlet scurried backwards and out the door. I shook my head and sipped the coffee.

"Knife-fighter, huh?" I heard Clay Allison's voice and I shot him a cold glance down the bar. His face turned white.

"Just asking," he said, and he raised a cautious hand. "I was coming back to help last night." I just nodded and looked away.

An unnerving stillness settled about the place, broken only by an occasional cough from Mackay. I finished my coffee and slid the cup across the bar.

"The blonde-haired woman rode out before dawn," I said to Briggs.

"She what?" Briggs snapped his eyes to mine. "What on earth was she thinking?"

"I don't know. She went for help," I said. I heard Sonny laugh. I looked down and saw he'd been listening to us; and I walked over, kicked him a solid thump in the stomach, and stepped back to Briggs. Briggs looked surprised. "I'd go after her, if I thought it'd do any good."

Briggs rubbed his jaw. "It won't. Best we can hope is she either made it through or died quick. These boys play rough."

"They ain't seen *rough,"* I said. I picked up Briggs's silver dollar and flipped it beside my empty cup. He looked at it and grinned at me. I just stared at him. "They'll be here today, Briggs. I've brought them to you. They'll either be madder than hornets and ready to fight, or else they'll offer me a deal to sell you out. All's I ask is that you go along with me till it's time to make our move." I turned and started for the door.

"I will," he said, "so long as it don't get between me and the law."

"The law went out of business, Briggs," I said from the door. "Last night, about the time you pitched me the apple."

I'd started away from Fortenay's and back to the wagons when I heard a hushed voice call my name. I looked toward the alley and saw Goodlet cringe back. "Please, I have to speak to you."

I walked over. "What is it, Goodlet?"

His voice trembled. "Mister Beatty, we have to stop this madness before it goes any further." I just looked at him; he held up a shaky hand. "I couldn't tell you in there because of that crazy Briggs. But Quarrels can be dealt with. He'll reason. I know he will. He just wants his brother back."

"It ain't that simple," I said. Goodlet had no idea about the money. "He's got my horse." I started to walk away.

"But he'll give it back, I swear it—I know he will."

I stopped, looked at him and took a deep breath. "I wish it was so. But Briggs ain't giving nothing up. You saw what he did to the mayor—"

"Then give Briggs up. You be our law here—"

"There's no way," I said. "And you better hope Briggs don't hear this kind of talk." I turned and headed for the wagons.

Almost there, I heard Mackay cough behind me. I looked back. "Mister Beatty, wait up," he called out; and I stood there as he walked briskly through the dust. He stopped and stood panting for a second. "I declare, sir, keeping up with you will wear a man out."

I glanced around. "What is it, Mackay? I'm in a hurry here."

"I know." He took a hold of my shirt sleeve for balance and tried to catch his breath. "I feel I *must* offer my assistance."

I shook my head. "Listen to you, Mackay. You sound

like a mule's kicked you. What's being out here in the sun going to do to you?"

"I may look a bit off my game. But, sir, I'm as crisp as a new dollar—"

"Nothing doing, Mackay. I'm sorry, but you ain't up to it. Go play cards or fix some teeth or something." I saw a strange gleam come into his eyes, and I felt something hard poke against my ribs. I looked down between us, saw the Uhlinger still in his vest pocket, but saw a short-barreled Colt cocked and pressed against my ribs. I raised my face slowly and let out a breath. "All right. You're a slick draw. You got me. What does that prove? This ain't no card table shoot-out coming. It's a full-blown gun battle."

He uncocked the pistol and it disappeared inside his coat. "You, sir, are a stubborn, narrow-sighted individual." He shook his head and turned loose of my sleeve. "Come on. At least let me accompany you to your wagon fortress."

I grinned, and we walked toward the wagons. "Why are you so damn determined to get into this anyway? Everybody else is running the other way."

"Call it my southern contrariness, I suppose. But how can I just stand by idly when so much is going on?" He coughed. "Life must be lived, experienced to its highest level of intensity." He made a sweeping gesture. " 'I reply in sweet refrain to both the pleasure and the pain.' " He coughed and smiled.

I returned his smile as we walked on. "Is that something they taught you to say in dental school, something to tell folks right before you yank their heads loose?"

Mackay laughed and coughed. "You have to admit, it provides a certain amount of comfort for one without hope."

"We're not without hope here," I said, as if he'd been talking about our situation.

"Indeed not, sir."

Inside the wagon barricade, Jack stood cleaning a shotgun with an oily rag. "Where's the kid?" I asked, looking around for him. Jack nodded at me and shot Mackay a glance. "Morning, Mackay." He grinned and spit. "Kid's gone off to brag about last night."

"Damn, I wish he wouldn't do that," I said.

"Why not?" Jack grinned. "It'll keep everybody in line." He turned to Mackay. "Will you be staying for tea?"

"Nothing would please me more, but I'm afraid I've exhausted all effort with Mister Beatty here."

"He's hardheaded. I coulda told ya." Jack looked the shotgun over, laid it down, and picked up another. He glanced at Mackay as he broke it open. "Why do you want to get mixed up in this, anyway? Thought gambling was what piqued your interest."

"Careful," I said to Jack before Mackay could answer. "He'll start giving you a bunch of dental talk." I grinned at Mackay.

"You pull teeth?" Jack spoke as he ran the rag along the barrel.

"That *was* my profession." Mackay stifled a cough. "I have forsaken it for the allure of the West . . . among other things."

"Folks out here need their teeth pulled too." Jack slipped shells from his pocket and loaded the shotgun. He eyed Mackay. "You've got bad lungs, don't ya? So you figure you got nothing to lose."

Mackay didn't answer.

"Your patients didn't take to you being in their faces, breathing and coughing on them, right?"

"Jesus, Jack!" I felt my face redden.

"That's quite all right, Mister Beatty. Your partner has a keen level of perception." Mackay smiled. "I spend a good deal of time denying my condition, as if that will somehow make it go away. But it doesn't hurt to have it presented to me from time to time, especially in such rare candor." He spread a wide smile.

"Just saying what I see." Jack shrugged. "I mean no offense."

"No offense taken," Mackay said. He turned to me, and rubbed his hands up and down his coat. "So, then . . . having bared my soul. What do you say, Mister Beatty? Is there room for me here in your merry band?"

"A man with nothing to lose is a dangerous man to be around, Mackay. Even more so if he's *looking* to die."

"On the contrary, Mister Beatty, I'm not *looking* to die. I'm looking to *live* . . . every precious second that I can. I've not blindly reconciled myself to the inevitability of Madam Death's cold embrace. I simply enjoy the luxury of flirting with her with no fear of reprisal." He rolled his hand and curtsied like a stage performer.

I grinned and scratched my head beneath my sweat band. "I ain't sure what you said"—I glanced up at Jack, saw him barely nod his approval—"but if this looks like fun to you, grab some iron and hang onto it."

By ten o'clock, sunlight glistened on the dirt street, pressed its weight on the backs of the construction workers, and rose back upwards from metal and pitched roofs in a swirl of angry heat. The noise of nailing, cutting, and unloading material never stopped, not for a second, and the sound of it forged a dull pain in my forehead.

I looked around at Mackay sitting on a handkerchief in the dirt with a shotgun across his lap, practicing his deal with a worn deck of cards. The kid leaned on the far end of the wagon puffing a Mexican brown, and Jack walked back and forth with a rifle cradled in his arms. Briggs had untied Sonny from a wagon wheel and taken him to Fortenay's for water. I turned back and watched the cluttered street.

"Reckon this bunch will get out of the way long enough for Quarrels to attack?" I heard Jack say as he walked past me.

"I don't know," I said. I squinted my eyes shut for a

second and squeezed the bridge of my nose between my thumb and finger. I shook my head, trying to shake off the headache and the noise. "Beats all I've ever seen," I said. "You'd think people would clear the streets for a gun battle." I let out a breath and gazed back up the street, searching for any riders who might weave their way through the piles of lumber and the thrashing humanity.

I looked down the street and had to blink and look again in order to believe my eyes. "Aw hell," I said under my breath. Then my voice kicked up a notch. "Jack, quick! Look at this."

I spoke over my shoulder without taking my eyes off the white flag weaving through the workers and the stacks of lumber. Jack leaned in on one side and Mackay on the other. "So they've decided to deal with us," Jack said quietly.

Up the street, the old ladder maker stepped out of the alley and stared up at three riders carrying a white flag tied to a rifle barrel. He scratched his head and watched as they rode toward Fortenay's.

"This beats all," Jack said, and he chuckled under his breath as he laid his rifle across the wagon and leaned his face into the stock. "They don't even see us here. Pow," he said, sighting down the rifle. Then he looked up and grinned. "Ever seen anything like this, Mackay?"

"No indeed! See why I had to be a part of it?"

The kid knocked the fire from his Mexican brown, coughed, and dropped it in his pocket. "You okay there, Hank?" I called over to him. He grinned and spun a finger in the air.

The riders started to step down at Fortenay's, but a miner came out and pointed toward our wagon barricade. When they looked our way and turned their horses, they had to wait until two workers carrying a long board crossed in front of them. I looked around and saw Mackay walking to the end of the wagon. "Where you going, Mackay?"

"I thought I'd flank them, sir," he said over his shoulder. I shrugged and looked back at the riders. They rode closer, gazing about, checking rooftops and doorways.

"Where's Briggs?" the kid asked. He slipped out his pistol, spun it, checked the action, and held it down his side. I noticed his hand seemed steady and sure.

"He's at Fortenay's," I said, glancing about the busy street. "Good thing they didn't go in there. They could've taken Sonny and this would have all been over." I watched quietly until the riders were within ten yards, then raised my rifle over the wagon to let them see it. "That's close enough," I called out.

The middle rider stopped, then stepped his horse a couple feet closer while the other two hung back and eyed our barricade. The front rider carried the white flag tied to his rifle barrel; he gestured across our wagons. "What's this?" He raised his rifle and propped it up on his saddle.

"You know what it is," I said. "Now speak your piece. We been ready for you all morning." I stared at him. He was a tall man with a pencil-thin mustache and eyes that shined beneath the shadow of his hat brim. Even from Briggs's crudely drawn poster, I could tell this was Jake The Rake. The other two must've been a couple of flunkies just sent to cover his back, although from the stories I'd heard, The Rake wouldn't need cover. He turned his head slightly, spit, ran a fingertip across his thin mustache, and turned back to me. "Ned says to tell you this can all be straightened out." He glanced at each of us behind the wagon, then back to me. "If you're the one who lost your horse, Ned says tell you all you've got to do is pick it out and you'll get it back." He smiled, a thin tight smile that offered nothing. "All's he wants is his kid brother, Sonny"—his tight smile narrowed—"and anything *else* you have of his. We're reasonable people. Nobody has to die."

I shot a quick glance around the street, didn't see Briggs, then stared back at The Rake. I wondered why he hadn't mentioned the money. "It ain't that simple," I said, "and we both know it." I watched his eyes as best I could to see if we both knew what we were talking about. "A federal marshall has Sonny. I got nothing to do with that. I just came for my horse." I glanced across the three of them and back to The Rake. "You know the rest."

"Yeah, we know old Briggs is here. We just gotta get past that part, right?" The Rake raised a finger to his hat brim and pushed it up an inch. Since he wasn't mentioning the money, I figured we had a separate deal going between us somehow. "Ned figures you got in this because of Diamond Joe, and everything went to hell from there." He smiled; it was the smile of an undertaker sizing a client. This was a cold and dangerous man. "He's not real pleased with Joe for letting all this happen."

"Diamond Joe's still alive?" I was truly amazed. I glanced at Jack, and back to The Rake.

"Yeah, but he probably wishes he wasn't," The Rake said. "I've never seen a man so ruined. Says you caused it all . . . even burnt down his house and stole his wife."

"You had to be there," I said. I glanced around but still saw no sign of Briggs. Maybe Briggs had seen them ride in and was laying low with Sonny. "Tell Ned I've got no say about letting his brother go. But if he's interested in anything I *might* have, I'm willing to dicker—"

"Like hell," Jack said under his breath. I gigged him with my elbow.

"I hear you," said The Rake. "Ned says tell you horses bring a high price in this country." He backed his horse and glanced over his shoulder at the other two. I saw Mackay step out of a doorway. He leaned against a post with the shotgun hanging on his arm. The Rake's eyebrows raised slightly when he looked at Mackay. Mackay tipped a finger to his brim and smiled.

"You a part of this?" The Rake called out to him. There seemed to be a twinge of concern flickering across his eyes.

"I, sir, am the proverbial *innocent bystander.*" Mackay nodded cordially and raised his cigar to his mouth.

"Wait a minute," said one of the riders, sidestepping his horse a couple of feet. "Nobody said nothing about—"

"Shut up," The Rake snapped. He turned back to me. "If all you want is your horse, I'm sure it's for sale. But that means you clear out of here as soon as you get it, and leave the rest of it between Ned and the marshall."

I glanced about the street; some of the workers had stopped and watched, but most were still working, banging hammers and sawing wood. "You'll be facing a whole town here," I said. "These people are ready to defend what's theirs. I might do better just waiting it out and—"

"Nice try," The Rake said, cutting me off. "Right now, you stand a chance of buying back your horse and riding out. Don't start pushing your luck. Some of the boys ain't real happy about the mess you made of their friends last night."

"They ain't seen nothing yet," I said. "If I don't get my horse back—"

"Hold it right there, Rake!" I heard Briggs yell. The Rake and his men jerked their eyes toward him as he stepped from Fortenay's and started walking with his big Dance pistol raised, leveled, and cocked. I cursed under my breath. Mackay stepped off the boardwalk and reached for Briggs's arm, but Briggs ducked past him and kept walking. "You three are under arrest. Skin 'em slow and pitch 'em down."

The Rake looked at me. "You better do some quick thinking, before Ned changes his mind. We're five miles out, near the high pass—"

"You hear me, Rake! I said drop your irons!"

"Briggs, goddamn it!" I cocked the rifle just to let The Rake know that I'd cover Briggs if they tried anything. "They come under a white flag. We're trying to work things out. Get the hell in here!"

"Damn!" Jack said beside me. I heard the kid let out a

short squeal and jack a round into his rifle chamber.

Briggs's hand stiffened on his pistol butt.

"We came to settle up," The Rake said, glancing at me and tightening his hand on his rifle. Out the corner of my eye, I saw Mackay raise the shotgun and slowly open his long dress coat. I caught a glint of sunlight on the pearl handle of the Uhlinger and the short-barreled Colt.

"I know, damn it, hold up!" I said to The Rake, and I quickly turned to Briggs. "Marshall, for God's sake! Give me some room here!"

Briggs raised his free hand to silence me. "You've done your part, now the law'll take over." Most of the hammering stopped. The sawing died down slowly.

"He's dead," I heard Jack whisper.

"Briggs," I said, as calmly as possible, "this is only three of them . . . sent to talk, is all."

"We'll take what we can get," Briggs said. "I'm not bound to honor a flag of truce with the likes of such blackguards."

"Yep," Jack whispered, "he's dead all right." All the while, as Briggs spoke, Mackay had stepped closer and closer behind him, until he was in arm's reach. I saw Mackay make a slight sign to me with his hand, and I nodded my approval. The Rake saw it, too, but he and his men sat tensed, ready for anything.

I raised my hands, holding my rifle in one, and started around the wagon as I spoke. "Now everybody stay calm here." I watched Mackay lean forward behind Briggs. "Marshall, you've gotta let this thing go for now—" When I rounded the wagon, I stopped ten feet from The Rake's horse. "This ain't no time to go throwing down—"

Mackay threw the shotgun around Briggs, pinning the marshall's arms to his sides. A shot exploded into the ground from Briggs's big Dance pistol. I spun toward The Rake and his men with my rifle cocked, to keep them from taking advantage. Briggs slung himself back and forth.

"Turn me loose, you damn fool!" But Mackay hung on. I leveled my rifle up at The Rake.

"Okay, Rake," I said, "get out of here, quick." I glanced at Mackay holding Briggs, his coattails wiping back and forth as Briggs struggled against his grip.

The Rake backed his horse, turned it and spoke down to me in a lowered tone. "Five miles out . . . think about it."

"I will." I nodded. "Now get out of here." And I covered them as they weaved down the street.

"Damn!" I let out a tense breath, stepped over, and took Briggs's gun from his hand while he struggled with Mackay. "Marshall, this was for your own good." I nodded to Mackay. "Let him go."

Mackay turned loose and took a step back. Briggs shot a glance over his shoulder at Mackay, then back to me. "My own good? You don't know what a terrible thing you just did, Mister Beatty. You never . . . *never,* trust the likes of those kinda snakes! Now give me back my gun and let's get after them."

I stepped back. "Not until you cool off, marshall. They came to talk. You said you'd give me room here—"

"Don't tell me what they're trying to do! They came looking for an edge. Like as not, you've just got somebody killed here!"

"Beatty!" I heard The Rake's voice from up the street and spun toward the sound. "While you're thinking . . . think of this." Before I even located The Rake, I heard the shot.

I crouched with my rifle ready, glanced around, saw Briggs standing stiff as a poker and Mackay crouched beside him scanning the piles of lumber and delivery wagons with his hand inside his coat. "I . . . told you," I heard Briggs say in a choked voice. I turned just as he took a step forward. His hand went to his chest and he pitched forward into the dirt. A circle of blood spread across his back as I lunged toward him.

"Oh, no!" I grabbed him as soon as he hit the ground and turned him over quickly.

"My goodness," Mackay said, sliding in beside me, tearing open the marshall's shirt and pressing a wadded-up handkerchief against the gaping wound.

"Sonsabitches," I heard Jack yell. I saw him run to a horse at a hitch rail, jerk the reins loose, and jump on its back.

"I . . . told you," Briggs gasped.

"Lay still, marshall," I said. I glanced up at the construction workers gathered, and I saw Carmilla standing beside the kid. "Somebody get a doctor, damn it!" Carmilla turned and ran off toward the unfinished doctor's office. "Tell him we're coming," I shouted to her. "Help me, Kid!"

The kid jumped in with me and Mackay; the three of us picked up Briggs and carried him toward Doctor Eisenhower's. The construction workers crowded around us and we had to force our way through them. Briggs's blood left a trail behind us and soaked the handkerchief on his chest. "Hang on, marshall!"

Past the crowd, I saw Jack pounding out of town after The Rake and his men. "Damn it, Jack," I said. Someone slung open the doctor's door. "Kid, go help him . . . stop him!"

"Yeee-hii!" The kid turned loose of Briggs and disappeared as Mackay and I struggled through the narrow doorway.

When we'd laid Briggs on a long table, Doc Eisenhower shoved me out of the back room. Mackay threw off his coat and had started rolling up his sleeves. "I have some limited medical training. I can help," I'd heard him say to the doctor before the door closed in my face. Now I paced back and forth, slapping my hat against my leg under the cold stare of Carmilla who leaned against the wall with her arms crossed. "Okay," I said finally, stopping and returning her cold stare. "Whatever you're thinking, spit it out."

"There is nothing to say." She slung her hair back from her face. "What do you have that is so important to Quarrels? It is not just his brother." She nodded toward the closed door. "What are you keeping from the marshall—from all of us? What is going on between you and Quarrels? Why does he send in his best gunman just to talk—?"

"Nothing," I snapped. I ran my hand across my wet brow. "Nothing that concerns you." I paced back and forth. "I only want my horse back." I glanced at the closed door, heard Briggs moan, and I paced more. "Jesus," I whispered, and I looked back at Carmilla. "I wouldn't have had this happen for the world." I heard my voice crack and felt my throat tighten. "I mean—"

"Of course not. But now it is too late. You will scheme, betray, do whatever you have to do for this horse? You will have people die?"

I started to say something when the front door opened and Margaret stepped inside. "I just heard—" She held one arm across her sides. "Is it the marshall? Is he . . . ?"

"He's shot bad," I said. I gestured toward the closed door. "One of Quarrels's bunch shot him. It was . . . my fault, I reckon." I paced back and forth; Margaret stepped in and stopped me with a hand on my arm.

"No . . . no, it's not your fault. Don't blame yourself—" She tried to lay a hand on my arm as I paced by.

"And your pig of a husband is still alive," I heard Carmilla say.

"Joe? Still alive?" She glanced from Carmilla to me. "But you said—" Her hand fell to her side.

"I know," I said, and I paced again. "Evidently nothing will kill the son of a bitch."

"Well, I'll be damned." Margaret's voice turned flat in disappointment. "You told me he fell off a cliff—went through the roof." She looked at Carmilla but spoke to me. "Said he was probably dead before he splattered all over the floor . . . is what he said." She jerked her head toward me in exasperation.

"Look, I'm sorry," I said. I stopped pacing and turned facing them, Carmilla with crossed arms and a hateful stare and Margaret with a hand on her hip and a tight expression on her face. "I was sorry when I told you he was dead . . . now I'm sorry to tell you he's alive."

"Then . . . he'll be coming for me," Margaret said.

I stopped and turned toward her. "I'm afraid he might."

"But he'll kill me! Mister Beatty, what will I do?" She looked to Carmilla and me with pleading eyes.

"I'm sorry, Margaret," I said.

"Will you kill him for me, Mister Beatty?" She reached out a trembling hand. "Please! When he comes here . . . kill him. Will you . . . will you, for *me?*" I saw the look of fear and desperation in her eyes.

Carmilla straightened from the wall and looked her up and down.

"Jeez . . . Margaret," I said.

"Why in the name of God did I ever get mixed up with you?" She threw her hands over her face. I stared at her, not believing she would say such a thing.

"You can not blame him because your husband beat you," said Carmilla. "Blame yourself for allowing it."

I looked back and forth between them. Margaret lunged forward and grabbed my arm. "I'll pay you! Please kill him," she said in a shaky voice. "I have some money in a bank in Santa Fe—my father left it to me—" She turned my arm loose and wrung her hands. "I'll get it and give it to you!"

"Don't," I said. I raised a hand, looked at the two of them, shook my head, stepped out the door, and headed to Fortenay's On The Frontier.

• 19 •

When I walked into Fortenay's, I saw RC Allison leaning against the bar, watching Sonny Quarrels. Sonny sat shackled to the bar rail, eating from a plate someone had sat before him. "Gonna cut his head off?" I heard Allison ask. His words were distinct but struggling against the early stages of a whiskey slur.

"No," I said without looking around. I stared down at Sonny and saw a smile crawl across his face.

"I heard what happened to ole Briggs," RC said. "Damn shame. It'd never happened if I'd been there. I was on my way out there to help you, you know. Hell, I love a good fight."

I turned and stared at RC for a second, then back down to Sonny Quarrels.

"So that's that," Sonny said in a low voice, as if the two of us shared a secret. "Briggs is done for. No reason to hold me now, huh?"

I just stared at him.

"I know you've got the guts to cut his head off." I heard RC but didn't answer. "If you don't, by God, I will." I heard him bang the bottle on the bar.

I glanced back over my shoulder and saw him talking to himself in the mirror. "Don't worry about him," Sonny said quietly. "He's still too sober to do anything. By the time he's drunk, I'll be gone, huh? Ain't that right? And you'll have your horse back." He raised a piece of cornbread to his mouth. "Pretty slick the way you played it. Even kicking me around a little to make it look good?" He winked.

I studied his eyes and realized he had good reason to think that Jack and I had set Briggs up. We'd told him we wanted to make a deal. I reckon he thought this was it. I started to tell him otherwise, but I stopped myself. Why not let it end, I thought. With Briggs down, with The Rake already telling us that Ned wanted to settle things, there was nothing to stop me from cutting Sonny loose and trading him for Buck. Nobody but Briggs cared one way or the other.

"We'll see," I said. I felt terrible saying it. It was as if I really had set the old marshall up. "Briggs has the key somewhere. I'll have to get it—"

"Good boy," Sonny grinned. He nodded up toward the bar. "Now, run me off a beer and pass it down here. We'll drink to Briggs on his road to hell."

I felt my jaw tighten and fought the urge to bury my boot in his grinning face. I tried to fake a smile but my face only twitched. From the street, I heard a long squeal as pounding hoofs skidded to a halt. "In a minute," I said. I turned and walked outside.

Jack was stepping down from his saddle when I stopped at the edge of the boardwalk. "How's Briggs?" He turned just as sunlight flashed off my badge and hit him in the eye. He threw up a hand as a visor. "Damn! Can you tone that thing down a little, before it blinds somebody?"

"Sorry," I said. I tried adjusting the badge but it did no good. I started to take it off, but felt bad about it for some reason. "It's touch and go with Briggs, but looks like he'll make it." I glanced past him at the kid, still in his saddle. I saw the reins to the two flunkies' horses in the kid's hand, and I leaned and saw their bodies draped over the saddles. Flies swarmed. The kid grinned and shook the reins. "Got 'em both, *pow! pow!* one shot each, one in the head, one in the heart. First shot went in right here—" he tapped a finger on his chest "—came out just above his—"

"What about The Rake?" I turned to Jack while the kid rattled on.

"He got away," Jack said, running a hand across his brow. He leaned close to me as I saw the kid slap himself on the head and rock back in his saddle, imitating how the bullet smacked the outlaw, giggling with delight. "It's time we settle up with Ned and get on down the road, don't you think?" Jack glanced around.

I just looked at him. He shrugged. "I mean, with Briggs down"—he waved a hand around the street—"and nobody giving a damn, let's get Buck and *vamonos.*" His voice dropped almost to a whisper. "You know we can dicker a good chunk of the money, even if we have to give part of it back." He smiled and slapped me on the shoulder.

Across the littered street, I saw the mayor on crutches being helped along by Sheriff Kersey, whose face and hands were still hidden behind a thick wrap of gauze. When they saw me look toward them they quickly ducked out of sight. A few workers had stopped hammering long enough to stare down from rooftops at the two bodies, then shrugged and went back to work.

I let out a breath. "Yeah, Jack. It's time to haul up." It was the same thing I'd been thinking, but somehow, hearing Jack say it made me feel even more like I'd betrayed Briggs. "Nobody here gives a damn."

Jack cocked an eye. "You ain't getting one of your, 'let's do something good just for the sake of doing it' attitudes, are ya?"

I looked down and shook my head. "Naw, I reckon not."

I saw Mackay and Tripplet walk up and look at the two bodies. Mackay had the shotgun in the crook of his arm. "Shoulda seen it," the kid said to them. "*Pow! pow!* One shot each. One in the head, the other . . ." He rattled as Jack and I stepped inside Fortenay's.

"The kid's a killer, straight up and cold-blooded as a scorpion," Jack said, letting out a breath. "He even scares me."

I stopped just inside the door and looked at him.

"I mean it. He killed both them boys, rode 'em down and shot 'em before I got a chance."

"You meant to do the same, didn't ya?"

"Yeah, but I was wild-eyed mad over Briggs. The kid wasn't. It was just a lark to him. He was just having fun." He shrugged. "They coulda been gonna surrender, far as I know."

"Hey! There's my buddy," Allison called out, seeing Jack come in.

"Aw hell," Jack said between us. "What's RC doing here?"

"He was guarding Sonny for Briggs," I said.

Allison let out a whoop and slapped the bar. "Tell this peckerwood bartender where-all they've heard of me." He banged his glass on the bar, splattering Gustav with a whiskey spray.

"Hello, RC," Jack said in a flat tone. He tossed a hand as we walked on to Sonny Quarrels. "Hell, they've heard of you everywhere. Spain . . . China . . ."

"See, goddamn it! I ain't afraid of no sumbitch." He toasted himself in the mirror.

"He's getting drunk quicker than I thought," Sonny said. He rattled his shackles when we stopped and looked down at RC. "We need to make a move here." He looked up at Jack and nodded at the bar. "Pour me a beer."

Jack's face twitched, same as mine had done. I thought I saw his boot start to swing back, but he stopped himself. "Sonny. Don't think we're friends, you and me. You'll just get your feelings hurt."

"Yeah?" Sonny sneered. "When my brother—" His voice

cut off as Jack's hand shot down, snatched him by the throat, and jerked his head up until the shackle chain snapped tight against the bar rail.

"Have the decency to keep your mouth shut while Briggs's blood is still warm—"

I grabbed Jack's arm just as his pistol flashed from his holster and swung back in a high arch. "Ease up, Jack!"

Sonny's face turned blue; his eyes bulged. "Turn him loose, Jack! He can't breathe!" I yelled.

"Attaboy," Allison yelled. "Give him a butcher knife."

Jack shoved him back and let him go. Sonny's head clipped the brass bar rail and a muffled ring resounded along the floor like a halfhearted church bell. "Don't open your mouth again," Jack said, "or I'll feed you to that lunatic."

"Get ahold of yourself, Jack," I said. I shook his arm. "You gotta watch him while I go get the key from Briggs."

Jack spoke to me, but with his eyes riveted on Sonny's. "Then hurry up, or I'll let RC roll his head outta here like a cantaloupe."

I backed away. "Just watch him, Jack." I turned and left, glancing back on my way out.

The raising crew had just leaned a long pole against the side of Fortenay's as I left there and hurried toward the unfinished doctor's office. I saw Fortenay walking back and forth in the street with his head cocked to the side, inspecting his newly straightened building and brand new sign. "What do you think of her, Beatty?" He beamed and waved a hand as if nothing else was going on in the world.

I looked back, up at the new sign, and nodded. "Nice," I called out, "but he spelled your name wrong."

"Goddamn it!" Fortenay bellowed.

The kid had slipped off his horse and stood holding his hand under one of the dead outlaws' chins. He swatted flies and pointed to the bullet hole for Tripplet to get a better look. Tripplet leaned forward with his mouth gaping. He reached out, tapped the outlaw's forehead, then jerked his finger back and rubbed it on his pants leg. Mackay stood off a few feet near the wagons, a thumb hooked in his vest, cradling the shotgun, puffing a cigar, and scanning the street in both directions.

Above Fortenay's, Carmilla stood in the window. I knew she was thinking about Greta, wondering if she'd made it, wondering if she was ever coming back.

I had to get the key from Briggs and get the shackles off Sonny. The thought of letting him go sickened me; but I saw nothing else to do.

When I stepped down from the boardwalk to cross an alley, Erlander and three of his men stepped out. I nearly bumped into them. "Excuse me," I said. I tried to sidestep them.

"Hey, not so fast," Erlander said. He grabbed my forearm and I jerked to a halt. "We was just talking about you."

I smelled a vapor of whiskey swirling about him like a dark cloud. I jerked my arm free. "I've got no time for ya right now," I said. I tried to walk on.

"Make time," said one of his men, blocking my way. His hand slid into the nail apron around his waist. The rest of them gathered around me slowly. I looked from one to the other, and saw nothing to do but stand my ground.

"Yeah," said Erlander. He took a step forward. "You're starting to cost us money here."

"You're drunk," I said. "Let's talk later—"

"Who do you bastards think you are?" said one of the others. "Some of the merchants were aiming to give us a draw on our pay today. But after that cutting last night . . . they're holding up, to see what happens when Quarrels's bunch rides in."

"Boys," I said. I spread my hands slowly. I reminded myself of Briggs. "I'm about to get everything settled here. Now don't do something stupid."

"Settled how?" Erlander tapped a finger on my chest; I

looked at it and he pulled it back. "Like you settled it last night, cutting them boys—?"

"Them *boys* came to kill y'all," I said. "Now go on about your business. . . . Let me take care of things."

Erlander took a step back and laid his hand on the pistol in his belt. I noted that after shooting Bryce, he no longer carried it in an apron. "With the mayor and the sheriff crippled up, I'm speaking for the town. We want you all out of here, including Briggs."

I shook my head. "Can't move Briggs right now. He's in bad shape. It could kill him." I was just saying anything I could, figuring to talk everything down and get their minds off fighting.

"Then let him die out in the desert," Erlander said. "We've got money coming and building to do. Don't think I won't leave you laying—" his voice cracked and he swallowed hard "—dead in the street." I saw his jaw muscles clench tight. His eyes looked haunted and wild.

I looked him up and down and realized that killing Bryce was working on his mind. But instead of facing the terrible thing he'd done, he'd poured whiskey over it, and tried to numb his brain to it. Now the whiskey had taken a strange turn, and it had his blood pumping, ready to prove to himself that he could do it again. "I see," I said in a quiet voice. Without any sudden move, I drew my pistol slowly, watching all of them, but keeping my eyes on Erlander's. "You're wondering how Bryce felt when you smoked him, ain't ya?" I cocked my pistol slowly, hearing the long metallic click beneath my thumb. "Wondering what was the last thing he saw, the last thing he thought . . . last thing he felt." I leveled the pistol inches from his face, staring deeper into his eyes. "Wondering if he knew he was soiling himself . . . and tried to keep from it."

"What do we do, boss?" one of the workers said in a whisper. But Erlander didn't answer. Sweat ran down and dripped from his nose.

"Everybody wonders . . . the first time," I said quietly. "They get drunk, go crazy, try to deny it, justify it, even try to apologize for it in their minds. Them that believe in God ask Him to forgive 'em . . . and them that don't . . . well, they ask anyway. Some go looking for somebody to take 'em out of their misery." I waited a second and tightened my finger on the trigger. "Is that where you're at right now?"

"Boss?" One of the workers whispered again, but Erlander took a shaky step back, still staring in my eyes. He hesitated a second, took another step—his men moved to the side—and another, then turned, threw a hand to his mouth, and disappeared back into the alley.

I let the pistol slump to my side; I uncocked it. I wouldn't be a lawman for all the money in the world, I thought, letting out a breath. "Now listen to me," I said, raising my voice to the other workers who stood staring with their mouths open. "You boys ain't gunmen. . . . Neither is your boss. Y'all handle the cutting and nailing and I'll take care of the rest."

All but one of the workers backed away and drifted into the alley. "What'd you do to him?" the last one asked, nodding toward the alley. I noticed his hand still in the apron.

"Talked sense to him, is all." I nodded toward his apron. "Now you raise your hand out of there real easy-like and get back to work." I saw his hand come up slowly, empty, and he rubbed his fingers together. "And be careful on them roofs." I was just saying words to wind things down. "I once knew an ole boy, fell off a roof and landed straddle of a buck saw."

"My God," he said, watching me curiously and wondering why they hadn't done what they started out to do. He crossed himself and stepped back into the alley.

Me too, I thought. I wiped a hand across my brow, glanced back and saw Mackay watching from near the wagons. He grinned, clamped the shotgun under his arm, and clapped his hands together slowly and silently. I shook my head and walked to Doctor Eisenhower's office.

As soon as I stepped inside and closed the door, I clenched my hands in front of me to keep them from shaking. The old doctor sat sprawled on a wooden bench, wearing worn-out house shoes, a foot propped up on an ottoman and a bottle of whiskey in his bloodstained hand. "What in the world is wrong with you, young man?" His free hand hung over the arm of the bench and jiggled a skeleton hanging from a peg on the wall. "You look like you've swallowed a bucket of spiders." The skeleton rattled like a muted wind chime.

I ran a shaking hand down my shirt. "Place is getting on my nerves." I thought I heard my voice quiver. "How's Briggs? Can I talk to him?"

"Yep." Eisenhower raised one of the skeleton's bony hands and waved it at me. "But he won't answer." He threw back a shot and hissed. His big belly rolled, then settled. "He's still out. It's the best thing for him right now. What's got you so jumpy?"

"What's got me—? Do you know what-all's going on here, doctor?"

He chuckled. "All you young lawmen are alike, skittish as hell until you get some experience." He glanced at the skeleton and jiggled its hand. "Right, Clyde? Ole Clyde here was a *Tejas* Ranger for many years. Made the mistake of dying here in *Nuevo Mejico.* Nobody would pay to bury him." He picked a piece of lint from the skeleton's kneecap, examined it and flipped it away. "Took two days to boil him down. Looks good though, don't he?"

I just shook my head. "You didn't see a key in Briggs's clothes, by any chance?"

"Yep. That and some change, a dried-out buckeye, and a picture of his boy." He fished inside his vest pocket and pitched me the key. "Figured you'd need this."

I caught it. "Good, I need it to let Sonny—" I stopped

and shot him a glance. "His boy? I didn't know he—"

"Aw, yeah. Of course his wife died years ago. And his boy got murdered, shot in the head, working as a deputy down in El Paso." The doctor turned up a swig of whiskey and gave me a knowing look. "It's a story you oughta hear."

"Oh . . . ?" I sank down on a wooden chair, already getting the picture. "Does Briggs think Ned Quarrels killed his boy? Is that what this is all about?" I shook the key in my hand.

"Yep. Short and simple. Ned had it in for Briggs for busting his head a few times while he was in jail. Ned got out. Briggs's boy got popped once through the head, close up, ambushed from a dark alley three nights later." Eisenhower let out a breath. "Briggs figured two plus two makes four. He's been after Ned ever since."

"Jesus." I reached and took the bottle. I started to take a drink but stopped. "It's all a personal score between the two of them."

"With Briggs down, I thought you oughta know."

"Thanks," I said. Again I started to turn up a shot; again I stopped. "But I'm in too deep to walk away."

"Sometimes it's best," he said.

"But I still have to get my horse." I rubbed my chin, cleared my throat, and pitched him the bottle.

"Sure you don't want a dose of this old *smooth and mellow?"* Eisenhower swished the bottle back and forth. "It might get the spiders out of your belly."

"No." I shook my head. "All I want is a good dose of Missouri."

The old doctor chuckled, swished the bottle again, and threw back a shot. "It'll even melt their webs."

"No," I said, standing. I noticed Clyde the skeleton still swayed slightly, his thin calcium arms hanging at his sides, his hollow eye sockets staring like two small caves that came together and opened up into a much larger world, a world whose map was yet to be drawn.

"Not right now. I'm on duty."

20

"I ain't afraid of no sumbitch, drunk or sober," I heard RC Allison say when I stepped inside Fortenay's. He tossed back a shot of rye, let out a whiskey hiss, and watched me walk over to Jack and the kid. On the floor, Sonny nodded toward RC. "He's getting too drunk." Sonny shook his shackles; his eyes pleaded. "Get me out of here!"

"No key," I said, wanting him to sweat a little, and I looked up at Jack and the kid. The kid puffed on a Mexican brown. I wanted to tell Jack about Briggs's personal vendetta with Quarrels, but not in front of the others. It was time to strike a deal with Ned Quarrels and leave. If Briggs lived, he'd have to settle his own grudge with Quarrels. I wanted no part of it.

"I've killed more men than you've got uncles and aunts," RC said with a wave of his hand.

"Yes sir," Gustav said with a quiver. He stood tense, ready to pour whiskey on a second's notice. But when he reached out to fill RC's glass, RC smacked his hand away and snatched the bottle.

"Killed more darkies than teats on a possum. More redskins than flies on a hog." He belched. "I've killed 'em all, all sizes, shapes, and colors. Mexicans, Chinamen. Hell, I'd *eat* a Chinaman if I was hungry enough. No different than eating a deer." He raised his glass in a toast. "Kill 'em all. . . . More room for the rest of us."

We all three stared at RC; the kid laughed under his breath. "Bottle brave."

"C'mon," Sonny pleaded at our feet. His voice turned into a whimper. "Get me outta here . . . he's gone nuts."

Sonny was right. RC was boiling drunk and apt to do most anything.

"No key," I said, and I looked back up at Jack.

I started to speak when I heard a commotion from the boardwalk, and Jack and I turned toward the door. I saw Mackay shove Goodlet inside. Goodlet tumbled to his knees, then stood up shaking. His face was white; his hair ragged. He turned to me, wide eyed. "Beatty, tell him!" He pointed a finger at Mackay. "Tell him we had a deal going!"

"What deal?" I stepped forward looking from Mackay to Goodlet.

Goodlet spread his trembling hands. "You know . . . to let Sonny go. To get your horse back. I took it to Quarrels for you." He tried to form a trembling smile. "Rake took care of it, didn't he? Everything's okay now. Briggs is down—"

"You low son of a bitch." I took a step forward, felt Jack grab my arm, but I shook loose. "There was no goddamn deal!"

"Kill the bastard," RC shouted. He stepped out, but I shoved him back against the bar and stalked Goodlet backward across the floor.

"My oh my," Mackay shook his head and leaned his shotgun against the bar.

"Please, Beatty," Goodlet cried, "you said you wished there was a way—" I snatched him by his collar and slung him. His long coat spun around like a dancer until he crashed against the wall. Before he could move, I grabbed him again by the collar, slung him to the floor, and cocked my forty-four in his eye. "You set him up—got him shot! I oughta blow your goddamn head off!"

"Shoot him," yelled the kid.

"Easy," said Jack. "Don't make a mess here." He reached around and laid a hand on my forearm, pressed my arm away from Goodlet. I turned loose, stepped back, and felt myself tremble with rage.

"Get out of my sight," I said, and I turned, with Jack right beside me, and started over to let Sonny loose.

Mackay stepped in beside us. "I left Tripplet watching the street. I thought you'd want to know that Goodlet and the workers have formed some sort of alliance"—he waved an arm—"for the good of the town."

"Look out!" I heard Gustav yell; the three of us spun, drawing, but just in time to hear the kid's gun explode and see Goodlet spin a circle. Mackay's shotgun flew from Goodlet's hands. Another bullet slammed into him; he staggered backward. Shot after shot, the kid's forty-four walked him backwards, crashed him through the large glass window and out on the boardwalk.

"Goddamn!" I glanced around. Gustav stood frozen; RC raised a drunken toast toward the broken window. A piece of the frame swung back and forth and fell. Fortenay ran out of the kitchen, stared at the broken window, and fumed. The kid reloaded as he walked out the door. We heard shot after shot, then silence.

"Told you the kid's nuts," Jack said.

"Get me outta here," Sonny said from the floor.

I looked at Mackay. "There never was a *deal* for me to give up Briggs. I wouldn't do something like that." I saw Carmilla staring down from the stairs. Outside, the kid must've reloaded. We heard him shooting again. "Jesus!" I started across the floor. "How long is he gonna shoot him?" I jerked Mackay's shotgun from the floor and pitched it to him. "Try to hang onto it," I said, headed out the door.

"Certainly," Mackay grinned. I thought I saw a strange gleam in his eyes.

The kid had reloaded for the third time when I stopped beside him. He pointed the gun down at what was left of Goodlet's chest. "Don't, Kid! That's enough!" But he fired again anyway. I grabbed him, spun him around, and snatched his pistol. "The hell's wrong with you?" The Mexican brown dangled from his lips.

He grinned. "He meant to kill ya. Always wanted to drop a hammer on a politician."

I shoved the pistol down in his holster. "Thanks, Kid, but that's enough." I looked up and saw Erlander and his crew running up the street toward us. They slowed, seeing Goodlet dead in a spray of shattered glass, then spread in a half circle around the front of Fortenay's.

"Who shot him?" Erlander jerked the pistol from his holster and let it hang down his side. "I want the son of a bitch—" He stopped and looked at the smoke rolling up from the tip of the kid's holster. "You did!" He jerked the pistol up toward the kid, and before either of us could make a move, Jack's pistol roared beside me and Erlander's hand snapped back, spraying blood. The crowd jolted back.

"It was an accident," said Jack, stepping forward, fanning the crowd with his La Faucheux.

"Accident? Look at him!" A finger pointed at Goodlet's riddled body. Blood poured from Goodlet and dripped off the boardwalk into the dirt.

"That's right," I said. "So don't make nothing of it. I know you sided with Goodlet. And that's what got Briggs shot. You've all butted into law business. If Briggs dies, I'll kill every one of you son of a bitches!"

"Bunch of murderers," someone said. Erlander squeezed his bloody wrist.

"You're goddamn right!" I stepped forward. Mackay and Jack stepped forward on one side, the kid on my other. I saw Mackay break open the shotgun and drop two shells in it. "Murderers, lawmen, I don't give a damn what you call us. Until this is settled, I want you all to clear the hell out of here! This job is canceled until further notice!"

"You can't make us leave!"

I reached over, snatched Mackay's shotgun. "The hell I can't!" I jumped from the boardwalk, jammed the butt into a thick round belly, then smacked him in the face as he bent double. He flew backwards into the crowd. I turned the shotgun, fanning it; the crowd moved back. I stalked forward. Erlander turned and ran, leaving a trail of blood from his wrist. "You want more accidents?" I tipped the shotgun and blew a barrel in the air above them. The blast hit the sign on the unfinished barber shop across the street. It ripped loose, fell straight down, landed on a rain barrel, and crashed through the window. The crowd broke and scattered.

"RC, are you in on this?" someone called out as they ran.

"That's right," I heard RC say behind us from the door. "We ain't afraid of no sumbitch."

"I'll have the army when I come back," Erlander bellowed from a block away.

I'd already turned back to the boardwalk, but I threw the shotgun up and rounded out the other barrel. "You better have, you son of a bitch!" Splinters from Fortenay's new sign showered down around me. I stomped back inside the saloon, pointing at Goodlet's body on my way. "Get him away from here, Kid."

"I ain't touching that bloody sumbitch," he said. "Hell, I shot him!"

"That's right, young man," said Mackay, "so *you* must tidy up. Had I shot him, it would be my responsibility—"

"Then shoot him a couple times, and *you* move his ass," the kid said. "I ain't gonna."

"Look out, goddamn it," I heard RC say. He staggered toward the door. "I'll get a rope and drag him away. Never liked him."

Fortenay looked from the broken window.to me with a flat expression. He watched as I brushed splinters from my shoulders. "Sorry," I said. Then he turned rigidly, like a man in a trance, and walked back into the kitchen without a word.

"If you don't get me outta here, I'm calling off the deal." Sonny's face twitched; his hands trembled. I looked down at him, drew back a boot, and kicked his head against the bar rail. It rang like a bell.

Out of nowhere, a boiling darkness swept across the sky, bringing with it a sharp wind filled with stinging sand and rolling clumps of mesquite. I unrolled mine and Jack's rain slickers from our saddles and pitched his to him. We both put them on and gazed up at the sky. "Now, even the weather's gone to hell on us," he said.

We stood out front of Fortenay's and watched RC stagger around as he untangled a long rope. I told Jack about Briggs's son, about Ned Quarrels killing him. When I finished, Jack hooked his thumb in his belt and stared out at the street. The wind twisted up dust devils and spun them around. He shook his head slowly. "We never shoulda got involved."

"I know," I said quietly, watching RC loop the rope around Goodlet's foot and tighten it. "All over a horse." I raised my collar and looked all around. "And just look what it's grown into." I let out a breath. "I think everybody here's crazy but us."

Jack cocked an eyebrow at me; my face reddened. "I know how that sounds, Jack, but I mean it. I've never seen so many crazy people in one place. Look at RC. *'Eat a Chinaman'?* and look at what that crazy kid did to Goodlet."

"Lucky for you," Jack chuckled, "or you'd be dead. I can't believe Mackay just left his shotgun unattended—"

"I know." I rubbed my jaw. "But that's another thing,

Jack. Didn't you load that shotgun this morning before you gave it to him?"

"Sure. I'd never give a man an empty gun."

"Then why did Mackay load it when he stepped out here?"

I saw realization sparkle in Jack's eyes. "You think he leaned it there . . . just figured Goodlet would go for it?"

"Why else would he unload it?" I shrugged. "I hate to think it, but there it is."

Jack chuckled. "Well, he *is* a dentist. I reckon he'd do most anything." RC shook out the rope, drug one end to his horse, and tied it to his saddlehorn. We watched him stagger, then struggle into the saddle.

"Think you can hold this bunch while I go meet with Ned?" We'd already decided I would ride out and strike a deal. I was just going over it with Jack before I left. I would ride out alone, find Ned Quarrels's gang and make arrangements for our trade. He'd get his brother and part of the money. We'd keep part of the money, and I'd get Buck. Ned wanted Briggs, but I figured he'd settle for his brother and the money.

"I'll get as crazy as the rest, if I have to." Jack shrugged. "You know me." We watched the street as construction workers filed past two and three at a time with their nail aprons and belts slung over their shoulders. They shot a glance at RC rigging up Goodlet's body, then gazed at us with sour expressions and drifted out of town toward Cimarron, their collars up against the wind.

Kersey's deputies rode by in a buckboard without glancing our way; each held a hand on their hat to keep it from blowing off. Kersey leaned up from the wagon bed, his head still wrapped like a mummy. He saw us and dropped back down.

"You've got the money in a safe place?" I pulled out my gloves and slipped them on. I didn't want to know where the money was, in case things went wrong and Quarrels tried to torture it out of me.

"I *know* how to hide money." Jack winked. I saw RC start to drag Goodlet away, but the rope was wrapped around the porch post. Jack nudged me, and we stepped out off the boardwalk, out from under the porch overhang. "RC, wait," Jack called out, but RC sat slumped in the saddle staring straight ahead.

He nudged the horse forward; the rope drew tighter and tighter. The post groaned and bent, then jerked loose at the bottom, snapped out off the boardwalk and thudded straight down to the ground, still supporting the overhang but dropping it two feet. The buckshot-riddled sign broke loose and slammed into the ground.

Goodlet's body slid across the boardwalk until his foot came to the post, then his leg twisted upward around the post like a climbing snake. "Wait, RC!" I yelled, but it did no good. When his horse stalled, he gigged it harder, until the post snapped loose. RC rode away as the overhang collapsed, jarring the building; and Goodlet and the post bumped along the wind swept street, his dead foot tapping to some strange kind of music. Tripplet stood near the wagons, watching, writing like mad.

I glanced at Jack, squinted my eyes shut for a second, and shook my head. "Well . . . good luck here," I said. I stepped over to the hitch rail, slid up on the mare, and reined her away through the swirling dust. I looked back once and saw Jack shrug and spread his hands as he climbed over the collapsed overhang and into Fortenay's saloon. Fortenay stood in the door with a blank expression.

A mile out of town, the wind brought a deluge of rain that blew sideways in blinding sheets, but I struggled on, leaning low in the saddle and letting the mare stay on the road by her own instincts. For nearly a half hour, lightning shot down and danced in the sky like a silver whip being cracked by the devil. Then, as suddenly as it hit, the storm disappeared behind me over a low rise and growled above Gris.

By the time I rounded the turn at the bottom of the high pass, the evening sun had reappeared and glistened against the tall, reaching fingers of stone. A rush of water shot out from the bottom of a long crevice, cut its way across the road, and ran down into a raging creek that had only been a dry bed the day Jack and I raced back to Gris ahead of Quarrels's men. Though it had only been two days, it seemed like a long time ago.

I let the mare stop and drink in the rush of runoff from the crevice while I shook out my hat and duster and studied the wet trail before me. Before I tapped the mare forward, I heard the sound of hoofs splashing toward me from up around the next turn; I drew my rifle, slung my wet bandanna around the barrel so Quarrels's men wouldn't see me and just start shooting, and nudged the mare across the stream of runoff as the riders made the turn.

"What the—?" Three horsemen pulled up, sliding sideways, startled at the suddenness of coming upon me as they made the turn. Their horses circled quickly to keep from piling up on one another.

"Easy!" I yelled, throwing my arms up and waving the rifle with my wet bandanna on it. Though they drew their pistols and cocked them, I could tell they wouldn't shoot. "I come to see Ned."

"Scare the living shit out of somebody!" The first rider's eyes were still wide and darting about; his face was stark white but splotched red. The other two looked at him and laughed under their breath. He looked embarrassed, then angry. He glared at me.

"To see Ned?" One rider closed in on my left. "You the son of a bitch that did the cutting?" He eyed the knife handle sticking out of my boot. The other rider stepped his horse close up on my right.

"I turned a deal with Goodlet. Now I'm here to talk." I tried to watch all three at once.

I saw the first rider's hand shaking. "You can't come sneaking in—"

"I ain't sneaking, goddamn it! I came in under a flag." I shook the rifle and the wet bandanna. "See? I didn't mean to scare you."

The other two laughed at him. "*Scare me?* Why you son of a—"

"Take it easy, Tiny," one of the men said, and I realized the big man was Tiny Boyd. The rider on my right jumped his horse between us, staring at him. "God, Tiny, you oughta see your face." He glanced at the rider on my left who kept me covered. "Art, look at his face!" I realized that "Art" had to be Arthur Claypool.

"Damn, Tiny," Art said, glancing at him, "you gonna be all right? You look like you just dropped a load in your—"

"Shut up, goddamn it! I'm all right! I just can't stand being snuck up on."

"I wasn't sneaking up. I came to see Ned." I looked at him closer; his face had turned blue around his mouth and under his eyes. His hand shook something awful. "Damn, mister. You really *don't* look so good."

"That's it!" He swung his pistol toward me, but the one closest grabbed his arm and shoved it in the air.

"Tiny, he's got our money! You know Ned wants Sonny back! Now settle down"—he looked Tiny up and down—"before you give yourself a failure." He looked back at me with eyes like gun sights. "So you're quite a hand with a blade, huh?"

I just stared at him. Tiny let his pistol slump in his lap and ran a shaking hand down his jaw. "Okay." He backed his horse a step and the other two reined around, one on each side of me. "Let's take him to Ned." He breathed deep and held a hand on his chest. "But y'all ride ahead with him." He glanced at them with a distressed expression. "I'll be right behind you." Then he shot me a dark stare as I gigged the mare forward. "You better hope I don't become ill over this."

We followed the trail upward a mile or more, then turned off onto a narrow path and worked our way around spilled rocks until we reached a wide opening that soon turned into a clearing on the other side of the rock wall. From atop the rock wall, two riflemen had watched us wind our way along, then stood up and ran on ahead of us once they recognized their own men.

We stopped at the edge of the clearing, and saw several of Quarrels's men rekindling a campfire, some of them shaking out their rain gear and slapping their hats against their legs. The Rake looked our way and nudged a tall man standing beside him. I saw Diamond Joe drop a cup of coffee and reach for the pistol in his belt, but the tall man stopped him, yanked his pistol from him, and shoved him backward into the mud.

Diamond Joe rolled in the mud and had a hard time getting up. His left arm was in a sling and I saw heavy bloodstained bandaging through his torn shirt. When Rake and the other man turned toward us, I recognized the tall man by the scar on his face. It was Ned Quarrels, without the round, penciled-in eyes or the curled lips.

"Look who's here, Ned," I heard Tiny Boyd say behind me. I felt him shove me hard from behind; I almost came out of my saddle, but I caught myself and swung the mare around facing him.

"Damn, Tiny," said one the other riders. "Why'd you do that?"

"Yeah, you stupid bastard!" I glared at him. "I oughta bust your goddamn head."

"I was knocking him off his horse."

"But you *didn't,*" said the other. "You better get some coffee or something. You look like hell."

I turned the mare back toward the campsite, and saw that Ned and The Rake had mounted and rode over to us. The others came walking over slowly, spreading out, with their rifles cradled in their arms. Diamond Joe walked a wide half circle around me.

"We finally meet," Quarrels said. Him and The Rake reined up ten feet away. I saw a slight twitch in his jaw as he sized me up and spread a dark smile. I glanced quickly around the area, searched the string of horses tied in a row twenty yards away, but saw no sign of Buck. "So you're the one holding my brother."

"And *our* money," The Rake added.

"And I'm here to straighten things out, just like you asked," I said, glancing from one to the other.

Ned eyed me closely. "You damn sure look familiar. Who are you?"

"I'm Beatty . . . James—"

"Don't hand me that." Ned sliced a hand through the air. "I knew better than that when I saw what you did to Diamond Joe." He studied me even closer. "You the one knifed my boys?" I slid a glance past Diamond Joe and back to Quarrels. Joe ducked his scarred and battered head. He looked terrible.

"I stuck a few coyotes," I said, and I stared at him.

"Yeah?" Ned studied my face. "Well, I've seen your picture somewhere." He rolled a hand. "One of them fancy, well-drawn posters—"

"He jumped me!" I heard Tiny say. " 'Bout caused me to have a—"

"You're too jumpy anyway," Ned said to Tiny Boyd. He looked back at me for a second and I saw his eyes light in recognition. "Hell's fire!" He pulled his horse back a step. "You're Jesse James, ain't ya?" I noticed the riders on either side pull away slightly.

"Then it's no wonder he got the drop on me," Tiny Boyd said in a low tone.

I just stared for a second, wondering if I should tell them

any different, then shook my head. "No, I'm not Jesse James, but I am kin to—"

"So you're Jesse—by God—James." Quarrels let out a breath and eyed me up and down.

I shook my head. "I'm not Jesse . . . I'm his cousin. We look some alike, is all. I'm Crowe . . . Miller Crowe." I glanced around at all the riflemen and raised my voice. "But if something happens to me or my horse, you'll *all* get a chance to meet Jesse and the rest, *up close.* And you won't like the circumstances at all."

Jake The Rake jumped his horse forward a step, beside Ned. "Don't listen to this sucker, boss. Whoever he is, I set him up like a duck at a county fair." He sneered and spit. "He handed me the marshall on a silver platter—"

"Shut up, Rake," Ned said. "That's what he meant to do. Goodlet set it up for us." He glanced back to me. "We're all outlaws, we all think the same."

"What about the two of our boys his partners shot yesterday?" Rake glared at me.

"That was just for show . . . right, Jesse?" Ned spread an evil grin.

I stared back and forth between Ned and The Rake without answering. "How are we gonna settle up, Ned? The marshall's down, I've got your brother and the money. I want my horse and two-thirds of the money—"

"Two-thirds?" Quarrels shook his head. "You're out of your mind."

I ignored his answer, pointed a finger at Diamond Joe, and spoke to the whole gang. "That man made threats against my horse, so I'll tell you-all right now. Anything happens to my horse . . . deal or no deal, I'll do you-all like I did them coyotes." I stared, hard-eyed, from one to the other.

"See, boss? See how he is?" Tiny spoke in a low tone. "No wonder I was—"

"Get out of here, Tiny," Ned snapped. He stared at him

as Tiny walked his horse around toward the campfire. "You look like you've soiled your saddle."

"About our deal," I said, staring at Ned.

Ned rubbed his chin. "How much is two-thirds?"

I felt my ears perk up at Ned's question; I looked at The Rake and saw he had no idea.

"There ain't no deal," The Rake said, "not for two-thirds—"

"Who runs this bunch?" I stared at The Rake, then Quarrels.

"I do," said Quarrels, "but Rake's right. Two-thirds is too damn much." He glanced at The Rake. "Ain't it?"

I studied their eyes. "That's just a starting point. I'm willing to dicker. Say . . . half of fifty thousand? That comes to thirty-five." I watched closely.

"Where'd you learn to count?" Quarrels shot a shrewd glance over his men, then back to me. "There's only *forty* thousand to begin with—"

"My mistake—" I shrugged, held up my fingers, and moved my lips as I counted them back and forth. "So . . . half of forty thousand. That's only twenty-five thousand."

"That's more like it." Quarrels shot his men a smug glance.

"I get twenty-five thousand and my horse. You get your brother and ride on." I watched their eyes closely to see just what I was dealing with.

"I don't like it," said The Rake. "We're the ones took the risk getting that money—"

"Then you oughta taken better care of it," I said, bold as brass. "Part of being an outlaw is having enough sense to not get robbed."

The Rake glared at me through eyes filled with daggers, but Ned just stared and nodded. "I can't argue that." He crossed his arms on his saddlehorn. "You gave us a stirring, the way you slipped in, captured Diamond Joe, and stole our money."

I snapped my eyes to Diamond Joe and saw desperation sweep his brow. Jesus! He was taking off with the money the day we caught him. Now he swallowed hard and took a step back, wondering if I was going to tell Ned what had really happened that day. "Don't trust nis sufa-bintch," Diamond said in his sick duck voice. I saw he was ready to come apart at the seams. I grinned at him, just enough to let him know that his life or death lay delicately on the tip of my tongue.

I looked back at Quarrels. "Yeah . . . well, my partner and I are good at what we do. Have we got a deal?" I didn't look back at Diamond Joe, but I figured his knees nearly buckled.

"Don't do it, boss," The Rake said. "Let me kill this sucker. We can always steal more money."

"Shut up, Rake. You wanta get my brother killed? Sonny wouldn't do me that way if it was the other way around." Quarrels glared at him, then back to me. "All right, I'll do it. But I get the marshall."

"Why?" I shrugged. "He's dying." I wasn't about to tell him I wouldn't give Briggs up. I'd wait until the rest of the deal came together, then spring it on him.

"It's between me and him," Quarrels said. "He thumped me on the head the whole time I was in jail. Then accused me of killing his boy. I *gotta* beat on him some before he dies."

"You saying you didn't kill his son?" I watched his eyes.

"His boy killed himself. I was drunk in an alley and saw him do it. Briggs just won't admit it. He forced him into law work and the boy couldn't stand it. So—" Ned raised his finger to his head and snapped his thumb like pulling a trigger. "Briggs has been loco—blamed me ever since."

I sat silent for a second. "Whatever you want to do, then. You bring your new string of horses with you to town tomorrow. I'll pick out mine. You take your brother, your part of the money, and the marshall. Deal?" I wouldn't tell him what Buck looked like for fear Diamond Joe would hurt him in spite.

Quarrels smiled and nodded his head. "Yeah, we've got a deal."

I let out a breath and relaxed. It was done; I'd pulled it off. Now all that was left was to make the trade. I glanced once more across the string of horses on the outside chance that I might catch a glimpse of Buck before I left. But I didn't; instead I saw something that made the skin tighten on the back of my neck and my hand tighten on my reins. At the far end of the string, I saw the swishing tail of Greta's silver-gray donkey; past the donkey I saw Greta laying on the ground with her hands tied behind her. She wore a bandanna gag. Her eyes pleaded toward me.

I looked back at Ned, trying to stay calm. "One more thing," I said. I pointed at Greta. "She goes back with me."

"No." Ned grinned and shook his head slowly. "She's ours. I'm keeping her for my time and trouble." I heard the determination in his voice. "We been looking for a light-skinned woman." He grinned. "Rake's searched for one from Roswell to Taos." Laughter rippled across the rifle-men.

"I see," I said; I took a deep breath and nodded. Any move I made right then would've only gotten me killed. "Then I reckon you got one." I touched a finger to my hat, avoided poor Greta's eyes, and turned the mare back to-ward the trail.

"How about some coffee before you go?" Quarrels called out, but I couldn't answer. I dared not open my mouth for fear the sound of my voice would spark the bloodletting urge that lay just one thin layer under my skin. I only raised a hand and kept walking the mare away.

PART IV — ◆

Worth of a Woman

21

Darkness overtook my spirit riding away from Ned Quarrels, out through the narrow pass, down to the winding trail. Three riders had followed me as far as the lookout guards, then dropped back and rode away. They weren't worried. As far as they were concerned, the deal was made.

At the fork of the trail, I pulled the mare over into the shelter of a rock crevice, slipped down from the saddle, and stared out across the sky. I did not want to think about what I was going to do, for to consider it might well scare me out of it. Come morning I would have the money, but how could I ever spend it without seeing Greta's face? I'd have Buck, but how could I ever look at him and not see the woman's pleading eyes? I spit and ran a hand across my mouth. Jack would be disappointed, I thought, then I almost laughed at myself for thinking it. What would I care? Hell, I'd probably be dead.

When sunlight turned to a molten glow and melted behind the Sangre de Cristos, I turned the mare out of the crevice and rode slow and quietly back up the winding trail toward the narrow pass. A mile from the lookouts, I hid the mare along the edge of the trail, hung my hat and holster around the saddlehorn, shoved my forty-four down the back of my trousers, and headed out on foot, edging along one side of the narrow pass.

It was dark by the time I reached a spot beneath the lookouts. From there I crept along in the shadows, out of the starlight, and worked my way gradually up the ridge on the right side of the pass. Each step I took, I waited for a second and prayed that no rocks would spill loose beneath my boot heels and tumble down behind me. At the rim of the ridge, I slipped upward over it, and lay flat on my belly like a snake until my breathing stilled and my eyes adjusted to the starlight.

I crawled silently for twenty or more yards until I saw the outline of a guard ahead; then I took a deep breath and inched forward silently.

When I'd pulled him back against me, held him tight with my arm around his throat and felt his life fade away into the night, I rolled him back from the edge, picked up his hat, blanket, and rifle, and continued along the ridge until it slanted down toward the campsite. There I watched and waited until I lost track of time.

Finally, two of the men stood up, belched and scratched, and pitched their coffee into the fire. One crossed the path and started up along the other side. The other one started up the path toward me. "I hate sitting up there," he said over his shoulder. "Nobody's stupid enough to come looking for us anyway." Muffled laughter rose up around the fire.

As he walked past the rock where I lay in wait, I flipped the blanket up over my shoulder, stepped out behind him, threw an arm around his throat, and lifted him up on the glades knife until his boots quivered and scraped at the ground. Then I drug him off the path and waited, judging how long it should've taken to change lookouts. When I felt it had been long enough, I flipped the blanket down over my bloody chest and walked calmly down into the campsite with his rifle cradled in my arms.

"Better get ya some coffee, Chester," said a voice from

the fire as I walked past fifteen feet away. "Bet it's cold up there."

I grunted and walked on. Chester would never feel the cold again.

I slipped unseen into the long string of horses, settled them with a gentle hand, and untied a tall-legged bay gelding. Leading him in the darkness along the inside of the string, I worked closer to where Greta sat on a blanket eating beans from a tin plate. Six feet in front of her Art Claypool squatted with a rifle under his arm. "I always say a little diddling's good for a person." He snickered, stretched out an arm, and pinched his fingers toward her. Greta drew back from him, wide-eyed. A few yards away, I saw men asleep in blanket rolls. Snoring hovered above them like bubbling tar and steam whistles.

I ran a hand along the big bay's back and draped his reins over a rock. Here goes, I thought. "Art," I said in a mock voice, stepping forward with the lookout's hat brim low over my eyes.

"Hunh?" He turned his face up to me; I saw his brow arch and his mouth fly open just as he caught the force of the rifle butt between his eyes. He spun a complete flip backwards and landed on his face, knocked cold. I jumped for Greta. "Come on," I hissed, reaching for her; but her plate flew into my face and she let out a scream that could curl rope.

"Jesus!" I shouted. "Greta, it's me!" I dropped the rifle and grabbed her around her waist as she tried to stand. Her hands were loose but her feet were still tied. Snoring ended in a snarl; blankets flipped away. Men stood up by the fire. She screamed again and smacked me with the tin plate. Beans flew.

"Get him!" I heard shouts, then a bullet screamed past my head.

"It's that goddamn Jesse James!" A bullet thumped the ground.

Greta swung the plate again; I ducked, jerked the pistol

from behind me, and cracked her across the forehead. Another shot whistled by; I swept her up and ran to the big bay. The bay reared. I pulled him down, leaned Greta against him and fired two shots at the men wallowing up from their blankets. Then I slung Greta across the bay, leaped up behind her, and reined and spurred, jumped the horse over the fire with a long rebel yell, and headed toward the pass, knocking men in every direction.

I swung my arm back and fired a wild round, saw Diamond Joe screaming, rolling through the fire with flames and sparks licking up his back. A shot took the lookout's hat off my head as we pounded out of the light into the darkness of the winding pass.

"Wake up, goddamn it!" I shook Greta against my chest. The big bay tore the earth apart; but in seconds the men would be mounted and on our heels. There was still one lookout on the other side of the pass. I prayed he couldn't hit a moving target. Greta stirred, screamed, and tried to throw herself off. I held her. "Greta! It's me! Help me some, goddamn it!"

I reined the bay to a sliding halt, snatched up the glades knife, and slashed the rope around Greta's ankles. I helped her right herself and nailed the bay forward as a shot blossomed and exploded from the ridge line. We sailed on; I heard another shot from above, but it ricocheted off a rock far behind us. This time someone shouted up from the pass, "Lindsey, it's us! Don't shoot!"

I ran the bay flat out, dangerously, until we reached the spot where I'd hidden the mare. There I reined up sharp, sliding the bay around and down on his haunches as he stopped. "Here!" I shoved the reins into Greta's hands, slid down off the bay's rump, felt his coarse tail swish across my face, and I slapped him hard as he bolted himself up. "Go!"

In the distance, I heard another rifle shot from atop the ridge and a voice yelled up from the pass, "Goddamn it, Lindsey! Please! It's us!"

I ran, jumped up into the mare's saddle, slung my holster belt over my shoulder and spurred her hard. She shot away like a comet. My hat flew off the saddlehorn, but I caught it, slapped the mare with it, and pounded away, drawing and cocking my rifle one-handed.

We didn't slow down until we reached the creek bed. There I had to grab the reins to the big gelding and tussle with Greta to get her to stop. "Let go! Get away! Don't touch me!" She lashed the reins across my arm, but I held on and slid both animals to a halt.

"Greta, it's me, goddamn it!" I slapped her shoulder with my hat. "Why won't you listen?"

"I know it's you!" She tried to jerk the gelding away; I held firm. The horses thrashed in a short circle. "Don't touch me!" Greta's voice rasped and trembled.

"Well, pardon-the-living-hell-out-of-me!" I bumped the mare against the gelding, snatched Greta off and dropped her on the ground. I slid down holding both sets of reins, and jerked her to her feet. "We can't spend these animals out, or we're dead."

She jerked away from me and tightened her arms across her stomach. "Please! Please . . . just don't touch me." She held one hand out to keep me away.

"Lady, goddamn it! If you don't settle down, they'll be *touching* us both . . . *soundly!"* I slapped my hat against my leg and looked back in the darkness toward the pass. "We've got enough lead to make it to Gris . . . if we check our horses down and keep our heads."

"You—you came to get me?" Her breath heaved.

"Yes—" I looked at her. "As it turns out, I did." I thought of Buck. I thought of the money. I thought of Jack waiting in Gris, expecting me to work things out. I thought about just sitting down and never getting up. I let out a breath. "We got worried. I came to get ya. Just felt I should."

She raised a hand to the welt on her forehead. "You hit me?"

"You was fighting me!"

She touched her forehead carefully. "But still—"

I shoved my hat down on my head and gritted my teeth.

It was near morning when we stopped at the outskirts of Gris. I reined up at the end of the street, let out a night-bird call, and waited quietly until I heard Jack's reply. Greta sat beside me on the big bay. Both horses were winded and blowing hard. Froth dripped from their bits. They slung their heads and snorted. I gigged the mare forward and Greta followed me to the wagons. I saw the curious look on Jack's face as I reined up. He must've saw the look of concern on mine.

"What the hell's wrong?" He looked me up and down and glanced at Greta. "Kid," he said over his shoulder, "help the woman down."

"I will help her," Carmilla said, running up from Fortenay's, shoving her shirt down into her trousers. She must've been watching from the window. She looked up at me with a tear streaming down her cheek, and offered a tight smile. I tipped my hat, pulled my rifle, and slipped down from the mare.

"Here, Kid. You can have the horses." The kid quickly put out a Mexican brown, stepped in and took both sets of reins. I turned to Jack. "They're coming, Jack. The deal went to hell. They had the woman. I couldn't leave her there. Sorry."

"Damn it! Couldn't you make the deal and pick her up in the trade? You're a dealer, for godsakes—"

"You want to ask them, Jack? They're about a half hour behind me, if their own guard ain't killed them." I pushed up my hat. "They just wouldn't go for it." I shook my head. "Everything else was going fine. But I couldn't leave her there."

"Well, hell." Jack followed me to the pot of coffee between the wagons. "What's the chances of packing everybody up and making a run for Cimarron?"

"Slim to none. Our best chance is to get them in here and shoot the hell out of them. That's all it comes down to."

"Think they'll hit soon?"

"Most anytime. If I was them I'd wait till after daylight, maybe wait till the sun's in our eyes." I saw RC Allison laying on a blanket by a wagon wheel. His eyes were as black as a raccoon's. "What happened to him?" I asked Jack as I poured a cup of coffee.

"He got too drunk and wouldn't settle down. I had to pop him one."

"Jesus," I said. "*This* is our crew."

Jack nodded at my bloodstained shirt. "You're ruining all your clothes. How many did you get?"

"Two," I said. I sipped the coffee. "Three, if I can count almost giving Tiny Boyd heart failure. Four, if you count Diamond Joe burning up in the campfire."

Jack whistled low. "That poor sumbitch."

"Yeah. That *poor sumbitch* is the one to blame for all this. He deserves whatever he gets."

"Well, at least you whittled them down some." Jack picked up a rifle from against the wagon. "There ain't near as many as there was. They're down to about a dozen men, the way I figure. That ain't so bad. All's we've gotta do is kill them and we'll still come out ahead."

"That's a dandy attitude, Jack." I pitched my coffee away.

"Beats complaining about every least little thing, don't it?"

"Yeah, I reckon." I smiled. "I don't know what to think of Quarrels's bunch. They ain't real smart. Ned's dumber than a cross-tie. Diamond Joe was robbing him the day we caught him, and he made Ned believe we took him hostage and threw him off the cliff."

"No kidding?" Jack flipped his pistol from his holster and checked it.

I checked my rifle. "Jake The Rake can't count the fingers on both hands without missing a thumb."

"We ain't talking about arithmetic here. He only has to count to two to shoot both your eyes out. He's supposed to be the fastest gun alive."

"Faster than you?" I looked him up and down.

"Watch your language." Jack grinned, and spun the La Faucheux into a shiny blur that ended in his holster.

"Well . . . then what are we worried about?"

Jack shook his head. "Not a damn thing."

I glanced around. "Where's Sonny?"

"Mackay's watching him, over in the livery barn. Did you know Mackay ain't his real name? His real name is Johnny Holliday."

"He mentioned it. Why?"

"Why? 'Cause he's supposed to be a bad sumbitch, is why. I heard of him last year. He took a couple Texans down real quick, one with a knife, one with that little Uhlinger. They say even Dave Rudabaugh's scared of him. He skinned clean out of Texas when he heard Mackay was looking for him."

"Gypsy Dave? I doubt it." I smiled. "Hell, Jack. You've seen how Mackay coughs his brains out. He does well to stand up on his own."

"Then maybe he killed 'em between coughs, sitting down." Jack shrugged. "I'm just telling you what I heard." Jack picked up the shotgun, checked it and leaned it against the wagon. "You don't have to stink and wear rawhide to be a dangerous sumbitch, you know."

"Heard anything more on Briggs?" I looked past Jack and saw the kid trotting back from the barn.

"Doctor says he's come around some, but he's awful weak. I don't think he's doing so good."

"Too bad," I said quietly; and I looked all around the

dark street as the kid stepped in between the wagons.

"What's wrong with him?" I heard the kid ask Jack as I stared away from them toward Fortenay's saloon.

"He's just worried about everything," Jack said.

"Aw, hell," said the kid. "Ain't nothing in life worth worrying about."

"I ain't worried." I turned and faced them. "I was just thinking."

"You looked worried to me," Jack said. "Looked like you was standing there wishing you'd treated your mama better when you was a little boy."

"I reckon everybody does that . . . sometimes." I felt my face redden as Jack shot me a curious glance. "I was thinking how good that cable would be strung across the street here, good and tight, for when Quarrels comes tearing through."

"Think Fortenay's will fall if we take it off?" Jack glanced over with me.

"It's about gone anyway." I looked at the pile of debris that was the porch overhang, and the new sign laying broken in the street. "Do you care?"

"Not much. He's in need of major repair. He can set up in a tent for awhile."

"Okay, Kid, let's get it and hook it up." I looked at him; he'd just lit a Mexican brown. He took a draw and stuck it toward me. I raised a hand. "No. Let's get the cable, quick, before Fortenay steps out to pitch a bucket of water."

"That thing'll weigh a ton." He fell in beside me and we headed to the alley beside Fortenay's.

"There's *some* labor to anything you do, Kid. It ain't all just lounging around, waiting for somebody to shoot at you."

He held the Mexican brown over toward Jack as we walked to Fortenay's. "Get that stinking sumbitch out of my face. If I wanted to smoke horseshit, I'd get a pipe and go to the barn."

"This ain't no Mexican store-bought," he said, trying to talk and hold his breath.

"I bet it ain't," I said.

"You better watch that stuff, Kid," Jack said. "It'll have you goosing butterflies."

The kid laughed. "It don't do nothing to me no more."

I looked at him, eyed him up and down, and shook my head. "I bet it don't."

Carmilla and Margaret Alahambre stepped out of Fortenay's as Jack and the kid rounded the alley to the cable. "I must talk to you," Carmilla said.

"What now?" I stood still; she walked over and stopped three feet from me. Margaret stayed a couple of feet behind her, wringing her hands.

"Greta told me what you did." Carmilla's voice was softer, more friendly than I'd ever heard it. "How you risked your life to find her and bring her back." Carmilla's eyes turned misty. "That was very brave. I thank you for it."

"Well"—I cleared my throat—"it was something that had to be done, is all." I tipped my hat and started to step into the alley. I wasn't about to tell her my real purpose in going there.

"Did you happen to see my husband?" Margaret's voice sounded meek.

"Yeah," I said. "He was ablaze . . . last I saw him."

"Then he—he's dead?"

"Don't hold me to it," I said. "We all know how he is."

"Mister Beatty." Carmilla laid her hand on my arm; I stopped again. "I won't forget what you did for Greta. And I'm sorry for all the things I've accused you of."

"Well . . . no offense, ma'am, but you have been a little quick to judge." I smiled and stepped away into the alley.

Jack stood holding onto the cable while the kid stood atop a ladder unhooking the other end. "It's about time you done something to warm that little filly's heart," Jack said in a quiet voice. "I was starting to get concerned about ya."

"Lot of good it'll do me now," I said. I walked over and steadied the ladder.

"It always pays to be on good terms with beautiful women." Jack pulled the cable and it fell to the ground with a thud. "Even peculiar ones."

"Peculiar is right," I said, turning loose of the ladder and bending down to the cable. "Greta is afraid to be touched."

"No kidding? Wonder how long she's been that way." Jack reached in to help me.

"Who knows? Who cares?"

"I do." Jack chuckled. "I've always admired peculiarities in a woman."

"Then you and her oughta marry and raise a family. She's a straight-up lunatic, far as I can tell."

The kid climbed down. The three of us gathered the cable, carried it twenty yards from the wagons, and stretched it across the dirt street, from a heavy stack of lumber to a post outside the barber shop. When we finished, Jack and the kid headed back to the wagons. I walked over to the doctor's office to check on Briggs.

• 22 •

When I knocked on Doc Eisenhower's door in the gray hour of morning, he opened it a crack, saw it was me, and almost jerked me inside. I saw a club hanging from his hand. "Never stand in front of a door like that," he said. "What if I had a gun and thought you was one of Quarrels's boys?"

"You've got a point there," I said, not wanting to discuss it. "How's Briggs?"

"Not as well as he should be. Maybe his age is working against him."

I walked halfway across the floor toward the door to Briggs's room. "Can he ride?"

"Sure. But it'll kill him."

"So will Ned Quarrels."

The old doctor shrugged. "Then why'd you bother to ask?"

I nodded toward the door. "Can I see him?"

"Why not?" He stepped over, turned the knob, and pushed the door open with his club.

I looked down at the club. "You don't really expect to stop Quarrels with that, do you?"

"Naw—" He wiggled the club. "I'm not a fighter. This is just to let him know I'm not afraid. They won't bother me. Hell, they'll need my services, same as the rest of you."

I stepped into the dim lit room and saw Briggs turn his

head toward me as the floor squeaked beneath my boots. I swept off my hat and crossed the floor quietly. "It's me, Beatty," I said. "Are you awake?"

"Beatty," he said in a weak and shallow voice, "am I dead?"

"Why no, marshall. In fact, I think you're getting—"

"Then put . . . your hat back on." He coughed and pressed a hand to his bandaged chest. "Nothing worse . . . for a wounded man . . . than people standing over him . . . holding their hat."

"I guess you're right," I said. I dropped my hat back on my head.

"Marshall, I'm awful sorry about you getting shot. You was right. I shoulda never thought I could deal with the likes of Ned Quarrels." I wouldn't tell him that I *had* dealt with Quarrels, or that it had gone well until I decided to take Greta from him.

"You did the . . . best you could." He reached out a weak hand and patted my arm.

"Well"—I cleared my throat—"anyway, he's coming. I need to get you out of here."

Briggs turned his head back and forth slowly. "I ain't leaving. I still . . . gotta settle with him." He tried to raise up, but I lay a hand on his shoulder, stopping him.

"This was all over your son, wasn't it?"

"No. It was . . . all over the *law*. Ned killed my boy . . . but that's another matter."

"Quarrels claims that your son—" I started to say something but stopped myself. There was no point in mentioning suicide. It wouldn't change his mind even if it was true.

"I know what he claims." Briggs looked up into my eyes. "But I know what he did." He fanned a weak hand. "I always . . . know about these things. Just like . . . I knew who you are."

I offered a smile and nodded my head. "Well, you was right." I couldn't believe I was actually admitting something to a lawman. "I am an outlaw. I am Miller Crowe, and I—"

"Crowe? Ha." Briggs almost laughed, then grasped his chest. "I thought that at first . . . till I seen ya work. Crowe couldn't found his way to *Nuevo Mejico* . . . let alone butt heads with—"

"Damnit, Briggs, I'm telling ya—"

"You two might favor some. But I know who you are." He closed his eyes and smiled. "I know now . . . both you and your brother Frank."

"For Christsakes—" I rubbed my forehead and pinched the bridge of my nose. "Marshall, I hope you don't think I'm Jesse James. Because I ain't. I swear I ain't. And hell, my partner don't look nothing like Frank James. You saw the posters."

Briggs's smile spread slightly. "Your brother's smart. Too smart to wind up on a wanted poster."

"*God,* Briggs, you are *so* wrong, I don't know where to begin."

"How many of Quarrels's boys . . . have you took down already?"

I ran it through my mind. "Over half, I reckon."

"And you've still . . . got Sonny?"

"Yep, we've got him—"

"You've still got the payroll money?"

I didn't answer; a silence passed. "I thought so," Briggs said. His voice was fading. "Don't worry . . . I said I'd give the forty thousand to see . . . a couple of the boys lock horns with Ned. It's been . . . worth every penny." He folded his hands across his stomach and smiled. "Now go get your horse . . . Buck." I just stared at him. There was no point in trying to tell him anything. There was no point in even trying to move him. He wouldn't last the day.

"Get some rest," I said; I patted his folded hands and stepped away, turned, and walked back to the other room.

"So . . . what do you think, Mister Beatty?" The doctor sat sprawled on the wooden bench with his arm slung over, waving the skeleton's hand up and down.

I narrowed a gaze at him. "Why didn't you just tell me he's dying?"

"Because I don't know that it's true." The doctor raised his brow. "Only God knows the truth"—he chuckled; his belly rolled and bounced—"and people like Briggs and yourself, of course."

Fortenay was awake, red-eyed and greasing down his hair when I stepped through the door and headed to the stairs. "Did you hear any commotion in the alley or on the roof?" He looked at me from beneath a lowered brow, pulling a comb back across his head.

"Nope," I said, avoiding his gaze. I felt a slight tremor beneath my feet as I loped up the stairs.

Just as I turned into the hall toward Carmilla's door, I almost ran into Margaret Alahambre. Startled by my sudden appearance, she gasped and swayed. "Sorry," I said, and I caught her by the shoulders. "Are you all right?"

She fanned herself with her hand. "Yes. I just wasn't expecting anyone—"

"I know," I said. "I'm getting everybody up and ready to ride before Quarrels gets here."

I started to step around her, but she grabbed my arm. "Wait, Mister Beatty." I turned back to her. She glanced around and lowered her voice. "I know you couldn't say anything awhile ago with Carmilla around. But . . . you really killed Diamond Joe for me, didn't you? I mean . . . he didn't *really* fall in a fire."

I just stared at her. "No, Margaret, I didn't kill him. I'm sorry. But things were happening fast. We had to get away. I looked back and saw him on fire. It looked pretty bad."

"Oh . . . and you couldn't make time to just put a bullet through him. I mean, you were in such a—"

"Listen to me, Margaret." I shook her by the shoulders, not hard, but firm. "You've got to calm down and put him out of your mind some. This'll drive you crazy if you let it."

She raised a hand to her lips. "I know, I know. Forgive me. It's just that I feel so trapped. What if he's alive? What if he forces me back to him? What if he just waits until all this is over—"

I put my fingertips beneath her chin and raised her face gently. "You'll be leaving here today. . . . You'll soon be on your own . . . so go somewhere and get a divorce. . . . Make it legal."

"On my own? Alone? Oh . . ." She looked frightened at the prospect.

"And you'll do fine." I took my hands from her shoulders.

"But a divorce?" She shook her head slowly. "Mister Beatty, no judge will grant a divorce because a man beats his wife. They'll tell him not to do it again, of course. But what else can they say? I'm sure the court thinks a man has a right to beat his wife now and then—"

"I don't know about none of that," I said, shaking my head. "But surely you can get far enough away that he'll never find you."

"In other words, *run,* run and *hide.* Hide like an animal the rest of my life." She shrugged and lowered her head again. "That's all a *woman* can do, I suppose."

I lowered my hand and withdrew it, not knowing what else to say or do. If Diamond Joe was still alive, it sure wasn't my fault, God knows. But I made a mental note that if he was, and I ever drew another bead on him, I'd keep shooting him until there was nothing left to shoot at . . . shoot until they had to carry him away in a sponge. Surely to God that would do it.

"I'm sorry," I said; and I tried to step around her toward Carmilla's door.

"I suppose if *she* had a husband, you wouldn't hesitate a second to blow *his* head off."

"*Jesus,* Margaret." I swung a finger from Carmilla's

room to myself. "You don't think?" I wiped a hand across my forehead and stepped back toward her. She stepped back. "You've got this all wrong . . . very wrong."

"Sure I have." She glared at me with one hand turned backwards and thrown to her hip. I saw her shoe toe tap angrily, causing the hem of her dress to flutter like the wings of a hummingbird. "I despise you, Beatty! And I hate myself for ever being weak enough to come here with you . . . for ever falling for your *Mister-smooth-talking-so-polite-yes-ma'am-no-ma'am* ways—"

"Now hold on. As I recall, I didn't exactly ride in to sweep you off your feet. Seems like there was a whole lot else going on at the time—"

"Yes, and you took advantage of it, had me thinking I could depend on you . . . trust you to help, to look after me." Her face twisted into an ugly mask in the shadows of the hall light. She snapped back a hand and swung it at my face, but I caught it and held her wrist, then caught her other wrist as she swung her free hand.

"Settle down, now!" I pushed her away; she jarred against a door, pushed away from it, and stood ready to come at me again.

"You dirty—"

"Here now!" I heard a voice as the door swung open behind her. Mackay stepped out, running a hand back across his hair. We both looked at him. He looked us up and down and smiled. "My, my, Mister Beatty, *wherever* do you find the time?"

"Where's Sonny?" I glanced all around as if I'd find him somewhere at our feet.

"Soundly chained, in the livery barn, sir. Tripplet is watching him. I came up for a fresh handkerchief." He patted his breast pocket.

"Good," I said. "I want you to get him and bring him here. I'll be down in a couple of minutes—"

"Lucky for me you're here, Mister Mackay," Margaret

said, cutting me off. Her expression turned incredulous. "I believe he was actually going to strike me!" I saw her arm fold across her injured side.

"Oh . . . but we can't have that, now can we?" Mackay stepped in between us, swept an arm around her waist, and guided her away from me toward the stairs. He glanced over his shoulder at me. "You are a scoundrel, sir!" But he grinned, arched an eyebrow, and winked. "Don't you worry, dear Missus Alahambre—"

"It's Margaret, please—"

"Dear *Margaret,* then." He nodded curtly as they stepped out of sight and into the stairwell. "I pray you're feeling better?"

"Much better, thank you, Mister Mackay. May I call you Thomas?" I heard her ask.

"I insist."

I breathed deep, shook my head, and walked back to Carmilla's room and knocked softly on the door. "It's me, Beatty," I said.

"Come in," I heard her say; and I slipped inside and saw her sitting on the side of the bed pressing a cold rag to Greta's forehead.

"He . . . hit me." Greta raised a finger toward me.

"Jesus," I said under my breath.

"Shhh." Carmilla said, pressing Greta's arm down gently. "If he did, it was only because he felt he had to."

"Uh, ma'am," I said, stepping closer. "I'm having the kid take both of you to Cimarron, just as soon as you can get yourselves ready."

Carmilla looked around me. "What about you . . . you and your friend?"

"We'll hold them here," I said. "We can hold them long enough for you to get away . . . I'm pretty sure—"

"And then what?" She stood up with the wet rag hanging from her hand. "They will kill you? I cannot ride away and leave you here to—"

"Ma'am." I raised a hand, cutting her off. "There's no time to talk about it. This is how it's gonna be. I want y'all ready to ride before they get here. Please go along with me on this."

She bit the inside of her lip, studying me, then stepped forward. "We are like sisters, she and I." She nodded back toward Greta as she stopped a foot from me. "I will never forget what you have done." She laid a hand on my shoulder.

"It had to be done," I said softly. I pulled back the dark veil of hair and smoothed it behind her shoulder. It was soft and light, like running my hand across a draft of warm air. I felt strange being close to her, touching her hair, and I did so the way a person touches something precious and rare, savoring it. And only as I touched her did I realize how badly I'd longed to touch her ever since the first day we'd met. She was something distant and forbidden to me, and I felt myself stroke her hair and hoped I'd remember the feel of it for a long time to come.

I left her and went downstairs, stopping on the third step from the bottom and looking around the saloon. Daylight spilled through the broken window in an early morning haze. Jack leaned in the doorway, watching the street with a rifle hanging from one hand and a beer and a biscuit in the other. The kid stood with a boot propped on the broken window frame. A rifle lay across his knee; he flipped a bullet up and down like tossing a coin.

RC stood against the bar, his eyes swollen and black, staring at a full bottle of whiskey as if seeing his future in it. Tripplet stood beside him, writing in his pad.

At RC's feet, Sonny Quarrels lay chained to the bar rail. He stared at me wild-eyed. "I'm tired of all this moving back and forth," he said in a trembling voice. "We're s'posed to have a deal—"

"Shut up!" RC reached over and grazed him with a boot heel.

At the table near RC and Tripplet, Mackay sat dealing cards slowly to Margaret Alahambre, leaning forward and smiling at her from behind a black cigar. Margaret flicked her eyes past me and back to Mackay with a smile of deep satisfaction. Somewhere in the distance a rooster crowed.

Down the bar from RC and Tripplet, of all people the banjo player from Lambert's stood leaning half across the bar with his banjo hanging down his back, talking to Fortenay and tapping a finger from one knot to another on top of his bald head. Fortenay stood listening to him with his arms folded on the bar. I saw him nod. He ran a hand back across his greasy hair and patted it in place. "You didn't pick the best time to come here," I heard him say. "But either way it goes, once this mess is over, somebody will be thirsty. Some good music oughta pack 'em in."

I felt a tremor run across the floor, followed by a heavy thud, and I froze. "The hell was that?" I glanced at the faces along the bar, then remembered the cable we'd taken from the side of the building. "Everybody who's leaving better get going. Everybody's who's staying better get armed."

"That was just the building settling," said Fortenay. "The rain softened the ground, but it's nothing to worry about. It's well braced." He spread his arms. "You've all got time for a little eye-opener before Quarrels gets here."

"Oh, you've returned!" Gustav said, stepping out of the kitchen behind the bar. He raised a finger. "One second, I'll be right back."

I stood for an anxious second, looking from one to the other until Gustav returned carrying a stack of paper in his hand. "Here's some recipes I thought of since the other day." I saw the worried look on his face as he held them out to me. "I thought—after this is over . . . maybe you—" He looked down at the floor.

"Thanks," I said. "They'll come in handy. But what about you, Gustav? Don't you think you oughta get out of here before the shooting starts?"

He proudly jutted his chin. "I'm a good chef, Mister Beatty. A good chef doesn't run from anybody."

"Goddamn right," I heard RC say; and I heard him pull the cork from the bottle of whiskey. I smiled, walked over beside Jack in the doorway and looked out with him.

"I reckon we all handle things our own way, don't we?" I said quietly.

Jack nodded. He still wore his long duster buttoned all the way up to his chin. I heard him chuckle as he watched me shove the recipes in my pocket. Once more the floor trembled and thudded beneath us. Jack glanced around and spoke to me in a lowered voice. "If this place falls over on its side," he said, "I'd like to find me a whore and dance on the mirror." He nodded over his shoulder at the banjo player. "Think he knows 'Bound for the Rio Grande'?"

I glanced around at the battered banjo player, then back to Jack. "If he *did* he wouldn't be here," I said.

• 23 •

I'd leaned against the wagon, bone tired, my face cradled in my arms; in spite of all that was going on, I'd dozed off. Somewhere in my drifting state, I'd pictured myself laying in a cool shallow stream with the water flowing over me, cleansing me. Then I felt a hand shake my shoulder. I raised my face, squinted against the sun's glare, and saw Jack standing beside me with his rifle cradled in his arms. "I hope you're in the mood for company," he said. "We got some coming."

I straightened up, rubbing my eyes, forgetting for a second what the night had bequeathed to me. "What time is it?" Then I looked around the small area between the wagons as realization set in.

Jack spit and shook his head. "Time? It's time to get up and get shot at." He picked up my rifle from against the wagon and shoved it to me. "Ok, *deputy,* show your stuff." I heard a loud slapping sound beyond the wagons and I ducked slightly before seeing it was only Gustav pitching a bucket of water from the boardwalk in front of Fortenay's On The Frontier. I saw him cast a nervous glance up the cluttered street and disappear back inside the tavern. "Everybody's a little edgy today." Jack smiled.

"I reckon," I said. I slapped my hat against my leg, dropped it on my head and tightened it down. "Still cold?"

Jack's duster was still buttoned from his throat to his waist, then thrown back behind his pistol butt. He sniffed and ran a finger beneath his nose.

"Yeah, after that storm . . . I hope I ain't coming down with something," he said.

We stepped over to the wagon and looked out across it. It only made sense that Quarrels would come in from this direction with the sun in our eyes. Because of our small numbers, I didn't figure he would come in from both ends of town. One quick run was all he'd think we were worth. And in that one quick run, we had to take down him, The Rake, and as many riders as possible before they knew what hit them.

If that didn't work, my plan was to then pull back to Fortenay's, slip out through the back to the livery barn, and help the kid take the women and make a run for Cimarron while Quarrels pounded the hell out of the tavern. Quarrels would have a few men strung out around the town, but I figured the kid would get the women through while Jack and I kept the gunmen busy. It wasn't the best plan in the world, but it was all I could come up with.

I glanced around and saw the kid sitting up on the edge of the other wagon absently twirling his pistol. *"Damn it,"* I said under my breath; then I spoke out to him. "Get down from there, Kid. You make a perfect target." He tipped a finger to his hat with a stupid grin and slipped off the wagon. I shook my head and turned to Jack. "Why do you suppose he's still in on this?"

Jack grinned and spit a stream of tobacco. "Crazy, I guess. Just looking for something to do."

"Here they come!" I heard Carmilla call out from above Fortenay's; no sooner than she said it, I heard the crack of a rifle shot from the distance. Above the piles of lumber and delivery wagons, I saw hats bobbing up and down and felt the earth tremble from the impact of many hooves. Then the sound stopped suddenly.

"Jesse James! You rotten, back-stabbing son of a bitch!" Ned's voice rolled like thunder down the mud street.

"Here goes," I said, jacking a round into my rifle chamber.

"Goddamn!" the kid yelled. Jack and I both looked over at him. His mouth hung open. "Jesse James? You're him? You're Jesse James?"

"No, Kid," I said, "so don't start thinking it."

"I heard what he called ya—" He looked from me to Jack. "Is he, really?"

"Don't make a big thing of it, Kid," Jack said. But I saw the kid spin in a circle, pitch his pistol high in the air and catch it. "Gaw-hod-damn!" A grin wrapped around his head. "If he's Jesse"—the kid pointed at Jack and jumped up and down, his eyes wide—"you must be Frank!"

"Please, Kid." Jack held up a hand to calm him down.

"Morning, Ned," I yelled out down the cluttered street. We waited, listening to the ring of silence in the morning air, but we heard no reply. I felt a slow steady throb in my forehead, like the low beat of a funeral drum. "Been expecting ya, Ned, so ride on in and let's settle up." I glanced at Jack; there was still no answer.

I saw Fortenay run from the front door of his tavern carrying a box piled high with bottles of his most expensive whiskey. He stopped for a second and yelled back over his shoulder to Gustav, "Put a fresh keg on the beer tap. They'll be thirsty, either way it goes." He glanced our way, ducked his head and pounded off between the stacks of building material. I saw the banjo player slip out the door and disappear like smoke.

I caught a glimpse of The Rake riding his horse slowly to the edge of a pile of bricks and leaning around cautiously. "Half of forty thousand ain't *twenty-five,* Jesse."

I felt my face redden. "I never claimed to be a bookkeeper."

"Did you really do that?" I glanced at Jack and saw the

incredulous look in his eyes. "That's the craziest thing you've ever done. Half of forty thousand is—"

"Damn it, Jack, they believed it . . . at the time." I saw The Rake's horse step back out of sight. "It don't matter. There was no stopping this from the get-go."

"Yeah, but my God"—I heard Jack cock his rifle—*"twenty-five thousand?* That was insulting."

"Then, the next time . . . you handle it, okay? I get tired of having to do everything my damn self—"

"We're taking what's ours," The Rake said, "including Briggs's hide." He waited a second. "So, do you want to live or die?"

"Now that's a stupid question, Rake, even for you."

There was a tense silence, then Jack turned to me. "Listen to that," he said.

I listened for a second; we heard the low rumble of hooves jar the ground. "Here they come." I felt the funeral drum pound in my temples.

"Yep. Time to go to work." Jack turned his head and spit out his wad of tobacco. "Or is this a part of the *'everything you have to do yourself'?"*

"Sorry," I said. "I suppose I'm a little overwrought here." I nervously slid my free hand across my shoulder harness, down to the forty-four at my waist and around over the hideout pistol in the small of my back. A rifle slug thumped against the wagon; I heard the kid let out a crazy laugh, caught a glimpse of him reaching up and firing a round into the group of riders swinging around a stack of boards forty yards away. For a split second, time seemed to stop, then it started moving again . . . only torturously slow, like we were in the midst of a bad dream. Six riders bolted from the bottleneck of lumber and spread out abreast as they pounded toward us.

Jack had turned and started away from me as I fired a round and recocked my rifle. I shot him a glance. "Jack—" He glanced back over his shoulder. It seemed to take him forever just to return my gaze. "Be careful." My voice was drowned by a volley of fire.

"Shit," he said, and he grinned. His voice sounded long and tedious. Then hell exploded.

Three front riders didn't see the drawn cable until their horses slid sideways to avoid it. One horse caught the cable at knee level and spilled over it sideways in a spray of dust. The other two stopped short and sent their riders flying in the air. A shot exploded from Jack's rifle and a rider hit the ground leaving a mist of blood in the air.

I hit one of the stalled riders in the chest as he jerked his horse back and forth along the cable. Two others had dropped from their horses, and they took cover behind a stack of nail kegs. More riders bolted forward from among the building material. Some left their horses and spilled across the lumber and delivery wagons like an endless army of ants. Orange puffs of smoke exploded.

I pounded out rounds until my rifle was empty, felt a storm of lead slap against the wagon, and felt a streak cut across my shoulder as I ducked down and threw my rifle aside.

"Stay back!" Jack yelled at me as I ran toward him and the kid. I stopped. With my forty-four in one hand and my hideout in the other, I lunged up on the wagon and emptied them both into the swirl of men, horses, and dust, then dropped back down as a chunk of shattered wood stung the side of my face. Shots bounced under the wagon, kicking up dirt; I rolled away from them until I felt the wagon wheel against my back. "Stay back," Jack yelled again. I saw him drop down and shove cartridges into his La Faucheux. I couldn't tell him I was only rolling toward him to keep from getting hit.

I saw the kid stand straight up on the edge of the wagon. He let out a long yell, fired repeatedly as chunks of firewood exploded at his feet and bullets whizzed past him. I shoved bullets in my forty-four and saw the kid hit the ground. I thought he was dead for a split second as I snapped my pistol closed and raised up to fire, but then I heard him laugh and let out another crazy cowboy yell.

I fired four quick shots and saw two men fly backwards against the nail kegs. The kegs rolled away. Jack and the kid dropped two more men as they scrambled for new cover. "I'm here, goddamn it!" I heard a voice yell from the boardwalk at the end of our wagons. I caught a glimpse of RC staggering toward me, bare-chested, waving a pistol and a shotgun . . . drunker than a skunk. "I ain't afraid of no sumbitch!" I snatched the shotgun from his hand as he staggered past me, leveled it across the wagon, and emptied a barrel into the chest of an oncoming gunman.

"Hold your fire, goddamn it!" I heard Ned Quarrels shout from somewhere behind a stack of roof sheeting. Two more rounds thumped against the wagon; RC stopped and staggered in place.

"They don't want no part of me! Yeee-hi!" He pulled off a round straight up. The kid jumped up and fired three quick rounds, then ducked back down. There was no fire from Quarrels's men, and I shook my head to still the ringing in my ears.

"I said, hold your fire, damn it," Quarrels yelled.

"Screw you, Ned," the kid yelled. "I don't take orders from—"

"Hold it, Kid," Jack said. I ducked, shoved RC out of my way, snatched up my rifle, and ran up to Jack, reloading. I heard RC cursing in a slurred voice behind me.

"Jesse!" Quarrels yelled. "Make them stop. . . . Goddamn it! Let's talk."

"Marn-gret, is nat nuu?" I heard Diamond Joe's terrible duck voice yell toward Fortenay's.

"What do you want, Ned?" I shouted. "We're kinda busy here."

"Is nat nuu, Marn-gret? Darl-ren?"

"Shut up, Joe, goddamn it!" Quarrels bellowed; I heard

a loud thump and a deep grunt, then, after a second of silence, "Jesse, I want my brother. . . . let's talk."

"Jesse?" I heard RC behind me. "He called you Jesse?" I heard him belch and mumble something.

"Yeah, RC," I said over my shoulder. "Now set down and shut up."

"That's right, RC," I heard the kid say. "He's Jesse—fucking—James, you idiot! And this is Frank. Now think about *that,* you drunk son of a bitch."

"Is that true?" RC's voice sounded weak.

"It's a long story," I heard Jack say to him.

"I wish I'd knowed that to begin with—"

"Ain't as easy as you thought, is it, Ned?" I yelled over the wagon while I reloaded my other pistol and shoved it into my belt. He'd rode in red-hot, strapped for a quick killing. Now that we'd thrown it back in his face, he'd cooled some. "Are you ready to surrender?"

I heard Ned chuckle above the silence of the street. "That's a good one, Jesse. I'm just thinking . . . it'd be better to stop this thing right here. You already see the outcome. All I want is my brother—"

"What about our goddamn money?" I heard The Rake bellow at Ned.

"What about him killing Chester and the others?" somebody yelled.

"Everybody shut the hell up!" I heard Ned shout, then silence for a second. "You wanted your horse . . . you can have him."

"Nice try, Ned. What about the woman? Thought you wouldn't give her up."

"Keep her, Jesse," said Ned. I heard grumbling among his men.

"And the marshall? I thought you wanted him pretty bad."

"Well . . . can't always get what we want, can we? If he's dying anyhow, that'll be good enough."

I heard a rustle of footsteps, leaned down, and looked under the wagon, saw a gunman crouched and sneaking across the street. I popped a round into his foot and heard him squall like a panther.

"That's cheating, Ned," I said. "I'm starting to think you ain't an honorable man."

"Everybody stay put!" Ned yelled to his men, then spoke to me. "He did that on his own, Jesse. But you can trust me now. We got off on the wrong foot here. I was awful damn mad about your arithmetic . . . and taking that woman. But we can settle here and now with no hard feelings."

"No way, Ned. I double-crossed you on the deal. Now I'm afraid to trust you. Now I gotta kill you. Can you understand that?"

There was a long second of silence. "Goddamn it, Jesse. I'm giving you everything you ask for—"

"Don't beg these sons a bitches, Ned," I heard The Rake say. "I'm taking you straight to hell, Mister Jesse—by God—James. That's all the deal I've got for ya."

"Good luck, Rake," I called out. "But to be honest with you, I don't think you've got a chance here. You've just got a bunch of boys stupid enough to die while you and Ned sit back and hide. Once we kill them, you two will turn tail." I waited a second, then said, "You boys see that, don't ya? Ned and The Rake ain't exactly *leading* this charge . . . are they?"

"What's he mean, Ned?" I heard a voice from behind one of the nail kegs in the street.

"Shut up," The Rake yelled. "He's trying to get you rattled."

"Rattled—shit! I'm shot in the damn foot here."

"All right, Jesse," Ned shouted. "Have it your way. If you want to die over this . . . it's up to you. I ain't offering again."

"Ned . . . I'm a lawman now"—I looked at Jack, grinned and winked—"and this town ain't big enough for both of us." I saw Jack grin and shake his head.

"You're a crazy sucker, is what you are," The Rake shouted. "And I'm gonna be the man that killed ya." I heard the sound of horses and men backing away among the building material. "Next place I'll see you is in hell!"

"Whant 'bount my winfe?" Joe yelled. "Marn-gret, nuu hear me? Lent's go home and manke up."

I jacked a round into my rifle, and I motioned for Jack and the kid to follow me to the boardwalk at the end of the wagons. RC stood leaning with his hand on a wagon wheel and staring at the ground. "What about him?" the kid asked, when he and Jack joined me.

"Leave him be," I said. "He's too drunk to die."

"Where we going?" The kid looked all around. "Are we running away?"

I pulled him by his arm. "No, Kid. But you're gonna take the women and make a run for Cimarron, remember?"

Jack shoved him along. "Just go on, Kid. It'll come to ya." Jack glanced at the blood running down my arm from the graze. "You're hit, you know?"

"It ain't nothing." I ran my hand down my arm.

"*Damn!* I love this," said the kid. "Getting shot don't even bother y'all! You *are* the James brothers!"

Inside Fortenay's, Carmilla and Greta stood near the rear door ready to make a run for the livery barn. Gustav poked his head up from behind the bar, saw us, and ducked back down.

"You better hightail it out of here too, Gustav," I yelled.

The kid ran beside me and we threw open the back door, jumped out behind a pile of bricks, and searched the rows of roof sheeting, nail kegs, and buckets of roofing tar for any of Quarrels's men. When I saw there was none, I looked up and shrugged. "Maybe Quarrels *really* is dumb," Jack said as they hurried away.

"Careful, Kid," I said, and we backed away toward the barn with our guns scanning the building material.

Carmilla slipped in beside me. "I must stay and help you—"

"No. Just go with the kid. You'll all be all right."

Mackay sat watching, seated on a nail keg with a shotgun across his lap under one hand and holding a hand of cards and cigar in the other as we slipped inside the barn. Margaret Alahambre stood beside him with her hands on his shoulder. The quart of bourbon sat on the ground at his feet. Sonny Quarrels lay shackled on a pile of straw. He sat up; his hands raised toward me. "Make a deal for godsakes! What the hell's wrong with you?"

Mackay shot out a foot and slammed Sonny backwards. "My, my," he said to me, as I bolted the door behind us. "That certainly was a *loud* confrontation. I trust you managed to hit someone?" Beside him, a few feet away, Tripplet scribbled fervently on a pad of paper.

Carmilla and Greta worked quickly, checking the saddled horses, leading them from their stalls, and tying them near the front door. "We whittled 'em down some," I said. "They see we ain't a bunch of school children." I untied the bandanna from around my neck and tried to wrap it around under my arm.

"Here," said Mackay, standing. He stepped over, took the bandanna, and wrapped it tight. I stood impatiently as he tied it and patted my shoulder. "There now, all done."

I didn't know when Ned would hit again, but it wouldn't be long; now that he saw we weren't an easy kill, I figured he'd take us more seriously. He knew we'd try to get ready for him. He wasn't about to give us the chance.

"Where is our good friend and colleague, Mister Allison?" Mackay looked all around as if he'd missed seeing him.

"Staggering around drunk out there somewhere," I said. "We didn't have time to fool with him. He'll be all right. Nothing happens to a drunk. They all seem to know him."

"Yes, indeed." Mackay smiled. "Everybody knows RC."

I looked at Mackay and nodded toward Jack. "My friend tells me a lot of folks in Texas knows you, too. I'm sorry I misjudged you."

"I've tried to tell you, Mister Beatty. I'm not without a certain amount of resource." He glanced at Tripplet and back to me. "Nothing worth writing about . . . evidently. But I have managed to hold my own here in this vast and desolate land."

"Then do me a favor," I said, leaning in close. "Hold Sonny till the end. If everything fails, and you're the only one left, trade him to Ned for Briggs. Briggs deserves to die in peace."

"Consider it done," said Mackay. "Where is our dear old marshall?"

"Still at Doc Eisenhower's," I said. "I figured it was the last place Ned would look for a wounded man."

Mackay coughed and nodded. "Good thinking."

"Thanks, Doc," I said.

I started toward Carmilla as the horses and Tripplet stepped up in front of me. "Just one quick question, Mister Beatty. When Quarrels and his men first rode in, did he offer you one last chance to surrender? You know"—Tripplet rolled his thick hand before him—"sort of like the old *Alamo* situation?"

I straight-armed him out of the way and stepped over to Carmilla. Glaring back at Tripplet, she handed me the reins to Lambert's big mare. "You should give this *writer* a gun and let him learn the story for himself." For no reason at all, she raised a hand and brushed my hair back from my eyes.

"Thanks." I looked at her for a second. "But forget him, and get ready to ride." I led the horse over to where Jack and the kid stood peeping through a crack in the barn. We heard the sound of horses pounding up toward Fortenay's On The Frontier. I shot Jack and the kid a glance. "I hope Gustav hightailed it like I told him to."

When we'd mounted inside the barn, I looked down at

Mackay smoking his black cigar and motioned for him to swing open the rear door. "Thanks for your help, Mackay. See you again someday."

"Or," he said, "as they so colorfully say in these parts, 'See you in hell.' "

"I hope not," I said.

Margaret Alahambre stepped beside Mackay and wrapped her arm around his. He tipped a finger to his hat as I glanced past him and saw the snarl on Sonny's face. His shackled hands were clenched into fists, and he lay in the straw staring at me.

I looked back when the mare stepped out of the barn and saw the others come out behind me, Jack with the saddlebags of money lashed behind his saddle, followed by Tripplet who rode with his pencil and pad in hand. Behind him, Carmilla, followed by Greta, then the kid, glancing around with a rifle propped up from his saddle. "I'm counting on you here, Kid," I called back to him. "Don't let them catch you."

He didn't appear to have a care in the world. "Don't worry about nothing. They'll have to kill us first." I saw a Mexican brown hanging between his fingers. Smoke curled and crawled on the back of his hand like a gray snake.

I saw Greta stiffen at the kid's words. "Don't worry," Jack said. "He's just blowing off." He reached out and patted Greta's shoulder. She flinched at first, but then nodded and ducked her face as Jack brushed back her hair. "He'll take care of ya. I promise. And *if* I live through this"—Jack squeezed her hand gently—"well . . . we'll just see." His voice trailed into a whisper. Greta tapped her fingertips beneath her big blue eyes.

We slipped along quietly between the building material and scattered debris, and I pulled up beside Carmilla and stopped. "Ride hard," I said to her. I looked into her eyes; her eyes glistened.

She nodded. "This seems so unfair. You saved my friend, and yet I must leave you here to—"

"Just go," I said. I saw the kid take the lead, and I reined back the mare and slapped Carmilla's horse before she could say anymore. Just as they rounded past a row of abandoned tents, Jack and I turned our horses back toward town.

"This is it, Jesse!" We heard Ned call out to Fortenay's from the street. "Come out now, or I'll torch this dump to the ground."

"Boy, he really is stupid," said Jack, gigging his silver-gray up beside me.

"So far, so good," I said quietly, knowing that every second counted in getting them a head start across the desert and back to Cimarron. I planned to circle behind what was left of the gang and hit them hard while they were busy pounding hell out of Fortenay's.

But then, no sooner had I said it, I heard a voice answer Quarrels from inside Fortenay's. "Come in and get me, you varmint!"

"Who the hell—?" Jack and I stopped our horses cold in their tracks and stared at each other, stunned.

"Gustav?" I shrugged at Jack.

"Varmint?" Jack shrugged in reply.

"You'll never take me alive!" I heard the voice again; it *was* Gustav.

"Then I won't plan to," I heard Ned Quarrels yell. "I'll just burn your ass out of there."

"Damn it all!" I jerked off my hat and slapped it against my leg. "What *the hell* does Gustav think he's doing?"

• 24 •

As soon as we hit the street, I slid the mare to a halt on her haunches and slipped from the saddle before she stood back up. I jerked down my shotgun and slapped the mare away. Up at Fortenay's, rifles pounded the building, tearing off chunks of wood in a spray of splinters. Quarrels's men hadn't even bothered to take cover. They stood half way across the street, firing as they walked closer. I counted eight of them. Two of them carried torches. The cable we'd strung across the street had been ripped down and thrown to the side.

"Here goes." I threw the ten-gauge up and pulled off a round. The shotgun thundered above the rifle fire and caused all heads to jerk toward us.

"Look at this, boss," someone yelled.

"Hold your fire," I heard Ned Quarrels say, and I saw him step his horse around from behind a stack of lumber with Jake The Rake right beside him. I stood with the shotgun propped on my hip as they rode toward us slowly, followed by the men on foot, spreading out as they came. My heart thumped in my chest. Out of the corner of my eye, I saw RC leaning against a post with a bottle hanging from one hand and a pistol from the other.

"Damn, Jack. Is this all that's left of Quarrels's bunch?"

"It's been a busy day," he said. "You've done some serious dickering."

I glanced at him and raised my forty-four, checked it, and kept it cocked back, my thumb across the hammer, ready to drop it when I drew a bead. In my other hand I held the shotgun propped up from my hip. "What do you think?"

"About what?" I saw him lay his hand near the La Faucheux, and it crossed my mind that after today, he'd never draw that fancy gun again. He shot me a grin. "I think you better hit three out of four of everybody you shoot at. That's long odds against this many, even for me."

"So, you're saying I don't have a chance here?" I took a deep breath and let it out.

"This ain't the time to explain the arithmetic of gunfighting. Can you take out that fat son of a bitch with the shotgun?"

I looked at Ned and The Rake leading the wedge of gunmen up the dirt street. Beside him, Tiny Boyd walked along with a shotgun at port arms. "Yeah," I said, "that's Tiny. He don't like me anyway. What're you gonna be doing?"

"Going for Quarrels and The Rake."

"Which one first?"

"I ain't sure. Maybe both at once. I'll see how it goes."

"Let me know something here, Jack. I'll get whichever one you don't."

"Just keep that shotgunning son of a bitch busy." Jack took a short step forward.

"And then what . . . that's it? I can just go home? Tell me what you got in mind, goddamn it, before they get here!" I stepped up beside him.

"Whew! You're getting on my nerves." Jack let his cocked hand go loose and shook it out, then recocked it. "When the wedge opens, shoot everything on your side, starting from the nearest and back." He shot me a glance. "Do I have to tell you everything here?"

"I just wanted to know your plan, is all." I looked him up and down. "Why don't you go ahead and draw your pistol now before—"

"Settle down, *goddamn it,"* Jack said. "I hate it when you start acting like this."

"All right, Jesse!" The Rake yelled from thirty yards away. "One question. Live . . . or die?"

"Why does he keep asking me that?" I whispered out the side of my mouth. "It's plain stupid." I leaned near Jack. "You know, if he wins, he's gonna *really* think he killed Jesse and Frank James."

"Yeah . . . and Jesse *really* will kill him."

"I told you they're dumb."

Ned and The Rake jerked their horses, pulled them up at thirty feet, in respect for the wide pattern of my ten-gauge. Ned spun his horse sideways, and raised an arm to halt his gunmen. "Well, now," he called out. "You're full of surprises today." He nodded his head back toward Fortenay's. "Who's that back there?"

"Just a chef . . . a bartender." I stared at him and The Rake. "You know how they can get." I raised my voice and called out at Fortenay's: "You all right in there, Gustav?"

"I'm not Gustav, I'm Beatty . . . James Beatty," I heard him call back, trying to disguise his voice. "I'm a horse dealer—"

"I'm out here, Gustav . . . but thanks anyway."

"Oh," said Gustav, in a weak voice.

I squinted, shook my head, and looked up at Ned. "He ain't done nothing. Just let him go."

Ned tossed his head back at the torchmen. "Light it up."

"Wait!" I stepped forward. "Let the cook go."

Ned spread an evil grin. "Ready to deal again, huh?"

The Rake sat silent, tensed as a coiled viper.

I shot Jack a glance, saw he was ready for whatever call I made.

"Yep." I let out a breath. "Let the cook go. You take

your brother and half the money. I get my horse and keep the marshall. That's all I can do for ya." I watched and waited.

"What about the woman?" Ned stared cold-eyed. "I really wanted her."

"Yeah, and that's where it all went wrong on us." I stared right back. "Forget her. She's gone. She never was a part of it. You've heard my last offer."

He pushed up his hat brim with a long finger and spread a dark grin. "That would've worked earlier. But now you've shot up most of my men—"

"I ain't afraid of no sumbitch, drunk or sober," RC blurted out from the boardwalk. "I've killed Chinamen, Mexic—"

"Shut up, RC, goddamn it!" The Rake yelled. Clay Allison stared through a drunken fog.

"—And you've cost me a lot of time." Ned finished and shot RC a dark stare. "Go sober up, RC. This ain't none of your concern."

"All right then, by God. Don't say I didn't tell ya." RC nodded and leaned back against the building.

I felt my finger clammy and tense against the trigger on the ten-gauge. Ned shook his head and grinned again. "Now I gotta have it all. I get Briggs, the money, my brother, the woman . . . *hell,* your pocket watch if you own one." I heard a ripple of laughter among his men. The Rake stifled a laugh and stared at me with eyes like poison darts.

"That's foolish of you," I said, "giving up everything else just for that old lawman. But I'll give you Sonny, *all* the money, you forget about torching the cook, and give me back my horse. I told you, the woman's gone."

"Not as foolish as it is for *you,"* Ned said, "over a damn chef."

"A good chef is hard to find," I said. "Now what do you say?" I looked past him, then back into his eyes. Ned turned in his saddle without answering, waved the torchmen away from Fortenay's, then waved a hand toward a stack of roofing. I saw Diamond Joe lead Buck out into the street and start forward. I felt my chest tighten and resisted the urge to run to him. I knew that Ned was only baiting me, hoping I'd see Buck and forget everything else.

Buck saw me, threw his head up, and nickered. Joe held the lead rope tight, keeping him from bolting to me.

"I figured *that* was your stallion," said Ned Quarrels. "That's the worst son of a bitch I ever seen. I'd have given you a hundred dollars to take him back . . . before all this got out of control."

"He's got his ways," I said, waiting as Diamond Joe walked up beside Quarrels, leading Buck. Now that I saw Buck was all right, I hoped to bargain Quarrels away from killing Briggs. Neither of us had mentioned Briggs in the last offer, so I figured Ned was still as dead set on taking him as I was on not giving him up.

"Where's my winfe, gondamn-nit?" Diamond Joe's hand went to a pistol at his side. His face was a mess. His clothes were burnt and torn to shreds. I saw that his chest was wrapped tight in bloodstained bandages.

"Easy, Diamond," Quarrels cautioned him.

"She's gone," I said. "What'd you expect, you rotten son of a bitch? You can't beat a woman like she's a—"

"That's enough," Ned Quarrels said. "Either deal, or die like a dog in the street."

I stood firm. I wouldn't give up Briggs. I felt like telling Jack to make a run for it but I knew he wouldn't. If we had to go down this way, I only hoped that Buck would get away and the kid had enough sense to get the women to Cimarron.

" 'Like a dog in the street'? My, my, Ned Quarrels, but aren't you the dramatist today." I heard Mackay chuckle from somewhere behind me, and I heard his soft footsteps come closer, out of an alley from between stacks of building material.

"You said you weren't in this, Mackay!" The Rake's expression changed as Mackay stopped beside me fifteen feet away. I could smell the cigar smoke in the breeze. I saw Sonny land on the ground in front me with a grunt.

"Boss," someone said from behind Ned Quarrels, "we never figured on Mackay being in this—"

"Shut up," Ned snapped over his shoulder. He gazed at Mackay. "What's your angle in all this, Doc? I got no fight with you."

"Oh, merely an observer of the human condition," Mackay said; I heard two hammers of a shotgun cock beside me. "But I wouldn't want to see Mister Beatty or his friend here fall on unfortunate circumstances. Good poker players—like good chefs—are hard to find."

"You're making a bad mistake, Doc," said Quarrels. "This son of a bitch is Jesse James . . . that's his brother Frank."

"I won't even attempt to tell you how wrong you are," Mackay said. "But let me caution you, that unlike our dear RC over there, I have pushed sobriety to a dangerous level this morning. I'll simply empty this shotgun into Sonny and be done with it."

"There's still eight of us, and only three of you," Ned warned.

"And yet, *you're* the only one who's counting," said Mackay. His voice had changed to a murmur as he raised the shotgun to his shoulder and aimed it down at Sonny Quarrels. I saw he meant to kill him, and I felt my hand drift down with my ten-gauge.

Diamond Joe stepped back, pulling Buck with him. Buck tugged against the rope and snorted. Behind Quarrels, his men spread out more. The Rake's hand slid to his pistol; he stared straight at Jack. Jack's hand hung calmly near the La Faucheux.

"Aw Jesus—" I breathed to myself, ready to drop the first

round into Tiny Boyd, then Ned, then go for my pistol. *"We're all gonna die here."*

"Wait, goddamn it!" Ned threw up a hand. Mackay kept the shotgun pointed but looked up at him. "Everybody hold it!" Quarrels's hand trembled. Rake stopped, with his thumb already across the hammer, ready to swing the forty-four up from his holster. "We'll deal," said Quarrels. "Let's stay calm. I'll settle for Sonny and the payroll. To hell with Briggs. Diamond, give him his horse! Go ahead!" Ned sounded rattled.

"What abount my winfe, Marn-gret?" Diamond Joe leaned toward Quarrels.

"That's your goddamn problem, you stupid goose-mouthed son of a bitch—!" Quarrels bumped his horse against Diamond Joe, almost knocking him to the ground. Buck snorted and reared, spun and kicked, barely missing Ned's face. "This whole goddamn mess is your fault. Now give him that ornery goddamn horse before it kills somebody!"

I let go a tense breath and felt my finger relax on the trigger as Diamond Joe stepped forward and led Buck closer. "Now," Quarrels said, nodding down at Sonny, "uncuff him and give us the money." Diamond stopped and jerked Buck to a halt. Buck jerked at the rope, ran around Diamond Joe and stopped behind him. Joe gathered the rope quickly and held Buck close beside him.

"Easy, boy," I called out to Buck, then turned toward Jack. "Okay, Jack, throw in the money."

Jack stepped back slowly to his horse, slipped the saddlebags from behind his saddle, drew back, and hurled them into the street. Jake The Rake slipped down, picked them up, and started unfastening the straps.

"Now give me my horse," I said. But Diamond Joe only stood there with a strange grin on his face.

"After all nuu done to me? Funck nuu!" He reached up quickly, snatched Buck by the halter with one hand and flashed a long dagger from under his coat with his other. "I'll knill 'im!"

"Turn him loose, Joe!" shouted Quarrels. "You stupid bastard!"

I bit my lip, saw Buck try to raise his head against Diamond Joe's grip on the harness. "I want nuu to see nis," Joe shouted at me.

I leveled the shotgun. "Goddamn you!" But before I could pull the trigger, Buck reached down, his mouth opened wide, and took all of Diamond Joe's ear between his teeth with a loud chomp, and swung him off the ground. I heard a tortured scream from deep in Diamond Joe's guts and the sound of ripping flesh as Buck slung him up and dropped him without turning loose of his ear. Buck threw up his head and spit out the ear with a four-inch strip of skin and scraggly hair hanging from it. Joe screamed, like any man scalped alive, and rolled and thrashed like a snake on a griddle with his hand on his bloody jaw.

Ned stared with his mouth slightly open; Buck stepped forward, nodding up and down, and stomped a hoof on Diamond Joe's knee. It snapped like the cracking of seasoned hickory. "God almighty," said Ned. He leaned out and stared in disbelief as Diamond Joe screamed louder. I moved quick and snatched Buck's rope when he trotted to me. I heard Mackay chuckle and cough; then I saw The Rake look up from the saddlebags and wave a handful of wadded-up newspaper.

"Another goddamn double cross!" Rake yelled, slung the saddlebags away, and drew the pistol from his side as he ran and dived behind a pile of bricks.

"Damn it, Jack!" I yelled, dropped Buck's rope, swung the shotgun, and emptied it into Tiny Boyd, then ducked back beside Mackay with bullets whistling past me and slapping the ground. I saw Buck rear up, then hit the ground running. Diamond Joe rolled away screaming. Ned swung his horse away, leaning low on one stirrup, using the horse as a shield and gigging it into an alley.

Mackay dropped two of Quarrels's men, threw the shotgun down, and pulled out both pistols from beneath his coat. I blazed away with my forty-four and the two of us backed away into an alley. Clay Allison, drunk as he was, fired one shot straight through a gunman's head, then just sat down on the edge of the boardwalk.

Jack grabbed Sonny and held him as a shield, then crouched in the street, firing as the gunmen took cover. "Get out of there, Jack!" Ned had circled through an alley and came charging out from behind Jack. "Look out!" I yelled, and fired at Ned, but missed. Just as Jack stood and shoved Sonny away, Ned swung past him, hanging low off the side of his horse. He emptied the pistol into Jack's chest; I saw Jack fly back a step each time a bullet hit him.

There was only Mackay and myself, and he had taken a graze across his arm. But seeing Jack go down, I lost all sense of danger and bolted toward him.

"Don't shoot, you'll hit my brother," Ned Quarrels bellowed to his men. I saw Buck circle in the street, rear up, and let out a long neigh, then drop and scrape at the ground like a bull, slinging his head and threatening everything in sight.

I ran yelling to Jack, emptying my forty-four at the gunmen on my way. Sonny Quarrels ran a few steps, picked up a pistol, and pointed it down only inches from Jack's face. He cocked the hammer. "Son of a bitch!" I pointed the forty-four and pulled the trigger as I ran, but it only snapped on an empty chamber. In a second that seemed like an hour, I dove out at Sonny, swung the forty-four high, and came down across his head with a solid blow. He rolled one way and I another, then I crawled quickly back, jerked Sonny up in front of me by his hair, snatched up his pistol, and jammed it against his ear.

"I'll kill him! Back off or I'll kill him!" Sonny groaned and tried to shake his head. I glanced at Jack and saw the white of his coat lining puffing out of four bullet holes right at his heart. He was still as stone. A breeze licked at his hair and threw dust on his face. Jack was dead and it was all I could do to keep from pulling the trigger and blowing Sonny's head off. I even started to, but then I glanced down at the chamber of the forty-four in my hand and felt a chill go up my spine as I realized that, like my own, it too was empty.

The firing stopped and I saw Ned's horse circle in the street. "Hold your fire," he called out. He gazed at me holding his brother with the gun in his ear. "Jesse, don't do it. Let him go. You've got your horse . . . you've got the marshall and the money. For godsakes, you've won . . . don't kill him. He's just a kid. I'm sorry about your friend . . . but goddamn it, look how many of mine are dead." Buck ran in a wide circle, up on the boardwalk, kicking and stomping.

"Back your men out of here, Ned . . . everybody but you, or I'll splatter his brains all over the street!" I prayed that no one would see the empty chamber.

"You heard him . . . everybody back, mount up and pull back. Get the hell out!"

"Where's Marn-gret?" I heard Diamond Joe shout from behind cover. "I lonst an ear and my leg's bronken. I ain't leabing winthout—"

"Get out, Joe, or I'll kill you myself!" Ned Quarrels screamed. He was losing his grip.

I watched Quarrels's men creep slowly from behind cover, take up their horses and fade back into the stacks of building material like demons slipping back to hell. "See, Jesse . . . they're leaving, all right? Now let him go. Okay? He's my kid brother for christsakes!"

Sonny groaned and turned his face up to me. "It's . . . empty," he said in a groggy voice.

I shook him by his hair. "Shut up or I'll knock your head off."

"Who's up—?" I heard RC yell in a drunken voice. "I'm up. I shot a sumbitch . . . but no sumbitch shot me."

"Shut up, RC!" I thought I heard a slight groan from Jack's body, and I leaned closer to him, still holding onto Sonny Quarrels. I saw Jack's hand move slightly, then I saw his eyelid flicker. "Mackay," I shouted, "Come help me . . . he's alive!"

"The gun's empty," Sonny Quarrels yelled to his brother. "Come get me, Ned!"

"Damn you!" I shook him, started to bust him in the head, but realized it only proved what he'd said. Ned stepped his horse forward; I braced the gun against his brother's head. "It's not empty, Ned! Take another step and I'll prove it."

He reined up. "All right, I sent them away. . . . Now turn him loose." I heard Buck nicker and snort, and heard his hoof crash against the side of Fortenay's On The Frontier.

"Not without the money, you dumb bastard," Sonny yelled at his brother. I jerked him again.

"Drop your iron, Ned, and hurry up. My friend's alive. If he dies, Sonny goes with him." I jerked Sonny back and forth roughly.

"All right." Ned let the rifle fall from his lap, drew his pistol with two fingers and dropped it in the dirt.

I stood up, pulled Sonny up with me, and shoved him forward. He stumbled and ran forward. "Damn it, Ned, why'd you do this? We had 'em cold! Why'd you let him out-dicker you?"

"To save your life, goddamn it!" Ned pointed toward a horse milling in the street. "Get it and let's go!"

"You horse-trading son of a bitch!" Sonny turned back toward me shaking his shackled fists; and instead of going for the horse he made a dive for Ned's rifle.

"Shoot him, Mackay," I bellowed, knowing I couldn't get to a loaded gun before Sonny got to the rifle. A shot spit into the dirt beside Sonny as he grabbed the rifle and rolled away.

"I'm coming, Sonny!" But Ned stiffened in the saddle as he started to spur his horse. I heard the explosion behind him and saw him snap forward as a red ribbon of blood uncurled from his chest. He flew off his horse into the street and tried to raise himself. "God, Sonny, I'm hit . . . hit bad!" He managed to wobble up onto one knee. He threw a hand up to Sonny as Sonny ran toward him. "Help me!"

Sonny scrambled across the dirt; I shoved bullets into the pistol. Ned rocked back and forth on his knee, "Help me, Sonny!" Sonny stopped beside him and grabbed the reins to Ned's rearing horse. Ned grabbed his brother's leg as Sonny jerked the horse down. "Sonny, help—!" But Sonny kicked him away as another shot spit into the dirt.

Sonny leaped for the saddle but missed as the horse spun. Ned doubled over in the dirt. "Please, Sonny!"

"Fuck you!" Sonny screamed, stepping on his brother's back and up onto the horse. Ned raised slightly and another explosion resounded along the dirt street. This one caught him full in the chest, raised him almost to his feet, spun him around, then dropped him face down like a bundle of rags. I looked up from the boot print on Ned Quarrels's back and saw Marshall Newton Briggs hanging with one arm around a post outside the doctor's office. From his right hand, the big Dance Brothers pistol hung toward the ground in a cloud of curling smoke.

I ran to Jack, slid down beside him, and ripped open the heavy coat. I heard Buck's hooves thunder along behind me. "*Jesus, God!* Hang on, Jack, please . . . hang on!" I saw an ugly graze just above his right temple, saw the holes in his duster and ripped it open, saw the holes in his vest and ripped it open. Saw the holes in his shirt, ripped it open, too. "What the hell?" There was no blood on his undershirt. I ripped it open . . . and stared wide-eyed at the stacks of bullet-riddled money tied around his chest. Buck poked his muzzle down in Jack's face and blew out a wet breath. I shoved him away; he nipped my shoulder.

"Son of a bitch!" I let out a tense breath and slapped Jack's face back and forth to revive him. He groaned again, this time longer, and this time his eyes flickered and stayed open for a second.

PART V — ◆

Price of a Horse

• 25 •

"Jack! Can you hear me?"

I shook him and saw him wince. "Yes . . . but I can't see you." His eyes wandered aimlessly. "I'm blind!"

"You took a bad one upside your head, and four right in the chest." He stiffened and grasped my sleeve. "But you're all right," I added quickly. "The money saved your life."

He relaxed down into the dirt with a pained smile. "I always knew it would . . . someday." I saw he was coming to his senses.

"Why'd you do that, Jack? Didn't you know they'd find out?"

"I . . . figured if we won, we oughta get paid . . . and if we lost . . . what difference would it make?"

"Makes sense to me." I took off his bandanna and wiped his bloody forehead. Buck walked up, poked his muzzle in Jack's face, and tried to nip him.

"Get that goddamn . . . horse outta my face."

"Get back, boy." I nudged Buck away; he snorted and stomped a hoof.

Gustav and Fortenay came running up, then slowed and stepped cautiously closer. "Is he—?" Gustav pointed a finger at Jack.

"He's all right," I said, "but he can't see. I need you to

take him to Doc Eisenhower's office. There might be more of Quarrels's bunch around."

I stood up as they gathered Jack between them. "I'll be right there, Jack."

Mackay and I walked among the bodies with our pistols raised. When we reached Ned Quarrels, I saw his hand twitch, and we turned him over. Blood ran from his lips. "Where's my . . . brother?"

"He left, Ned." I leaned down on one side and Mackay on the other. I thought about taking him to Eisenhower's, but I looked into Mackay's eyes and saw him shake his head slowly.

"Lie still," Mackay said in a soothing voice, patting Ned's shoulder. "It won't hurt much longer."

"Sonny'll be . . . back for me," Ned said, struggling for breath. "We're . . . brothers." He turned his face from Mackay to me. "All this . . . for a horse?" He coughed and shook his head; his eyes began to fade. "Hell . . . of a price . . . for a horse."

"I know," I said. I looked around at the dead, strewn about as if hurled down from heaven by the angry hand of God. "But you're the ones who paid it." I watched Ned struggle for one more breath, then one more, then the one that didn't come. Up the street, I saw Buck trot in a wide circle, slinging his head, nickering, prancing like a circus stallion.

Mackay closed Ned's eyes and stood up. "Poor Ned . . . he only wanted his brother, as it turned out. All the rest meant nothing in the end. He simply couldn't deal with you."

"Yeah," I said, turning toward Eisenhower's. "After the dealing's done, you see where everybody stood."

"Indeed," Mackay said in a hushed tone. "Quite a bit like poker. It must be an interesting profession . . . horse trading."

"It has its moments." We walked past Briggs, hanging

from the post, a slight smile on his lips, his dead eyes staring at Ned, his pistol cocked for one more round. "Let's lay him down, Mackay." I heard my voice falter. "He shouldn't be hanging here like this."

"Of course," Mackay said; he reached out, uncocked the big Dance Brothers pistol, and shoved it down in my empty shoulder harness. We took Briggs from the post, closed his eyes and leaned him against the building. An explosion of rapid gunfire resounded in the distance. We both flinched and turned in that direction. In a moment, we recognized Sheriff Mace Bowman at the head of six riders. They rode out of a shimmering swirl of sunlight and bounded toward Gris at an easy gallop.

"I might have trouble explaining who I really am," I said to Mackay. "So don't feel obligated to back me up—"

"Nonsense, sir. You're James Beatty. I defy anyone to say otherwise." Mackay looked me up and down with a smile.

"We kicked ass, didn't we?" RC Allison staggered up beside me and tried to throw his arm across my shoulder. I ducked it and he nearly fell. "I got to tell you, Jesse—"

"Shut your goddamn mouth!" I snatched RC by the hair on his chest and jerked him close. "This is law coming here. Don't start any of that Jesse James talk."

"Hell, it's just ole Mace," RC shrugged. "I told you he'd be back." I shoved him away.

Mackay chuckled and coughed as the riders drew closer. "I don't think I'll use an alias from now on . . . seeing the complications it's caused you. From now on it's simply John H. Holliday, DDS, for me. Or . . . *Doctor John,* if you will."

"Yeah," I said. "It gets confusing going under an alias. . . . makes people set unreasonable expectations on ya."

Fortenay stepped out of the doctor's office, saw the riders, smiled, and rubbed his hands together. "I hope that banjo player's still around."

Margaret Alahambre slipped up beside Mackay and wrapped her arm in his, looking carefully around at the bodies in the street. "Is my husband here?"

Mackay smiled and patted her arm. "If not, we have plenty of time to find him. Be a dear, now, and go find me a bottle of whiskey." He glanced at me and smiled as she scurried off toward Fortenay's. "So nice to find one already trained. I'm amazed you let her slip past you." His smile widened; I shook my head.

When Mace Bowman and his riders reined down, I saw Briggs's deputies, One-eye Ingram and Dick Duggins among them. They led two horses with bodies slung over them. One was Diamond Joe's, the other was Sonny Quarrels's. Blood dripped from the top of Sonny's head and into the dirt, slow and steady, as if marking the endless passing of time. Mackay walked up and pulled Diamond Joe down into the street. "My, but won't Margaret be pleased."

"I told him you'd be back, Mace," RC said. I stood staring up with my hand on the big Dance pistol. Mace Bowman took note of it, kept his hands clear of his holsters, and pushed his hat up.

"I shouldn't have left ya like I did," Bowman said. He had a hard time looking me in the eyes. He shrugged. "I had the *damndest* hangover—"

"You know who this is?" RC stepped away from me with his finger pointing. I tensed up, ready to put a bullet through him. Bowman must've seen it.

"Yeah," he said quickly. "He's that horse trader that Briggs had so much faith in." He looked down at Briggs's body and back to me. His eyes narrowed and darkened. "Was Beatty any help to ya, RC?"

"Hunh?" RC looked bewildered for a second; Bowman nodded toward the bodies in the street. "Aw yeah," said RC, catching on. "A lot of help. I couldn't done it without him—" He hesitated a second. "Well . . . I *could've,* but he *was* a lot of help."

"Good," said Bowman. His eyes settled with me, and turned to Allison. "I told your woman you was taking care of things here. She's looking all over for ya. I gotta take you back, you know."

RC grinned. "We got time for a few bracers first, don't we?"

"Sure you do," Fortenay called out.

I let go a tense breath. "Did you see The Rake anywhere?"

"He got away," Bowman said. "I'll get him if he ever shows up in Cimarron. I don't work like Briggs. I stay in my jurisdiction. That's what got him killed."

"He thought Ned killed his son," I said. "Was that true?"

Bowman looked from Briggs's body to Ned's, then swept his eyes past the all the dead in the street. "Sure, why not?" He shrugged.

"That's a hell of an answer, after all this." I cocked an eye at Bowman.

He shook his head. "That was a hell of a question . . . after all this." A second of silence passed, then he said, "Did you get your horse?"

"Yep." I thumbed over my shoulder toward Buck, prancing in the street.

"Anybody find the money?" Bowman watched my eyes.

"Nope." I held his gaze until he glanced away.

One-eye Marvin Ingram stepped his horse up and looked down at Briggs's body. "Does this mean we're off the hook?" He looked at Mace. So did I, curiously.

Bowman saw the question in my eyes and smiled. "Ingram and Duggins ain't real deputies. Briggs was holding them on a theft charge. He had a habit of deputizing prisoners. Never got many volunteers, you know. You must have really impressed him, if he left Marvin and Dick behind for you."

I just stared at him.

Margaret Alahambre scurried past Buck on her way back

from Fortenay's. He stomped the ground, threatening her. She glanced over her shoulder as she hurried to Mackay with a bottle of whiskey. "Something should be done about that animal before somebody gets killed," she said. I looked up at Bowman and the two of us shook our heads.

"Look, darling!" Mackay pointed to Diamond Joe's body with a playful smile. "Your husband! Colder than the proverbial cucumber! Aren't you thrilled?" He took the bottle from her and pulled the cork.

Margaret took a cautious step. "Is he—I mean, are you sure?"

Mackay spun his shiny pistol and offered it to her butt first. "Be my guest." He smiled; Margaret rubbed her hands up and down her dress, considering it.

"Should I?" She reached toward the pistol, then drew back.

Mackay shrugged. "Of course. Just a couple of shots to ease your mind. He *is* your husband, after all."

"Jesus," I said. I turned and walked into Eisenhower's office.

"The hell was that?" Jack asked. We'd heard two pistol shots outside as I stepped over to him. The doctor had cleaned his forehead and wrapped it in heavy gauze half way down his nose.

"Just Margaret . . . settling her marital problems," I said. I looked at Doc Eisenhower. "Is he going to be able to see?"

"In a day or two. He can see now, but it's fuzzy. Best to keep the eyes covered against the sun till they can focus better."

"Ready to ride?" I looked at Jack and saw his hands folded across his chest. I saw the lumps of money through his shirt.

"Been ready," he said, smiling beneath his bandage.

I turned to Eisenhower, pulled five silver dollars from my pocket, and held them out to him. "I want Briggs buried,"

I said. "I better never come through and see him hanging on your wall."

"Oh, don't worry. There's plenty of pickings in the street." His belly bounced as he wheezed out a short laugh. "But I don't know who'll bury him."

"There's a banjo player around here somewhere," I said. "You know how they are. He'll dig a grave for free just to get to play something over it."

On our way out of Gris, I swung by Fortenay's, called Mackay to side, and while no one was watching, I slipped a roll of dollars in his hand. "What's this?" He chuckled as he looked down at the money. "Are you a philanthropist, among other things?"

"No," I said. "I can't even carry a tune. This is just a couple thousand I want to give you for helping us out." I grinned. "High pay for a dentist, but you do good work."

"I really shouldn't take this," he said, as the money disappeared into his clothes. He leaned close. "The fact is, I'm partly responsible for what happened. I'm the one who caused Ned to rob the stage in the first place."

"How's that?" I glanced at him.

"I ran into The Rake in Taos and told him about the false stage seat." He shrugged.

"Jesus," I said. "Why'd you do that?"

"*Drunk,* sir." He hooked a thumb in his vest. "Drunk beyond RC Allison's wildest dream." He stifled a cough. "I played cards with the gentleman who designed and built the stage seat. He seemed to think it would be the latest rage among the security companies. But, as we now see . . . "

"Well, don't worry," I said. "I'll never breathe a word of it."

"Thank you." He smiled. "I have a friend in law enforcement, you see. It would be *most* embarrassing."

It was evening when we rode into Cimarron. I'd led Jack's silver-gray most of the way, but he insisted on holding his own reins as we crossed the town limits and headed to Lambert's Saloon.

"Hello there," said the kid, from the boardwalk. He pointed to Jack. "What happened to him?" He wore a battered top hat he'd gotten from somewhere. It sat lop-sided on his head.

"Don't make a thing of it, Kid," Jack said, before I could answer.

The kid shrugged. He stood next to Frank Tripplet out front of Lambert's Saloon, holding a rifle propped on the boardwalk with one hand around the barrel. "I just had my picture taken posed like this." He stiffened in a pose. "How you think it'll look?"

"It'll look fine, Kid." I didn't have the heart to tell him that his top hat was too crooked, and his clothes were dirty and too big for him. The two of them stepped out from the boardwalk. Tripplet reached up to help Jack down, but Jack kicked at him and slid down on his own.

"If you wanta do something, lead me to the bar," Jack said to Tripplet. I slid off Buck and nodded the kid toward me as Jack and Tripplet walked into Lambert's Saloon.

I spun Buck's reins and held the lead rope to Lambert's mare. I reached in my pocket and took out the roll of money. "I want you to have this, Kid," I said; and I held the money out to him. "You did good."

"Aw heck, Jesse—" He looked down, embarrassed, and scraped a boot in the dirt. "I was glad to help. I don't want no money."

"You oughta get something," I said. "What *do* you want?"

"Heck, all I want is to be better with a gun," he shrugged. "It was good practice for me. Maybe we'll do it again sometime—"

"Damn, I hope not." I let my hand drop and shook my head.

"You look worn out, Jesse." He laughed, and took the

lead rope from my hand. "Get us both a beer. I'll take the mare."

"Thanks, Kid." I slapped dust with my hat.

I walked in Lambert's and saw Jack and Tripplet at the bar.

"Can I ask you a few questions?" Tripplet flipped out a pad and pencil.

"No," I said. "I'm tired and thirsty." I looked at Lambert's son and held up two fingers. "Beers . . . cold and deep, and keep 'em coming till I'm too short to reach 'em."

Tripplet shrugged and sipped his beer. Lambert's evening crowd stared at us for a second, then turned away. Henri Lambert stepped out of the kitchen wiping his hands on a bar towel, saw me and smiled.

"Just the person I wanted to see," I said, smiling back and reaching into my shirt pocket. "I want to give you something for lending me that mare. She's one *damn* fine animal. I couldn't ask for better—never *seen* any better."

"I'm glad you liked her." Lambert beamed, then glanced around at an empty hook on the wall behind the bar. "Has anyone seen my top hat? It was right there."

Tripplet chuckled. "The dishwasher took it. Said he wanted to see how it fit."

"I'll kill that little weasel—" Lambert slapped the bar.

"Don't worry," I said. "He'll bring it right back. He just took your mare over to the—" My voice stopped and I stood stunned for a second, realizing that we'd never see Lambert's hat, or his mare, ever again. "Goddamn it!" I jerked off my hat and slapped it on the bar.

"You gave my finest animal"—Henri Lambert's face swelled red—"to that thieving, good for nothing, Billy Antrim?"

"Billy Antrim? I thought his name was Henry McCarty."

"It's William Bonney. He told me earlier," said Tripplet. He fingered through the pad. "No, Bonney's another alias. It is McCarty."

I shrugged. "I just called him Kid, for some reason."

"I don't care if you called him Victor—fucking—Frankenstein! You owe me a thousand dollars for my mare!"

"A thousand dollars?" I stared at him with both my hands on the bar. "For that mare? Hell, she ain't worth twenty dollars. She's short-winded—gun-shy—couldn't run—wouldn't rein—"

"Pay the man." Jack chuckled and shook his bandaged head.

I pulled the roll back out and licked my thumb. "All right, Lambert, here's the deal. You get a thousand for the mare, but we get a room for the night, a steak dinner, and a bottle of your finest whiskey—"

"No room." Lambert shook his head. "A detective agency wired ahead and reserved all my rooms. They're on their way to Colorado, looking for the James brothers." He spread a sly grin; I let the roll of money fall on the bar. "They'll be here anytime. But I'll throw in dinner and whiskey, if you're gonna stick around—"

"I'll save that posse the trouble," said Jake The Rake's voice from the door.

Chairs scraped, boots and slippers scuffled, as we spun around from the bar. Jack's hand started for the La Faucheux, but I caught his arm and stopped him. Lambert dropped behind the bar; Tripplet slid away as if the room had tilted. I stepped forward with one hand out and my other near the big Dance pistol. "The deal's over, Rake. The Quarrels's are dead, the money's gone. Better luck next time. Let's not do this."

He reached up a finger and ran it across his thin mustache. "Aw yeah . . . we're gonna do it. I'm coming out of this deal with something. So don't even bother running your mouth, *horse trader.*" His jaw twitched. "You and your brother get a bullet in the brain, I get the reputation and the reward money. That's my only offer."

"What's he doing?" Jack asked. He tried to step forward beside me, but I shoved him back.

"There ain't a way in the world I'll convince you that we ain't the James brothers, is there?"

"Not a one." The Rake's voice was flat and resolved. His eyes said his hand was ready.

"Then skin it," I said; and in that second I saw in my mind all that had happened in the past week. It all spun in a swirl of blood, badges, bandages, women, horses, and money. I blinked once to clear it away.

"He's too fast for you," Jack whispered. "Let me have him. I'm better *blind* than you are—"

"Thanks . . . *a lot,* Jack," I whispered with a sigh and shook my head. "That's real encourag—"

"You've never done this before, have you, Jesse?" Rake spread his evil grin. "I mean straight up, one to one?" I didn't answer. "I didn't think so," he said. "I'm wondering if your reputation is built on hot air and chicken feathers. Nobody skins iron from under their arm like that." He nodded toward my shoulder harness.

"I do," I said. "Always have."

He stepped sideways, circling the room slowly. I did the same, knowing he was trying to rattle me. He opened and closed his fingers slowly near his gun butt. I kept my right hand on my chest near the Dance, as if pledging allegiance to hell.

"So . . . tell me, how does it feel?" He would taunt, try to rattle me. I saw it and began working my mind, figuring him out, looking for an edge. "What does death look like, this close up? Feel them buzzards picking at your navel? Hurts, don't it?" But I never answered; I'd let him talk till his talking stopped. Then he'd never talk again.

"First man I ever killed . . . it was just like this," Rake said as we continued our waltz in a slow circle. "He died hard. Took him over ten minutes . . . teeth blown out, air sucking through the back of his neck. Couldn't swat the flies from his mouth. It was ugly . . . real ugly."

I saw a flash of something sweep his eyes, and I realized that in the process of rattling me, he'd seen the picture in his own mind and it stalled him. He hesitated for just a split second; and in that split second, I snapped my hand around the big Dance pistol, and slung it forward.

My hand seemed to struggle, as if forcing its way through the clear heavy matter of the universe. But The Rake's hand moved quicker than a hornet. His pistol was out, up, and cocked. Mine was still swinging around in a slow arch that seemed to take in the whole room. I saw the barrel level toward me, larger than a field cannon. I heard the explosion, saw the blast of smoke and orange fire, and braced against the impact that would rip through me and carry me away.

My pistol stopped swinging. I froze. I wanted to cry, to scream, to tell the world I was sorry and to tell it good-bye. But instead I saw the bullet hurl toward me, growing larger as it neared. My eyes fixed on it, judged where it would strike me. But it dropped farther and farther . . . until it slapped the floor in front of my boots and rolled between my feet. I let out a long trembling sigh and just stared at it. My knees slapped against my pants leg like the flutter of a dove.

"The hell's that? The hell happened?" I heard Jack but I couldn't answer. I looked up at The Rake and saw him shaking the pistol with both hands; his face was actually green, his eyes wide and pleading. He threw open the gun and spilled out the bullets.

"What's going on?" I heard Jack behind me.

"Taos?" My voice sounded strange in my ears as I stared at The Rake and stepped forward, raising the Dance.

"Uh-huh." He nodded; his voice was a meek whine. His eyes pleaded for a second chance as his fingers searched his belt and jerked out some older-looking bullets.

I cocked the Dance. "No way," I said; and I took a breath to calm my pounding heart. "I *ain't* going through this shit again." The Dance bucked once in my hand. The Rake spun around and wobbled to keep from falling. I saw the cloth lining of his coat shower out and down like windswept snow. Snow, in a spray of blood.

"Did you shoot him?" Jack stepped forward, but again I shoved him back. The Rake took a step toward the door, then stopped and turned, trying to raise his pistol from the grave. I dropped the hammer on him again; he spun and sat straight down on the floor.

"Goddamn it!" Jack shouted. *"What's going on?"*

"Don't shoot him no more!" someone yelled, as I stepped forward cautiously. The Rake rocked back and forth, and finally just slumped with his hands laying out on both sides, palms up. The pistol slid away. I walked around him with the Dance still pointed and cocked. Smoke curled from the barrel, drifted up my arm, clouded around my face, and burned in my nostrils.

"Is he dead or what?" I heard Jack call out. "Tell me *something* here!"

"Yeah—" I reached out and put the barrel against his forehead. "Oh no!" Lambert pleaded. "Don't blow his brains out in here!" But I just nudged the barrel against his head, shoved him, and let him fall backwards like a downed tree. "He's dead," I whispered.

• 26 •

Frank Tripplet stepped up beside me as I guided Jack to his silver-gray and laid his hand on the saddlehorn. "Beatty," he said, "I hate being blunt, but I might as well tell you." He followed me around to the hitch rail. "Either you let me come along with you and give me your version of what happened in Gris, or I'll write it in my own words and call it *The Adventures of the James Brothers.*" He spread a shrewd grin. "How's that for a deal?" I took the reins and stepped over beside Buck. Tripplet spread his arms. "After all . . . what will you do, sue me?"

"Naw, Tripplet"—I swung up in the saddle—"I won't sue you. We both know that. But I'll go buy a bear somewhere." I smiled and pushed my hat up. "And I'll find you, and feed you to him, one piece at a time . . . over a two-week period . . . starting at your toes." I smiled, then let the smile fade; I stared at him a second to let him know I meant it. "How's that for a deal?"

Jack chuckled beside me, turning his silver-gray.

"Can't you tell I'm only joking, Beatty?" He forced a frightened smile.

"Me too," I said, but my expression didn't change.

"One question, Mister Beatty," he said, as I reined Buck around toward the dirt street. "Off the record." He ran a finger across his heart. "If you and Clay Allison ever really got in a grave and had a knife fight . . . who would win? Be honest."

"I would," I said. "Because I'd be polite enough to let him go down the ladder first . . . then I'd shoot him in the top of his head and throw the dirt in over him." I chuckled and shook my head. *"Get in a grave and have a knife fight. Jesus!* That's the craziest thing I ever heard of."

"Good answer!" Tripplet laughed and slapped his leg. I looked back and tipped my hat as Jack and I rode away.

"One more thing—" Tripplet yelled as we rode down the dirt street.

"Why don't you shoot him?" Jack spoke out the side of his mouth.

"Looks like I'll have to . . . to get rid of him."

"—What about the kid? What'll you do if you ever see him again? Hunh? What'll you do?"

I didn't answer, but Jack slung his bandaged head around and yelled, "No comment."

"No comment?" Tripplet yelled and laughed. "That's the kinda answer a politician would give."

Jack chuckled. "He wouldn't talk to me like that if I wasn't blind."

"Quiet Jack . . . the statesman," I said. "With an imagination like that, Tripplet oughta be writing fiction, like that ole rebel boy, Samuel . . . what's his name?"

"Clemens," Jack said. "But he goes by the name Twain." Jack chuckled again and gigged his horse forward. "He's like you. He goes under an alias."

"Yeah . . . I like that about him," I said, gigging Buck forward.

That night, we sat close to a low flame deep inside a thicket of pines along the valley trail. Jack pulled his bandage up on his forehead and rubbed his eyes with his thumb and finger. "Doctor said a couple of days"—he rubbed his eyes again—"but it ain't taking that long. You know, it sounds strange," he said, "but in the end, everybody back in Gris got what they wanted the most."

I thought about it a second and nodded, studying the flicker of firelight and the glowing bed of embers. "Yeah," I said. "Briggs got Ned Quarrels, Ned got his brother freed, Margaret got to see her husband dead, you got your money, and I got Buck."

"Oh? *My* money?" Jack said. "Didn't you want the money too?"

"Yeah, but not as much as I wanted Buck . . . not as much as I wanted to get Greta away from Quarrels. And not as much as I wanted to keep Ned from killing ole Briggs. I reckon it was all these things that kept me in the deal. Maybe that's why we're still alive. Everybody wanted something, but they wasn't willing to give up a thing. We was willing to dicker, and we ended up on top. That make any sense?"

"Not a lick," Jack said. "But it don't matter."

We sat in silence for a few minutes until we both heard a slight rustle in the pines a few yards away. "Stay still," I said, and I dropped and rolled away, out of the firelight, drawing the big Dance pistol and cocking it. I heard the heavy thrashing of horses through the thicket and realized that whoever it was wasn't trying to sneak up. "Who goes there?" I stood up slowly, watching the dark woods.

"Mister Beatty? Is that you?" I heard Carmilla's voice and felt a warm glow sweep through me.

"Yeah, it's us, Carmilla. Come on in." I glanced at Jack and saw he'd pulled the bandage back down over his eyes.

"Greta?" Jack's voice sounded gentle, searching. "Are you there?"

"My goodness," said Carmilla, stepping her horse out into the small clearing. "You were certainly hard enough to find. Are you hiding?" She gathered her wool poncho, smiled, slipped down from the saddle, and caught herself by putting her hands on my shoulder. I steadied her with my hands on her waist. Greta rode in on a small red donkey and slipped down on her own. She stepped over to Jack, started to put a hand on his shoulder, but stopped herself.

"Is that you, Greta?" Jack reached out a hand and felt around in the air. "Greta, are you there?"

She stepped back. "Yes," she said quietly. "It's me. I'm here."

"So," said Carmilla, shaking me by the shoulders. "You leave without even saying good-bye? Is that what you do?"

"Sorry," I said. "We didn't see y'all at Lambert's. I figured you'd gone on to the lodge." I took her reins, led her mare over, reined it beside Buck, and walked back.

She smiled and tossed back her hair. It was glistening clean and scented of peach blossoms. "We would not stay at Lambert's. There is a colony of Friends near there—"

"Quakers?"

"Yes. They took us in." She smiled and stepped back. "I'm so happy you are alive—" She glanced around at Jack. "Both of you." She looked at Jack's bandages, then back to me, and bit her lip in sympathy.

"Don't worry about him," I said. "The doctor says—"

"—It could be a long time before I see again . . . if *ever*," Jack cut in and finished my words in a humble tone. "But it don't matter, so long as you women are safe. That's always been the main thing here."

I looked over at him, then back to Carmilla. "It's gonna be hard on him until he gets used to it." Past Carmilla, I saw Greta reach out and lay a hand on Jack's shoulder.

"Why didn't you stay in Cimarron and rest for a few days?" Carmilla reached up and brushed back my hair. "Look at you. You haven't even had a bath."

"I know," I said. I wasn't about to mention the detectives coming. I cleared my throat. "The truth is, we're both broke." I shook my head. "I'm ashamed to say it—" I hoped she wouldn't notice the bulging saddlebags beneath my saddle near the fire.

"After all you did for everyone? Someone should have put you up for a few days. That is what's shameful."

I looked down and rubbed my toe in the dirt. I couldn't really think of *anything* we'd done for *anybody,* but I wasn't going to say it. I did save Greta, but what person wouldn't have done the same, given the circumstances?

I heard another rustling in the woods and I spun and almost shot the banjo player as he stepped into the clearing.

"Whoa!" He threw up a hand.

"Oh," said Carmilla. "I should have told you. We met him along the road. He was coming from Gris. You would not believe it, but Fortenay's fell to the ground!" She waved a hand. "He saw it!"

"It was terrible," he said. His eyes grew wide. "I was burying the old marshall . . . and *pooof-booom!* The whole place just fell over! I was supposed to play there tonight."

"That's awful. Plumb awful. Anybody hurt?"

"Well, naw. No more than usual, in a place like that."

I gestured toward the fire. "Get you some coffee, old buddy. You've been through a lot."

"I sure have." He ambled over, took a cup from his coat pocket, filled it from the steaming pot, swung his banjo around from his back, and sat down.

"Where will you go now?" Carmilla looked deep into my eyes. Behind her I saw Jack reach out a hand and carefully touch Greta's face. She stiffened at first, but then let his hand feel down to her neck, then out across her shoulder.

"Everything's so strange to me," Jack said in a weak and wistful voice.

"I don't know, Carmilla," I said. "Back to Missouri . . . rest awhile, get ready for whatever life has in mind for me, I reckon."

"Nonsense. That is a long ride. And who will help you with your friend? It could be a long time before he can see again . . . if ever."

I saw past her, watched Jack's hand wander down to

Greta's breast and press it gently; then his hand jerked away. "Oh! I'm so sorry," I heard him say in a hushed tone. But she took his hand in both of hers and pressed it against her bosom. Her cheeks flushed in a red glow.

"No, it's all right. You have to learn to feel with your hands what you cannot see with your eyes—"

"We'll just have to manage," I said to Carmilla, looking into her eyes, but still watching Jack as his hands learned to see what his eyes could not. "We're strangers here. There's no place for us to just rest and heal." I sighed, shook my head. "No . . . we'll just have to keep moving . . . pressing on, I suppose."

"You must come with us to the lodge. It is the least we can do." She ran her hand down my cheek and rested it on my shoulder.

"But what about the women, the other members? Won't they be upset if they—"

"They will not be back for another month. That is plenty of time." I saw firelight glow and flicker in her dark eyes.

"Well," I said hesitantly. "If it's not putting y'all out. He could use some rest and some care—we both could." I sighed, walked over to a pine tree, leaned my back against it, and slid down. "I'm *so* tired. . . . Broke . . . no friends . . . no place to stay. . . . I don't know what we'll do. . . . "

Carmilla walked over and slid down beside me. She leaned near my ear and whispered. "*I* came looking for *you,* remember? Please, don't overplay it."

I looked at her, saw her smile, felt my face redden, and I chuckled and shook my head. "Sorry," I said. "Old habits, I reckon."

"I've invited you in—" She slipped her arm in mine. "Just relax. . . . Let us enjoy each other without pretense. It is really very simple to do."

"Yeah." I let out a breath. "You're right. . . . It is."

"Of course," she whispered; she laid her head against my chest and closed her eyes. I breathed the heady scent of peach blossoms, of her, and of the wide clear night.

I looked over at Jack. "Looks like we might stay a couple of weeks at the lodge. Hopefully, you'll be back to yourself by then."

"Let's hope so," Jack said. He turned his bandaged face all about. "I'll need some special care and consideration. I'll need to learn so many things all over—"

I felt Carmilla chuckle against my chest and squeeze my arm gently. I looked at the banjo player. "Feel like striking up a tune?"

"Sure." He sat his cup down and ran a thumb down the strings. "What would you like to hear?"

I grinned. " 'Bound for the Rio Grande'?"

Carmilla chuckled again and shook her head softly against my chest. "Don't be so cruel," she whispered.

A silence passed. I looked up, saw a breeze sweep in and stir the stars around the tops of swaying ancient pines.

"I have trouble remembering the words to that one," he said.

"Just do the best you can."

Another silence passed. In the distance a coyote yipped, long, mournful, and sweet; its voice lingered and danced on the high, thin air above *Nuevo Mejico.*

"You won't hit me, will ya?"

"We ain't that kinda crowd," I said, and I raised Carmilla's wool poncho and spread it over us both. Buck nickered low; I looked over and saw him nuzzle Carmilla's mare. *Ole Buck,* I said to myself. It felt good seeing him there . . . like the sight of home at the end of a long day's ride.

I looked at Jack as Greta took a blanket from the back of her donkey and walked back to him. "Yep, special treatment," he said. "You can't rush these things, you know." He turned his face toward me, raised his bandage, winked, and pulled it back down. "*Now* it makes sense." His hands reached out, searching the air before him. "Greta," he said helplessly, "are you there?"

◆ EPILOGUE ◆

"Excuse me," said an elderly gentleman with a white mustache. "Aren't you Beatty? James Beatty?"

I turned my good eye up to him, studied him, raised a hand, straightened my tie, and kept my hand on my chest near the Colt automatic in my shoulder harness. "Do I know you, sir?"

He spread a tired smile. "It's been years. The last time I saw you, you threatened to feed me to a bear?"

"Frank Tripplet," I said, and I took my hand from my chest and extended it to his. "It *has* been awhile."

He gestured toward a chair; I nodded, and he sat down. "I can't tell you how many times I've wondered what became of you," he said. "You're one of the last of the old bunch, you know." He flagged a waiter.

"Old bunch? What *old* bunch?" I gazed at him.

"Oh, you know, the rowdies, the gunmen, the old"—he raised both hands and wiggled his fingers up and down—"*we've been everywhere, done everything . . . here's how it really was,* bunch."

I shrugged slightly. "Did you ever get a book published?" He didn't realize it, but I already knew that after my cousin Jesse's death, his wife, Zerelda, allowed Frank Tripplet to write a book about the James brothers. He wrote it, but

Zerelda had to sue him and the publisher to ever get a penny for the story.

"Nothing like *we* could've had," he said. He shook his head. "I could've made you a legend. Take what happened in Gris, add a little here and there . . . throw in some Indians—" He stopped as the waiter sat down a cold mug of beer.

"You don't make legends," I said. "Legends make themselves, *then* you write them up." I smiled and watched the foam on his beer creep down and spread on the table. "You blew your chance when you didn't write about Holliday, or RC Allison. Or Billy The Kid," I added, just to rub it in.

"You're right. But who could have ever guessed—about skinny Holliday, or drunken RC . . . or that *stupid*-looking kid." He clucked his cheek, studied the mug, then raised it. "Anyway, here's to them. May they all burn in—" his words stopped short in the draft of my cold stare. "Sorry . . . I'm a little bitter." He took a short sip. "But you and I really could've done something big."

I looked at him and thought of Clay Allison, of how someone finally agreed to having a knife fight with him in an open grave. Allison got so drunk and excited about it, he fell out of his wagon on the way there, broke his neck and died on the spot.

"I doubt it," I said. I finished my last sip of beer and took a silver dollar from my vest pocket. I thought of Holliday, of how he'd died, young and sickly, coughing out his lungs in a sanitarium after facing down some of the toughest gunmen in the West.

"You're leaving?" Tripplet saw me reach for my cane. "I just got here! I wanted to ask you about The Kid. I heard somewhere that you and he—"

"Then you heard wrong." I flipped the silver dollar from the edge of the table. "I never seen him again after Cimarron." The dollar landed in the middle of my empty plate, rang like a bell, and spun there; I propped both hands on my cane and watched it spin. "Damned shame what happened to him though."

Tripplet lowered his brow. "Some say there was a *horse dealer* there who saw what was coming and could've stopped it."

"Nobody sees what's coming," I said. I watched the coin slow down, wobble, then rattle down, then stop. I pushed myself up on my cane. "If we did we'd all be legends." I shook my head. "Or else none of us ever would."

"One question," Tripplet said. I'd turned to leave, but I stopped. "What about your partner . . . ole what's-his-name? What ever became of him?"

"Someday, I might write a book myself, Tripplet. If I do, he'll be in it. You'll hear our whole story."

"If you do, will it be the truth?"

"If it ain't, will you know the difference?"

"If I *do,* do I get my money back?"

"Read it first . . . then you tell me."

"Damned *horse trader* . . . " I heard Tripplet chuckle as I walked away. I smiled.

"Always was . . . " I said over my shoulder.

Over the years, I'd remained close to Carmilla. Although we had started out as natural enemies, somehow, fate in its rare, strange and random mercy, led us to become lovers, then friends, then *good friends,* then eventually . . . warm memories. She went on to become a leader in the Anti-Violence League, and I like to think that in some way, I might have served as her inspiration toward such a noble undertaking. I'll never know. I do know that just thinking of her filled many a cold and lonely night for me, as I huddled near a low flame somewhere in the deep woods, where a wanted man takes refuge, seeks his solace in the ember glow, talks to the stars, and reconciles himself to what he is; and prays to find his salvation, somehow, someway . . . before the stars begin to answer.